Love In Relief
(L'Amour en Relief)

Guy
Hocquenghem

Love
In
Relief

(L'Amour en Relief)

Translated by
Michael Whisler

Preface by George Stambolian

SeaHorse Press
New York City
1986

First English Language Edition
Originally published in French *L'Amour en Relief* by
Èditions Albin Michel © 1982, Guy Hocquenghem

First English Edition

Cataloging-in-Publication Data

Hocquenghem, Guy, 1946—
   Love in Relief (L'Amour en Relief)

   Translation of: *L'Amour en relief.*
   I. Title.
PQ2668.0215A413   1985   843'.914   85-2347
ISBN 0-933322-26-7

The SeaHorse Press, 307 West 11th St., N.Y.C. 10014

Contains Strong Language and Adult Situations

To those readers searching in vain for a Translator's Note,
STOP HERE: You are welcome, for there are no more to
follow, after these brief words from our sponsors—

Thanks to:
> the wise and beneficent typesetter;
> the good graces of George Stambolian's
> > incisive preface;
> the patient editorial resourcefulness of
> > Felice Picano;
> the foresight of the original French publisher,
> > Editions Albin Michel;
> the author, who may one day forgive my
> > ruthless slaughter of his brain-child;

and of course
> the late Mademoiselle Tanette Prigent,
> > who started it all, for so many;
> Mrs. Lillian Masters, for her expert guidance
> > in the aural realm;
> Mr. and Mrs. Whisler, for their unfailing
> > encouragement;
> Ledger Heavilon, for psycho-social advice
> > in the early daze;
> Mark Blasius for his persistent efforts
> > in bringing this unusual tale to the
> > attention of the English-language public;
> Doug Ireland, and to anyone who has ever tried
> > to live in a foreign land...

Need I add that the resemblance in this fiction to any persons
living or dead is purely coincidental and is a product of the
reader's fertile imagination? Thus let it read, and may he live
long and prosper with no rationing of food.

The Translator
Indianapolis,
March on, 1986

PREFACE

The hero of this novel is so beautiful that everyone who sees him wants him. He parts crowds in Paris discos and sells his body on the boulevards of Los Angeles. A wealthy old heiress protects him, a brilliant scientist lusts after his brain, a madwoman obsessed by love pursues him like a shadow, and a cat as mysteriously intelligent as an Egyptian god accompanies him wherever he goes. He trips on drugs, becomes a professional surfer, an actor. He records his life on cassette. There is a twist—he is blind. His beauty is a spectacle for everyone but himself. When he makes love, he does it as if he were reading Braille, in relief.*

*What would happen if love really were blind? Hocquenghem proposes that our world would be radically changed. His hero, Amar, does not judge others according to inherited standards of beauty. He is not influenced by the self-conscious images people fashion for themselves to attract attention, or to gain power. He offers himself with equal ease to men and women, young and old, the beautiful and the ugly. For him, each individual is first of all a body to be explored: "People's skins are my images," he says. Amar lives within that flux of polymorphous and nonexclusive desire whose revolutionary potential Hocquenghem described so effectively in his first book—until now the only one known to American readers—*Homosexual Desire.

Hocquenghem showed in this earlier work how homosexual desire could liberate all desire by challenging the phallic-centered organization of society. He also warned that the identificaiton of homosexuality as a separate category and any attempts at social acceptance and integration could lead to ever more complex forms of repression. Although Love in Relief *presents many different kinds of sexuality, it is interesting that Hocquenghem's hero remains free of a specific sexual identity. Amar's blindness places him in a politically neutral—and for Hocquenghem's purposes ideal—minority because it has not been overcharged* with social significance. On the other hand, few conditions in life are more feared than blindness or more subject to withering expressions of pity and false comprehension. By refusing to conform in any way to the role assigned to him by society, Amar becomes a spokesman for all minorities. Like the homosexual in Hocquenghem's first book, he assumes the function of a "cultural troublemaker" whose very mode of existence questions the habitual certainties of existence.

The culture Amar succeeds in troubling is, of course, Western culture, particularly in its most evolved form: the ultra-American culture of Los Angeles. With a keen sense of paradox, Hocquenghem drops his hero inside the world's image factory where he reappears as that inconceivable creature, a beautiful man unconscious of his appearance. This society of Spectacle exposes Amar to the twin diseases of the West: the drive to reduce all things to images and the passion for classifying each phenomenon. Caught up in our image systems and divorced from the sensual immediacies of reality, we are the ones who are truly blind and who blindly exploit others. By remaining literally in touch with reality Amar gains access to the only cure—he goes beyond appearances, beyond sexual and social differences, ultimately beyond sex itself and the society it engenders. He creates a new form of thought and becomes a new Tiresias prepared to guide us toward the reinvention of our culture.

Hocquenghem's talents as a journalist, filmmaker, theoretician, and political activist are all present in this novel which, like its author and its hero, resists classification. Love in Relief is an erotic adventure story about a handsome gigolo, and a philosophical tale with political punch recalling Voltaire and Sartre; a case history unexpectedly told by the patient, and a Murder Mystery in which victims pursue the assassins of their minds; a bildungsroman whose hero progresses through ever more startling discoveries, and a Science Fiction vision that transforms contemporary America into a land at once perfectly recognizable and utterly strange. Finally, Love in Relief is intricate and carefully composed music, a sonata for two voices—a madwoman, Andréa, a blind man, Amar—each resonating against the other, both so strong they outlast the worlds they describe.

—George Stambolian

When I consider how my light is spent
E're half my days, in this dark world and wide,
And that one Talent which is death to hide,
Lodg'd with me useless, though my Soul more bent
To serve therewith my Maker, and present
My true account...
John Milton

CONTENTS

Love In Relief
(L'Amour en Relief)

The Importance of Being Wanted

HANDSOME?

How could I say if he is handsome?

That would seem like betraying him. When you get to be like he is, you forget flowers, clouds, people's faces. When you're like he is, everything has to disappear, in a few days, a few months.

I don't want to describe him. I never describe him. Superstition. When I close my eyes, I become like him, and I don't want to talk anymore about his eyes, like golden walnuts, his curly hair, black curls with a touch of violet ... or even his smile, his half-smile, questioning, with an eyebrow arching as he turns when he hears someone coming up behind him, the sly grin of a ready accomplice.

He gets just so close then fades away. The death of his benefactress didn't bring him back to me. He gets just so close, as he has always done since the first time I ever saw him, three years before on Kerkenna.

What was it like on Kerkenna, Amar's home? The sea was always turbulent around the island. I never thought of the Mediterranean like that, green and furious. It crashed upon the black rocks, gleaming like shiny seals, crashed over the pumice flows, the island's specialty.

On Kerkenna the only scene fit for a postcard was at the bottom of the sea, every nook and cranny filled with a rainbow of butterfly-fish and enormous, ferocious spiny lobsters. And then there were the cliffs near the house, where birds the color of a quarry flew crying through the sky.

That summer, the Soul Sisters took a long time deciding

whether or not to take me with them. I wasn't certain the invitation was serious. The year before they had taken me to visit one of their aunts in Auvergne. In fact, they were taking me along so I would feel like I was in the way. They're always afraid I'm going to steal one of their lovers, lovers they have so much trouble snagging. Now me, I arrive, and in the twinkling of an eye I can tag the best looking guy of the lot, the one they've been trying for weeks to work up to asking for a cigarette.

The guy abandons them once he sees a woman. They'll never forgive me for that.

Still, they decided to take me with them. I was just coming back from London, where I had a duel at dawn with a hanger-on as they so elegantly put it. I don't remember if they were as hard as I make them out to be. I've never seen them since Kerkenna. But, I was with the three of them when I first laid eyes on Amar.

I ran into the Soul Sisters in Paris, on my way to London. When I got to their place on Boulevard Saint Germain they were ever so nice. They never hold back on sweetness, especially if you're just coming or just going. I had just called it quits with Léopold. When he was introducing me to his mother Léopold called me Andréa. He thought it sounded so much more Montparnasse.

I had met Léopold at Saint-Nazaire the year before, when I was passing through for a weekend by the sea ... after having slipped away from the hospital in Nantes during an outing. I just stuck with him. Léopold never guessed where I came from, even that time when we'd gone off to Paris and ran into Philippe. Philippe is my doctor. We even had a talk right in front of Léopold, and he still didn't figure it out. But I didn't go back to the hospital with Philippe. I knew he'd never call the cops.

Léopold's family owns a company that makes *petit beurre* biscuits. Provincial upper middle class, full of their little prejudices, they lived in a big English-style villa with three gardeners to keep up the front lawn that nobody ever uses. I stayed there three months, after I became pregnant, and never once dared to put my chaise longue out there. Springtime chirped, the sparrows squabbled in the grass, and I could always sense his mother behind the heavy curtains, upstairs, watching me. She had a way of rapping the window with her knuckles that made kids and birds flee for their lives.

All got up in her fancy gray suit that matched her gray hair, Léopold's mother drove her own gray 2CV, and treated me well enough, sort of like a daughter-in-law. Until she became more sure of herself, and started making me feel like an intruder.

You could find her every morning at breakfast time on the veranda overlooking the sea. You ought to see all they had for breakfast: toast, omelets, salads of every color, at least three plates stacked one on top of the other, and real silverware for every person. English again. Well, I can never stand anything but black coffee for breakfast, especially after hitting the clubs in Nantes the night before with Léopold. It was right about that time that the workers at the family factory occupied the plant. May of '68. The old lady didn't know what to do. Then, during all the strikes, she decided she'd be nice to me. That meant thinking of me as a cow, one she wanted to fatten up for the sake of the child soon to enter the family. She would pucker her lips every time I refused a mountain of eggs carried in under a silver dome by one of the help.

At the end of May, things got worse. She "wasn't born yesterday," she once said right in front of me. The riot squad had finally reoccupied the factory, and now here she was trying to get me to say I wasn't even sure the kid was Léopold's.

Léopold was a sort of a blond lug with a flat nose, twenty-seven years old, and still taking off his shoes when we'd come in a little late from a night out in Nantes, to keep from waking up the old lady. In those days I preferred someone just a bit slow, like Léopold, as a lover; especially someone who could really make love well, full strength like he was getting back at all the rest. During the day he was scared stiff of his family.

He wasn't tall, but well-built, thanks to tennis; he had a small mouth and a big prick. He turned me on, he was dumb, and he turned into an animal when I undid his tie with only one hand and slipped a finger in his fly. I was young, and I thought sex was just for fun.

When he began to mention London, I felt like the idea came from his mother, and that he was a little ashamed. I understood that my Saint-Lazaire fling was over, or nearly over, and that was okay by me. As for keeping the brat, at twenty-five I didn't quite feel cut out for playing nursemaid, dealing with diapers and burped up milk.

So, I went to Paris to catch a plane to London. I met the Soul Sisters at a party. I was supposed to stay a day and instead I stayed a week in their cream colored apartment, watching my belly swell. They were the ones who came up with the bright idea of getting me married to Léopold. A brilliant idea since it would get me out of their hair. But they weren't the ones who'd have to marry that crumb from a biscuit factory.

Maybe that would have been a good way to end up, but I wasn't ready to end up. Sure, I would have really liked to have a classy match, just to see the faces of my seven brothers and sisters in their little miners' shacks when I came back to Hayange, Madame Léopold in a Mercedes.

But, that bunch were my only friends in Paris. I spent a lot of time with gays without really having sought them out. I always had a better time with them than with other people, even taking into account their spite and indifference. I was a parrot among apes. We didn't have a thing in common except the lovers we all squabbled over tooth and nail. It was a great time, in short. They were more direct and natural with me than any lover ever was. And I lived the same illusions they did: the satisfaction of being able to count the men you've had, the importance of being wanted.

So, I was in London to get rid of the heir to the biggest cookie fortune west of Paris. Léopold came to see me. I didn't want anything more to do with him. I was really in the pits, drained. I rolled over against the bright enamel wall to keep from having to talk to him. He disappeared, leaving me with a barred check, of course, the kind I wouldn't be able to cash right away. Not a very big one either. Fortunately, a group of women supporting the newly aborted sent me a money order at the hospital. And my friends from Boulevard Saint Germain? They sent me an orchid via Interflora, wrapped in plastic. They let me pay the international surtax.

After five days, the clinic threw me out; I was still bleeding. The day after my d. and c. I had started trying to pick up the male nurses. When I got back to Paris, I had a choice: since I had just had an abortion, the ultra snobs from Women's Lib were fighting over me. I decided upon the Boulevard Saint Germain.

We went out every night drinking up my abortion checks. Finally, generously, they asked if I wanted to go on a vacation with them. With what was left from the biscuits, we could rent a house for practically nothing on Kerkenna, a Tunisian island I only knew about because of its earthquakes. It seemed that Kerkenna was the ideal retreat for a young abortee.

It was the summer of '68, the summer of broken down barricades, when we arrived on Kerkenna. After a few hours they had all forgotten I was invited too, *and* that I had just gotten out of the clinic. They treated me like they treated each other—no holds barred. And if any victims ever carried their own misery, it was the Soul Sisters, so I just had to make do. I've slept with so many so-called real men, men who thought they were God's gift to women, then laid all the weight of their confessions on me, crushing me with misery and inner weakness. The Soul Sisters were the only guys I've ever known who didn't need an ounce of pity, World War Three men of steel.

As for the resort, approaching Kerkenna by boat reveals what looks like a bunch of slag heaps from an industrial city in the North transplanted to the sunny skies of Tunisia, because the island is completely volcanic. Most tourists get fed up after they turn an ankle in the hardened minerals. It looks like a big smelting plant. Not a good-sized tree to be seen. Lava dust everywhere, vines spreading all over the ground, sticker bushes and little caper shrubs. That's the kind with purple flowers and bitter little berries that I tried to eat.

The town was bombed by the Americans in '42. Crumbling walls, gutted and empty military barracks pitted with bullet holes, where the kids take their goats. No one has heard a word about post-war reconstruction. All over the island you stumble across bomb debris, pieces of rusty metal sticking up out of the ground, and the cement of the bunkers that encircle Kerkenna blends right into the rocks. According to the brochure, Kerkenna was used to close off the gulf, back then, a stationary aircraft carrier the Allies bombed the hell out of.

It looked like war everywhere: battlefields between the volcano and the sea. The only foreigners were some Japanese scientists looking for certain kinds of lava only found on their islands or here; and some crazy, bearded snorklers who'd flown thousands of kilometers with harpoons, just to kill some fish.

The big attraction in our isolation was the road, melting in the sun on its way to town. I watched the "traffic." At first I would hear a mosquito buzzing in the distance, then get louder. The heat would make the landscape tremble. The motor would change speeds down below the house, snort, groan, and a scooter would pass, tossing pebbles onto the front of our terrace.

All they have on Kerkenna is scooters. It's the only form of horsepower they know. The Tunisians on the island were like Italians to me, only a little more wild—and more virile. As for my traveling companions ... Arabs drove them off the deep end.

For the first few days this household, in which I was the only female, was pretty calm. Intimidated by our surroundings, we watched each other. In spite of the sun, I was cold all the time. There was something chilling in those fields of rock. The water was cold, too. I had brought along all of Françoise Sagan's novels: I was there to rest.

We had rented a house at the top of a cliff with a view of the sea. A little unmanned lighthouse marked our property on the right: a toy lighthouse, black and white—the only sign of life. That, and the lights of vehicles on the road. Each evening the beacon played over a greenish sky.

The Soul Sisters had given me the only room set apart from the rest—a real nun's cell—in the former cistern. There wasn't a single fresh spring on the whole island. But the owners had cut a window in the big stones, and had plastered and whitewashed the vaulted ceiling.

Naturally, by the end of the week the others all wanted it. They couldn't stand each other any more, all three of them in one big room, a former stable, where they had hung up sheets as dividers. As usual with gays, they'd all slept with one another at different times when they were running around together. But none of them could stand to hear each other beating off alone in the dark.

Come to think of it, they were really pretty conventional, especially with me. They wouldn't even let me sunbathe in peace on our blue and white faience terrace. From the terrace you could see peasant homes: little piles of rocks that nearly blended into what looked like a moonscape. The pile to the right covered our landlords. They were no longer poor, due to decent market prices for the capers they grew. One woman showed me around inside her home. Under those rocks they had a stereo and a T.V., and along the light blue walls were red and gold benches in velvet.

Below our house the road peeled in the sun, enormous holes in the asphalt across from our doorway. Trucks carrying field hands or fish vendors had to slow down in front of the house which gave them time to look me over, laughing, so I had to nudge up my towel to cover my breasts. The traumatized trio would storm in saying I was giving us a bad reputation with the islanders. Pure and simple jealousy. If the workers had seen them stripped down, a piece of cardboard stuck on to their noses to keep from getting burned, there wouldn't have been such a fuss.

It was on this same road that I came to know Amar. Well ... that *we* came to know Amar.

We had rented a scooter when we arrived on the island. Even today when I hear the sound of a scooter—which is less and less often—I get a knot in my chest. A scooter ... the huge open sores in the tar, gravel, little wheels slipping, spinning...

We waited all afternoon in the heat, dust and grease of the service station. But finally we got hold of a blue Vespa with two lines of gold metal-flake paint, ending in arrows. All three of us hopped on and ground up the hill, terrifying the donkeys along the road; under the sun we were three sheets to the wind.

They mostly speak Italian on Kerkenna. It's really funny, Arabs speaking another language as badly as they do French. They feminize objects, saying la Vespa, la Kodak. For me the scooter was a nasty little male.

Everybody had a turn. Me, too, even though they all said it was bad for my convalescence. When there are four of you and only one scooter, problems begin when you want to go into town evenings. The two who got to go left the others fuming in front of an oil lamp, trying to chase off the day's collection of mosquitoes. I was left more often than I should have been.

There really wasn't very much to do in town at night. You could watch the boat come in from the mainland and whistle at the new prisoners who still hadn't realized what they'd fallen into. You could go to the film club at the local church to see a lot of old Roman-toga and Hindu movies which broke all the time, and hope that Amar would be among the viewers when the lights came up. You could climb to the blockhouses surrounding the port—complete with Arab poems, graffiti of cocks and hearts and arrows all over the walls, and the smell of crap. You could have an ice cream at a brand new bar by the port, and could try to get Amar to come along—without his friends…

But I'm getting ahead of myself. At first we behaved ourselves pretty well on the pretext that we'd all come for a rest. We went for hours without talking, watching the cross the lighthouse beams formed above our heads, the blades of a big white helicopter in the night silently sweeping the house.

Each remained inside himself, speaking softly, caught up in some secret regret, not daring to mention that boredom already reared its ugly head in spite of the sun and beach, the postcards to people you never think to speak to when you see them.

I sent off two a day to Philippe, my doctor, who accumulated a collection of spiny *rascasse* fish and sea urchins in Technicolor. Then there was the tomato stained Tunisian newspaper in French we bought in town. It didn't seem to talk at all about the France of the summer of '68; pages dragged on about the opening of model olive groves while there were only a few lines on French elections. The others kept looking for news about the Sorbonne, where for a few days they had founded a Committee of Gays, among numerous other groups, Armenians, Domestic Workers, etc. The Sahel Desert advanced ominously, but the puddle of articles on happenings in France dwindled every day, under the sun. So, they cooked—cooked in the morning, after siesta, arguing over whether or not to add which herbs, forgetting everything else.

The appeal of cooking wilted away when there was just enough cash left to buy starches. So we organized, taking turns going out on the scooter every evening: the hunt was on again. I don't know what could force them to go to Kerkenna at midnight unless it was an all-out search for cock. I could hear the scooter coming back late, zigzagging up the hill through the locusts' whine. No one talked about men, but cruising was once again the main attraction. They had come back from coming back. They couldn't remain widows of the Spring of '68 forever. Then, one evening, they even stopped going to the trouble of making noises in our waterless bathroom—where there was only a wooden pail. Sometimes, one would plaster a little smile of satisfaction upon his face when he got up at two in the afternoon. Pure bluff. He hadn't done anything in town the night before: it was just to aggravate the others. I could never understand what in the world they could find at night in the middle of nowhere, in a port without boats, in a town without cafés, in streets without lights. Strange. The most virile men, the most courageous, would think twice before going to some of the places they went to every night. And it was precisely that kind of man they hoped to meet wandering around down there.

At night, I would watch the lighthouse sweeping across my pink nylon curtain and hear the Vespa as its motor stopped at the bottom of the hill whenever they brought someone home with them. The Arabs are hush-hush and they didn't want anyone to wise up to what was going on—especially me. I'd roll over in bed and imagine the night's catch, the scrungiest wino of the port no doubt, getting a decent blowjob.

One lover moved into the house: a waiter from the café in Kerkenna. He arrived on a bike one day at lunch time. We were beginning to be short on money and were eating pasta with olive oil and dried fennel picked along the edge of the road. When the Arab boy entered, all of them blushed. He must have been a regular, taking turns with each. When anyone borrowed my room, I had to shake out the blankets and sheets 'til they were shreds, throw the window wide open; but their filthy odor still remained.

Some time later I was peeling some cucumbers the landlord had given us. Evening was falling upon the terrace. Amar appeared in the doorway. I'm sure he hadn't come by accident. Our house must already have had a reputation.

It all goes back to those holes in the road I've already mentioned. Like leprous sores, they grew bigger every day, digging the tar skin away to its pebbles. Because I was there, the holes in front of the terrace had become a joke. Old men on bicycles would turn their heads to look at me and nearly break their necks.

That evening I wasn't watching them go past. I was peeling cucumbers. I could hear the scooter climb the hill: two of the others coming back from shopping. I was keeping track of the changing gears because they were supposed to be bringing me back cigarettes. When I raised my head, I felt dizzy from hunching over the basket in that heat. I squinted. Someone was in front of the sun, invisible, a halo of golden rays in place of his head, a black silhouette with long legs astride a bicycle. Even so I could see his smile, a white spot in a black hole. My first memory of Amar is blinding. There was the sound of metal as another bicycle arrived, an old rickety woman's bike, crashing into one of the holes. Amar turned around. He was waiting for the boy riding up.

He wasn't the same Amar as today. Not quite fifteen, too tall for his age, his trouser legs climbing his calf. His friend was three or four years older and really ugly. Of course the ugly one did all the talking, offering whatever a tourist could possible want. They were stopped between two holes in the road, Amar perched on his old bike. The older one righted his and they looked my way. That angered me and very nearly ended the whole story. Since our arrival, in the midst of those queens I was the wise virgin who might have just aborted some little Jesus. I told myself why couldn't I at least try. So I began to cruise this young stranger whose face I could make out by now, just to piss the others off. You see, Amar was a queen's wildest unadulterated dream.

He didn't make a move. He just smiled, his arm around the waist of his horrible friend, looking at me. His friend's face was chock full of zits, but Amar didn't seem to pay any more attention to them than he did to the insects buzzing around our heads.

I turned around and saw all the other occupants of our house silent. One was by the cracked-open door, the other two near the scooter, whose motor must have stopped from the shock. The one in the doorway had been watching Amar longer than I. At least that's what he claimed later on, so he could say he was the first to see him. But I'm the one that got up. I wiped my hands on my blouse and signalled for them to come in.

They leaned their bikes on the wall, and Hocine—that was the ugly one's name—came first.

Now that I could see them clearly, as they sat on our two chaise longues, Hocine was even more repulsive; Amar kept stroking him absent-mindedly, like you would a familiar pet. All the boys from there hold each other by the little finger. I don't know if Amar was used to Hocine's ugliness or indifferent to it, as I later came to think. He acted like he didn't notice. Perhaps all those caresses were to console Hocine, letting him take part in Amar's success. Amar was the tourists' main attraction. At least that's what we decided after they'd left late that night, talking for hours about them.

The hanging naked lightbulb gave me hideous wrinkles and turned Hocine's zits into enormous pocks, but it left Amar just as handsome. My friends thought it was like a play: Hocine played the jewelbox, Amar the diamond. He probably would have opened his long lashed eyes wide if he could have heard us after he left that night. Anyway, Amar acted naturally. He was "with" Hocine. "It's like my brother, like the sea and the waves," he would say in that high-school French he used and even knew how to write, in capital letters.

Within ten minutes we had exchanged names and addresses. We had shared pasta—our daily pasta. After spending the previous night making fun of those queens who dressed up in white djellabahs trying to pass themselves off as Moslems, the Soul Sisters spent that evening learning the Arab names for water, for bread, for wine, for every object on the table—and the numbers from one to ten. They dragged out a bottle of wine they had hidden and insisted that the evening continue, but Amar and Hocine stood up and buttoned their jackets. I hardly said a word during the meal and they hardly looked at me. A tall white woman with no veil, one who even drank wine: I suppose I must have seemed questionable to them.

In the next month, Amar and Hocine went along with us every day to a cove where we tried to catch little black fish that looked like miniature marine bulldogs. Amar didn't come in swimming. He would take off his shoes and squat on a rock. Hocine reread for the hundredth time an examination manual for the French Postal Service because he wanted to work in Paris.

Some days Amar wore a blue djellabah; other times he dressed in jeans and sneakers like everyone else, following some rhythm none of us understood, but having to do with religious holidays or family visitors. He went home every evening, no matter what we suggested, home to that mysterious house nestled under a boulder, the top of a fig tree sticking out of it, a house we never entered. Only his mother lived with him. His father was in Villeurbanne, near Lyon, and had been in France for nearly twenty years—since 1949, to be precise, the time of the last earthquake. The people on Kerkenna dated all their personal events by cataclysms. Amar's mother had been abandoned by his father, who had taken away Amar's sisters—each of them by a different wife.

The photos of the sisters that Amar let us see showed a kitchen from a low-rent highrise, with a T.V. set and some man with a moustache and black hair. Not bad the others said. He was surrounded by a blotch of brightly colored fabric, which was the series of sisters dressed to the hilt with hennaed hair, silver jewelry, and lines of floating blue dots tattooed in the corners of their eyes. Amar was the only boy in the family, which visibly depressed him sometimes. Too heavy a responsibility. It prevented him from drinking and partying, obliged him to have to work hard in three more years, after he turned eighteen.

The Soul Sisters never failed to boast of their good connections; they knew queens who worked as process servers in some ministry and only had to stick out a hand to come up with a blank residence cards so Amar could live in France. As their tempting multiplied, they asked themselves, "Amar comes to see us because he's interested, doesn't he?" They had discarded the idea the very first time because he always turned down their invitations at the café. Now they thought they might still be in luck—with their imaginary jobs in Paris. Once there a big scene happened. Two of them wouldn't speak for a whole day to the other, "cold wicked queen who sees scheming in everything," while the other one sneered about their "disgusting colonial naïveté."

At that time, none of us had the means to outdo the others with wealth, or to conquer Amar by providing him with work or a place to stay in Paris. My companions didn't have any real careers yet. They did a bit of painting to earn their living, mostly trashing up friends' apartments and calling it redecorating. There was some work as extras in films. At worst, they sold fries at the flea markets. Later on, when they make a little money, they'll still call themselves "students," to make themselves sound younger to foreigners.

Amar liked all of us, the whole bunch, the way he liked the music on our stereo, and Hocine. But all these people that he thought of us as an indissoluble mass of friendship, when left to themselves hated each other sooner or later. Because of him.

To begin with, each maneuvered to separate Amar from Hocine: not a conspiracy to be proud of. We took him to the island's French restaurant, a fake chalet under the palms run by a couple of Swiss. Impossible to get Hocine in because he was wearing sandals, not dress shoes. Supposedly the Soul Sisters only had one pair to loan out, yet each had at least two pairs of white Italian moccasins stashed away. They said they didn't want to get them ruined.

At the beach no one spoke to Hocine, and I noticed that Amar became more and more troubled. Finally Hocine stopped coming and Amar didn't say a word about it, as though Hocine had never existed. Yet no one dreamed to think of Amar as insensitive.

Amar seemed to have trouble experiencing emotions without physically touching someone. Hocine was there as long as Amar could lean on him, hug him, pinch him, stroke his hair. From the moment Hocine was out of range of touch he was forgotten.

When Amar was finally all ours it was everyone for himself. My desire was more one of protecting him, of mothering him under the dwarf olive trees at siesta time. I was more excited by his face than his body. I'd never felt that kind of love. What I was undertaking became my reason for having come to the island. I began to feel how dangerous the others might be for him.

The disputes and mistrust among us began with Amar's arrival. Where are you going? Who's been using my cream and didn't put the cap back on? You had the Vespa yesterday ... I stopped loaning out my room. No one ever explicitly said he wanted to sleep with Amar. But I checked to see if I could lock my door.

These three queens lost in sex couldn't even touch Amar's arm without jumping. They became like little girls; they who had reached the point where the only thing of any importance was sex—which made them really sort of tragic—and less than a hundred years among the four of us.

When the moon was already high in the sky, we'd go on foot as far as the "Eye of Venus," a lake in the volcano crater filled with warm salty water bubbling up from underground springs. It was said that the sea flowed under the mountain to mix with the entrails of the Earth. Past the little hill that formed the crater, you could hear really loud music from the island's only discothèque, for the people in local hotels.

A shrewd businessman from Tunis had opened the disco the summer before. An open-air dance floor of colored glass tiles at the edge of the lake was lighted from beneath. Music echoed in the mountains as enormous, laughing Dutch women hung onto Lebanese and Greek playboys from the beach, and tossed wilted jasmines into the black crater waters.

We didn't have to pay. We were chic compared to the other tourists; white suits for the Sisters, blue muslin for me. Amar was proud to be with us. He introduced us to his friends who sat bunched at the entrance between the flower pots that lined the dirt path, where they ridiculed the clumsy dancers in streams of Arabic—puppets colored red and green by the dance floor tiles. I would go see the D.J., who played sambas for us, and the Astaire Sisters would put on dance demonstrations for busloads of dumbfounded tourists.

We also used to go to the big rock table on the northern part of the island, a huge white flat rock with a gentle slope that suddenly plunges into the sea at the foot of a cliff. On the scooter at night, we replayed the game of wolf, goat and cabbage to get down there—a delicate balance of the proper combination of driver, rider and whomever waited at each end of the moonlit cliff. The water was phosphorescent and warmer than in the daytime. The rock was warmer too, and the trick was to try to be the last one to remain there with Amar watching the cliff in the growing obscurity, waiting for the moment when a rock would come loose with a sinister crack, followed by a plop in the black water below.

The weather began to change and the great September storms arrived. We stayed shut in between the sheets hanging flapping in the wind, dissecting *Le Monde*, playing cards in the big room.

In France, buses were filling again with people on their way to work. We were still on vacation like the nightowls who meet the garbage men in the morning. Vacation from what, since no one had a job? France had forgotten us on the island. The Soul Sisters talked about going to live in Italy, or looking for jobs as teachers in Tunis. The two younger ones took to getting plastered in town every night. They left me alone in my room to watch the rain beating upon the windowpanes. In the big room, the surviving sister popped open bottles of Coke, the only noise I heard. No one had slept with Amar yet. To keep an eye on each other they'd reached an agreement: they'd wait until he made up his mind, or till we were trapped on Kerkenna by winter.

We passed evenings like a family, discussing politics—I didn't understand any more about it than Amar did. One day he let me put make-up on him; emerald-green lips and eyelids, his cheeks touched with sparkles. He took one look at himself in the mirror and ran straight to the outside faucet. He came back laughing, make-up running over his brown skin, his hair matted down by water.

Being stuck inside those long days made us all more irritable. The two drinkers had stopped cooking; the other one refused to do the dishes, shutting himself up every afternoon to write. The dishes weren't a problem any more, anyway, because once when they found Amar washing them himself, to try to prevent any more scenes, they broke every dish.

It was confession time. They paraded into my room one after the other. They now had only one desire: to clear out—taking Amar with them, of course. One morning when I opened my window, the air was full of the smell of wet caper trees. One of the Sisters asked Amar to go away with him by boat to Sicily, at least for a few days, "and after that we'll see." But Amar didn't want to understand "we'll see." He asked what was going to happen to us who stayed behind. Not that I even counted anymore, now that my abortion money was all gone. For a long time we had been living in suspense waiting for money orders the post office took weeks to deliver. We passed our time waiting in siege at the only window there, surrounded by flies.

In the big room, the two lushes devoted their time to playing games of *crapette*, chugging warm Rosé, doubling up laughing if anybody said a word to them. All our conversation in French became really cutting, even if the words meant nothing themselves. That only left the dozen or so Arabic words we practiced in front of Amar that weren't insults.

Since Amar only understood the French he'd learned at school and wrote it better than he could speak it, you could say anything in front of him as long as you did so in a nice tone. I got the same treatment a thousand times; they'd say dirty stinking cunt or nigger whore as though they were saying "pass the salt." It was especially searing one afternoon when they had drunk a whole case of little bottles of *bourra*, a local White Lightning. The oldest Sister was stretched out on the bed next to Amar, who had also drunk a little too much. He started to put his hand on Amar's chest through the half opened shirt, sobbing warnings about all the rest of us hypocrites who only wanted to sleep with our guests. As usual, Amar acted like he didn't understand. This time he sprang up and asked if we would loan him the scooter.

Every boy on the island wanted to borrow that scooter. We always refused. You only had to see them drive once to understand why. There are people who go right to the edge because they don't think as much of risk as we do: Amar was one. The Sisters had spent the entire afternoon trying to get him drunk on *bourra*. I tried to say no they mustn't let him do it, but they told me that of course the scooter belonged to everyone and it wasn't up to *me* to decide.

The squabble went on; two wanted to take Amar for a little spin without letting him drive; the drunkest of all said it was ridiculous, nobody needed some tired old queen for a tutor— among other horrible things. I put my hands on my ears and shouted at them all to just shut up. Before I knew it they'd left, slamming the door.

Only then did I remember the night before when I had gone down to Kerkenna to shop and the grocer had helped me change a flat rear tire; he'd noticed the spare was bald. I got up to tell them but when I reached the corner of the house I saw that the one who had stayed with Amar was now kissing him on the mouth. I hiccoughed and realized I'd had quite a few myself. I slipped away to go lie face down on my bed so the hiccoughs would stop. I put pillows over my head to block out the noise of the motor they were still trying to get started. They couldn't get it to go. I promised myself that if it started to turn over I'd go warn them about the spare, praying to the stars above that it wouldn't, because at that moment I hated them too much to even speak.

I raised my head. It was awfully quiet. I ran to the window and saw the Vespa coasting far away down the hill, the passenger's white shirt flapping in the breeze as he hung onto Amar, who leaned across the handlebars. The bike jerked as he threw it into gear, and the motor sputtered on. I began running to catch them, but they were only a white spot climbing the turn in the distance.

I headed back to the house walking through black volcanic rock as gray daylight fell out of the clouds. The other two Sisters were sacked out in the big room next to an empty bottle. Night fell. I must have slept a little. I heard a police siren in the distance, which stirred things up in the big room; the empty bottle fell to the floor. I didn't turn on any lights; I wanted to stay in the dark. The siren came closer and the car stopped in front of our house. It wasn't the police at all but an ambulance. Its headlights reflected off the terrace, now glistening with rain. The queen who'd gone off with Amar climbed out of the ambulance, his arm in a sling, a bandage on his chin. I grabbed hold of him screaming "Amar!" He grimaced in a comedy of pain as he shook me loose. The others came out of the big room, rubbing their eyes. I forced myself to be nice and asked the victim if he'd been hurt in an accident. He said it was nothing, really, just a shoulder out of joint. "Thank God my face was spared," he added, imitating a starlet confronting the press. I felt it was a poor moment for that kind of humor, and I broke down, so in the end I was the one they had to comfort.

Amar was still in the hospital. As he was trying to dodge a hole in the darkness, the Vespa had smashed into the wall of a villa at the edge of town. The next day all eyes were dry. It was clear, without anyone having to say it, that the time for our departure had arrived. We walked to the owners' farm to let them know and to call the hospital. It was impossible to get a single detail over the phone, except that Amar was fine. If that was true, why were they keeping him?

The wind settled down. It was gray and muggy on that mountain of lava. We stayed outside on the terrace and all of a sudden there was a veritable army of bikes and Vespas climbing toward our house. They remained in front of the house, none daring to come in. From the field across the road two of Amar's relatives yelled out some things in Arabic that couldn't have been very nice. Finally, one of Amar's buddies stepped up to present us with a request: because Amar was under eighteen, in our declaration to the police we had to say that one of *us* was driving the Vespa. His friends weren't trying to threaten us as we'd thought, but rather were pleading with us. But the police didn't ask us for any details. We were the only ones outside of his family, who thought that we were in any way responsible for the accident. The boys were only trying to keep Amar from getting into trouble. They all seemed to think it was his fault; his craziness, that craziness about machines all the kids of the island possessed, which mangled and scarred them every summer, and which they spoke about objectively, sadly.

When they left, we felt ashamed, although no one knew exactly why. We packed our bags and left a call for an early taxi. The morning that we left Kerkenna, we settled in at the café looking at the deserted dock through windows dripping streams of rain; the terrace awnings hung swollen with water. The waiter was in a real snit because of the weather, because of the end of the season.

When there was a break in the rain, we ran to the hospital, splattered from puddles in the road, passing between grim houses whose walls were normally light pink or pistachio green. Everything had been soaked, gotten darker, even the people's skins, which looked more gray than brown.

The hospital was located at the end of the quay between a storeyard of old military trucks rusting since the war and abandoned villas with crumbling cement columns, showing off inner reinforcements. I had bought some coffee-liqueur candy and the others never stopped telling me how bad it was for someone sick. We passed a little crowd in front of the hospital: taxi drivers waiting, nurses with dirty smocks sitting on window-sills, old men in pajamas with stubbled faces standing around under the awning, looking up at the dull sky, picking their noses.

At the entrance, one side of the glass door was shattered and filled in with old newspapers and adhesive tape. No one would talk to us in the corridors, so we had to go back downstairs to find somebody who worked there and who could tell us what room Amar was in. When I asked the man about the liqueur candy he smiled and claimed some himself.

There were visitors entering and leaving rooms everywhere carrying food, blankets and babies.

The second floor was a little calmer. In front of Amar's room a "SILENCE" sign cried in the desert. That was where all the noise came from—a radio, five or six people reading the newspaper aloud or in animated discussions. At first I couldn't even see Amar because some character in a smock was standing in front of him. A nurse was washing her hands, and several of Amar's pals who had been in front of our house the night before were sitting around the bed, smoking cigarettes. They stared holes right through me. The whole island was judging me. Hocine was there too; he gave me the cold shoulder.

I sat down on a plastic stool and looked at Amar—I was unable to say a word. He had one leg in a cast, held up high by some contraption hanging from the ceiling. A blood-stained bandage coiled around his forehead didn't hide his closed and swollen eyes. What struck me most were his hands, tied to the sides of the bed as though he would be tortured. An old woman squatted near the window. All I could see of her was her back, heaving to the rhythm of her sobbing.

Amar's torso was wrapped in some sort of stretch cotton net with wide meshwork, and underneath his skin was brown and smooth, his muscles flexing as he stretched out his hands mechanically trying to get loose. He spoke loud, off-stage, in Arabic, probably telling them all to let him out of there, p.d.q. I could hear doors closing, hospital slippers shuffling in the corridor. The old woman—his mother—started to hit her head against the floor. Amar didn't open his eyes. It was hot and sticky in the room, and a fly landed on him, started to suck the clotted blood at the corner of one eye. I wanted to go. The old man in the smock, Amar's doctor, gestured as he talked, and the fly took off.

All of a sudden Amar began to yell, tried to get up, clenched his fists, pulled at his bandages. I was hypnotized by the play of his muscles under the network of cotton; even in the middle of all that, it turned me on. He kept repeating the same phrase in Arabic over and over, louder and louder. He opened his black and blue bloodshot eyes; they were alive, they moved, they looked at me. I quietly asked Hocine, squatting on the floor and clenching his teeth, what Amar wanted. He whispered dryly that Amar was asking why we were all hiding from him, but the doctor put a finger to his lips to quiet me. Hocine had begun silently to cry. I was suffocating. I wanted to get up, felt a searing pain tearing the base of my abdomen. I looked down and saw my dress stained, blood dripping down my legs and onto my sandals. The nurse rushed over, letting the faucet run over, as I slumped down in a faint. When I understood that Amar was blind, the poorly healed scar from my d. and c. had reopened.

Mrs. Hallowe'en

I woke up and knew it was morning. Sometimes in California, when hitchhiking was slow I would fall asleep on the sand. The heat fell softly around me, the ground under my sandals crunching, warm crystallized sugar, taking solid form beneath my back with the humidity of twilight or dawn's early light. I woke up because the sun touched my hand, and I was waiting for it to dry the salted drops of dew upon my face.

When I say that, I am talking again like people who can see. It really felt more as though I, not the dew, was evaporating, gently lifted toward the rising sun. In California, I began to feel my skin, to become my skin. Its sensitivity had abruptly changed, multiplied by each pore, crazed by this salted electricity, wildly excited by sun and sea. My skin. Even through a T-shirt, walking along the freeway at night, across the sound-filled horizon, the music from the snack bar at the crossroads I assume, and the roar of motors like huge bumblebees flying all around me, I could still pick out an oncoming car by the heat of its headlights climbing my back. There would be one moment when this heat became searing, almost a burning. I would turn to face it, imagine the big shining eyes looking me over as the driver slowed down across from Rudolph Valentino Park, not quite daring to pull up alongside me.

Meanwhile Zita would climb upon me to insult the four-wheeler in cat talk, mechanically clawing my shoulder as she meowed.

Amar is not exactly my name. The name my mother used to cry for hours in the little courtyard shaded by a fig tree with a painted white trunk where the laundry hung to dry. My real name is U'mar, like the second Caliph after the Prophet: the one *you* call Omar because Europeans never can pronounce Arabic vowels.

My mother raised me alone. My half-sisters went to Europe before I was born. I carry *her* name. As a last name, my mother used the name of her village.

It was the Europeans who called me Amar on Kerkenna. Later, I could have corrected my name, but it had become a part of me. Amar clung to my flesh. People who did not even know each other made the same mistake. *O*mar. Mrs. Hallowe'en would have said I sounded like a bridge player.

It took me years to be able to speak the Europeans' languages very well. When people asked me my name at first in America, I had to ask them to repeat the question, a terribly humiliating situation which I avoided like the plague.

One evening I cannot recall without shame I was on the twenty-second story in a hotel. I have been around so many elevators that I can recognize what country it is by the style of the elevator car. The hotel was beside a large port. Beyond the huge, cold bay windows the lake teemed with the drone of skimming boats. From time to time I heard a noise quite clearly; a siren, a cry drifted up like a piece of paper caught in an eddy of wind, rising to our windowsill. I was lying next to a presence who gurgled who knows what and held my hand.

I thought she was calling me. I leaned over her outstretched body and had her repeat what she had said. Too late, I understood. I had made this woman explain to me she'd been saying "I love you."

Since then I've learned English. There was a long confusing time during which I debated with myself in silence, or near-silence. I entered and left rooms and bedrooms and all my conversation passed from my hand to the hand pulling me along to a table, a car, into a drawing-room, from one group to another. Groups of odors of dignified older people, elegant voices speaking incomprehensible idioms, nasal and proper. These groups came nearer, then drew away again, atolls of noise, under Mrs. Hallowe'en's towing. Sometimes an arm, an evening gown or sports jacket would linger next to me, dragging me into halls, elevators, cars with silent chauffeurs. I never lacked the reassurance of her cane, tiny conspiratorial taps for my benefit, an audible telegraph destined to keep me posted. Mrs. Hallowe'en was old, so old I never really knew her age. I cannot read the identity of others. As for whether the Central European nobility beneath which she hid her Jewish origins was authentic, that was beyond my reach.

Born on the banks of the Danube, she had married a governor of Minnesota, himself a product of public assistance who had risen to the Capitol.

His name, which his widow had kept, meant in English the Feast of all Saints, or All Dead, or whatever. It was the result of some orphanage director's inspiration when he was searching for a name for his young pupil.

I have sometimes heard receptionists say that it was a perfect name for Mrs. Hallowe'en, that she could have been a model for the cut-out pumpkins the Americans use to frighten their little children. She wore dentures and a wig, and she carried a cane.

She called me "Amar," so Amar I remained. When we were first together I was Amar because I was too shy to say anything about it. Afterward I made this sacrifice for her—an extreme sacrifice. When I was a child if someone pronounced my name wrong it was not in error, but as an insult, one I corrected with my fists. But after my accident I liked to listen better than to speak, to be called than to call myself. On Kerkenna when I was crazy about speed and quarrels like the others, I was more interested in proving my indifference than in being violent. The French would say I am a fatalist; doctors that all invalids are passive.

I often feel the modification of my name is a sign. Since my accident, I have become so much another person that I am in a sense reborn. Mrs. Hallowe'en brought me into the world a second time, and things changed to the point that I was no longer sure I was an Arab. She often spoke French with me, pre-war French. Perfectly multilingual, she later taught me "*le fluent* English." Too late for me to ever know who all those people from Acapulco to Copacabana were, those permanent exiles from their palaces, senior citizens with rich and heavy names from European history, ambassadors, left-overs from before the war who made up her world. I am probably the last person to have slept with the Austro-Hungarian nobility.

Mrs. Hallowe'en was American by marriage. Some days after we first met she offered me my first tape recorder. Since then I have spent years in front of every kind of tape imaginable. I have never been without a tape recorder, true faithful dogs to the human voice. Mrs. Hallowe'en insisted I spend days on end in hotel rooms repeating unknown languages. I had my whole life to devote to study if I wanted to. Mrs. Hallowe'en was immortal, or tireless at the very least, and I drank in the sum total of human knowledge, murmured by thousands of anonymous voices.

I had always studied out loud. I have said I was different from other people from the simple fact that I cannot understand something *not* read aloud. More different because of that than from the fact that I do not see.

Even today I scan what I am writing, murmuring low between my teeth. Koran means "reading," but only Europeans ever imagined reading which is "mute."

Like all young people on Kerkenna what with scooters, jukeboxes and Egyptian and Hindu films, I didn't have much time for the old bearded men in turbans who my mother would often go to see for fresh afternoons of silent meditation. But without ever being pious I have long been a believer. Repeating the *fatihat al Kitab*—the first verses of the Islamic profession of faith—so many times formed within me a physical link between the Text and the proclamation, between my brain and my lips, even though I no longer believe in any god.

Since I learned that Amar means "to love" in Portuguese, I gave up trying to correct my name. They are right, those who see me, who name me. After all, those on the outside speak better of me than I can. Between them and my consciousness they describe a frontier. It has a different name depending on which side of it you look from. I too look at the frontier from my confused interior confines. Mrs. Hallowe'en taught me never to be afraid of words of the sighted ... I say "I'll see you tomorrow," without any worry. I "look" to see what time it is in Braille on my digicassette. The sighted cannot claim to have a monopoly on attention to time and to appointment schedules. Mrs. Hallowe'en also insisted I turn toward the person I'm speaking to. On Kerkenna in the months following my accident, no one had the least idea of my new needs. My mother wrung her hands; I was surrounded by neighbors who fed me like a baby, forgetting that I had seen before, that I could recognize a tool, a spoon....

Mrs. Hallowe'en was patient and systematic. She discovered

at the same time as I did all the humorous gadgets in the world of the blind. The most expensive were not expensive enough for her. I had a talking alarm clock which told time out loud. I had a photoreceptor, the size of a pen, which vibrated on contact with a light source in a room. There was a parrot especially trained for the blind by an old Spanish man in Florida, worth thousands of dollars because it knew how to warn in Spanish at traffic lights so you could cross the street. I walked around the Bahamas with that bird on my shoulder, a creature that perhaps knew how to recognize colors because it had so many itself.

Mrs. Hallowe'en taught me how to drink without spilling a drop using a whistling glass which indicated the weight and the level of the liquid. She taught me how to use the telephone, how to find zero on push-button phones which I prefer, or on the older dial models, and also where the other digits were by adjacent positions. I have used telephones frequently, and tape recorders, and today the digicassette; a Braille typewriter recording this text.

Mrs. Hallowe'en had the patience to teach me Braille over long evenings playing games of dice. She had bought a special set with the dots in relief. I've now learned how to write on the Braille-writer with its six keys, but I have never really tried the stylus and perforated board used to write Braille by hand, and I can't read the letters easily. Record, reread addresses, take down memories ... What good does it do? I never reread, and I think the human word is made to run, to never retrace its path.

During all the time I lived with her, I barely learned to sign my name, and Mrs. Hallowe'en needed my signature for legal papers. She did not want to force me to stumble through using my fingers like an invalid, nor could she stand to see me walk with a white cane. According to her a pair of canes together would have been a laughing stock, a public ridicule. We tried everything: a kind of folding cane, an antenna fixed in back of my buttonhole, anything to help me forget my predicament. One summer I went around with an electronic yo-yo which emitted sound in front of an obstacle, a kind of radar which cost a fortune.

When I say "obstacle," I am especially referring to holes and excavations which are the only real obstacles for me. Missing manhole covers, descending stairways ... I very quickly learned to sense a wall, a dead-end, a closed door without the aid of any contraption. What I really fear is the hollow world, not the three dimensional world; not the world in relief, but a world riddled with mortal chasms, eaten up by plates of nothingness where I might fall. Since the accident, taking a tumble is my obsession of fear. Mrs. Hallowe'en built for herself out of me an invalid *de luxe*, a young robot all the sales girls fell in love with: her gadgets made me look like a Martian, an extra-terrestrial come down to offer my body to Earthlings. That is how one of her friends put it once, at about the third drink before dinner. After a year or so, Mrs. Hallowe'en gave me small amounts of money to take care of certain expenses, then she got me accustomed to receiving "gifts" from her friends. I had to learn how to calculate again. I had an abacus with silver beads, a cubarhythm with a hundred little ivory cubes, and finally a crazy videocalculator—a pocket-sized tape recorder that spewed out the sums of my computations when I hit certain keys. Those machines taught me how to do without machines. Without being able to do figures in my head I would never have been able to lead an independent life. There, as elsewhere, Mrs. Hallowe'en was paving the road to tomorrow. . . . Over three years' time, in her capable hands, a little peasant boy from Kerkenna became cosmopolitan. Thanks to her, I know the pleasure that comes from arranging flowers, whipping up a canvas of scent and texture, what you call color. She patiently reconstructed my education, a framework entirely conceived to enhance my future freedom; an education of refinement and intelligence for which I have not returned to her a hundredth of its value in love.

The second evening after we met, we were in the huge dining room of a palace. It was warm, and somewhere an orchestra was playing *bossa nova*. Mrs. Hallowe'en was explaining to me how to explore my plate with a fork without making any noise, and how to find the chair a well-intentioned waiter pushes up to you, by slightly drawing back your heel until you touch its legs.

I have never stopped learning since that night. I discovered tinkling glasses, plush carpeting, the odors of food and flowers, the velvety voice of the maître d'. Even someone who does not see can perceive all that.

Practices, customs are much more to me than mere practice: they are the guides which allow me to have nearly normal contact with others. I hate it when visitors do not announce themselves or do not talk.

She would show me to my seat, in airplanes as well as in theatres, by putting my hand up on the seat back, letting me know that space was mine and that from there on I was on my own.

During the short time I stayed on Kerkenna I no longer knew how to dress myself, to wash or how to eat alone. She had the patience to respect the revulsions of a little Arab afraid of pork hiding in every meat sauce, she followed the ritual of my toilette; first my chest, then my head, and finally my feet, as prescribed in the Koran. Those first months I continued to recite my prayers five times a day, and to say *bismillah* like an ongoing mantra. She let me do it, up 'til the day when I forgot it myself.

My beard began to grow. She took to guiding my arm every morning in a repetition of shaving which soon became an integral part of my toilette.

I tell myself sometimes that I am nothing more than the sum of Mrs. Hallowe'en's attentions and preoccupations who continues to live through them. She rebuilt an existence for me that I had never known.

Sometimes I get people mixed up, especially those from the beginning, from the first years. So many voices, so many people leave you with your emotions suffocated. But hers is the first clear identity to leave its imprint after Hocine left me sitting in front of the hospital in Rome while he went off to find a taxi.

I never took the initiative to get away from Kerkenna. The whole island took up a collection to send me to Europe for a medical consultation. Finally, my mother sent me with Hocine to see a famous professor in Rome. I went along with it but I was already sure that nothing could be done.

It seems as though I was really little more than half-animal when the accident happened, nearly unconscious, paralyzed with shyness. For me, the world stopped near the wharf of our little sun-parched port where dogs slept in the dust awaiting the arrival of the daily boat.

That summer some European tourists came to the island. They were my first white friends. I do not even remember their names. The girl's, maybe. She had an Italian man's name. They disappeared after the shock that left me in the Kerkenna hospital.

The following winter was a numbing time for me when, from sunrise to sunset, I heard groans of mourning in the background amid the noise of earthenware utensils being put away: the wails of my mother. Bad luck had hit me from behind like an evil spirit surging out of the desert then slipping back into the sandy wind after its stroke of misfortune. Using my hands I could feel my shaved head, the little scars of sutures just above my neck where my head had struck the scooter's handlebars. The hair on my scalp was already starting to grow back in, it bristled against my palm. For some time I did not speak. I scarcely moved. The doctor at the Kerkenna hospital, completely at a loss, himself suggested that I be examined in Italy. Hocine carried all those people's savings from the caper harvest inside a knotted handkerchief. In exchange, the great professor confirmed that I was definitely stricken with blindness arising in the brain. He also added that contrary to what had been feared, no other brain center was affected. I had not become an idiot. That was the only certainty I could hope to take back to Kerkenna with me. But without light, Kerkenna was nothing.

Others told me that I was, as they say, "blind." I got used to it but I was never convinced. At first at the hospital, I thought there was simply something screwy with my vision. What, I didn't know. I was not in darkness but in a world without color, without shape, with the persistent impression of a simple fog just on the verge of breaking up. Scooter wrecks are so natural on Kerkenna that at first I was sort of proud, before I understood that I would never see again. Proud to the point of being grateful to those Europeans who were the source of my downfall, and who made me into a hero. When I had understood my blindness, I resigned myself to God's will. I could not figure out what I was being punished for. I had not looked at lightning—my mother had warned me on stormy days not to, convinced it would burn your eyes. I later discovered in a European dictionary that going blind there, too, is considered a punishment. They cited Oedipus, Orpheus and a sorcerer named Tiresias, who once looked upon his goddess mother as she was bathing nude. I never desired my mother, not even in dreams.

I wandered around conking into the walls of the house, repeating to myself that I must have been at fault, but without knowing how. Distances overlapped; my mother got into my way, stepped into my path. I ended up sitting still, going back into myself where I could still "see" myself, if only a bit.

So I began learning to be blind. When my friends—Hocine, everyone—thought I was walled up in sadness, silently suffering on the edge of suicide, I was merely immobile. Draped in my *djellabah*, I sat in the sunshine petrified by stupefaction, in the midst of the new universe which was, they told me, non-visible. I stretched out slowly, very slowly, exploring the shadow my arms made on the ground.

All I knew about blind people were those heroes of tales my mother used to tell when I was a little kid. I would go over the story of Baba Abdallah, with his white beard and his broken voice, blinded by a powder box, punished for his curiosity, and for wanting to place upon his *right* eye a magic cream intended for his *left*. Well, I had never tried to discover the treasures Baba Abdallah had lost. I had never committed any serious sacrilege, except maybe sometimes drinking wine, or yelling *Dinemuk!* to the woman selling newspapers at the port. I was not blind: it was a lie. One day or another to come I would be punished for having pretended to be blind, like that hero in another tale: caught *in flagrante delicto* imitating a blind beggar, he fended off a mob by denouncing the truly blind as charlatans. Where was the difference between acting blind and really being blind? Unable to say, I was chilled at not being able to escape fraud: one day the whole island would know I was nothing but a fake.

Kerkenna ignored me. Having known her before my accident, she now seemed to manifest an absurd indifference to the experience I'd had of her. Without knowing for certain I was blind, I felt that something was missing that I had known before on Kerkenna. Why go back?

I was nervously fumbling with the dark glasses the hospital had given me which felt too heavy on my face. I couldn't see what good they did. I was standing in front of the hospital that night on the edge of a sidewalk. It must have already been late. Hocine had left a long time before to search for a taxi. A man—the hand of a man—took me authoritatively by the arm. For more than two months I'd been dragged around, dressed, washed by others' hands—my mother's, those of the hospital staff. I followed this new hand and found myself on the sidewalk across the street, unable to go back, completely at a loss.

I smacked into the iron fence of a public garden where the cumbersome charity of those who always want the blind to cross streets had led me. I sat down wondering how I would ever find Hocine. Later that night, another hand—a young one this time— guided me along more sidewalks, and on to a sandy path. The traffic noise was damped by murmuring trees. It was cooler, and we walked a long time before the hand sat me upon a bench and began to touch me.

Since the accident, I had been touched constantly. However, my sexuality seemed dead. On the island, even those girls who had once lavished me with caresses and oral sex during my adolescence no longer dared touch that part of me which had become sacred since the day I could no longer see. When this hand opened my fly, I became excited. I felt a pair of lips, an unshaven chin. Then there was some disturbance, the noise of running in the distance and the hand abruptly withdrew. I heard footsteps disappearing in the night.

I zipped up the wash-and-wear pants my mother had bought from a wandering merchant on Kerkenna and I moved forward a bit randomly to the edge of a large expanse of tarmac where cars ambled around in a zoo of backfires. There, at the edge of the gardens of the Villa Borghese, I met Mrs. Hallowe'en.

I heard a rather shrill and nasal voice yelling insults in American from the other side of the tarmac. Then I felt something softly flowing against my leg, rubbing against me before it jumped onto my shoulder. It was her escaped cat.

Mrs. Hallowe'en limped. She claimed it was an old injury from the First World War. I heard her walking, scattering the automobiles. The imperious gait of an old rich woman who has adopted a cane not to lean upon but to add rhythmic tapping to her walk.

She called me. I did not understand English, but she was so authoritative that I moved forward, guided by her dancing cane; only then, she later told me, did I emerge from the shadows and she saw my dark glasses.

I have always thought, and heard said, that she did not really limp. Just as I did not try to make her pronounce my name correctly, I did not contradict her own little inventions. That evening she hammered the ground with precise little taps, moving around me as I put the cat back onto the ground. Then she spoke to me in English, French and Italian, telling me that this part of the Villa Borghese was no place for me to be hanging around, given my age and disability. She spoke firmly. I could not understand how the Villa Borghese at eleven o'clock at night, at her age, could be a place for her. We walked around cars where, according to her, Italian lovers were making out with salesgirls from big department stores. Across the way, lit by the lights of passing automobiles were a dozen down-and-out boys trying to supplement their income. She had thought I was one. Mrs. Hallowe'en stopped a taxi with a couple of whacks of her cane, and we drove back down to a big noisy *piazza* to drink cognac at an outside cafe, because she was worried about how pale I looked. While we lingered amidst odors of rancid cooking, the desk clerk in the palatial old hotel said he couldn't do anything for me. Mrs. Hallowe'en threatened to cause a scandal by sleeping in the lobby; they wouldn't allow the handicapped into this hotel where they made you pay a hundred dollars a day for a room without air conditioning. A great ruckus of Italian voices broke out around me, and the manager went off and returned with his copy of the Italian penal code, which defined the blind as "persons juridicially incapable." He repeated these words with immense satisfaction, and then allowed us to go upstairs, to the accompaniment of the rustle of banknotes which must have been an incredible tip. Once inside the elevator Mrs. Hallowe'en decided we would leave this country which denied the handicapped their rights. Six hours later, early in the morning I left Rome, having known little more of the city than the hotel, the road between the airport and the hospital.

During those few hours I'd made a very important discovery: the accident had not left me without sexual feeling; but it had made me indifferent to the criteria to the problems of the sighted. For example, I didn't wonder if Mrs. Hallowe'en was ugly. She undressed and bathed me. She lathered me up in every hotel tub in the world. She led me to bed, wrapped me in a perfumed dressing gown. I heard a plop in the glass beside the bed, the water making a bizarre bubbling noise. For three years, she removed her dentures every evening at my side, before conscientiously sucking me off, without any attempt at other kinds of sex. She had a proficient technique, and ever since her I've come to like to be sucked. Since that time I've come to believe that it is the simplest form of sex for somebody blind.

I was born to sex under bizarre circumstances. From the time

I became a being who could make love, I could no longer see. The people I later knew always believed my amorous adolescence in the company of Mrs. Hallowe'en had been monstrous. They had no idea what desire without sight is. She was the real reason for my survival: because she provided me with care, access to erotic sensation. At her side at night I often thought of kissing her on the forehead as she slept away, snoring, murmuring in German, sweating in wrinkled sheets. How could I judge her? She was my entire life, down to the smallest detail: my deepest intimacy.

Someone like me is never alone because I am never sure that I *am* alone. Mrs. Hallowe'en led me to understand that my "interior," my innermost self was from then on hers, too, as it would eventually become a part of others after her death—after three years of southern hotels from Florida to Brazil, Bermuda to California.

Mrs. Hallowe'en's death in San Francisco meant a greater change for me than the death of my own mother. Not that I didn't love my mother, but from the time on Kerkenna that I could no longer see, she was a different woman—a mountain of desolation with clumsy gestures which reduced me to an inconvenient package. The fact that I did not try to see my mother again before her death was not due to insensitivity as Mrs. Hallowe'en once reproached me. My mother was dead to me the day she disappeared from my view.

Later, after I turned seventeen and once my mother's death was legally confirmed, Mrs. Hallowe'en obtained my freedom through a court in the city of Key West. My mother was crushed by the rock above our house which an earthquake shook loose: Kerkenna taking revenge upon my escape. Mrs. Hallowe'en took me from my family only to give me back my self. This emancipation required nothing more than a simple legal process. Since those first days when she had me explore our hotel rooms wall by wall—everything within arm's reach, the very space around me, my environment—she had taught me to use all my fingers, to reconquer space. Getting up, lying down, even sitting ceased to be the nightmare of an animal caught in a sticky canvas of obscurity. I returned with delight to the normal exercise of my physical body. Nothing is more absurd than the prejudice I'd suffered on Kerkenna, in which space for the non-sighted was nothing more than a series of traps from which escape was unknowable, simply because *one* orientating sense had been taken away. Through Mrs. Hallowe'en, I found a place in the world again; not the same place as before. I was better than the sighted: now I could feel the world as volumes in truly sensual depth, not pale, flat deceptive planes, but *in relief!* I could perceive the most ordinary objects in depth. She had me touch and retouch everything until the muscles in my fingers and hands were sore, as the sighted sometimes get headaches from too much reading.

In the confusion that followed the accident this one thing at first escaped my attention. More than others I'd moved around, breathed, in three dimensions. I'd never reduced the world to its merely visible side; now I explored it minutely in all its facets, before forming ideas about it.

The only objects that still escaped me were mirrors. One day on Kerkenna my mother broke every mirror in the house; she had surprised me passing longing hands over its glassy surface, trying to find the memory of my double. One evening with Mrs. Hallowe'en I had fun imitating the movements of a man looking at himself in a mirror. There was no point in being afraid of mirrors, afraid of visual illusions. The only difference between a sighted person and myself is that I do not let myself be taken in by that error which makes him see perspective in an object when it's really flat. That's where I have a superior view—I can sense an object without being shown it.

When I saw that I had a place in the world again, I must point out that in the beginning this place conformed precisely to that of Mrs. Hallowe'en and her cat. By modifying my manner of perceiving I mentally followed her steps, her cane, her space, her animal as though they were mine. Her cane she used especially for my benefit, as a warning, as a means of touching and exploring the surrounding world by sound, both alerting me and teaching me. Why should I need a cane when Mrs. Hallowe'en traced out the path?

She preceded me by half a step everywhere, a shadow in front of my own sensitivity, that paled with the years. The edge of a sidewalk, the steps to a train ... I never confronted them first or alone. She never pushed me ahead. I would slide behind her at doors. Politeness disguised our tactics. Keeping contact with me she would tap her cane on every obstacle; I had only to follow.

Since my accident heat and taste had undergone a complete transformation. After a few unfortunate incidents where I burned my fingers upon heating coils or matches, my skin became a long-distance thermometer. Taste, especially in the company of Mrs. Hallowe'en, took on incredible complexity. Our words for taste are reduced to simple contrasts: bitter/acidic, sweet/salty. Not enough words exist for the series of tastes which are colors to the sightless; my possibility in description is reduced almost to black and white. Even in lovemaking, my mouth became the essential seat of pleasure. Upon the trembling edge of lips unfolds the most mysterious, the most refined of impressions, that which can be compared to fluttering bird wings taking to the air. Exploring the world, my lips more than any other organ served as my guide. Mrs. Hallowe'en used to say that the greatest number of points of sensitivity in the body were squeezed together there, a cushion of vibrating pins.

The luxury she had me living in did not surprise me. A kid straight off an island of fishermen is not truly conscious of all that; and I was not impressed by the outward signs of a respect and power that I could not see.

From time to time, remorse crept up. I imagined the *imam* of the little mosque on Kerkenna blustering into his beard to my mother about the new kind of life I was leading. After her death these scruples vanished. Even the *imam* would have been secretly proud. Living on the good graces of a woman is nothing to be ashamed of. Did not the Prophet himself marry the widow Khadidja for her money?

Occasionally, Mrs. Hallowe'en had me touch little rectangles of plastic where her name was engraved in relief, and which furnished her with tickets to anywhere by a magical transcontinental system rivalling any of the fairy tale genies of my childhood. Borders to cross were purely on paper, which she would fill out for me in majestically carpeted first-class waiting rooms. She would declare on them that I was adopted from the Red Cross, or I was a war refugee, according to the whimsical documents one of her friends—a high official at the U.N. and a Chevalier of Malta (a title which set me dreaming)—cooked up for her.

From the day of my emancipation, she got me used to having my own money and to accepting gifts from her friends. My only means of really "knowing" people, of forming a "mental image" of them, is to make love to them. At that time, most of the bodies I explored were elderly. That did not shock me. I would describe them to Mrs. Hallowe'en and we would burst out laughing when we compared the image I had formed with the descriptions that she provided. Every such adventure left me with banknotes with numbers upon them I could not read.

For anyone else but me life with Mrs. Hallowe'en could have seemed the ultimate in artificiality. Over the long haul, I familiarized myself with all those nuances of the practiced culture of the well bred man such as must have existed in Europe before the last war. We never stopped at a hotel which did not require coat and tie in the dining room. I came to recognize silk from synthetics, good wine from imitations, gold from other metals. Mrs. Hallowe'en had an attachment for gold of a European exile who has gone through all the wars. I had never even seen gold, so for me this metal that my toilet articles were made of was only a particular patina, polished, warm, far from the brutal cutting iciness of steel or the granular softness of silver. There she was covered with jewels, and I covered in her gold. We ought to have been attacked during the long walks we sometimes took in the middle of the night. At night? Yes, I chose to live at night, which is so convenient for me. Because Mrs. Hallowe'en was an insomniac, we lived mostly between dusk and dawn. It became my turn to guide her sometimes in dark alleys or along deserted shores.

The word "blind" in English, like most words meant to describe me, gives the impression of confusion, of bumping into things, of struggling no end. I'm not at all confused. I'm even able to guide a sighted person in the dark. All the confusion and stumbling are provoked by sighted ones around me, who oblige me to carry some distinctive sign of my blindness to keep them from knocking into me. I have never been able to get used to someone calling out "Careful!," which they are so generous with, after the fact. A warning always said too late, signifying nothing.

So, we needed a way to make me recognizable as blind. . . . We had a difficult choice, Mrs. Hallowe'en and I; she did not want to see me in those frightful dark glasses from the hospital and had thrown them out the window the first night; nor did we want a white cane or some other similar, humiliating sign. I took to walking around outdoors with closed eyelids, since for all a sighted person can see, my eyes are normal: the muscles move, the reflexes and pupil all appear ordinary. With my eyes closed, I become for them a blind man. But closing my eyes is only a trick to me; I'm never bewildered.

I have heard everything, undergone everything that a blind man who doesn't look it can undergo. Walking with my eyes closed and hesitating at a street corner, I would feel a coin slip into my hand. Every time I'm treated like a blind man, I open my eyes, which puts charitable souls into a rage.

Mrs. Hallowe'en took me to see both eminent physicians and the worst quacks. I began to know my medical file by heart. My organs of vision seemed intact; however they had become useless. A laboratory in Florida undertook a series of injections with a radioactive substance which was supposed to outline my optic nerves, to make them visible to X-rays. The doctors hoped to establish the exact location of the break in my optic nerve. They never succeeded: on the other hand, after those injections, the reactions of people on the street to me, at night, was sometimes astonishing. I couldn't understand why they turned around flabbergasted. Then one evening as she leaned over me Mrs. Hallowe'en screamed. She claimed my eyes were glowing faintly in the dark: they'd become phosphorescent.

I don't know if it was around that time that I began to feel handsome. I always supposed I was handsome, if only because my mother and the entire island said so. Between the kid who listened impatiently to the compliments of old men sitting around in a circle gravely smoking their hookahs and the man writing this text, two thousand years have passed. I know that I am handsome, a curse or a trick my body plays on me, since I cannot see it.

The sighted feel beautiful seeing a face through the deceptive aid of mirrors, a face encountered only indirectly. I know that I am handsome from their voices, the voices of those who speak to me. My beauty is the emotion which makes them babble, a mysterious effect enveloping me like a gas. I know I am handsome because I imagine myself to be, without looking at any facsimile of myself. I might have done that in the months following the accident, trying to memorize my own features. But I didn't: I forgot my self.

I lost the anguish of visual memory quickly enough. A new

sensitivity was born. Even when my hands were trying to "imagine" some body I had met, I wanted less to judge if it were beautiful than to establish total contact. One body next to another remains my way of knowing others. Without this contact, between her, or between him and me, there is too much hypocrisy, a mass of syrupy hypocrisy that I always sense in the voice speaking to a blind man. For me, every voice simply reveals what is hiding, making the admission stand out crystal clear.

Then, there are the voices after lovemaking, the tones bubbling over with gratitude and confidence, recounting their lives, their most secret desires. Making love to someone blind, for those voices, is making love to a corpse that can listen.

Mrs. Hallowe'en often told me that I described people-voices, beings not of flesh and blood but of wind and lamentation. But this was not due to my lack of perceiving their moist skin, their odor. Their moral being was reduced to their sound for me: more precisely reduced to how their voices either harmonized or contrasted with the grain of their skin.

A voice is to me what a face is to you: an indelible imprint, the surefire path to the quality of someone's presence. I used to be able to make serious errors with voices. Don't people make them with faces?

To set my emancipation into motion Mrs. Hallowe'en contacted the rest of my family. I learned then that my mother had died alone, none of her children at her side. I did not cry. Someone that I don't hear suffering does not exist for me; what I do not touch scarcely touches me. My family came back into my mind only two years later when I received a thick envelope smelling of patchouli and containing pages torn out of a school notebook. At the bottom, a powder fine as dust had fallen between the pages.

It was kohl. I remembered what I'd learned from my mother: make a point of the end of a matchstick and soak it in the mineral; then lift it to your eyelid, so lightly you almost can't feel it. Upon contact with the stick my eye became irritated—as it had on those holidays of my childhood, the powder spreading between my lashes. I felt the moisture of tears gather on those membranes that were hiding the world from me. Soon I would shed real tears.

That letter from my half-sisters made me want to speak Arabic, to compare my old world to the new. I decided to go see

these sisters I'd never met. They had sent their address in Paris.
They wrote in French. Mrs. Hallowe'en and I went to Europe for
twenty-four hours. When we arrived, I mistook Djamillah for
Alissa and vice versa. Naturally I attributed Djamillah's four-
octave voice to the older sister.

Noise bothered me more in Paris than anywhere else; the
streets there, the traffic along the big avenues (which seemed like
huge corridors jammed full of crowds) were more compact, more
tightly pressed into a narrow space than anywhere I'd been. I
stayed inside a hotel near the Tuileries Gardens, and instead of
the sights of Paris, I explored the monuments of my sisters' faces.
They came to meet us at the airport, and I did not leave them the
whole day. We had a little Tunisian house installed in part of the
suite rented by Mrs. Hallowe'en. Pillows and *colochons* were
placed in a square on the floor against the walls. Alissa brought a
canoun made out of a big tin can with her, one of those enamelled
metal teapots, and goblets with handles like we used in Tunisia.
Summoned by an outraged maid, the hotel director found us
seated traquilly in the midst of a cloud of charcoal smoke.

Since my birth, my sisters had lived in Lyon with our father,
cloistered those first years as though they were still on Kerkenna.
They had broken away from him by sleeping around with the bad
crowd from Villeurbanne. I could not understand by what
mystery they had exchanged their faces—faces that I knew, used
to know, only by photographs. How was it I didn't recognize
their voices? Why, compared to a vague memory of the portraits
my mother sometimes showed me on Kerkenna, did Alissa seem
younger, sweeter than her little sister? Perhaps I made the same
kind of mistake every day! My fingers told me about shapes and I
arbitrarily compared them to hazy memories. Perhaps after all
my world coincides with that of the sighted only at the price of a
gigantic misunderstanding. I will never know if the objects I
touch are the same ones you see.

The meeting with my sisters concluded with a party, and poor
sparkling wine in one of the most fashionable spots in town; it
definitely put me on guard from comparing a visual past with my
present. My family was included in this. Anyway, my father
hadn't even bothered to make the trip from Lyon. To him, a blind
man could only bring bad luck.

This was my only attempt at "finding my roots." If I had felt such confusion seeing my sisters again—and they were only half-sisters, after all—and my visual memory of them was so off-track, doubtless things on Kerkenna would have been disastrous had I tried to go back there to see my mother. My sisters told me that her solitary death had been something of a relief to the rest of the family, rebuilt around a second wife and mother in Lyon. Both sisters admired me, but they didn't hide the fact that no one in Lyon really worried about me. To them I was just another invalid.

Mrs. Hallowe'en and I left for San Francisco the following day. California was to be fatal for her. Two weeks after we arrived she took me to the huge Golden Gate Bridge. I liked the sea as much as she did. The vastness of such a panorama reaches me, too: a shock of immense space upon my face, as I turned toward the western sea.

Few passersby troubled our promenade. A woman's footsteps passed beside us. The bridge resounded deafeningly with the wheels of automobiles. It swayed slightly, as though hesitating in its flight toward the Pacific. All of a sudden Mrs. Hallowe'en's cat, Zita, must have taken off again. At the same moment that I felt the gusting of a truck past me, Mrs. Hallowe'en ran forward limping. I heard a scraping of high heels upon the concrete in front of me then a muffled cry. Perhaps I was imagining things, but I heard cracking bones, a skull shattered; and the soft plump of her handbag bouncing into the gutter, her abandoned cane rolling off the sidewalk's edge. I cried out her name; it was echoed back to me in the mirror of concrete pillars. They later told me that her body had plunged into the Pacific channel.

We were in America. The footsteps I heard swiftly faded into the distance. I called for help. I flagged down a car whose motor purred behind me. The driver, contemplating what few remaining traces were left of Mrs. Hallowe'en, reproachfully said to me, "Was she your guide?" I had the strong feeling he thought it should have been me—the blind one—and not her who should have been smashed to death.

They never found the cat, nor the truck driver. When the police arrived, the patrol sergeant in command placed a tissue paper in my hand. I began to blow my nose; that's when I noticed water under my fingers. For the first time since my accident, my eyes had formed tears.

I only truly understood what I had lost in Mrs. Hallowe'en when I began to live that institutional life which it seems is normal for the blind. We cry before we know what there is to cry about.

That same afternoon I was taken away, police sirens screaming full blast, by two cops who smelled of hair oil and who chewed gum, spitting their words at the two-way radio. Instead of driving back toward town, we made a u-turn on the bridge and went the other way. We stopped a half hour later in front of a house. When we got out of the car I searched—in spite of myself—for the sound of Mrs. Hallowe'en's cane. The cops followed me; they didn't know one was always supposed to walk in front of me. I crossed a garden with dirt paths, passed a glass door, and in an air-conditioned room a friendly young woman sat me down and offered me an orangeade. She then took upon herself the responsibility of telling me of my protectress' death, which I had already perfectly understood. Mrs. Hallowe'en had been taken away by a simple twist of fate; exactly as she had first been brought to me, providing a bitterly ironic satisfaction and locking my thoughts together as the woman stroked my hair and finally told me that her husband had returned. He was the Juvenile Court judge.

I felt brutally yanked back thousands of kilometers by all these people: they dripped with pity; they spoke to me, touched me, as you would a small child or some tiny pet. I had forgotten all that. Even as an apprentice, my relations with Mrs. Hallowe'en had been free and adult.

The judge was a young man with a weak voice who smelled of deodorant and who spoke of me as a "he" to the wall across the room, or to some listeners that I didn't see. Once again, I had become nothing, an object.

Until her death Mrs. Hallowe'en always used the formal "*vous*" with me, in French and "*voi*" in Italian, which we both spoke fluently. However imperious she was in word and gesture, she never considered me a minor, a kid: perhaps a savage, but an independent savage. The young man smelling of deodorant brought me into his office. He told me he was a judge. I detest this mania they have for repeating things to me they've already said in my presence, as though by not seeing I'm also deprived of ears. He told me not to be afraid of him. If the circumstances hadn't been so sad I would have burst out laughing in his face. Why should I be afraid of him? To me, judges, policemen, doctors are mere names, abstractions. The uniform they use to terrify others ... well, that intimidation simply can't reach me.

The judge explained that I was now an orphan. My father had never recognized me, thus I fell under *his* jurisdiction, or that of his colleagues, from which I would never have recourse or escape. In vain I held out my American residence permit to him, my emancipation from the Florida court. In Florida, the law does not protect minors as in California. At any rate, he added softly, my "handicap" gave him the right, even the duty, to put me under his protection. Of course he wanted to recognize the validity of the certificates from the United Nations, given by Mrs. Hallowe'en's friend, which had declared me a political refugee. The judge spoke of her condescendingly, convinced that for the past three years I'd been in the clutches of a madwoman. He offered me psychiatric sessions right away, to "decompress." I thought I understood that a will had been found in her purse which left Mrs. Hallowe'en's entire fortune to her cat. The judge expressed extreme caution with respect to the validity of that heir. But the cat had apparently been killed in the accident too, leaving me high and dry.

I remained silent. The judge told me that since court was closed that day, he was hereby declaring court in session (and I did hear him scratching out his signature) remanding temporary custody of me to an institution whose name I could not quite catch in Santa Barbara. This decision was made by virtue of some law about endangered children and permits prolonging of the status of minor up to the age of twenty-one. It was either that or they would send me back to Tunisia. Anyway, he added, meticulously rubbing at a spot on the paper, there was really nothing repressive in these measures. We were only putting things back in order. The State would allow me—as a refugee—a financial allotment to cover the costs of the institution. I might even submit an application for retroactive benefits for all those years I'd spent in the United States at the expense of a benevolent third person, instead of having had the salaried companion-guide to which I'd been entitled. With even more persistence, I might obtain a pension for life.

I remained confused about so much generosity, skeptical of so many promises. That night, I slept on a sofa-bed; the judge had pinched his fingers unfolding it. I wanted to cry more, but tears would not come. For the first time in three years I was sleeping alone. I stayed awake a long time, listening to insects rustling in the garden, a slowly rising nocturnal sound in the cool night air. I threw off the rough army blanket and walked over to the guillotine-like window. I could walk alone, though the spirits of Mrs. Hallowe'en and her cat were still with me. Those men, that woman who had grabbed me by the arm after the accident had not been out of contact with me for an instant, hiding this primal discovery.

Perhaps I'd already been walking alone for a long time, deluded by the easy confidence Mrs. Hallowe'en made me feel even when she pulled her arm away, as though it were unimportant, continuing a conversation we had begun or going through a doorway or climbing the stairs. Now I stood alone before the open window absently searching for moonbeams upon my skin, meditating upon my newfound liberty.

The Valentine MacPherson Institute was atop a hill covered with pines that whistled in the Pacific breeze, just above Santa Barbara Beach, upon which the entrance colonnade opened. The view was breathtaking, making all the visitors exclaim in wonder and leaving all the residents completely indifferent. Upon entering the institute, you were accompanied one last time, as though it was saying *adieu*, by the California panorama.

The whole building operated on infrared and photoelectric cells. The furniture and walls were rounded, and the straight stairways had carpeting which warned you at your first step with a soft buzzer. The posts and trees in the courtyard were surrounded by a flexible plastic covering to prevent accidents.

When I entered I was saluted by the discreet puff of a double-door run on compressed air. The doors to all the buildings operated on the same system. From the library to the gymnasium, passing by the Fathers' offices or the woman director's office, every passageway was furnished with either light or heat detectors which did the work of the eyes for us, preventing all collisions.

MacPherson, founder of the institute, had wanted it wholly conceived on the most up-to-date standards. This generalized foresight, destined to facilitate the boarders' lives, satisfied most of my companions. I, who knew how to open doors in the real world, found these precautions useless. In each room the lamps were out of reach, the windows were opened and closed by electric levers, hot and cold water were armed with warning sounds. We students were to avoid all efforts at adaptation. A loudspeaker—something like that I sometimes hear on the radio in the limousines Mrs. Hallowe'en rented—broadcast from one half hour to the next a program of guidance. Instead of announcing congested freeways, the director's voice reminded everyone of sports times and discussion groups, it whispered sermons at bedtime inspired by the Angel of Blind Purity; or she read some of the residents' poems, celebrating the songs of the local birds.

The park and walkways between the buildings were furnished with differently shaped tactile indicators placed on wooden posts at about the height of your hand. Spheres led to workshops, cones to the gymnasium, crosses to the chapel.

We met in this chapel for assembly once a week in a group prayer for Valentine MacPherson's soul. Her father had been the largest agricultural machinery manufacturer in the West. She had become blind and deaf at only six months old nearly a century before when a combine-harvester machine being demonstrated had exploded. As an introduction to our course, the professors related her life to us. It was years before anyone around her got the idea of making her touch certain objects, or of communicating by means of a tactile code. One month after this occurred, she knew the entire alphabet-in-relief. A year later she was writing proficiently. One day, the doctors came up with the idea of having the little mute touch their vocal cords during her speech exercises. She, in turn, would imitate the movements of the voicebox and tongue and so began to talk; she became a curiosity to the entire world. The adventures of this learned ape was an exemplary epic at the institute that every student ended up knowing by heart.

The chapel was as electronic as everything else. Stereophonic loudspeakers sang motets, ventilators wafted clouds of incense. The public standing behind us witnessed with astonishment the play of lights, while we each stood in our places dressed in white robes.

The institute was lit up day and night, including our rooms, as a permanent offering to God: the spectacle of our innocence. And of course this measure simplified the task of our surveillance.

In the middle of the central court of honor a statue of little Miss MacPherson chattered on every day about falls and scrapes. I spent hours in front of this statue, "conceived," according to the pedestal, "so that the sightless might forever keep the memory of the daughter of their benefactor." The hair, clothing, even the statue's skin was made of some indestructible material which felt almost real. The sculpture's features seemed exaggerated, a caricature, so that we could get a better idea of it. Naturally I could not resist touching the eyes. I noted with disappointment that the sculptor had been satisfied using glass, confusing the visual and the tactile. I heard a brief whistle to make me get down off the pedestal: that was how the director communicated orders to the residents.

I was to hear this noise—an exasperating familiar call to order of an ever-present surveillance—hundreds of times over the course of my stay.

The courses did not interest me; after having verified that I knew nothing of the location of Calcutta or the exploits of George Washington the director placed me in an elementary class. The first week, I was especially fascinated by the library where I could forget my sorrows by reading. We had afternoons free. I could not read Braille and I never really did manage to learn it. That manner of reading is too slow for me. The simple thought of all those texts hidden under that delicate pointed lace made me dizzy. But I did treat myself to an orgy of cassettes, which I was already accustomed to using. Those captivating voices—older women for the most part, anonymous benevolent readers whose every cough I heard—and the sound of turning pages made me listen to study-texts as you would listen to a story. I knew some passages by heart and made a game of changing the readers' intonations.

I learned how to use a typewriter at the institute. Those for the sighted are not much different from those for the blind, which delighted me. I also learned how to use the ones which write in Braille using six keys, each of which represents a point, which you press simultaneously to form a character. I never could stand the tablet-and-punch my fellow residents carried around attached to their wrists, which reminded me of a beggar's wooden cup.

During class they made little insect noises as they perforated their paper. The machine only made a mechanical "ploc-ploc."

Later, people told me I could have no idea of what literature was, limited as I was to knowing it only in its verbal and sonorous defilement. I had left Kerkenna without ever really having read, though I pretty much knew how to write in French. I have always known how to write before knowing how to read; the only way I do read is aloud. The idea of a silent text still sends shivers up and down my back. Naturally, by the simple fact of knowing entire passages by heart, I am quite capable of standing back intellectually to consider the whole of the passage just as any sighted person would.

Going through the mountains of cassettes of a history of civilization I also discovered that most cultures have bypassed silent texts. Even the ancient Romans had their letters or books read aloud. Only modern European literature has been written expressly, one might say, to elude the blind.

My discovery of my companions came much later than that of the library, but as a consequence of my reading. I had passed an entire week without noticing anyone. I could just as well have been living alone if it weren't for the rustling of paper, or the sound of a closing book, like phantoms around me, and the song of the six-winged Braille scratching during class, just beneath the professor's voice. They began to complain when I insisted on trying to learn Braille by decoding my manual aloud in the study hall, while all of them read silently.

My classmates: for the first time I existed in the same night as other sightless people. We were united by that sole fact, a court of miracles of differing destinies returned to infancy.

I learned that there were more than one hundred thousand blind in America. Until then I thought I was the only one, or just about. The news was not pleasant. My companions had strange customs like always saying the first name of the person they were speaking to when they were in a group, a device which the Fathers had instituted to avoid confusion.

The fact that these people read Braille fluently—the compleat blind—translated for me the reclusiveness of their lives. They had no other experiences than dining halls, workshops, classrooms and rooms with glass doors where you never knew if the director was watching you during one of her surprise inspection tours or picking up stray pieces of soiled linen, or arranging chairs, or changing lightbulbs.

I speak of the compleat, the completed blind, because I discovered in this place—which existed only for a group, "the blind"—that this very notion was to be shattered into a thousand pieces. The selection of residents was almost arbitrary. Most of them were completely convinced, even if they were the only ones, that they were simply "vision-impaired." I know from my own experience that when you're blind you imagine yourself as seeing for a long time, maybe forever. During my first medical exam I was able to persuade the doctor that I "saw" his white coat perfectly well. It took an in-depth examination to discover that I had not the slightest visual perception. This affirmation by the doctors had never totally convinced me. No one ever really thinks he is blind, but there we were, living proof, all brought together and certain that there must be some mistake. Maybe we were right. Every one of us, in our own way, *could* see. I discovered that the act which the sighted call "seeing" is in fact the complex totality of an entire civilization written into our bodies.

In the Braille library I got to know Huong. He was half Vietnamese, the son of a G.I. He was alexic; sitting down at my table at lunch, he explained that he couldn't read or write in black print but was obliged—he could see perfectly well—to read and write in Braille. Others suffered from a spatial disorder, an inability to organize or localize objects. They were the worst because they were more incapable than any of us to properly orient themselves even by touch. Others were simply incapable of glancing; their visual attention became fixed in a stare, like the tall Canadian girl who always stood still in front of the first object she spied, and whom you could find no matter where you left her, hypnotized by a doorknob or a spoon. Others had lost their visual memory, and another group couldn't tell high from low anymore. In the eyes of the Fathers, all were blind.

Among those of us who could "see" without being able to use their visual perception, the most touching was David, a sweet and smiling kid about twelve years old. It was nearly impossible to shake him loose once you had met him. David's cries would break your heart as soon as you began to move away from him. David suffered from a complicated disorder with a mixture of perception problems of space and time. Whenever someone walked away from him at a normal speed, David saw them disappear in a flash, as though they had been instantly torn out of his visual space in dizzying motion which brought him to the edge of tears. You had to leave David half a step at a time, like an actor in front of a sped-up camera.

The most astonishing of my companions was a complete paralytic: a Thalidomide victim. The little torso already had fifteen years of vegetative existence. He had learned to get around in a wheelchair, even to move objects by letting out little cries, setting off some electrical mechanism linked to his vocal cords.

At the institute the Fathers of every nationality were kept in a continual frenzy by the director. Many of the staff members were unpaid volunteers, and this little charitable world of telephone calls and lost files, persuaded to offer its good work to God, stirred around Mother Superior.

The teachers spoke to us in that sticky-sweet tone that always made me stop and turn around, as though the remarks were being addressed to some small child behind me. A just impression. The Fathers weren't really talking to us: they were talking to something beyond us, above us. While their physical side was turned toward our bodies, their thoughts were off to God, whose favored witnesses we were. We were Salvation by Void: almost above sin—which neither kept them from watching us like hawks nor from suspecting us. Incapable of doing real evil, devoted sooner or later to mystical paths, to great music (the organ, preferably) we were the Mission-field par excellence.

They didn't quite trust me, but they weren't enemies either. Even the director softened up toward me. Something in me particularly moved them, which led me to take account of the power of my beauty. The director's dry hand always trembled a bit whenever she touched me, during her lectures upon my lack of sociability.

The idea that the blind are close to God seemed really comic. At the most extreme, the Fathers would have willingly accepted me even with my God, the God of the Koran. I obviously did not have the same religion as they did, not even the same kind of religion. I often think I unconsciously became an atheist; but a Moslem atheist will never be like a Catholic atheist. And when I no longer know a single word of the Koran, I will still believe in the legend of Hassan, his nine *djinns* and his magic wand. I will still purify myself with water, or at least with sand—with something that flows—after every act of daily life. I had been really stupefied to find no faucet in the W.C. but rolls of paper, in American hotels, something I had once thought due uniquely to Italian filthiness. I continued to carefully collect all the debris of my toilette, trimmings from my beard and nails, and to put it into little papers which I burned. "When you are ready for prayer, wash the face and hands to the elbow; purify yourself when you have satisfied your natural needs, or when you have had the contact of love..." It had been a long time since I had ceased to pray, but this invocation came back to me as an imperative, more powerful than any belief.

Without having been religious, I realized that having been raised as a Believer gave me an opportunity which my companions would never know. Most of them were dirty. They had no interest in their bodies and dressed any way, with sweaters on backwards, or covered with greasy spots; some wore pajamas all day long.

I did not have this ignorance of my body. I knew from the time I was a small child how important it is to purify oneself, what you call a toilette. Then, with Mrs. Hallowe'en, I learned how to put all the little things in order, the minute attentions that permitted me to eat in publice (I preferred to eat alone—a clumsy move like putting an elbow in my plate was always possible) without differing noticeably from a "normal" man. Most of my blind companions could not eat without turning over a glass, and considered all the elements of clothing outside their tactile field as irremediably lost. The many diabetics among the boarders—as if one infirmity brought on another in a cynical fate—carried a syringe filled with insulin around their necks, to administer their necessary daily injections to themselves. They smelled like rubbing alcohol, with a tincture of unmade bed.

This indifference to appearance was not a hatred of the customs of the sighted, which however are often incomprehensible to the blind. They let themselves go by obedience, by resignation, to the status of the Assisted Inept to which the Fathers invited them. Well, I wasn't one of them. If I scorn the rules of the sighted, I still know how to handle them, to conjure up that illusion and to be visible in the midst of them, if I wish.

The most distressing and by far the most numerous of the whole groups of boarders were the elderly. They were closed up in another wing, where we went once a week to shake the flaccid hands of those poor half-vegetable, abandoned creatures. They were a confusing alignment of definitive odors: old cologne bottles standing open too long, old housecoats worn an entire lifetime. A shuffle of slippers. A gurgling, almost a rale right next to us, signalled a nearly covered presence: an old woman perceptible only to the sighted who if it were up to us would have been forgotten and left to die.

The Fathers involuntarily helped us that day (at least those of us who still had a bit of vitality) to get a powerful taste of the future life of the blind according to their ideal: a life steeped in boredom, in impotence. Nine out of ten of the blind are old people. Once again I found myself the exception. These visits pushed me further in my determination to not become one of them. These senior citizens had been progressively, inevitably deprived of movement. The risks, the insurance premiums all pushed for their immobilization. They were rolling in reverse back into themselves, which is what produced that continuous scraping of chairs surrounding them. For the first time I became aware of that rolling-at-anchor in the others; most of the younger ones, blind since birth, were afflicted with it too. This rocking back and forth on themselves replaced all real movement, real exploration. It was the sound equivalent of the uniform of the institutionalized blind.

The residents who had been there several years spoke a definite slang, which had its humorous side. For one Father who always played the Pope whenever he gave classes, they said he had a fizzy voice. Blankets or hair were "sheep," soft to the touch; but it was also used for music, or someone's personality. Basic conversation revolved around the difficulty of getting out of that space they had closed us into: ineptness. An inept, I learned, is called "blind," a word we never used except in its original sense. An inept "rowed," that is he extended his arms for orientation, or he "got it"—he knocked into something. The fear of running into things paralyzed us all.

There remained speaking and being touched. I had discovered touch by myself and had learned languages. I did not need to be put to pasture in a pen. To the Fathers, my education as one of the blind had been done in a savage manner. We had to start again at zero, clear the slate if possible. They wanted to eradicate the imprint of Mrs. Hallowe'en. To speak, to be touched ... the Fathers were babbling mystics with roaming hands. The sort of vague religious tone they supplied to our "communication groups"—where we were supposed to talk about ourselves, all of us holding hands—filled me with repulsion.

I didn't like to talk about my past as the others did, or to be smothered with their compassion, each waiting his turn to "deal with" his handicap. They really meant to deal with their bad luck. In me—whose daily independence they admired—they paradoxically saw independence as a refusal to "deal with myself as non-sighted." My tongue remained paralyzed during these recitation groups. I had already discarded the self-blubbering some handicapped crawl in. I didn't *feel* blind.

The Fathers' doctrine, in the form of insinuating niceties, had contaminated those soft brains. In each of my companions' activities, they ended up acquiring a totally specialized talent. With the Fathers' encouragement, their little manias finally constituted their entire universe. The only people I talked to were Mexican twins, afflicted with congenital glaucoma. Still only vision-impaired but soon destined for full blindness, they were learning the techniques of the blind, useless at the moment, but which would shortly become indispensible. They were learning to be blind, and while they waited they took advantage of what sight remained to rip off jam packets from the serving line at lunch.

In the "activities," everyone was so absorbed by his own toy that the institute, seen from a helicopter, would have looked like an assembly of hermits. There was a sixteen-year-old virtuoso flautist whom they showed off on holidays; there were translators putting the Bible into Indonesian; there were experts in assembling electronic components who didn't know how to hold their own forks at the table. As a community, these people who demonstrated such astounding aptitude, turned into a chorus of fuzzy voices, objectively believing in their "infirmity;" most had never known anything of the universe beyond the inside of the park gate. Their real infirmity was in their isolation from the world.

Life at the institute was exasperating because of its systematization, laid on thick, which even today comes back to me as a bad taste. The professors had to count the residents so many times, and to instill into them the fear of forgetting an object or a word that they found it simpler to turn the students into maniacs.

The place was drenched in electronic spirituality. From time to time adventure would break out between two residents in the "youth" pavilion. Some of those I took to be kids were more than thirty years old, retarded adolescents. The Fathers did not tolerate relationships between residents of different "blocs" (impaired-vision boys, impaired-vision girls, sightless boys, etc.) except under certain mysterious conditions which resulted from an in-depth examination by the director herself or from dossiers and close interrogations, which sloshed around inside her head for weeks. You did not make love in the institute. But at the end of a long inquest a young man could look forward to marriage with a young lady. The Fathers were haunted by genetics: they searched the couples' genealogical trees for other cases of blindness. So—under the guise of hygiene—their fear and hatred of blindness was clearly manifested. Couples formed inevitably, which the systematic retardation of the place was unable to prevent under Catholic guidelines. They were tolerated better than the "domino" couples—as they were atrociously called, couples consisting of one blind and one sighted resident—at least the problem of poor genes was known; no further risk of contamination when all the eggs were from the same bad basket.

Old adolescents' trembling hands sometimes found each other ineptly under the table at breakfast time, knocking over coffee pots in the process. Passion was purely verbal. Even touching between "fiancés" remained above all symbolic. A little peck on the cheek was the most daring caress.

Incredible: of the hundred girls and boys in good physical condition with full faces and well-nourished bodies who were left after one subtracted the old people and the basket cases, not one had the slightest notion of what sex was. It didn't take me long to verify that first hand.

Maybe these guys had never even had a hard-on; the girls thought you got a kid by kissing when you're twenty-five. Yet their physical development was the same as any student in the country.

Fortunately, I began working out. I had never done physical

training until then, preferring to play soccer when I was a kid on Kerkenna. We all had our favorite soccer stars, born in the streets of Tunis. Sports opened a world to me closed to invalids, just as it opened the only door to success back home to the most down-and-out of our "disadvantaged."

I quickly became one of the most eager participants in sports. The gym teacher was a former speleologist, blind from birth, who had set up an entire system appropriate for us. He never left the sportsgrounds and gym. Christopher had lost several fingers underground in caves, far below the surface, but plain as daylight to him. Spelunking is the mountain climbing of the sightless he once explained to me in a terrible Oakland accent. He was repairing his "harmonic target." Oh, Christopher was black, I forgot to mention: I can't see black.

The "harmonic target" was a contest of adroitness where I won every prize. A big round target made of resonating wood had concentric circles each with a different tone, sounding sharper in pitch as you neared the center with every arrow. A cord hooked onto a central rim allowed you one chance to get a fix upon it before you drew the bow.

Christopher always began class by letting us position our-selves at random in the vast, sonorous gymnasium. We were supposed to call out to each other, answering once, to allow us to direct ourselves toward another person before calling out the name of someone else. The session lasted until we had covered the entire gym, taking possession of the space.

I hung from the rings, on the trapeze, in emptiness. Chris-topher's hand went with me. We jumped the horse. Christopher would call out a brief signal to indicate its position.

I didn't like it when we walked in a line to the rhythm of a record of African music, each with his hand on the shoulder of the one in front, a long blind worm squirming along the field. I preferred the bicycle races on stationery bikes, with weights which rubbed against the wheels to make hills, and an electric buzzer to mark the finish line. The real tandems, bikes that Christopher let me sometimes drive with his hands upon my arms, were usually piloted by the sighted person and pedalled by the blind.

We ran foot races, the clumsier of us holding onto a ring which slid along a wire stretched out beside our lanes, others

guided by our feet, by the simple difference between sand and
grass. A line of fringe caressed our sweaty brows to mark the
finish line.

I was on the baseball team. We wore armbands with bells, and
the ball that Christopher let fly sent out a continuous beep-beep
into the pure Pacific air above our heads. That summer I lived my
best moments of institutional life. In the locker room, in secret,
Christopher told me all about his expeditions. The Fathers
hardly wanted someone inciting us to wanderlust.

Christopher had recognized me, not as an Arab but as
someone who was not blind in their sense of the word. My
accident was *only* an accident, a rite, an initiation. I wasn't about
to construct my whole existence around one of those "blind man's
crafts," which permit the sighted to use our weakness to their best
advantage. Their ideal life for us would be a little blind couple—a
switchboard operator and a newsstand operator, or a cellist and a
radio technician—laying their white canes side by side next to the
fireplace. They would be involved in one of those post-insti-
tutional groups; the former residents return once a month for
"tea," as though they were sorry they ever left. I never wanted to
be "welcomed" again. I didn't want anything more to do with
good souls.

I became convinced that my abduction by Mrs. Hallowe'en
had been the great opportunity of my life. Had I stayed, like my
companions, under my family's care my mother would sooner or
later have put me into an institution, one a lot worse than where I
wound up. My only memories, my only desires would have
been—like those others'—strangled by two closed worlds. Families were the only visitors (aside from former residents) authorized to get into the institute. I had the luck to come in late
enough, formed enough, to retain my distance.

The residents who had been sighted once were completely
attached to their families: their letters, their visits. Their families
contained the only living beings they could attach a visual
memory to. I could think of nothing but the crazy and
anonymous world, outside.

All these students had as visual souvenirs were their family
photos, the images of those relatives whose letters a teacher
would read to them in a flat neutral voice. Absorbed in the
recitation, they would silently scan for these images, trying to find

a memory of themselves from that time back when they could still see: the touchstone of their tragedy. Most of them had long since ceased to have any interior "image," except in the form of a persistent recurrent regret which they confused with the picture of health.

I had nothing to look back to anymore on Kerkenna, and I would never return there. A dusty courtyard surrounded by fresh blue and white rooms, the crushed velvet of the divans where we had sat cross-legged for meals at the little round table, the school, the dust from scooters, the flies that got into the bar through parted curtains over the doorway: all that world stopped with my accident and would never return again. Then, I had been a young empty-headed colt, scared by his own shadow. Since then, I have already lived more than any other kid on Kerkenna will in his whole life.

In the institute there was a calm which astonished me: the incredible calm of the resigned. Personally, I had become neutral, a spectator to my imprisonment more than an actor in it. I was ready to attribute this calm to the other students' spontaneous numbness, since they had managed to transform every occasion to touch one another into religious *kitsch* or naïveté.

One day, inadvertently, I asked aloud why the grape juice they served us had such a bitter taste. An old-timer explained it was the saltpeter that the Fathers dumped into our drinks every evening. After that the only thing I drank was tap water from the courtyard near the gym.

All these people were sexual latecomers, and I've always been more advanced. The saltpeter, no doubt, but surely their unbelievable resignation, too. Well, *I* had a body, *I* had sexuality.

I would spend mornings in class, and afternoons in the library or at the workshop: a sort of big hangar in the middle of the lawns. It contained a sampler of work for the blind: offices with tape recorders dictating quotations from the cattle market to apprentice stenographers; the holy of holies of the institute with vibrating keys—a section for computer programming; a special workshop where the vision-impaired recopied books into large print for the institute's library. At the back was a photographic studio.

I had asked to be trained in photography and the director beamed with satisfaction because that meant I had come out of my "state of shock." They'd figured I was in a state of shock those first days because I refused to speak to them.

I became an expert in photo-developing chemical baths and their temperatures. I recognized the different trays by their odors. I selected paper by its grain. At first I would forget to turn out the light, or to close the door, which meant a certain number of foggy negatives. Then I had a buzzer installed—connected to the light bulb—which reminded me.

The huge building resounded as the students took part in a symphony of noise. The walls were too thin and the roof must have been made of iron. Out of the midst of the buzzers and bells, the hammering and machinery noise, an unreal music sometimes wafted up, above it all, hesitating, incomplete. Leaning over my pungent developing trays or hanging photos to dry I would hear a series of notes sounding like runs played at random, sometimes separated by a deafening shock. The descendents of black slaves who played the *gumbri* back in Tunisia spent hours like that: they'd have a great time playing chords on their instruments, accompanied by little slaps with the palms of their hands upon the body of the guitar.

One day as I was opening the photo lab, instead of going inside I turned and walked toward the music. With the Fathers' help, each of us was allowed certain standard routes within the institute. They didn't like you to stray from the path by yourself. To meet people there were encounter groups with all their pious sap. At any rate, two residents could never really be sure of being alone.

The musical noise continued, undisturbed by my approach. I added a final note to the score when I crashed noisily into what I thought was a wooden wall, but found to be the moaning body of a piano.

Beside it, squatting or stretched out on the floor someone was working, or had just stopped working. I asked who was there, and all I got for an answer was a mumble, until Jenny took the piece of wood she was using to repair the instrument out of her mouth. Jenny was learning to tune pianos.

She started in again, making the large injured beast moan under her nimble fingers, letting out an occasional "ouch" when a hammer landed on her fingers. She wouldn't speak first. I had to question her. She told me her story in half sentences while she continued her work. The students knew their handicaps by heart and loved to talk about them.

Six-year-old kids spoke seriously about their "retinal conjunctivitis" and other horrible things. Jenny wasn't really blind, either. She just could not identify objects. A hysterical blindness had made her lose vision of movement. Only stationary bodies or those just coming or just going when she was herself motionless, were perceptible to her. What's more, she only saw a tiny part of the visual field: only a bizarrely-shaped slit, the same on both retinas, "saw." Jenny imagined the world across this twisted slit which demanded long minutes from her as she held her breath to make it appear.

Jenny never did manage to see me: I was too mobile. She showed me some scores in Braille, where each note is indicated by a letter of the alphabet with the music written after it. I found her again in the following days. She continued to repair her piano, slowly climbing toward the high notes.

Each note of the piano is comprised of more than a hundred twenty pieces, and there are eighty-eight notes. While she was busy with her tuning key and wedge, Jenny let me stroke her breasts. She didn't seem to be more than fifteen, and my hands wandered over her blonde girl's skin which she said was covered with freckles. Bathed in sweat and dust, we rolled on the floor in our blue work clothes (embroidered with the initials of the institute). The piano hid us, letting out an occasional protesting vibration whenever a foot or an elbow knocked against its naked wires.

When the hammers were done she began on the keyboard, decoding the Braille score with one hand while playing a childish song with the other. She had a way of pulling her head down into her shoulders when I caressed her neck like a plaintive little squirrel who shivers at the slightest touch.

Her naïveté bothered me. After she was used to me, Jenny was very fond of cuddling. To keep her from seeing the blood when I deflowered her, I washed her myself with a sponge from the lab. She wanted to "tell the Fathers everything," which wasn't all too clear in her mind, anyway. She sincerely believed we were going to be married. If only because of our ages it was out of the question.

I must have been the very first one to touch her with desire.

She had never known adolescent sexual games as I had on Kerkenna. She thought that every time you touch each other lovingly, a trace remained, a brand which the Fathers could not help but notice.

At the highest note, our lips approached and touched, and I felt the slight trembling of her mouth. We embraced, reinventing the kiss, our tongues inside warm and humid hollows. For the first time I kissed on the mouth. Mrs. Hallowe'en had never kissed me, and neither had any of the friends she had loaned me out to. I was familiar with women's bodies and with their mouths around my sex. For the first time now I made love to someone near my own age, someone less than thirty years' older.

I dragged her off into the lab and locked the door. Nasty vapors from the fixatives swirled around us as we made love. Jenny tirelessly caressed my eyelashes, describing the little house where we would soon be living, peopled in several years with (why not?) little blind ones: our children.

My photography was going well, since by then they had started trusting me with the key. Despite the fact that they still considered me "anti-social," the Fathers and the director decided I was beginning to resemble the others. The little lone wolf would become a good sightless human being. I was starting to owe them something: my training was the principal. I might have become the little darling of the institute, or so it seemed. They kept repeating that I had the face of an angel.

They still kept reproaching me for my refusal to become confidential with them and especially for my lack of shame which outraged the personnel. With Mrs. Hallowe'en I was accustomed to think of the state of undress as strictly a function of the temperature—which in Florida is mild.

I am indifferent to clothing; it is only an obstacle between people's bodies and myself, a barrier similar to putting a sighted person in front of a screen, or a mask in front of the negative you're trying to develop ... let us say, like someone wearing dark glasses whose gaze you cannot see.

In September I passed my exam as photo technician with flying colors. The director had taken me herself in her Cadillac to the examination room, one hand upon my knee, the other on the steering wheel. The teachers organized a little reception in my honor on the lawn. Between a glass of hot wine and some cake I was presented to the Senator from Santa Barbara and his wife. She was saying in a hysterical voice (already a little drunk), "You could swear he sees, don't you think?" An old gentleman who turned out to be the son of MacPherson, founder of the institute, handed me my diploma and shook my hand between his two dried up old thrashing machines.

The next day, the Father in charge of the darkroom accompanied me to work. I thought he had found out what I was doing with Jenny. I coughed to warn her. She must have heard the Father's footsteps and stayed behind her piano, showing her irritation by a lot of wrong high notes.

You could easily guess when a Father was there by the swishing of his gown. But the Father only wanted me to develop a roll of pictures from the party the evening before. He smelled like licorice, and you could hear him sucking on his candies while he mused over the pictures. All of a sudden he grabbed my arm and said in a voice choked with emotion, "Do you realize what you have just developed there? Your own picture ... too bad ..." (that you can't see yourself) formed unconsciously on his well-shaved lips.

Usually, I didn't worry about the subject matter of the photos I was developing. Only their texture was important. They could have had me turning out pornographic film for all I cared.

But upon hearing that, I was seized by incomprehensible exasperation. I jerked up the soft and running proof and tore it to shreds, it ripped warm and noisy like a living being.

I abruptly stopped being interested in photography. Occasionally, I would return to the lab, but I always had the impression of being washed out since I couldn't even see the results of my work. Jenny, pressed against me, didn't understand what had brought out my anger. Resigned to being blind since birth, she admitted without discussion that the world of the sighted around her was superior to hers; she recognized that, not contesting the presence of some authority beyond the reach of her hypersensitive little palms. Since I had led her to discover sex, her entire universe was limited to me, to touching me insatiably, as if to assure herself that I hadn't disappeared. There was only one single body in the world—mine; and that, she imagined in her frail little brain, until the end of time.

*

So as to not be doing nothing, I asked to try kinesitherapy, an activity much in vogue among the institute's students. The massage room was hidden in the basement, a big, fresh, tiled room as noisy as a swimming pool with the slap of hands massaging muscles echoed by the walls.

As with many of the other students, massage was practically natural for me. I had the tactile familiarity of my own body. When I was a little kid on Kerkenna, in the *hammam* (what you would call a Turkish bath) the masseur had twisted my arms and had climbed onto my back—in the midst of wooden pails filled with boiling water drawn from a steaming basin. Vapor ran along the platforms and climbed the columns toward the shadowy vaulted ceiling. I had learned the importance of the body from those long massages every Friday. Mrs. Hallowe'en had continued this ceremony in her own manner by sudsing me in the sunken tubs of intercontinental hotels.

Unlike photography, there was no hidden sense in this activity. Everyone was equalized: I was completely mixed in with the sensual world.

After a few lessons I could "read" a body, and with my busy contented hands, work on sprains, cramps and other muscular weaknesses. Bodies trembled, became firm, admitted their frailties. To relax the subject, I spoke without interruption. Knots of pain, of nervousness slowly unravelled under my fingers. According to the director whom I treated for back pain, I had magic hands.

I often had to treat members of our rugby team that Christopher sent over. The club was renowned on the West coast: they played the Santa Barbara firemen's or policemen's clubs in amateur championships and often our non-sighted team walked away with the game. One Sunday morning, Christopher brought me a patient who had dislocated his hip in a demonstration match at the stadium. He stretched out on a mattress on the floor. His name was Enrico, and he muttered complaints in Italian-American.

All his muscles were stretched and painful because he had stayed out in the cold just after the demonstration. I massaged up the length of his leg, starting from his heels—stuck inside big mud-caked socks. Enrico was very muscular with thick solid muscles outlined under my hand like a flexible modeling form, supple and warm. Of course I had to examine the hip, but when I pulled on the elastic of his shorts he stopped my hand. I thought I had hurt him, and I started speaking to him in the Italian I had known since living on Kerkenna. Footsteps of the Father on surveillance duty approached. He leaned over me and let out a distracted groan of approval. I had begun to strike Enrico's right thigh with the heels of my hands.

The Father moved away, and I remembered that Italians were very modest. I sensed Enrico raising up on his elbows. Then, I knew he had a hard-on.

That didn't bother me in the least, but it seemed that for him it was torture. Enrico must have been one of the male nurses. The very worst fault for one of the personnel was to allow any resident to suspect sexual emotion. Touching him, I had recognized it. His brutal, ashamed manner of quivering upon contact with me was that of someone sighted. I went with him into the showers. I was surprised when he took the initiative. I felt his anxious eyes scanning the glass door of the locker room at the moment he began to suck me fiercely.

On Kerkenna, boys used to do things like that together. I tried to figure out what I liked about Enrico. For me love is at once completely abstract and very precise. I make my own synthesis of little dabs of skin, of organs that I caress: It has nothing to do with an image.

I had never had full sex with a boy except once when I was very small, with the teacher from the Koranic school. I would never have thought a young man like Enrico could do the same thing to me as Mrs. Hallowe'en and her gentlemen and lady friends had. I had thought it a custom of old European nobility. Even less did I imagine he would turn around for me in the shower stall so easily, as though he had always done it.

At first I was sort of cold. Enrico began exciting me by his tactile motions, the fumbling venturesome manner of the sighted; touches exploded under my fingertips, reassured perhaps by not being seen, as he now discovered with me.

I have never seen anyone having an orgasm. When we used to caress each other as kids in a shepherd's hut of dried rocks isolated in the cactus fields, I always closed my eyes just at the moment of orgasm; and I could never imagine looking at my cousin's face. Instead, I stared at a slice of the blue skies, a blade of sunlight falling from the heavenly fortress onto my nearly closed eyes; a sight I remembered a long time.

I never imagined how Mrs. Hallowe'en looked. The image of the image didn't excite me any more, as had still happened on Kerkenna. The image of the image, the mental repetition of the word "image," whose secret I was trying to pierce by chanting aloud, just after the accident. As if to say "colors," or the names of colors, forms, of bodies, would make you master them.

I only discovered pornography the day I bought some cassettes in Times Square—stimulating stories. I have always liked the people I am making love with to talk at the same time, even to say something stupid like "more, more." At least I hear them. I make love with people-voices, with people-skins. Enrico's scratchy chin on my chest and torso as our hands, legs, mouths were pressing against one another gave rise to electrical discharges in me, reflexive body movements, rapid contractions . . . the calm silence of rest in the smoke of our first cigarette.

Making love, more than a picture, suggests to me the idea of executing a piece of music; not the ethereal music that the residents' chamber music orchestra played *ad infinitum* in the little salon with the open windows, but a music of contrasts, thrown together, almost violent, where an irritating odor strongly opposes the smoothness of a skin; extended arm muscles contrasting with the supple softness of an abdomen.

There exists a policy of regard, a policy of seeing that paralyzes the non-blind. Enrico had a store of passion and tenderness with me that he surely did not have with his official little lady friend. When we make love there comes a moment when all of us are blind, and it's the strongest instant, the most exceptional moment. I had already known it as a child, at the moment when my body lost fear and timidity. I never felt fear making love with the sighted, with a body close, touching me; yet I feel it whenever I go into an unkonwn room where I have no idea of its shape or of what may be inside it.

This same fear, this same timidity reappeared unexpectedly in my relations with Jenny, since I discovered the immense importance I had become for her. She supposed herself and I alike: two condemned prisoners in the same cell. There was born in me an insufferable irritation which expressed itself bit by bit by impatience. Those blind hands skating desperately over my face, searching for the confirmation of resemblance, burning me, skinning me with the regret of something they did not know, whose key they sought in vain: my visible beauty, which the sighted talked about so much.

Making love with Enrico, then with other men and other women after him, I had the pleasure of unbalancing the naïveté of the sighted. They saw me as a child contemplates a too-precious toy, embarrassed by their own desire, afraid of ruining everything. With me, they finally succeeded in having what they had always wanted and could only attain by closing the shutters of their love nests, or by taking refuge at night in public parks to make love without any supervisory gaze. It seems that surveillance is born from a passing glance, or from two glances passing.

With Jenny, I got to know how it was for two to explore the **bars** of our mutual cage. With sighted lovers, blindness takes the upper hand, a perfection allowing them to close their eyes confidently. Inversely, I was "visible" in love only to the blind. My face took my infirmity out of view of the sighted: the same infirmity a blind lover could never forget. With Enrico, love was a consequence of my beauty, that final touch of the artist who creates a strong emotion.

Now that I was sure of being not a blind man but an invisible voyeur of the sighted world I started to talk to Enrico about escaping.

We made love everywhere around the institute, between two brooms in the kitchen closet, behind trees in the park, in the locker rooms of the gymnasium. I stopped going to see Jenny, and I could sometimes hear her, shuffling around in my corridor evenings, not daring to cross the threshold or to ask out loud if I was there, sobbing in a corner like a little mouse.

The first time I told Enrico that I had to get out of the institute and go to Los Angeles he shook the bed jumping up. I was waiting for darkness to get back to my room without being seen. It was hot in the employees' quarters. Their rooms were not air-conditioned and his sweat rolled down onto me. "Do you mean ... travelling by yourself?" We were speaking in Italian. I didn't even have to spell out the word "escape," which was off limits at the institute. I said, yes, I would be alone. He relaxed. He had been afraid he might have to go with me. "And without the

Fathers' permission?" I said I had a friend in L.A. who was going to put me up. I would come back to the institute after a couple of weeks.

Enrico didn't say anything. I think he wasn't taken in by the innocent way I proposed this little excursion. The idea of someone blind out in the world, without a guide, seemed so completely absurd to him that he washed his hands of the whole matter.

As a matter of fact, escape from the institute was so unthinkable that I could have walked right across the court of honor, suitcase in my hand and climbed into a taxi before the director reacted. Naturally I could have gotten LOST, but escape? You cannot escape what I am. And what other world than the institute would have me?

The residents' suitcases were all heaped together in a locked cellar, it was so completely evident that most of them would never be needed again. Enrico gave me a gym bag which I never got back to him. I filled it with a pair of tennis shoes, some shirts and other clothes, my toothbrush and my minicassette recorder. That morning I was wearing my jeans and some street shoes that Enrico had bought for me. My passports and residence permit were sewn into the lining of my coat. The shoes were too small and hurt my feet.

We went out through the garden door, and I recounted the five hundred dollars Enrico had paid for the link bracelet that Mrs. Hallowe'en had given me. I marked the bills with my nail: one slit for the singles, two for the fives, three for the tens, and a little notch for fifties. It was an old café waiter's trick. Of all the kinds I've come across, American money is the worst: all the bills are the same size.

We went along the roadbank. Enrico was surprised to see me capable of following the arc of the curve descending toward Santa Barbara on a road I had never walked before. Sometimes he stopped to look at me, forcing me to stop too, since I was being guided by his footsteps.

Following Enrico I dreamed about how easy it was going to be to slip in among the sighted—at least as long as they weren't watching me. All you had to do was cue in on the rhythm of someone's footsteps. Now there's an expression I really understand, "To follow in someone's footsteps." Then you only had to change steps, slide in behind another passerby, and thus be led down the road to wherever you wanted to go. Following a precise itinerary would of course require another tack. You would have to know the city map pretty well, and only use someone else's footsteps as a passenger, like taking several buses to get to the right direction.

As long as they weren't looking at me. As soon as they started thinking about me, their steps and the interest I had in following them were gone. So it did matter if they found out I was blind.

At the third turn, the smell of the sea overpowered the pines. Far away, the ocean was rolling, spray freshening the air. I faced the wind and breathed in deeply. It smelled like Spring, like on the bridge the day she died. It had been just one year.

One year of being shut up. Enrico started yelling to warn me: the noise of a motor was coming up the slope. The car slowed down when it reached me, then accelerated again, throwing gravel on my shoes with a whiff of warm air and exhausted gasoline.

Enrico had run up beside me. "She didn't see you!" It was the director's car coming back from the morning errands. I wasn't wearing the regulation shirt and shorts anymore. She hadn't even recognized me. She couldn't imagine me walking around OUT-SIDE dressed like an ordinary sighted man in the street.

Down below there was a bit of a crowd at the bus station. With Mrs. Hallowe'en I always liked train stations and airports. When she was furious about a delay or a strike I thought all the brouhaha of the crowd constantly mounting and falling was great, like the waters of a human fountain, punctuated by loudspeakers and odors carried on drafts of air and in strangers' clothing. This time there would be no one to come take me by the hand once I'd left Enrico; he was among the sonorous spectacle of a ticket window as I sat out of trouble on a bench.

Enrico came back to give me my ticket. For a minute, I thought I heard the toc-toc of a cane, felt Zita's shape against my leg. At the last instant, overcome with emotion, Enrico took me by the hand an begged me in the name of the Holy Mother and all the Saints to come back to the institute, where I should never say that he had helped me. I was surprised. I had already nearly forgotten him. While I thought about how to answer him, he left, clearing his throat as he shook my hand. I concentrated on the smells and the noise, on the crowd, shapeless and powerful, anonymous, the crowd again, at last.

Plaisance

When I came to for my last view of Kerkenna, I had in the foreground the bloated face of a Tunisian male nurse who reeked of fig liqueur, his hands rummaging around under my clothes, supposedly to help me. I shoved him away and recognized the walls of the Kerkenna hospital spattered with fly turds. They had taken me to this room when I fainted. A fat old Arab woman wearing at least five slips, one on top of the other, arrived and sat on my bed, making it crack, took my hands and calmed me down. The doctor—the same one who was taking care of Amar—let her continue while he washed his hands; he looked disgusted. For a man from Kerkenna, poking around in a wounded vagina must have really been something else. The woman took a little piece of coal out of her braided wool bag with some tweezers and lit it. She asked me to pull down the covers and pull up my gown; she took away the padding and waved smoke around the lips which by then were starting to ooze blood again, and then without warning she stuffed the coal in. It didn't hurt. I fainted again. There were a few jolts, fresher air. I was dreaming that Amar's mother and all his friends were after me, pelting me with glowing coals, pieces of lava from the volcano.

Days, nights went by. I found myself sitting up in an iron chair at Sainte-Anne, a hospital in Paris. My room was in the gallery which circles the courtyard planted with leafless, sick lime trees. Every time I came back I had the consolation of seeing one more dead stump sawed back clear to the nub. One more tree that hadn't lasted as long as me.

Philippe took me back as a patient, just like before I had left.

And of course, my three traveling companions—he let me know with a little smile of satisfaction—abandoned me the minute we set down at Orly in the Europ-Assistance plane he had sent. They had not been seen since.

I usually brought Philippe back tobacco for his pipe, which he would tamp down conscientiously without ever smoking it. The packets from all my trips decorated the wall above his desk. This time there wasn't any from Tunisia. It surely would have pictured a setting sun and palm trees, pipe smoke floating through the landscape.

I was saying anything.

I turned around to look at him. He had his big round faithful dog eyes fixed on my boobs and he didn't believe a word of what I was saying to him about Amar's accident. Deciding I was still too upset, he sent me back to my room. Clémence, the nurse from Martinique, got me again, groaning how *she* had never spent two whole months in Tunisia. She took me to a room on the second floor. I started to yell. I wasn't about to sleep there right in front of the parking lot. It was very bad for me. I wanted my room on the gallery again, the one under the rickety lime trees. She informed me that Sainte-Anne was not a hotel and that some new women were there anyway. Then, when she finally did give me back my old room, I discovered that all my good things had been stolen while I was away, specifically my blue-black silk dress and Léopold's jewels: the ones I called "my mother's jewelry," which in fact were his mother's and a gold cross that I never wore. Can't you see me wearing a gold cross?

I refused to take my medication, Clémence let me know what a pain I was, and gave it to me in a shot. I put up a fight just to make it look good, but it was the only thing I really wanted.

I woke up screaming, my arms groping in front of me and I kept on screaming, screaming in the dark, until Clémence turned on the lights and I was sobbing in her arms, crying that I thought I had gone blind. My wound wasn't hurting anymore. It had scarred over by itself, thanks more to the mumbo-jumbo of that old sorceress than to the antibiotics that I'd spit out on Kerkenna.

I started going outside again. I needed to straighten out my affairs which were in a horrible mess. All my Social Security papers had to be redone; I had to resubmit my Welfare application. It's a real career being treated for mental problems.

What I needed was a good secretary.

I could only count on Philippe. I decided not to see the fags again, the ones with whom I had left and who I considered responsible for the accident. Philippe was avoiding me, and I knew perfectly well why: I had caused him a lot of trouble.

Philippe had given up his career with the clinic in Switzerland to follow me to Sainte-Anne, losing a lot of seniority in the process. Philippe doesn't like me to leave, because things are always happening to me that he's jealous of. He agrees with my mother; she would have adored him. He didn't think I could actually fall in love with some Arab kid who was the victim of an obscure accident: an adult maybe, someone more his age. If he could have, with the best faith in the world, he would have strapped me down to my bed and pumped me full of shots and pills through a funnel, to stay close to me every day, with his droopy moustache, his sad eyes, that red hair in his nose ... I really like him anyway. He was helping me re-make myself. I was the patient that took up most of his time. The other females in the pavilion were all jealous and whispered how I was sleeping with him. Which was not true. I have my principles: I never sleep with my psychiatrist.

With the calm, the good food, and with sleeping well, I stabilized again. In spite of Philippe's threats, I could start going out again. He'd said he would never take me back again after another escapade. I wrote to the hospital in Kerkenna but got no reply. Philippe didn't want to loan me the money to get back to Tunisia. One morning I took my courage in both hands and phoned some girls who lived near the Bastille, and who had given me money from the Women's Fund. They told me to stop by and see them.

As a bit of reinforcement I had drunk a shot of calva, (calva*dose* as Clémence calls it) on top of my medicine, at the bar of the Hotel P.L.M. Saint-Jacques, just down the street, making the taxi wait. That made me all warm in the tummy. I was looking at an old Arab street sweeper dressed in blue with a red cap on the other side of the window. He could have been Amar's father.

I told the taxi to go to the Bastille and in the middle of a traffic jam the dirver pulled out his disgusting wrinkled up old cock and showed it to me in the rear-view mirror. I didn't leave him a tip when I got out. There wasn't anyone at home except the housekeeper's little girl who said that her name was Carmencita and that she was seven, and that her mother had gone out with Hermeline and Marie-Flor to do some shopping at the Aligre market.

Hermeline and Marie-Flor came back with baskets full of vegetables. We were in front of the T.V., Carmencita and I, eating yogurt and watching the noontime variety show.

They lived in a big, really somber apartment, once a studio with heavy, dusty curtains on all the windows, and they had Barbra records purring in the background all the time. It was a feminist building and even the trash cans had wreaths of flowers drawn around the names of the owners—Sophie, Françoise, Julie.

On the telephone they thought that I was coming to repay the money they'd loaned me in London. When they found me in their apartment, I cried into my yogurt telling them how the wound from my abortion had re-opened on Kerkenna: you really couldn't decently ask a woman-child like me for the money for her abortion. They fixed me right up with a "status," as they called it, in their place. So just like that I found myself with two mothers for a whole year; I who could never even stand my own mother.

At first I tried to ask them for money to go back to Kerkenna. I had never told them about anything but they made up stories all by themselves about falling in love with an Arab—they heard something from the big-mouth homos who worked in the same designer's shop as they did and who knew the people I had been with in Tunisia.

Hermeline was blonde with a big arching nose, crow's-feet around her eyes, tanned wrinkled skin, and droopy breasts. She had to hold them when she laughed really hard. She wrote the "Animal Rights" column for a newspaper where all the men were in love with her. Marie-Flor was a stylist, designing thousands of patterns of different colors to be printed onto fabric. She went to work on a moped, carrying planks of painted designs under sheets of acetate. She had short hair and a turned up nose and she never said anything. Hermeline talked all the time. Every time she surprised me in the same occupation as on the first day—eating yogurt in front of the T.V.—she'd exclaim, "It's not the price of the yogurt, but, really, couldn't one get into the habit of saying so when one eats a yogurt, so that at least one can buy some more?" The first "one" was me—and Carmencita, who was my real friend. The second "one" was Hermeline, out of breath, dragging her grocery cart behind her overflowing with yogurt, without a single one of those machos to ask if she needed help; and should one of them dare ask, she'd spit in his face.

They were all vegetarians: No doubt meat induces rape. They would spend hours simmering dark concoctions of vegetable juices which they sampled with gourmets' delight. Well, I fixed myself a steak and frozen fries that they'd bring back for me. They ate nothing but broth and puréed herbs and thought I was depriving myself of a great pleasure.

I spent my day in bed leafing through soccer magazines for immigrants that I went to buy at Barbès, seeing if I could find a photo of a North African jock who looked like Amar. There were these magazines lying around all over, which made Hermeline very nervous, supposedly because of the disorder. She couldn't stand the sight of all those superstuds giving her the eye from the cover of a magazine. What's worse, when you think about it, Hermeline would have wreaked havoc on Kerkenna.

Sure, I liked the women all right. The thing is, I can psych out women really easy. I don't fall for any of their pretenses, because they're all like I am, except they don't dare let it all out.

They fed me, dressed me, gave me a roof over my head, but not one cent. All the stuff they gave me didn't mean anything to me, anyway, because they never gave it without hesitating. Fortunately, I had my allotment from the more sociable Social Security for pocket money.

They finally found me a job as a salesgirl in a boutique at the corner of the Rue de Buci and a passageway onto Saint-Germain selling stuff from the Far East. All day long I would wrap up appalling bowls, bamboo tables, raffia handbags, all kinds of horrible things. I was working part-time, and I kept seeing Philippe every weekend. He had me on Mandrax: really great with a can of beer!

I was always thinking about Amar, and I couldn't tell anyone. If they knew that story, Hermeline and Marie-Flor would have thought me an Arab's whore, or a fag-hag, or practically a murderess.

Nobody must have felt too clean about the whole affair. The

proof of that was that my Kerkenna companions never tried to see me again. I went back to the "Rosebud" every evening to get myself offered drinks by the last of the bearded journalists and artists on Montparno. I even met a big couturier who wanted to make me his star mannequin. It seems I was the French Twiggy; I had a sculptural svelteness: absolutely sculptural, with a "p." I have a very nice body, long and smooth with small firm breasts like apples and not an ounce of fat. My head is less successful because I have no nose to speak of.

Beer in the evening, Mandrax, yogurt and T.V. in the afternoon—I was getting fat. Coming home late one evening, I found all three women "discussing my problem," as Carmencita whispered to me in the kitchen. All three because Carmencita's mother took part in all their meetings, in which they all considered themselves either psychologists or the Women's Court.

I walked in enraged. I insulted them. I slapped the concierge, spitting into her face that she was a stoolie, like all Spanish maids. Hermeline and Marie-Flor were completely blown away. They told me I was drunk, which was true. So I marched out the door and left forever. Only on the sidewalk did I realize that I still had little Carmencita by the hand.

We ran to the street corner to catch a bus. I climbed aboard still holding her by the hand. The driver said to me, "You sure do have a pretty little girl," and as I turned I could see the three women back at the corner wildly waving their arms in the air.

We travelled in an everchanging crowd. I had left on impulse, not thinking where we'd go. Carmen was very good, sitting up straight in her seat, looking out the window not talking. When we arrived at the end of the line—the Gare de l'Est station—she said why didn't we call her daddy. He'd been separated from her mother since Marie-Flor had begun organizing teas to combat Latin machismo. We did and he said to come meet him where he worked, not far away, near Stalingrad: his name was Antonio, he was in exile and worked for a newspaper.

We arrived at a grungy little street lined with an aluminum and glass high rise which took up the whole block. There was a photoelectric eye over the glass door at the entrance. When we got inside, Antonio had already forgotten about us, and the receptionist groaned that she didn't know anything about it, when all she had to do was go get him. She began to reheat a can of cannelloni on a gas camp stove, cutting off all calls on the switchboard. A tall thin type went by and Carmen jumped on his neck. He said, "Oh, it's you guys?" like he'd already forgotten us. He hugged the little girl a little absentmindedly, and added that he had called her mother: she had already started talking about kidnapping. He was telling me how Andréa, my name in Italian, was a man's name. He thought at first that some guy had taken off with his daughter. Finally, her mother told him to keep Carmen. She was leaving soon with her two bosses on a cruise to the Antilles for a seminar on the plight of the immigrant woman.

Antonio was tall with a scar in the middle of his forehead; he had a big sensual nose, and he gave you the impression of knowing what he wanted. He got off on everything he saw. He laughed when he was talking about Carmen's mother, like she was a bad joke. He had to yell to be heard above the general hubbub all around us. The night journalists were just coming back from dinner and were all hyper. Some were tearing up the telephones, going into nervous breakdowns; others were knocking over wastebaskets looking for lost articles; a couple of proofreaders were taking a shower and fucking in the john; the more stylish editors were dressed in Nifty-Fifties duds which looked like they hadn't been ironed since then. Covered with zits, they were seated behind typewriters pulling up their sleeves to show their needle tracks.

The filth was general, and when Antonio led us toward the back of the room to show us around the paper, we had to walk around leftover ham sandwiches and cigarette butts. I thought how unhealthy it was for a child. It could have been a subway station during a janitor's strike. Half the employees were hanging around not doing anything, sitting on desks watching T.V., laughing. Five or six people were typing like crazy on old machines like you see in the movies, plugging up their ears to concentrate. Their edition was supposed to be wrapped up in an hour and they had barely begun.

Between the john and a huge typewriter that was going all by itself and spitting out a roll of paper, was a room without any windows that stank from stale tobacco. Antonio took us in and introduced us to a fat guy with black fingernails who was crumpled up over the desk trying to choose a butt that wasn't too short from a collection of stubbed-out cigars. He offered one to Carmencita, lit his own and pushed aside the porno want-ads he had been reading while he picked his teeth. Then, taking some papers from the night before, he grumbled about how there was "a hell of a lot of filler." Antonio handed him a sheet he'd cut off the roll from the big machine and he let out a "Jesus H. Christ" and shot out of the room so fast I couldn't believe it.

Antonio worked in the back where there was the least amount of air. It was the part of the paper where they did layouts. All the work was done by girls, even though it was supposed to be a paper of the extreme left. Half of the girls, the French ones, were so ugly they could clear the sidewalks of the Rue Saint-Denis. The other half consisted of immigrant hoseheads who spent their time changing their make-up and popping out blackheads the minute Antonio's back was turned.

When I'd left Marie-Flor and Hermeline I kissed my job goodbye since they and the boss were buddy-buddy. In solidarity against them, Antonio offered to recruit me on the spot. Seeing those zombies all day long would have depressed me.

Antonio showed up in the cave again and the girls got back to work since he was in charge of them. They were typing in front of big blue cubes with flashing lights. Some of them just turned their backs to him and kept on exchanging suntanning secrets. He couldn't do anything about them. Since it was a leftist paper he couldn't fire them.

So Antonio picked up a heavy wooden case filled with drawing supplies and threw it on the floor right in the middle of all the machines. He marched straight to the spot where the newspaper dummies were made. Some guys with glasses and long hair were bent over glass tables, lit from beneath, which gave them terrible circles around their eyes. Antonio took one from that group by the collar and started banging him against the wall. I took Carmen over to have fun with the word processors: that's what the girls doing the typing were called. Carmen wanted to watch her daddy fight. She thought it was cool. Finally one of the word processor girls—she must have been at least thirty and an Arab—helped me pull her away.

The Arabess' name was Malika. She had a tiny triangular face with high prominent cheekbones. We went out together to eat pastry with Carmen. Malika was even skinnier than me—I only like slender girls—and had a very tiny mouth, and she looked very determined. We got back to the newspaper just as they were starting to tilt back their chairs at one desk after another, because they had just screwed up the edition for another day. Malika had gotten herself some *loukoums*, to satisfy her craving for sweets. She lay them down on the keyboard of her flashing cube, claiming she was like me and could eat anything she wanted without getting fat. She talked really fast, swallowing half her words. For the first time I found a girl I really liked. Maybe because she was Arab.

A *loukoum* fell into the machine and all the keys got stuck together. Antonio came back, but Malika just kept on laughing without doing any work. Antonio kissed her on the forehead, and she gave him a kiss in return. They went together. They began to talk about what they were going to do with Carmen. I sent the little one over to play with the rolls of paper coming out of the big machine that everybody pranced around, then I had her glue together the photos coming out already developed from another machine.

When she came back, five or six people were discussing what they were going to do with Carmencita and *me*—people who didn't even know me. I pointed out that if they were a sincerely leftist paper they would come up with a pension for me and find me somewhere to live, since I was a victim of society. Antonio burst out laughing looking at me while licking his lips and slapping Malika on the back. He was calling her "my little *loukoum*," and winking at me. At least I thought he was winking. I found out from the other girls that he tried to pick them all up, that you had to watch out for him.

On that note, Antonio started in on his wife, Carmencita's mother, calling her a cunt. A word processor with glasses went into a fit of hysterics and we had to make her drink cologne, the only thing that could bring her around. Antonio suggested that since I was with Carmencita I could come back with them to their place. I could be the babysitter. So we all went, leaving the paper like it was, with the chief pulling out his dandruff-speckled hair.

Antonio was living at Malika's in the Fourteenth Arrondissement.

Working all day in that cavern had gotten them used to living in a hole. The apartment was a semi-cellar at street level, half buried by a little apartment building stuck in the little Rue de Plaisance, and it never saw the light of day. You entered by a little door you could barely squeeze through two at a time into a hall where all the doorways were painted green and deep violet, covered with political posters.

Malika's room faced the street, and she kept the shutters closed all day. There was a mattress on the floor circled by dirty plates from lunch two weeks before.

The little apartment house's plaster was falling down everywhere as the walls sweated out the Parisian humidity—which is really great if you're a mushroom. Antonio said what about putting me in the hall that led to the courtyard. Across from the hall was a wooden crapper and an old sink where Malika fixed couscous and told me all about her life. We went up to the second floor to get some spices and I found out that Malika had fallen in with a bunch of intellectual ecology freaks who owned the building.

She didn't pay rent; she used their apartment as a bathroom. Jérôme was leader of the new residents of the quarter who had cropped up in the last two or three years, following May '68, and who hung on like mussels to those narrow streets cluttered with beams left over from all the demolition. From the window in Patricia's salon—she's Jérôme's wife—you could see the cruddy stone face of some modern marble-covered convention center towering over the ledges where she grew rosemary and thyme, without fertilizer.

Old people were taking over the top of their building: retired people from the gas company, old café waiters who stopped in the street to look at painted-over buildings covered with signs and already boarded up, what used to be the bistros where they had worked. Everywhere in the Rue de Plaisance the old people went to the top, like rats before a flood. On the respectable lower floors, unmarried sociologists like Jérôme and Patricia were knocking down walls to make the apartment of the "modern couple."

Malika was an adventurer. She knew all about ready-to-wear, she had been to Ibiza and she smoked grass left over from her lover before Antonio. There was a whole forest of it under her bed.

She was well preserved, a little dry, with an animal instinct that must have kept her in shape.

We put Carmen in their room, and Malika took me up to the second floor to ask for a bed for the little girl and a mattress for me. Jérôme, the guy that opened the door, was bald with a little blond beard and eyes that bugged out but always seemed like he was smiling. He was in the middle of trying to get a spoonful of baby food into a little kid who was spitting it all back out. Jérôme's wife, a tall blonde dressed only in a man's robe, was typing in the bathroom. We all went down to the cellar to look for a little bed for Carmen. Jérôme was scratching his beard, thoughtfully studying the hall without any windows where I was supposed to sleep. We went back up to his place and lowering his voice and looking toward the bathroom, he finally suggested that perhaps in the meantime I might take the main room above, which they wanted to make into a kid's room later on.

In the meantime ... I stayed there almost two years.

Next to the house a crummy café spread out a facade of brown-painted wood. The bar itself was real zinc, really pitted, marked all over with names and pictures scratched into the metal. The café was mostly frequented by Arabs. They would come and drink the first calva before the first subway at five-thirty in the morning, talking together, playing cards, or betting on their favorite horses in the races on Saturdays and Sundays. I had never paid that much attention to Arabs in Paris. I was really blown away by the difference between them—all overcoats and gray jackets—and my sunny memories of Kerkenna. I was at the café all the time with Malika. The old Arabs and young hoods (like the son of the woman who owned the café), talked to Malika as though she were an Arab girl. Madame Robert, the owner, and the old bags that came to mooch a little something to wet their whistles, talked to her like she was a neighborhood shopkeeper.

Malika and I used to have a lot of fun comparing each other nude in the little overheated room; Jérôme had loaned us an electric radiator we plugged into the light switch timer in the hallway. For the first time in my life a woman's body wasn't disgusting to me. However, Malika was no dyke, and neither was I.

Malika's good friend and owner of the café, Madame Robert,

had pallid copper skin and the fat on her arms hung down like breasts, sloshing back and forth above glasses of beer. They had a favorite topic of conversation: how their men beat them. Antonio only threw a few punches at Malika, who defended herself with a switchblade: Madame Robert's husband was a good-looking Algerian in his forties with a Mercedes and threads from the Belle Jardinière ... "maybe not Galeries Lafayette but still" ... and they *looked* a lot more like gardener suits after Madame Robert had covered them with a nice round of flying tarts. Her husband didn't live with her but in a brand new trailer that in the summertime he parked in front of the café, directly in front, just to piss her off. In the winter he left it on some property he owned north of town, at Saint-Denis, waiting for the time when he would have enough stashed away to go back home to Tlemcen, a rich man with a trailer *and* a car.

According to Madame Robert, he went as far as to take money from the old lady winos. She protected her little bunch of alkies who pissed in the courtyard of the building at night under dresses they never washed and then came back to sit in the café. Madame Robert would yell at them, and make them go throw a bucket of water to rinse it off: she thought she was their mother. The poor dears, when she was gone, they'd kick off, their mouths gaping open. Fridays and Saturdays they would take a ten franc note out from under their skirts and treat themselves to six calvas in a row: they were just back from getting screwed by some old Arab, somewhere behind a truck down the street.

At other times their lovers came in to treat them to a drink. I never would have thought those old scumbags could be whores, too. And those stinking old slobs had love scenes with Kabyle grocers, drinking splits of champagne, singing "Cherry Pink and Apple Blossom White" in their husky voices.

Strange atmosphere for a café, but not that bad. Madame Robert spent all day talking about her problems with her husband, who even stole the Welfare checks she got as trustee for the old girls. She kept their papers, their mail, their cash, and their clothes in plastic bags. Everything they owned smelled like stale wine. A man would have to lose every last shred of morality to take an old age pension!

Antonio wanted to sleep with me, and I could see Malika's chin harden whenever we came downstairs together from my room under the eaves. He wasn't very handsome. He always insisted: he could never talk in a normal voice and went around hollering all the time in Italian. He was a militant revolutionary in his country. I let him do it: we became lovers as friends, no frills. He drove Madame Robert up the wall, especially when he started scrunching up his eyes, swearing in Italian. He did have an enormous cock, but it didn't do that much for me. Sex had lost a lot of its appeal for me. I was sleeping with him to be nice.

Antonio wasn't the sentimental type; he wouldn't stick to me afterwards. He used to laugh because I closed my eyes whenever he went inside me, but he didn't know I was concentrating on Amar. If he ever suspected, he might have killed me for cheating on him like that with a ghost at the very moment he was making love to me. The day after we balled the first time was the twenty-fourth of December. I read an article in the paper that morning about an earthquake: there had been several deaths on the island of Kerkenna. For Christmas that year, we all went to a holiday lunch at Jérôme and Patricia's. She gave me some torn old lace curtains for my room which she had dyed with tea. The party was for the kids, especially Carmen, but Antonio started drinking all the wine and cognac and yelling insults at Malika.

Patricia turned away, as though Antonio's Italian curses smelled bad. Jérôme pacified the squalling brats by serving frozen turkey fricassée with pumpkin. This conflict between the ground floor and the second floor was inevitable. At night, I often heard terrible crashes of broken dishes whenever Antonio had stopped smoking joints—his feet up on the radiator, he aimed plates at Malika's head. She never stopped circling him, telling him he didn't have any balls, he was a dirty little wop she should have known better than to get mixed up with. This Christmas dinner she stood up as they were bringing in the cake for the kids and went to the bathroom, where everyone thought she was crying. She didn't come back. The bathroom used to be a workroom which they had fixed up and had a door leading to the stairway.

After the meal, Patricia looked for the earrings she had bought the Sunday before at the Vanves' market. She had left them in the soap dish, and now they weren't there. She began rummaging around everywhere in the big room. They weren't under the cushions covered with Greek fabric. Antonio kept on belting down cognac, snickering. Malika came back in time for coffee. You could have cut the air with a knife. Everyone in the room, except maybe Antonio who was dead drunk, was trying to keep from thinking Malika was the thief. Patricia ended up asking in a choked voice if she hadn't, by chance, "borrowed" the earrings. Malika exploded, knocking over the earthenware bowl she'd been using as a coffee cup. She was the one people always asked when something disappeared. She went downstairs, we could hear her indignant footsteps on the stairway. Antonio woke up enough to walk straight up to Jérôme, who backed away throwing up his hands. Antonio let it be known that if his stinking whore's cunt of a bourgeois wife didn't can it, he would tear the fucking place to pieces. He'd had it up to here with bourgeois racists. He left, too, slamming the door so hard on his way out that he knocked down the plaster Jérôme had just finished putting up.

Downstairs, I found Antonio holding Malika by the throat with one hand, the other holding a frying pan that hadn't even been washed, demanding the earrings, ready to smash her skull. I pulled them apart. Antonio had everything topsy-turvy in the place, which put it almost back in order. He found the earrings in a box of tampons above the sink, out in the courtyard. Malika got all her things together and asked if she could stay in my room. She never wanted to speak to Antonio again, ever, nor to anyone else in the building, except me. Antonio took me aside in the hallway. All I had to do was to move in downstairs; so I did. I was never afraid of him. The only time he ever tried to hit me, I pulled out my fingernail scissors and went for him where it counts.

Antonio let me do everything I wanted. He would whistle as he read Gramsci—an Italian politican—while I put things in order: stray political pamphlets, dirty pots, a bike in a million pieces, Carmen's jumpers. While he was occupied with the newspaper, I'd go up to Malika's to discuss what a rotten son of a bitch he was, as we smoked up the rest of her grass. Antonio gave me a lot of flak because he said I was one of the oppressed and I wasn't doing anything about it. I got used to him. He was a good lay, and since my trip to Tunisia, I didn't believe in love anymore. He'd been in exile for two years. The Italian government had it in for him for having machine-gunned a Communist cardinal. But he said it wasn't true, and came off sounding like someone entirely capable of doing it.

Antonio said why didn't we go to Milano to see his little brother, who—from his photos—looked like him, only worse. Antonio had bought a fake passport at Barbès which he had altered himself, one eye glued to a magnifying glass, using some clips he'd picked up down at the Fourteenth Arrondissement police station. We took the train from the Lyon train station, just like a little family, Antonio carrying the bags with Carmen's stuff, me, the kid and a package of sandwiches Madame Robert had made up for us.

Malika had slipped a little gold medallion and chain around Carmen's neck, the hand of Fatima, to protect her against hazards of the trip. It didn't work. We didn't get past Ventimiglia. The cops came into our compartment while the train was stopped at that border station. All the travellers were hurrying through the corridor and along the platform to see the gangsters being arrested. The police emptied boy scouts and an Italian soldier out of our compartment, and rummaged through everything, keeping an eye on Antonio. He asked them to let the mother and child get off, so I took Carmen by one hand, her things with the other. After all, I didn't have anything to do with his troubles. The head plainclothes cop dumped Carmen's bag upside down. In the middle of little socks and tiny panties were three pistols and several long pieces of modeling clay wrapped in paper. The guy said yes, it was *plastique* ... bombs.

Later on, I found out Madame Robert had squealed on Antonio. Carmen and I were turned over to a social worker who made us sleep on air mattresses in an office right there in the train station. Carmen kept saying the cops had old pistols and her daddy had brand new ones. The next morning we freshened up in the station washroom and her real mother arrived by plane to get back her little girl, and didn't speak to me once, as though I'd dragged Carmen off to a whorehouse and she'd gotten V.D. As for me, I told them I was a patient at Sainte-Anne. The cops became more respectful. They called up the hospital, and I got Philippe to order them to put me in an ambulance. Up rolled this super-comfy Citroen D.S. driven by two wild dudes in white coats. They took me to Paris, stopping at every café on the way, to prevent dehydration. When the ambulance finally rolled into Sainte-Anne's, Philippe had to hand over three thousand francs.

*

As we were walking to the stairway, Philippe said he had to admit my analysis was the most expensive he had ever done—at least the most expensive for him. Even so, he was rubbing his hands at having gotten me back again. Insensitively I had dropped him over the course of the last two years. He wanted to get started again right away with my analysis. I went up to his office where there wasn't a single new tobacco pouch. No one had replaced me.

I started off telling him my dreams again while he chewed on the ends of his moustache, full of little pieces of tobacco, then chewed on his new horn-rimmed glasses, and finally chewed on his pen: he had a ferocious appetite for inedible objects. At Sainte-Anne I dreamed about Amar. A woman who looked like Malika, but who was Amar's mother, was chasing me to punish me for having abandoned him. According to the analysis, I'd been dreaming about the same thing without remembering it for the past three years. Philippe didn't even believe Amar existed. He talked about *my* mother who didn't have a thing to do with those dreams, and he was happy as a goldfish in the troubled waters of my analysis.

I didn't recognize Sainte-Anne. Clémence had been canned after they'd found out she was knocking off the older more vegged-out patients in Pavilion Five with morphine. The lime trees in the courtyard had been chopped down, and the bare bust of some doctor dressed in a labcoat, founding father of asylums, stood alone in the middle of the green. The only thing left was the ether, the same good old smell of ether. I kept up my practice of making up "rotten cotton" in the evening, in my bed, with a bottleful ripped off from the pharmacy in the infirmary. The pillow became a cushion of clouds, soft and acidic, a source of music from Arabia.

Even the hospital's odor wasn't what it used to be. They were disinfecting everywhere with bleach. A hell of a meningitis epidemic had wiped out the few residents I knew.

I went back to my apartment in the Fourteenth Arrondissment as soon as Philippe authorized it. Patricia's fat little girl had taken my room while I was gone, but they apologized, she and Jérôme exclaiming in a single voice that sounded fake how much of a surprise it was to see me again. They thought maybe I'd been in prison.

Winter was just finishing making the chestnut leaves fall onto the pissoir in the Square Jean Moulin. They stopped up drains, channeling a lake of piss onto the sidewalk in front of the house. Patricia gave me back my room and I stared at the withered-up geraniums on the windowsill that no one had thought to bring inside: frozen dead.

Jérôme and Patricia showed me some flyers about a meeting called to form a committee to get Antonio freed, which they had gotten into right after he'd been arrested. Nobody came, because everyone owed Malika money for grass. Malika had reoccupied the downstairs flat by opening the one door that didn't have a police seal on it, the one on the courtyard. She came up to say "Hi," her eyes hollow, looking feverish. She wanted to avenge Antonio. She'd discovered he had been turned in by Madame Robert by seeing an inspector from the Rue Boyer-Barret going in and out of the café all the time.

In Algeria they would have put the old bag's eyes out. Something had to be done, and it was up to Malika and me.

I was sort of afraid of Malika. She didn't lose any sleep over that bastard Antonio, that's for sure. But she couldn't stand things being out of balance: justice had to be rendered.

In Antonio's absence, Malika had started to give parties on the ground floor, to which she didn't invide Jérôme, didn't invite Patricia; passing them all off as her tenants if they happened to pass by in the hall. After a few months, these soirées became much more chic than Patricia's eco-dinners on the second floor. Lines of taxis stood outside running their meters in front of our little painted wooden door late into the night. Sometimes, the whole street would peek out through their shutters and find to their amusement a big black limo, complete with chauffeur. Malika later told me it was simple to rent one for a day: for five or six people it's hardly more expensive than a taxi, but it's a real trip, as her new friends would say.

I hadn't really been paying enough attention to how people changed around me in Paris. They had taken up a new style, which Malika's visitors clued me in to. She invited M. Robert all the time and she began calling him Kateb, his nickname. She'd taken him into her band of partiers, which drove Madame Robert into an absolute rage. The party group was led by an old Spanish senorita with a head like a Mexican statue, who was the daughter of some famous painter and the only one of the bunch who had any real money. They woke up at five in the afternoon. They went to fashion shows, nightclub openings. Marie-Flor and Hermeline were with them a lot. Marie-Flor had become a beacon of fashion. One guy went along with them. I'd seen him at Antonio's paper. No one could tell if he was a hard-core adolescent fading before his time or an old bachelor embalmed by drugs. He wore glasses and black and white checked suits. Several suits, as he changed them every time he came, every one clean as a dog brush.

This guy arrived with a really beautiful Arab girl. It was obvious he wasn't sleeping with her. He must have been playing white knight, paying for her drinks. She didn't seem more than maybe sixteen, and had big lips, bigger than Bardot had at her age, the pout of a spoiled brat, a pony tail held with safety pins, black leather-look slacks, and she wore exaggerated, ultra-red make-up.

Malika introduced her as the little sister of Alissa, Malika's pal from the Lyon correctional house, the girl Malika always talked about. Her name was Djamillah, and M. Robert ate her up with his eyes: she must have reminded him of his younger days in Tlemcen.

A few days later Alissa visited: Djamillah had been a mere beginning. Alissa and Malika hadn't seen each other since the old days in the house of correction. Alissa started telling stories about the goings-on in basements of the government subsidized highrises where they had lived when they were young, or lifting stuff in supermarkets and fights with boys' gangs in vacant lots.

Djamillah and Alissa didn't look alike at all. Alissa was tall with a long nose and long hair, beautiful in her own way, serious, but not as sexy. The first week she was in Paris, Djamilla posed for a fashion magazine where the Spanish painter's daughter worked. She wore tiger-stripe stockings and had a bazooka in her hands, aimed straight at the camera.

The other girls weren't jealous. That surprised me. Running around with these Arab girls was beginning to get interesting. The big sister, even Malika, seemed like people who have pinned all their hopes and ambitions on their kid: Djamillah's success was theirs.

Malika's place was their general headquarters. I spent my

afternoons there watching them dress and make-up Djamillah. Jérôme and Patricia never said hi anymore, and M. Robert never left that ground floor flat. He couldn't have imagined—he, who had left Algeria twenty years before—that Arab girls could be like American actresses.

When I looked at Alissa and Djamillah together, it seemed they did look alike, in some way. It was hard to say just how; there was such a contrast. The day I saw Alissa being made-up, exactly like Djamillah, their common points showed. Both had the sames eyes: those eyes with long black lashes that go from velvety brown to angry black, passing through siena brown and ocean gray along the way. Eyes I had already seen on the beach at Kerkenna, keeping track of our disputes. But I mean, Arabs didn't all have the same eyes. Malika's were little shiny black pearls; the street sweepers' a gloomy muddy brown.

A pale light shone into the little courtyard. The crowd was sitting on the floor on old mats or leaning against the blankets hanging from the wall drinking straight vodka from used paper cups. It was quite select: a lot of people tried to get invited to our little hole on the courtyard. You could hear Arab music from Algiers on the old short-wave radio fading in and out in the background.

When I mentioned their eyes, Alissa and Djamillah both laughed. Then Malika said they weren't even of the same mother, but had their father's eyes. They got a photo of him, digging down through lipstick tubes and open eyeshadow in their purses: a man with a black moustache in his fifties wearing a suit. I had seen his head somewhere before, and without thinking, I asked where they were from. Lyon? Yeah, and before that? They weren't born in Lyon? "No, in Tunisia, on an island." They wouldn't say where, I had to insist. I couldn't possibly have heard of it, it was called Kerkenna.

They pronounced Kerkenna like the French, not like the people down there did, spitting out the first syllable and melting the other two into a single murmur.

Only Alissa had lived there and only 'til the age of six. Djamillah had left when still a baby. "Our father is from there," Alissa casually added. I got hold of myself and said I had heard they had earthquakes there.

Another photograph showed the family's home interior and

exterior, with a fig tree outside that I remembered grew up past the roof. A fat baby in a brown woolen robe stood up straight and looked right at the lens in one photo. Djamillah said that he was her brother, well, half brother, Omar. Amar, I nearly corrected, but bit my tongue.

On Kerkenna I met Arabs several times who said to me, "Oh, you're from Paris? Which arrondissement?" And when I said the Thirteenth (where Sainte-Anne's is) they'd bubble, "Oh, do you know such-and-such? He lives in the Thirteenth, too." At the time I thought they were *so* naïve that I didn't even bother to explain that the Thirteenth had as many inhabitants as Tunis.

Today, I understand they were right. Since I had been on Kerkenna, it was completely normal that Amar's family should come to Paris. Fate, even. I had never imagined Amar as being anywhere other than Kerkenna, hadn't ever thought of his sisters in Lyon. Yet they were this family from Lyon whose pictures I had seen three years before. Djamillah must have been in that photo. She'd really done a quick job of ditching her veil. At the time, the Alissa of the photos must have been in the house of correction. The old man sure enough was Amar's father. He was what they all had in common.

I swallowed my surprise. The shy young lad from Kerkenna who hardly dared speak French, and did so correctly when he did like a kid in front of class, was brother to these two lulus who drank vodka right out of the bottle.

The pictures were being passed around to everybody, and I was stuck between the cubbyhole for the trash can and the stove, the oven door opened for heat. I had so many questions to ask. His family surely must know what happened to him . . . of course they'd lived thousands of kilometers away from each other for years. Anyway, I knew that he hadn't died in the earthquake: they talked about him in the present tense. I was paralyzed. I got the absurd idea that they might have heard something about me. I could imagine Amar walking around in circles, on those lava roads or at the edge of a sheer cliff, condemned to remain a helpless adolescent by my actions.

I was afraid they would notice my silence. The Spanish woman started talking about her family. She wanted to know if their brother lived in Paris. The two sisters said, well you know they didn't really know him, as they left Kerkenna before he was born. Alissa added that he'd become blind, following an accident. The character with Djamillah said in a pasty voice that it was better to be blind than one-armed. No one even thought to ask who was taking care of this blind brother.

He'd stayed on Kerkenna alone. Their father's second wife—he was now on his fourth—had died since my trip. The conversation went on; bringing up the subject of her blind half-brother had made Djamillah sad, and she talked about writing him in Kerkenna. Malika ended up taking the whole bunch over to Madame Robert's café. I went upstairs to think. Since I had met them, it was a sign that I would see Amar again.

Malika had dragged them over to Madame Robert's café in order to finish off the place. She wasn't trying to give it publicity, but sort of to ruin her. Monsieur Robert took up his position behind the bar and offered one round, many rounds, on the house as he gobbled up Djamillah with his eyes. He got out bottles of whiskey, which were seldom used: the old winettes hardly ever ordered it. In fact, the old lady bums were more or less swept aside so the Spanish lady in an evening gown and her revel-rousers could have room at the three tables by the window, completely in a daze as they were at finding a café open at that hour in that neighborhood. Workmen passing on the street in the dawn's early light looked at the lit-up window with its dusty old potted rubber tree and its photos of Algiers before Independence, and they saw all these people you could have sworn were models mixed with that decor: women made up like vamps, with bobbed hair, chic outfits, men in rented tuxes. Out of shyness, in fear of meeting these people who hadn't been to bed yet, who had probably been out in nightclubs, dancing, they decided not to come in for the first calva of the day. The chauffeur, cap on, stood at the café door, opening and chugging down bottles of Jock'mousse which Monsieur Robert brought over from time to time.

The workers passed by and made the sign for crazy people. But Monsieur Robert wasn't the least bit worried about his wife's former clientele.

He had put on a blazer which was too small for him, and had a huge gold signet ring on one finger. Madame Robert went on about her business without saying a word, fetching glasses and ice, a belated victim of Malika's vengeance. Her chignon was askew and she was almost suffocating, she was so livid with indignation.

I was the one to finally speak to her. In her day—she moaned—Djamillah wouldn't have been more than a maid in her beautiful Algiers apartment. All she would have been good for was washing the floors, her pants pushed up her knees; and *him*, a man she had practically taken in from the gutter, in a marriage that had caused a scandal throughout the entire French community in the Algiers of 1951. Why, he was letting himself be led on like a boob by this creature. Once an animal, always an animal, and the Arab in Monsieur Robert was reclaiming its former strength. She could have forgiven him all the whores. She had always overlooked his little faults. But she was not about to forget him letting himself fall for some little *bougnoule* do-nothing, when he had been lucky enough to marry a French woman. She had been one of the first to marry a *maghrébin*. And now? I mean, you know, she got really racist about it, even more so after losing all her Arab workmen customers. There was some truth in what she said. Even had I the choice, I never would have married Amar.

Madame Robert developed bags under her eyes that dropped clear down to her double chin as her café became all the rage among the snobs. The gang would go to les Halles to eat, using money Djamillah borrowed from Monsieur Robert, who took it from the till. Madame Robert didn't try to hide her bruises anymore, bruises her husband gave her. One fine day, the street discovered the café closed. Malika said to me in passing that Madame Robert was in the hospital, with cancer throughout her body.

It was winter in Paris, sad and nasty. Heads changed hairdos and outlooks. The people that I knew, each doing his own little thing, now took themselves seriously and had telephone answering machines. Malika and the two sisters saw people in the fashion biz, broken down Japanese, leather freaks, and various other monsters. Hermeline managed to become famous by writing a feminist book titled "In the Deepest Part of Me." Jérôme and Patricia picked up a fat contract with the Environmental Affairs Ministry to reform grass roots recycling centers. They moved out to live in a château the government turned over to them. Malika and the sisters moved out too. Now that the second floor was empty and Madame Robert was on her way out, they didn't have anyone to harass.

Djamillah was sleeping with a rock singer, also from Lyon. They had a duplex in the Marais. So only me and an old woman on the top floor who never noticed new tenants were left in the leprous little building with closed shutters. And she hadn't ventured out into the stairway for the past ten years.

Why was I still there? Little by little a rift moved me apart from people my age. This rift had begun in Tunisia. All the time the others were working, succeeding, my flexibility was definitely being broken on that island.

Yeah, I stayed. I was in the right place at the wrong time. Too late to marry Léopold, who was exactly the kind of person my friends preferred to hang out with now, rather than with me.

For the first time I went back home on my own—to Sainté-Anne, I mean. Philippe had been promoted to assistant head doctor. He gave me a room all to myself with windows on the director's garden.

Two weeks later, the house on the Rue de Plaisance was flattened by a bulldozer.

Philippe didn't say anything when I told him I had run into Amar's sisters by chance: he didn't believe in chance. In the meantime he had joined up with a lady child psychiatrist who talked like some egghead. She would have sent any kid running at the sight of her. He almost seemed to apologize for her, like he should have asked my permission first. I'm probably the one person in the world who knows him best. He was really curious about Amar's sisters: he didn't believe in Amar, but he believed in them, since I said I'd show him them if he wanted. And, you know what else? He liked me to keep on with the same obsession, like some doctor who sits there rubbing his hands together when he sees a wonderful tumor he already knew would begin to grow.

About the end of winter I met Malika at the café of the Hotel P.L.M. Saint-Jacques and she invited me to a party in Djamillah's honor at a nightclub. I decided to take Philippe along. Because of that, I was sorry when Djamillah and Alissa told me on the phone that, incidentally, they'd come across their brother again. He'd arrived in Paris that very day and they were bringing him to the party.

I'm miserable at parties. This was like all the parties in those days. People who tried to be young, who thought they were having a wonderful time, and who looked more like they were attending a funeral.

I had come to see Amar and I was afraid of seeing him. I felt like I was being whisked back three years. I tried to figure out by what miracle he'd gotten all the way to Paris—and to this kind of place. The crowd at the building entrance—it used to be a theatre—made me think he didn't know how lucky he was when all was said and done, to not be able to see that miserable bunch of vulgar pretension in front of the box office.

Too-new white bib overalls, post-war gabardines that had wrinkled hanging in the les Halles shop windows, red vinyl *culottes* like you'd see hitching on the highway, lamé shorts and nylon lace: that's the kind of scenery into which Amar was going to reappear, like a diver suddenly coming up to the surface in the middle of a bunch of delirious men overboard.

They were dancing, taking advantage of the flashing lights to stand and pose in the dimness and to pretend they were not surprised but moving when the laser came back on. While others bounced up and down, Philippe and I—like most of the guests— were coming and going like ants on a mission from the second floor down to the first. In front of the glass doors that opened onto the boulevard, doormen dressed in grungy usher outfits were trying to make themselves look important to keep out riff raff from neighboring cafés.

The club, one of the most well-known in Paris, had an incredibly laid-back atmosphere for a place where even state ministers came to snort heroin.

You had to climb over bodies overcome by bad bubbly from the bar, littered in stairways and between plants cleared for their next harvest of cigarette butts. Philippe pushed aside the cadavers who slid gently onto carpeting covered with beer cans and broken glass. When they landed on a burning cigarette, they would jump around like fish out of water. The whole club was an immense human ashtray some lazy servant had forgotten to empty.

I was looking everywhere for Malika or the two sisters. I didn't try to find Amar. In the hubbub of freeloaders and pseudo stars who probably hadn't shone for thousands of years I looked out for Amar, afraid I might find him. I knocked into couples from the provinces with slicked-down hair, pharmacists' sons who had paid to see the beautiful people being wild. We went up to the second floor, to what used to be a balcony, where the heat concentrated the smell of sweat and piss. Chance duos in darkened corners were tickling one another's fancies, but they weren't on the balcony: that is, Amar and the girls.

Then on top of it all, Philippe threw a fit and refused to go another step. That's why he never did meet Amar. I planted him in front of the entrance stairs and went down to the basement. It was a cavern held up by mirror-covered columns accented with constellations of greasy fingerprints. Women were powdering their excess baggage, making it look like twice as much as was really there

The real hot spot, the real hard-core heart of the party beat was down in those toilets. The most tripped-out ones played potty-lady to get tips from spaced-out Pierrots, or glittery bargain-basement Monte Cristos. I went past the tinkle toyers, touching the peepees of guys who were totally out of it, and threw up in the sink. I went back up and Philippe was gone. I must have come too early: The others probably wouldn't show up before two a.m. On stage, a transvestite in a Rodier miniskirt was flailing around a wireless mike, imitating a record you couldn't hear. A big blue bank of neon lights rose and fell from the black painted ceiling above our heads. I went back to the bar, which had become an indiscriminate meat market beginning to stink. The waiters, mumbling and stubbled, were spilling buckets of champagne down the plunging necklines of party-goners. I cut through a group of retired police commissioners, leftist journalists, and models losing their padding. They stepped on my toes to steal bottles of lukewarm champagne. Since when can't a lady get a little respect! The whole bash had peaked a long way back if the only thing you could do to stay alive was to step on everybody else.

I was so freaked out by the whole thing I was ready to cry. Philippe had warned me that this kind of atmosphere was bad for me. Some queens offered me a line of cocaine and I'd drunk two whiskeys on top of my medicine, but I was definitely one of the more lucid there. People were cutting and recutting a mixture of drugs and booze 'til the end of the night seemed like a limp jelly of vacant stares. I sat down on the hallway floor in front of the checkroom, where there was a bit more air. Through the glass door the room was a psychedelic mess.

I heard a tap-tap on the carpet, like change falling. An old lady came in, so old you would have sworn she was an unwrapped mummy. This old witch had a hooked nose, menacing gray eyes that drilled holes right through me as they went past, and a cane that tapped the floor in front of her. The doormen moved aside respectfully before this nightmare. She was wearing an immense pair of butterfly glasses that stuck out on each side of her head like insect antennae. Under her fur coat, a white silk dress was plastered to her skinny legs, a summer dress for a young girl, not an evening gown for a grandmother in winter.

She was walking cautiously in front of a young man. It took me several seconds to recognize Amar. In my memory, he was a boy. Now he was taller, thinner, his skin lighter. He looked trimmer, his hair was cut shorter. Practically nothing Arab left. He wasn't wearing dark glasses and didn't have a white cane, either. He walked erectly, too erectly, like someone trying to show he's not afraid of falling.

They talked to each other in English. Amar wore a flannel suit that fit him like a charm, and held a pedigreed cat on a leash. Fascinated, I watched him walk, and I understood why the old lady was tapping the floor. Even while he was talking, Amar followed the sound of her cane. His arm too tried to follow the woman's. She held open the swinging glass door and his knee brushed up against her at every second. With his other hand, he held the leash, at the end of which this cat was pulling with all its might to get away. A fantastic cat, it must have come from Africa, sable-colored, bobbed tail, its eyes extended by black lines; eyes that glared at me. A white spot, shaped like a bird with outspread wings stood out on its forehead. The cat dragged behind, sniffing with a smirk of disgust whatever awful smells were in that mobile wall, a human wall in front of it. Amar gave a couple of tugs at the leash. Yes, his walk had changed. I still saw him running, nervous as a goat over the rocks. Now he moved with slow, fluid steps. He walked like his cat, and always seemed to listen for something— for the cane which was his guide. He was handsomer than on Kerkenna, the developed negative of what I'd only known as an outline. I made out Malika and the sisters at the club entrance, taking off their coats. Even though it was like an oven, the old lady hadn't seen fit to drop her mink. When Amar slowed down and was level with my face—backing a bit toward the door to wait for his sisters, I fixed him in my sight with the energy of despair. Seen from below he was really tall. I almost got down on my knees. Surely my staring would trigger something: a catastrophe, maybe. He went past before I had a chance to let out my breath, went past indifferently, concentrating on his steps, without me even being able to look into those vacant eyes.

I had a sudden rush of anger against this old lady who must dress him, breathe him in, every day—that ghoul with her fangs sunk into a victim who couldn't defend himself. He wasn't the young thief of Baghdad anymore. He could have been the son of an oil sheik who'd studied at Oxford. So I had seen him again, and nothing had happened because I didn't have the guts to speak to him. Someone else had taken him away, which I had never imagined possible. Someone who'd become completely indispensable to him, in his mind, someone who might have been me. Three years of waiting to see that slim back strapped into a jacket that looked like it was molded to him walking away. I got up, because Malika caught sight of me. Malika, who snubs everybody, tonight came to say hi and to introduce me to a group forming at the ballroom entrance. I had plenty of trouble getting her to forget me.

The two sisters and Malika were standing around this incredibly shocking couple that the American lady and the young Arab made: an Amazon guard around him. Djamillah was standing rigidly, total scorn painted on her aggressive pout. You couldn't be sure whether to read it as fear or pride. She brushed away the curious, with decisive swipes of her hand, like the prow of a boat, whispering two or three words to clue them in that Amar was blind and that they should move along. Alissa was wearing a silvery cosmonaut's tunic, and talked with Amar in Arabic, but he didn't answer her. He was smiling with that cockeyed smile he still had. Malika was the oldest of the three, and the worst dressed. But you could see on her stubborn little face that she naturally thought her gathered red dress was a joke. She wore it like a bag. She seemed to think of herself as a third sister, in charge of the others. At least she wasn't snubbing me.

In this huge crowd which was lily white, lukewarm, and

somewhere between zits and face lifts, the group of four Arabs—not counting the cat and the old woman who gave orders with the tip of her cane—navigated along, steady as she goes. A spaced-out guy in black leather swam behind, way behind their barge: Djamillah's sugar baby, the rock singer from Lyon.

Their little group was so bizarre that a curious throng followed at a distance. I joined in without even realizing it. From the moment they'd come in, the club had turned into a theatre again. Amar cut through the crowd as he moved forward, stirring up a whirlpool, a wave bringing back a touch of decency. I could see the effect that a few words from Djamillah had on people's faces: lushes were transformed into fine, upstanding young men and women from good backgrounds. In the far corners of the room the tapestry of timid queens and johns began to smile. And since the d.j. got the idea to aim the black light projector at Amar, he stood out sharply as he went along, unaware of the effect he made. The drunks were standing up, rubbing their eyes while their companions—once they'd finally swallowed their hysteria—whispered in their ears.

Because he was blind, Amar had saved all these people from the uselessness of being there. They had a big event they could spread around, the event of the evening.

Protected by his sisters, Amar was free to dream in the middle of all that uproar. I closed my eyes to imagine what he must be perceiving. A zone of whispering, then silence as he approached, whispering he must have heard hundreds of times announcing to all around that he was an invalid. But those closest were quiet, bothered because he was so good looking. When he went by, a silent zone was established, the negative of a sound projector, which broke up their fog of laughter and conversation, moving along with him in his circle of black light. Ice cubes stopped clinking, silent stupefaction ran before him like the dark spot a cloud makes upon the surface of a wave.

Behind me, some old man was annoyed, wondering aloud if the blind too were allowed into nightclubs. I envied Amar. He must go through the noisiest crowds surrounded by silence.

Uneasiness made a gap in the wild goings-on. Not only uneasiness at seeing an invalid with this old scarecrow for a guide. You can't look directly at complete darkness any more than you can at the sun. This beautiful young man walked around carrying his own cocoon of darkness. People who walked past him pretended not to look, as if to show, just in case his blindness was fake, that they knew perfectly well how to behave.

During the last three years, I'd felt as though I was guilty: the accident had happened because of me. That didn't seem to make sense anymore. It was as though Amar had always been blind. Amar was a priceless knicknack now, a deluxe gigolo to an old lady millionaire. The Parisians looked him over and he was totally out in the open—no dark glasses, but totally sheltered, too, since he didn't have any idea what a sight to behold he was.

That put a crimp in the partygoers' style. The people who could see were ugly, the one who couldn't was handsome. Really handsome, not just cute and well dressed. Handsome to the point of making a dent in the hard heads in that room, of being too heavy a note in that musical space—he who was seen without seeing. He smashed the screen of the ordinary play of sights and shadows they were used to. Anyone having fifty people looking at him would have gotten an inflated ego, just like that. But all he did was smile as he went past. He was the spectacle who doesn't need, isn't aware, of any spectator.

No booze, no pot, no pills were strong enough to make them forget this boy from another planet with no colors, no shapes; this boy who was so handsome he made the projector pale beside him.

For me staring means you're taking away, stealing the face you want, tearing a little bit of it away. That night I knew that every look Amar got was brutal, as violent, as bloody as if he were being carved up and skinned, so they could scatter him in a thousand pieces in fond remembrance of days past. His ochre skin, his curly hair, and those eyes, eyes I finally saw when he turned toward me, eyes with blue rims from the black light, eyes which looked phosphorescent. Eyes of a moving statue, without heat; useless and wonderful charms put in there as an ornament by a loving jeweler, bottomless eyes that could not see themselves.

They had barely made their way around the room in the midst of a geyser of silent admiration when the old lady made a bee-line for the door. They passed in front of me one more time, as if on an inspection tour and Malika made a little sign as she went by, like everything was all right.

So everybody is standing out on the sidewalk having loud an

lively discussions, with that insensitivity to the cold you get from sweating in a disco. I can't hear what they're saying, but I'm tortured by the thought they're talking about me.

Someone grabs my elbow from behind. I turn around, really pissed off. It's Antonio. They'd let him out for lack of evidence. He screams all kinds of insults in my ear for all those lowlife nightclubbers to hear. Across the way, against the shellfish stand in front of the darkened restaurant, their little group is talking, Amar giving his sisters nice long hugs. The old woman is tappng the edge of the sidewalk with her edgy cane. The cat is yawning.

Antonio, who hasn't seen anything, puts his motorcycle helmet back on and gives a swift kick to a trash can. I don't want to stay there by myself so when Antonio gets on his Honda I climb on behind him. Since a taxi has just loaded up the old woman and her invalid I yell out, "Follow them!"

The two sisters and Malika stay on the sidewalk. Malika turns around. A man in a uniform has joined them and is leaning on a yellow scooter that's been made into a kind of little truck, and has the post office emblem on it. When we go past Malika she doesn't notice Antonio, and I see that the driver is an Arab too. He's talking with her and the two sisters like they know each other.

My head is swimming and the wind is whistling, I don't have a helmet. Antonio scrapes his exhaust pipe on the turns in showers of sparks. We go up the boulevard in the bus-only lane, all the way up. We screech into the Rue Richelieu when Amar's taxi heads that way. At the Louvre, Antonio runs a red light to catch up with them on the Rue de Rivoli. Just before the Place de la Concorde, the taxi takes a right while Antonio, who has gotten completely carried away, brakes for all he's worth in front of the Ministry of the Navy. We skid toward the fountains and pour into the subway entrance. When I got up, I saw the taxi easing away from under the lit-up hotel marquee of the Rue Cambon across the street. Antonio was dragging his foot and groaning as he checked out his bike.

He got it back up on its stand, pushed the kick-start, and the thing sputtered a while and restarted. He motioned me to get back on but I yelled I would go the rest of the way on foot. Because of the helmet he couldn't hear anything. He rolled away, turning to look back at me and disappeared around the corner just as day rose behind me on the Rue de Rivoli.

I stayed sitting on those steps near the Tuileries gates to the sound of birds waking up and an occasional moped on its way home. After an hour or so, a little old man with a hat came from inside the park and opened the gates, standing well behind them as he pulled them back, like he was keeping out of the path of the thundering hordes charging in. But I was the only customer. I sat on a bench upon the terrace so I had a perfect view of the hotel door.

The sun came up. Office workers hurrying to their jobs glanced at me as they passed. Some kids came and some tourists who ate sandwiches on a bench not far from me.

I was numb. I hadn't gotten any sleep. When I saw the hotel door open up to let Amar and the old lady through, I got up from the cold stone. They walked toward the taxi stand below the terrace where I was stationed. A porter was following them, carrying bags that looked like safes constructed of plastic. Both wore overcoats, and the cat poked its head out of a flight bag that Amar carried—holes punched in it so the cat could breathe.

The guy from the hotel put the bags down and asked the first cabbie something. He had the old lady and Amar get into the second taxi, put the luggage in the trunk, and off it went. I ran down the steps and asked the first taxi driver if he was free. Yes, he said, if I was going in his direction. He didn't want to go clear out to Orly. I told him I wasn't going to the airport, just to Montparnasse. I asked how come he was talking about Orly: he had just turned down a run there. I couldn't ask him to go to Orly, so I changed taxis at the Gare Montparnasse. When I got to the aiport I looked over all the baggage check-in counters. I was beginning to think I had lost them. My eyes couldn't focus anymore and my hands were shaking because I hadn't had any sleep. I went into a waiting room but a steward politely threw me out, telling me it was reserved for TWA's first class passengers. Just as I was leaving, I saw the cat on the floor and their two silhouetted backs at the bar. The steward went away. All these people were waiting for a flight to New York announced on the departure board. The old lady took her cane and hobbled off toward the john. I hollered to the steward that I was just going to say good-bye to a friend and walked across the room as he shrugged his shoulders. I walked straight toward Amar. The carpeting and loudspeaker swallowed up my footsteps. I sat down beside him, like I was speaking to him, because the steward had an eye on me. Not a word came out of my mouth. Upon the bar, in a plastic folder, I could see two airline tickets next to Amar's glass. I picked up the folder while a hostess announced the flight to New York, and I looked at the first ticket, filled in with an American woman's name; destination San Francisco, in the United States. I left by the other door while the steward walked up to Amar, probably to ask if he knew me. In the terminal I got dizzy: I hadn't eaten anything since the night before. Next thing I knew I was hanging on to a phone, calling Philippe to come save me.

I wasn't even at Sainte-Anne for twenty-four hours before I tried to commit suicide. It was my birthday, and I swallowed maybe half the pharmacy. When I woke up, Philippe was at the foot of my bed crying, asking wasn't I happy with him at Sainte-Anne. I tried to make him feel better. It wasn't worth it to have studied all those years and to wind up like that. While he was blowing his nose he asked what would make me happy, so without a moment's hesitation I said I wanted to go to America. Philippe choked and sighed. Wouldn't I really rather spend a week in Ibiza? Several days later he came in with an enormous bouquet of dried flowers. Peeking out of the bouquet was a plane ticket to New York. He got an enormous hug for that, and he confessed, blushing, that if I didn't have any objection, we could go together to New York, because he wanted to take the opportunity to go to some congress on psychological illnesses in the Northwest, in Vancouver. Vancouver. Was that far from San Francisco? On the scale of things in America, not very. I told him how much I'd really like to visit San Francisco. Philippe sent his pedicatrician-woman to a friend with a clinic in the Cher. We took a Pakistani charter together from Roissy and the steward-esses all wore saris. Even the toilets smelled like curry. In New York all I saw was the terminal for connecting passengers. All the signs were in English in funny black letters on a yellow background. The cops had the same hats and clubs as they did on T.V. We didn't leave the airport. I found a flight to San Francisco right away and told Philippe why didn't he just go with me to San Francisco first; from there he could go on to his congress. He told me he'd never leave me alone in *that* town, it was out of the question. I'd never set foot in America before. So when we arrived in San Francisco, he wired his congress to tell them he'd be there a bit later than he had planned, wondering uneasily if they'd agree to reimburse our tickets anyway, as he'd gotten them free by agreeing to talk about my case.

Going across the hills of San Francisco I had the impression I had eaten magic mushrooms. Philippe and I had shrunk. They could have put fifteen people our size in the taxi. The Americans talked like they were chewing gum; at least it sounded like that. The apartment buildings on the street had only three or four stories, as disappointing as the ones in Europe, and were painted every color, like gigantic toys. We finally got there, thanks to having said "downtown," a place surrounded by bizarre sky-scrapers, so well done that at first glance I didn't think they were bigger than apartment buildings at home; once I started to count windows I understood the scale. Back behind, was a huge arched iron bridge, like the métro bridge back in Paris, but a hundred times bigger, stuck out into the bay, lost in fog. I wanted a hotel around there. The taxi let us off in a little street at the foot of some buildings where everything was Chinese, even the signs in the stores. It was an inexpensive little hotel for Asians, but cost as much per day as Sainte-Anne. Once we got into the room, I broke down again. I refused to go out, and for the first few days Philippe brought me hamburgers in plastic boxes shaped like rockets, sauce in packets, soya in cardboard boxes and watery coffee in sealed cups: I felt like I'd never gotten off the plane.

I thought about things, while watching a crazy color tele-vision. There were a million channels on it. I never knew if I was watching the same one twice. I'd never thought San Francisco was so big. I thought it was just a hippie village with a beach, and all I would have to do to find Amar was to make a systematic search of all the hotels. I looked up "Hotel" in the phone book. I didn't know which ones were chic; the list went on for three pages.

After watching T.V. commercials for a long time, I went out to see if America was really like that: it was. I ate in Chinese restaurants, fending off young karate freaks who wanted to pinch my boobs and who called me "Frenchie." And I really didn't look very well. I was all washed out and had a fever that I must have caught in the humid basements of the Fourteenth Arrondisse-ment. Philippe tried to take me to the nude beach. I stayed dressed so I wouldn't have to show my white skin. It wasn't warm enough yet. Philippe always wore his houndstooth suit, which went with his pipe and moustache. There he was, sitting in the sand in the middle of a bunch of tanned nudists, with his pantlegs rolled up. He wanted to leave for Vancouver. I took to my bed to persuade him otherwise. I didn't want him to have an inkling that I was there for Amar, and only for Amar. As soon as Philippe went out, I'd be glued to the phone asking hotels if he was their guest.

I didn't eat food, I gobbled it down, and I shit out all that cardboard paste without digesting it, practically still in the package.

The next week the congress at Vancouver was over.

To get some exercise, I'd bought a city map, divided it up into squares and took off exploring them one after the other. Well, I would have, but I didn't get past the first square between this huge avenue called Market Street, Chinatown, and the sea. Then Philippe rented a Volkswagen; just our size. We stayed inside it as it rained, trapped between huge cars all with closed windows, breathing in their exhaust. It doesn't smell like ours at all, it's wilder: they must like their petrol *brut*, like their champagne. We would go down to the port, and I would rest by the sheltered concrete boathouse watching the jetty, looking at the big black dock numbers in white squares, counting boats and looking over the crews. Philippe drove about thirty kilometers out of town every day on the other side of the bridge, to a valley called Marin County, where there was a Zen center. He had met a Zen master who spoke German, like him, and who was finally on his level. Philippe took me there once. Under the big cedars at the end of a valley in a landscape already nearly Oriental I was politely bored. There were huts made of light-colored wood with white window shades and I expected to see prehistoric monsters and flying saucers come out of the giant trees above.

Philippe tried every medication on me, and I tossed down homeopathic pellets prepared by the Zen monks which nauseated me. I imagined the guru putting in a secret ingredient—his own sperm. Since I didn't settle down, he took me to some consultations with a bio-energetics group at a little villa—well, little for them—on top of a hill called Pacific Heights. From the veranda I could take in the whole panorama, the huge red bridge which they call—I wonder why—the Golden Gate. They get red and gold all mixed up, or else it needed a paint job. We'd gone over that bridge to get to the Zen place. I couldn't see anything from the car because the Americans put their railings up taller than I am. I became acquainted with the wooden tramways, with black conductors who pushed big clashing levers with their whole bodies, and the invisible cable that rubbed under your feet.

The villa was up on the hilltop, because they said that's where you get the best energy rays. The treatment didn't do a thing for me. I remained limp and feverish. I let Philippe lead me around and stared at passers-by.

He would have preferred almost any reaction to apathy. For instance, I could go fuck some Americans. He started talking about my "cure," a word he never used before, as if to let me know that someday I would have to live without him. To make me afraid, to make me react. Today, just like yesterday, he's holding my hand, as I finish up this story, in the plane going back home. He knows the manuscript is for him, and he's impatiently waiting.

The meeting with Amar was the peak of my attack. Because I did find them; and I lost him just as quickly again.

I had gone back to Marin County several times with Philippe who spent his days there in a red kimono he'd bought. After I'd had my little fix of nature and its pills I got a young Irish Zen monk to take me back to the city. When we arrived at the big bridge we passed a huge blue limousine parked near the tollbooth. The chauffeur was reading the newspaper. He seemed surprised: it was still several miles. I replied in my halting English that I needed to walk.

The sun was fresh and dazzling, and I could feel a fever in my cheeks. The scattered fog had burned off and the waves crashed against the pilings that held up the bridge. They bubbled silently, below, far below, in a whitish foam, delicate, harmless as sugar frosting. On the left was a gloomy island, Alcatraz prison, which the Irish guy had shown me. To the right, nothing: the Pacific, all the way to Japan.

In front of me, two figures walked, fighting the wind, silhouettes I knew instantly. I walked a little faster. I was only up to the first piling, a long way behind them. The cat was crawling between them, its head lifted up against the wind as I came up from behind . It turned to look at me with watery blue eyes.

I took shelter behind the cement column. Lifting my head, I

got dizzy looking up at the huge spiderweb swaying slowly in the wind. From where I was, I could see about half of the bridge in front, right to the peak made by the slope of the metal arch. I waited for them to move on. Then I followed. Every once in a while a silent car with green glass rolled by like a hurricane, and I'd jump to the edge of the pavement scared half to death. Down below, a boat siren wailed like a lost cow in the fog, floating in sheets on the bay.

The straight lines of the bridge gleamed in the sun, rising toward the center, and I could see the two silhouettes arrive at the summit almost in slow motion, then disappear half-way, their legs seemingly cut off by the other side.

I ran to catch up. When I got to their level she gave me a hard look, like maybe she had placed me. Hardly likely, since she had only gotten a glance at me that one night in Paris. I didn't have time to think about it. The cat started to meow, the wind was blowing so hard I didn't hear anything. All of a sudden I thought there was a train on the bridge. It was vibrating, vibrating like it was going to fall apart. I passed by them.

I saw the old woman's hand let go of Amar's arm, and she stepped toward me like she was going to ask something. At that very moment the whirlwind came and a huge shadow covered me. A wall had gone up on my right in a second. I saw the cat running between the wheels of the truck and trailer, which made a sucking sound.

I heard cracking bones and clothing being shredded on my right. A bundle went flying over my head, it bounced on the guy wires that held up the bridge like a gigantic tennis racket; it passed over the railing and fell into the silence below.

The tail end of the truck arrived, the sun came back, and I found myself on the edge of the sidewalk contemplating an enormous chicken winking one eye and holding a drumstick over a barbecue, painted on the back of the truck that said "Kentucky Fried Chicken."

In the middle of the road, there was a ragged pile of stuff with brownish blotches I didn't want to look at. Amar had stayed in the same spot, his hand stretching out slightly for the missing cat.

I went back to help Amar. I could see a big blue car coming slowly by the first pylon, then putting on the gas. I shivered and went straight to the second pylon to get away from the mess, but saw the limousine stop, even with Amar, near what was left. Another car was coming from the other direction. A carload of cops slowing down. They were on their rounds, I suppose. They stopped near the purse and cane which had rolled into the gutter. One of them picked up a blonde wig skittering in the wind.

No one paid attention to me. I pulled myself together, listening to reason. I didn't know why I had run. I had to go back, to talk to Amar, to reassure him, to replace the old lady, to plead with him to forgive me my past.

I was ready to swear to the cops that I was his sister, his wife, his nurse. The old lady's death was my big break. I wanted to go back to that cop car, fast. But something caught hold of my dress. something trying to bite me, claw me desperately: the cat, which must have been a female to be that nasty. She wasn't meowing, wasn't losing energy making noise. She wanted to hurt me, to separate me from Amar. Completely out of my mind, I grabbed her by the waist. She squirmed and fought like a worm with razor plating. I threw her overboard, I mean, over the railing, and she went to join her mistress. I leaned over. You couldn't make out anything on the surface a hundred meters below: tiny gray waves as far down as an apartment house is high.

Over where the accident had taken place, the cops had enough time to take some photos and load up Amar. The police car u-turned across the bridge. The limousine was gone. I had to run against the wind to catch up. The police car started moving slowly, and I waved my arms, yelling. The wind blew it all away. The car left. Amar was out of my reach. By the middle of the bridge I ran out of breath, so I leaned against the balcony—the panorama overlook. In one corner was a telescope for tourists. I dropped all my money before I found ten cents and aimed the telescope on the police car disappearing in the distance. It was going into the shadow of a mountain and I couldn't even read the license plate number. I dropped my arms, and the telescope spun away, focusing on the base of the next stanchion. I could see the concrete foundations, furious silent ribbons of water smashed to smithereens. In the center of the circle of the lens, a small limber brown shape hopped from girder to girder along the red painted metal that formed the battery housing, climbing toward the light.

A Transparent World

I climbed on board the Greyhound and heard the silence form around me. As I tapped the seatbacks of the center aisle, walking over luggage piled on the floor that would have made a clairvoyant stumble, well-meaning hands pushed me toward the rear. I ended up in the back, next to the toilet.

The passengers settled in for the trip as seriously as if they were leaving on an airplane. I could hear advice being given, blankets being unfolded, the noise of sloshing thermoses.

At the institute I had gotten used to doing without a guide. The paths were all well swept; I knew them by heart. The entire time I was traveling I had to keep getting rid of charitable hands, those arms that take you by force to show you to your seat, that make you step down. Between Santa Barbara and Mexico, I had to endure an ex-pastor, an unmarried social worker, and two members of the Salvation Army. They forced their self-assured odor, their banal twittering, their useless help on me. I don't see why I had to be limited to dealing with charity professionals.

I wasn't too disoriented in the bus. But outside? With Mrs. Hallowe'en gone, I felt I needed some presence that would allow me to get my bearings instinctively, given the mysterious signals the sighted exchange, for their eyes only. When I'm traveling, a small percentage of the other passengers manage to act naturally with me, the way little old ladies act with young men my age. Perhaps they don't seem to feel as much pressure from fear of blindness. They accept not being able to see as too close or too far removed a thing to worry about. I uncovered an entire population of rejected lovers, bashful educators and social servants running around the roads of the United States looking for young folks in trouble. I had one hell of a time getting rid of them. From our first exchange, the retired pastor was amazed I travelled alone. To escape his sympathy I stepped out every time the bus stopped and walked around by the edge of the freeway, warmed by the sun.

I had forgotten that music murmured non-stop in America. Background disco from the bus driver's radio, singing announcements from supermarket loudspeakers, travelers carrying around portable radios. So many refrains, such a mixture to accompany my fugue, my flight.

I started up a conversation with a guy named Allan to get rid of the pastor. The bus was stopped at a gas station in the early afternoon not far from San Diego. I had studied the region on a relief map at the institute, where the freeway was a deep furrow between points marked as towns. Allan was just arriving from the East Coast. He'd been a student, but for the past two years all he wanted was to devote his time to his only love: surfing.

He went from beach to beach with a backpack which contained a tent, and with his two surfboards, fastened against each other—two being better than one—which he had lashed onto the top of the bus. Each year he managed to go across the continent, following the perfect wave, which only formed under certain conjunctions of tide and latitude. His speech was terse, rough. We drank cokes while the bus was fueling up.

Allan was getting off at the border, at Tijuana. In the beginning I wanted to go down into Mexico, but gave up that idea when I felt all the people shoving at the Mexican bus station. Allan said why didn't I come sleep in his tent on the beach. He had smoked one of those marijuana cigarettes he'd been stinking up the air with around me, but I followed him.

He was three years older than I. Indifferent to the sexual criteria of the sighted, and because people had gotten me used to the idea of exchanging my body for a service as perfectly normal, and also because making love was my best means of touching someone so I could "see" them, I did with Allan what I had done with Enrico.

We never said anything about it later, and if someone had pointed out to him that he was sleeping with another guy, Allan would have sworn in good faith that it was not true. His skin was cracked by the sun, and there was a scar on his leg—a surfboard had gotten him. The air mattress smelled like rubber; Allan's hair was stiff from sea salt.

He didn't have the slightest complex about my not being able to see. In his mind was room for only a certain wave swelling, pushing a body hanging onto a piece of wood.

Some imbeciles are always astonished when they learn I like sports. These charitable souls figure that the sightless are disembodied, mysterious harpies without skin, without muscle. At the institute, at least, sports were encouraged. Ever since I'd done kinesitherapy, body movements had become a pleasure I anticipated and calculated. Allan was completely alien to feeling pity for me. He saw me only as a physique, a body in motion.

We lived on this beach in bathing trunks for months in the sun, right 'til the end of Indian Summer. Allan watched me shave from memory and whistled in admiration.

After I'd explored the beach, while Allan played up on his board, I started swimming again, with no trouble. I had gotten rid of all that anguish I'd had in front of a horizon line that moved when I was a little kid. Once we were visited by the Coast Guard, who asked for our papers. Allan said he was a guide for the blind, and they didn't say another word. At the end of August, I asked Allan if he would teach me to surf.

He was all for it. His only qualm was that his insurance didn't cover me. I had to promise not to "turn against" him in case of an accident; that was his expression, which was pretty funny considering how well we got along together.

He was already having fun imagining himself piloting a blind guy out at sea. We began by practicing on the second board, held steady by a mattress of sand. I wasn't very comfortable on land and it went a lot better once I tried it in the water, first in a tranquil little cove.

I got to know the move you make to pull yourself out of the weight of the sea, how to stand up like a sail that you're hoisting. Allan would put his hands around my waist, showing me the twisting movements. Unlike a lot of residents at the institute I didn't have any problem with balance. From talking with Allan, I found out that I had a great sense of the vertical, basing it on things entirely different than he. I didn't take mental aim to construct an upper point and a lower point like he did. I was more directly conscious of my weight. I can walk a straight line without any cues if there are no obstacles in my way. I put together axes, angles, from within myself, without recourse to visual cues. I understand movement better than the fixed picture that a perfectly sighted person mentally makes. The motion of the surf, the combination of the swell, the wind and the oblique movement of the board: I didn't have to imagine them: I felt them directly like the tops of palm trees shaking and moaning in the wind were flowing waves rather than forms.

I like the beach. The sounds reach you simply and clearly, the least obstacle is easily heard. The canvas of the tent drank up the ocean's roar, muting it but not putting it out. The ocean's roar is the greatest show on Earth for me; the only thing that gives me an assurance of direction at every moment, the reassurance of an audible horizon.

That morning, the wind let up, so we swam out, pushing our boards until I got smacked by an enormous wave of water which knocked me over. The board, attached to my leg, came out on top of me and I could hear Allan's voice hollering an order. I knew I had several seconds to swim to the calm zone on the other side of the following wave that I could already hear swelling behind me. I had to get beyond it before it began to unfurl. I dived, sending my board before me with my hand, and felt the salt bite against my eyelids. I opened my eyes, and the cold was so green upon my cornea, it made me think for an instant that I could see. When I resurfaced, I heard the board splash in front of me.

The deafening detonation of the wave was running from left to right along the beach, as far as you could hear. Here the water was almost calm, a long gentle swell. Allan was guiding me with short calls, which he later had to replace with a little automatic siren. We swam back toward solid ground, and he began a detailed account, keeping an eye on the mountain of water growing behind us, lifting the back of my board. I could feel the force of the tide alive around my body, resisting the wave, half submerged in a thousand little currents.

Back at ground zero as the crest of the wave swelled beneath me as though ready for an immense sigh, I climbed upon the board in a single backbreaking leap. Allan's voice let loose an uninterrupted string of hurrahs. Behind me, on the right, a cold breeze had come up, while I stretched out my arms and weaved on my legs. The wind galloped toward me, but I was heading off at about the same speed, carried by the wave, that now started to fall apart at its apex in a spray that filled my mouth. Above, a crackling, then the cracking of breaking timber and rolling thunder. The wave was unfurling around me, above me, inside me. My hands, left and right, grazed the walls of the tunnel of water I was shooting through, nearly parallel to the beach, until it all finally collapsed beneath me, rolling me in sandy sludge near the shore.

When we got back to the beach dragging our boards behind us and laughing, we heard voices calling. As I got closer I could hear a whole group of people talking around our tent. Allan explained that I was blind.

When I came up dragging my board they all applauded. I wanted to go right back in, but Allan said we'd had enough for that day. We had taken a certain risk with that rough sea. So I had had my first applause. Surrounded by their deafening enthusiasm, I'd hidden my face in my towel, drying off. An old man who smelled like cold cigars put his hand on my shoulder saying he'd like to make my acquaintance. I told him it was already made. We climbed into his car, and he took Allan and I to eat in a Mexican restaurant, all fake leather and air-conditioned, where I ate two dozen grilled *gambas*. Our host drank bourbon after bourbon in a big glass without ice, tossing little bits of *paella* around him as he ate. He was really interested in me, asked if I was a minor, if I had any family or a tutor. At the beginning of the meal, Allan and I were skeptical. By dessert, instead of telling the version where Allan was my companion, I admitted that I was alone. The fellow seemed more or less satisfied. With his mouth full of rice he introduced his family: show people. His grandfather had been a student of P.T. Barnum. He was currently director of the park of nautical attractions at Marineland, near Los Angeles. He suggested that Allan come work for him, but Allan was planning to leave for the high tides of Australia, and he wouldn't miss that for all the money in the world. Olaf—this man—turned toward me and casually asked if I'd been surfing a long time. I told him he had been at my debut. He sighed and asked me to take down his address and to come see him again in four months when he was back in L.A. We returned to the beach, and I took down his coordinates on my minicassette. I had never taken down any addresses, except my sisters', in Paris.

Three months later, after three more months of surfing, I had to add on Allan's forwarding address in Sydney. It was all decided. He was leaving in just a few days. He had never been very wordy, and he became really quiet those last few days, leafing thoughtfully through surfing magazines. We surfed our way back up north, beach by beach.

For me, California was divided by music and the quality of the air. The radios on the bus, or in the cars that picked us up hitching, would have been enough to tell me where I was. Toward the north, the fresh air is scented with pines, the music of San Francisco is folk and rock; from Tijuana to San Diego, it's Spanish music, and in L.A. disco and synthesizers, and the dust of the South, like at home on Kerkenna.

We passed the last days of good weather on a beach at the far south edge of L.A. A line of shacks bordered the beach: cafés, dance joints with rippling roofs where the Chicano workers jumped around all night long and drank beer while they told me all about their country.

One was named Chino: the others told me he had slanted eyes, like a Chinaman. He came from the Sacramento Valley. He was old and walked around in sandals made out of a piece of tire tread that he made me touch. Before working in the Valley, Chino was from Chihuahua, a state in Mexico just on the other side of the border.

Chino harvested fruit on enormous farms and, when the season was over, took off for the border to do business, some sort of contraband smuggling. Chino brought me a beer the first night Allan and I were at the beach. I was really glad somebody had gotten the idea to offer me a drink. I don't really take to alcohol that much. However, I find humiliating that sighted habit of considering me a minor, off-limits to strong drink. Whenever I asked for a drink myself, I didn't dare ask for alcohol. I limited myself to Coke. Unlike the others, Chino didn't think that the fact that I wasn't able to see the bubbles should keep me from liking beer.

I'd kept up my surfing lessons with Allan, and I'd become capable of handling the same waves. We had contests to see who could stay up the longest, yelling out a warning just at the moment we fell in an explosion of foam.

I went along with the moods of the sea that carried me off into whitecaps foaming all around me. The stillness that precedes effort, the moment when you're ready to take off, had nothing in common with the paralysis of not moving on the ground. The gentle swaying of the waves recalled my suspended body to a feeling of self with absolute ease.

The waiting and holding time was often long. Allan chose his waves very carefully, following the good will that he read in each rise of the water, or on the back of the swell. Floating there listlessly, I was thinking how soon there would be no one to cry "Go!" to me any more. With only my senses, I would never know the exact moment when to clamp onto a wave by raising my body upright. Allan's departure also meant the end of a game with the wind, the sea, the stars. Sometimes we surfed at night, and then I was better than he was on the almost peaceful waves that followed a stormy day.

Chino had taken to keeping me company in the evening, whenever Allan hitched into town to try to find a girl. Chino wasn't his real name. He was from an Indian tribe that lived on the other side of the border. It was hard for me to understand his Spanish in that broken voice of his. He would draw figures in the sand with a stick. The scratching metal tip drove me up the wall, so I asked him to stop. He scratched his head, then started drawing again, and wanted me to put my hand on the designs. I could hardly feel a thing. They were hollowed out, and the sand caved in under my fingers, destroying their shape. He got down on his knees and took a long time making up a new design. I was getting exasperated. I thought it was all dumb. He got back up and asked me to touch it again. This time the lines were clear. He had made them in relief, with sand moistened with water. I looked at him, but he took my hand and made me continue tracing the line. At the end it came back on itself, then went off toward the front in a long curve, after an incomprehensible scribble at the far end. Toward the front I found a long toothed line, like a spur.

Pesca spada, he told me, in Spanish: sword fish. He continued to draw, and my fingers wandered in these valleys, hills, irregular little dunes, and there were ephemeral shapes, faces, trees, sinking ships. Chino was in seventh heaven. He began telling me what it used to be like where he lived, sputtering and spitting on the ground as he talked. He slapped his thighs, they resounded like dry wood. Everything about him was dried up by age and sun, even his smell, like burnt grass, like dust and wind. He was putting away an endless bucket brigade of beer that made a little psst whenever he pulled open a tab. Since the time I had left the institute, I had drunk very little. I'm careful with alcohol because it makes me lose my equilibrium and sense of distance.

I was asking him all about Mexico, where I had decided to continue my trip, imagining it as a Spanish speaking Tunisia. Chino knew only about his mountain, where Indians in white loincloths ran across mountain streams pushing bales of rags with their feet. To hear him tell it, they played and hunted all the time. The pile of rocks the Mexicans left them isn't good for anything. Mexicans who weren't "Indios" were enormous simple-tons riding horses only as big as they were, and they wore cartridge belts slung across their shoulders.

I wanted to go down there so badly I could taste it. You could die of thirst in the desert valleys, with their meager corn stalks withering under the sun, and gigantic boulders at summits where runners signaled each other with sweeping movements of their arms. From time to time, a traveler might run into a cactus pen holding goats, some women, or a half fallen-in church of dried out rocks. The Jesuits had grouped the entire population of the mountain areas around their missions, and Chino's two grand-children had been taken away and placed in their school. Like many another man, he had come down years before the last war, across the New Mexico desert to Santa Fe, and had packed into slums where junked cars served as chicken coops. He wandered from Tijuana to Los Angeles when he wasn't working in the Sacramento Valley, going from L.A.'s crummy ghettos to the border, looking it over with nostalgia, knowing he couldn't cross again. If the immigration people couldn't round up all the illegals any more, they could still keep them from crossing back again.

Footsteps in the sand. Allan arrived and we invited Chino to eat with us. Canned chili and hot dogs in a plastic package that we grilled over a kerosene lantern. Chino left to wash up and to put on his hat, like for a dinner invitation in town. He was perfectly satisfied being with us. He was telling how the Whites in the Sacramento Valley were such racists they wouldn't even shake a

Chicano's hand. I understood that Allan looked young, white, rich and well-fed from the almost respectful way Chino talked to him. He was more at ease with me. I was surprised to find that he took me for white, too, a European; our equality came from my being blind.

The next day Allan went to buy his boat ticket to Australia. Chino arrived in the early afternoon, and after having said hello and nothing else sat down.

He placed a little plastic bag on the sand next to me then drew back. I touched it and felt hard little knobs. I opened the bag and a mess of buttons like dry wood of all sizes fell out. Chino offered me one, and started to chew one himself. I bit into it, and it reminded me of licorice, except without sugar and really bitter, or like the peelings my mother used to make me chew to have white teeth.

Chino claimed that in his tribe, blind people were surrounded by superstitious respect; people thought that they could tell the future. We were sitting in front of the tent; the sun was warm and gentle. He started an endless chant in a mixture of Indian and Spanish words, continuing to chew the buttons and offering me more. After the first taste, the bitterness didn't seem so bad. Saliva seemed sweet compared to that initial bitterness that had made my tastebuds stand on end.

I turned toward Chino to tell him that he was yelling, his delivery was too fast, and they could probably hear him clear over by the shacks.

I turned my head to look at him so he would be quiet. At that moment I felt the first warning that something was happening. I had barely moved, but I felt as though I had made a complicated odyssey. Now I didn't know if Chino was in front of me or behind me, but I heard his voice all around me, like a blanket. He shut up, came over to me and put a hand on my knee. Was it the right knee? The left? The whole world turned like a spinning drum. Chino was talking. I couldn't understand anything he said anymore. I was able to get out a hoarse whisper that said he was talking too loud. He laughed and answered me in a whisper so loud it must have echoed up and down the beach.

He wasn't yelling: my ears had become extra-sensitive. The noise from the cigarette machine, far away, in front of the shacks, came to me with alarming clarity. My head was leaning forward to follow the coins as they dropped down, and I had a little convulsion when the machine spit out its noisy package. The suction of tires on the highway tar, the puffing of a boat, the laughing of swimmers, pierced my ears. Chino started to tell the story of a god of his tribe, called Peyote, or Coyote, the name of a cartoon character. He was a very small god, and he grew in completely desert lands on the high Mexican plateau.

He wanted to know if I was Catholic. My own tribe, I answered, admired a god who came from the desert, but fell into a black stone. The idea of a god who was a rock was really funny to him. According to what he said, his god must have looked like a miniature apartment-cactus. Both of us burst out laughing. It was indeed a cactus, the smallest member of its family. In the Spring they all went together in a procession singing and dancing to pick the cactus and to close up each one found in a cornstraw cage, which was then put on a little altar over the fireplace in their huts. The little god got drier and drier there in the shadows, saluted each evening by the family, shrivelling tranquilly on its pedestal, in the cage that kept it from taking off. At the beginning of Autumn they opened the cage. the drums were beat and the ground shook beneath bare feet—Chino imitated the dance, spraying me with sand. Usually the women crushed, kneaded, made the god into a powder, and mixed it with grilled corn in water and sugar. Everyone drank some of the mixture one moonlit night, a full moon like tonight, and then all winter long.

A whole day had passed since he had begun talking to me. It must have been dark by now, or that silvery night I was no longer meant to know. I felt the full tide climbing up the beach as clearly as if I were swimming in it, carried off by it. I said the word "drugs" out loud, and a vise of cold sweat gripped my temples. I was losing my footing, trying to make up my mind, in an ocean that surrounded me on all sides.

I stretched out on the ground, trying to run like mad to my inner self in search of my consciousness, to catch the center of those volatile impressions that ran away before me in a whirlwind.

This impression of being every place at once made me afraid: every place where a sound, even the very slightest—a cracking branch, an insect on the sand—every place where a miniscule movement was eating away at the order of things. I didn't see the backside of the world as Chino thought, but I heard its least detail monstrously enlarged.

I tried desperately to tell Chino what was going on. I found myself talking in Italian. I picked back up in Spanish. Chino was stroking my forehead, asking me how I was seeing objects. I answered him impatiently, still the same question, that obviously I didn't "see" them in his sense of the word, but I located, felt, observed them.

The interior of my self continued to slowly seep outside me to the mixed rhythm of my heart and the waves. I was desperate. The drug was blotting me out, completely differently from what it would do to perfectly sighted people like Chino. I was being gobbled up in the material world. Taking your bearings by sound—I tried to tell him—is using a more delicate compass than your eyes. I didn't have any visual reference point to focus on. I finally asked him to take me to a doctor.

Chino protested when I said the word drug. He got quiet when he saw that I was crying. Tears flowed over me, surprising and refreshing. I smiled through the liquid moistening my face. When I cried for the second and last time, I completely unwound. Something had melted: the fear of being abandoned or of disappearing. In the same moment, odors came back, very intense: a cigarette Chino had lit, popcorn on the beach, an odor of rubber to go along with the squishing tires in the distance. Chino asked me yet again how I was "seeing." All of a sudden, I saw, and I said, "I'm not in the dark. It's just that the world is transparent."

It seemed to me I had discovered an essential truth. I felt the line of the waves, the soft curve of the beach, a flash from a windshield on the parking lot to my left. I didn't see them as I had before my accident. The drug must have short-circuited something in me. Was that what people called "seeing?" I hesitated, trying to compare. There weren't any shadows. I was seeing transparent things; no color, no shadow, but I was seeing.

I rummaged desperately through my memory. These objects existed, I could describe them, except I didn't have to turn my head to be able to see them, and they were transparent. I didn't see: I believed I could see. Nothing had changed. The work of fiction my mind had dreamed up under the effects of the drug had deceived me.

I felt bitterness in the back of my throat, the bitterness of atrocious deception. I bent over to throw up, and I felt so weak I just accepted going on ahead. Chino had lit a fire and was fixing tea. Some kids were playing frisbee over on the beach. I was the plastic disk whistling through the air, the cry that makes the chest rise, the bare heels digging into the sand. I was trying to remember what it was that had upset me about the idea of being drugged. I wasn't really afraid of an accident—all I had to do was keep sitting on this beach—afraid only of losing control of my face, forgetting who I was. For me, being conscious of my own face is artificial. I can forget to make up, from inside, a face for the use of people who can see. For hours now I hadn't been controlling my face, so now I didn't know where the "I" stopped. A peaceful split was taking place. Two voices inside me were discussing whether this leg was me or not.

Was the experience I was having now more valuable than the other? Or wasn't it just the same thing, laid bare. No doubt I had always seen a transparent world, one I could melt into like sugar. My so called visual memories of Kerkenna were nothing more than retrospective illusions. I had never seen; nothing visible had ever existed.

I had adopted an attitude of mistrust for the world of the sighted for so many years that I had distanced myself from it. But I'd always admitted it existed, this real world, somewhere, in some way, a layer of reality I could not observe. Today I was putting that agreement, that contract I alone had signed, into doubt.

Chino began to sing. His chant accompanied the movements of his hands, and he was scratching the back of some animal kneeling between us. The voices from outside swelled up, invading me. My skin was extended to the surface of all things, and I was thinking that the seeing world was nothing but propaganda. From that alone—the fact of admitting a sighted world—rendered me non-sighted. I started laughing and couldn't quit.

Chino expressed his satisfaction by patting me on the back. He had been uneasy for a minute but now everything was all right. I was rolling on the sand, observing the miniscule respirations of larvae spitting out bubbles. Allan's departure was going to leave me alone, and Chino knew it.

He talked about dogs, asking me why I didn't have a dog as a guide and companion, like he had seen so many blind people with. I didn't like them: dogs reminded me too much of the blind beggars of my childhood. Those poodles, Labradors, German shepherds with rough coats that they wanted to force on us at the institute, who really were police dogs. They'd walk at your heels, telling you how fast you could go, stopping at attention at every street corner. I got up to imitate a guide dog, and Chino started laughing. Dogs were so stupid: they were only good for going over the same route over and over: they wanted nothing to do with exploring.

As I was imitating the dog, I heard a meow of protest. I sat back down. An animal started purring under my fingers, stretching out and yawning in the lightness of the humid evening's entertainment. Chino had conjured up or else had created a cat. I couldn't say how long it had been near. It had appeared little by little, like a fog settling in between us.

I had only petted one single cat in my life, a female. I automatically searched for the bobbed tail Zita used to have. And I recognized it while she rubbed up against me, seeming to be ecstatic as an animal can be who has been waiting a long time for some sign of recognition. I asked Chino hoarsely if this cat by chance had a white spot on its forehead, surrounded by earth-colored fur. A spot like a flying insect with outspread wings.

Zita returned? It was part of Mrs. Hallowe'en brought back to life. By what miracle had she found me, six hundred miles from the Golden Gate? What used to be short and pampered fur was all matted down, her stubby tail stuck up skin and bones. I had Zita back!

The effects of the cactus continued, the ground vacillating under my feet when Zita took a leap up onto my shoulders. I stuck out my arms to get my bearings—with me a sign of complete disorientation. In general, I try to keep from doing that. Zita meowed above my ears, and I knelt down to allow her to jump off. But instead of clearing away she rubbed my leg, like the day we first met, in Rome. I couldn't walk. I was paralyzed, all my reference points were mixing together. Zita rubbed against me again, like she was showing me the way to follow. She took off walking, still rubbing against my leg as she went. I hobbled along after her, keeping in step. She used to use this strategy when Mrs.

Hallowe'en let me take her out for walks.

Zita had found me: I was ecstatic.

We rolled around together in the sand. She licked me in a real outpouring of affection. I had just received my last gift from Mrs. Hallowe'en. We walked side by side, Zita turning around me without moving away. I had found a new guide. The cat had come to replace her mistress.

We went together toward the shacks from where the sounds of a Spanish street fair still cut through the night. And Chino continued to get soused, all the while congratulating himself, as though he had organized this reunion. Zita and I weren't ever going to be apart again.

Chino introduced me to his friends in one shack. It was hot under the corrugated roof which retained its daily quota of sun's rays. The Chicanos, completely drunk, began to dance, beating out rhythms on cans of food. Brutally, there was a terrible cry outside, then a series of squeals, and then a distinct blow that stopped everything. It seemed to me like the tin roof must have fallen on our heads. Chino took my hand and soaked it in something warm and sticky. I sucked my fingers, and it was sort of salty, gummy: blood.

Allan came back in the middle of the pig sacrifice and took me by the hand to lead me away while I was pulling on Zita, who was excited by the animal's opened entrails.

I fell asleep in the tent against Zita, murmuring insults at Allan. At first, Zita laid her head between her paws, like a sphinx, and I could feel her whiskers against my cheek. I wondered if I was asleep, because this stuff Chino had given me to chew was awfully stimulating. I played around with closing my eyes, without being quite sure if I was really closing them or not. I didn't run my hand over my face, for fear of waking her up.

In the obscurity of the tent, asleep or not, I was following the purity of my sensation: I had wrongly admitted this white screen—which was the absence of vision—to be the dark.

Without transition, I heard the noise of the morning birds in the tamarisks surrounding the tent. Zita had changed position, her paws on her thighs, twitching, hunting a mouse in a dream. The movements of her body, her eyes which I felt beneath their closed lids, had awakened me. The noisy birds became noisier. The white screen became a sort of gray, and the transparent world opened up like an iris, becoming iridescent. I saw a pigeon, violet in the rising sun on the white sand, through the opening of the tent. I saw colors, and I let out a cry of surprise that woke me up.

I hadn't dreamed in color for a really long time, and I felt that Zita's presence had served as the catalyst. I fell back asleep listening to Allan's deep breathing. The dream began again. I could hear the screaming of the previous evening's pig. Instead of stopping, with the whack of an axe, it continued, louder and louder, and stopped little by little, slowing down in front of our tent. It wasn't the pig's soul anymore, come back from Hell. Deep American voices were talking with Allan now; he had gone outside, still wrapped in his sleeping bag.

This noise was a cop siren. They dragged us off to the station several miles away, without even giving us time to fold up our tent. The sheriff was really in a fix. He didn't know what to do with me. He didn't have a thing on us that would permit him to keep me while he waited for a judge to put me back in an institution. Allan said his father was a lawyer. The sheriff asked me what I lived on. He hoped to be able to charge me with begging in his county. But I was legally responsible for myself, I had a valid long-stay permit, and more than two hundred dollars on me. He tried to explain that I wouldn't go far, then thought better of it, had me sign some release of responsibility, and set us free after threatening to have Zita put to sleep or given to the furrier.

We hitched back, gathered up the tent, and set up in an old abandoned wooden house in Venice for the few remaining days before Allan had to leave. The cat had discovered it when we were running on the promenade, Zita and I; she led us there through a fallen wall at the edge of the beach. All she had to do was brush against me to warn me of an obstacle. We zig-zagged between skateboarders carrying huge portable radios on their shoulders—scratchy sounding like slide guitars all around us—as they criss-crossed each others' loops on the concrete walk.

Allan was moody; he wasn't eating his whole-grains anymore, and he was getting sloppy on his workouts, done on a flat strip of land next to the sea. He couldn't hand me over to any one, couldn't abandon me without money in this new town.

The day before he was supposed to leave, Allan took me to Marineland, a big nautical amusement park on the coast, south of L.A., where we found our old friend Olaf. When we arrived I had to ask Olaf for money to pay for the taxi that brought us. He handed the money to Allan and told me I would start training that afternoon. I could move all my stuff into one of the little houses for the staff located near an artificial lake full of ibis, marabouts and pink flamingos.

Olaf gave us a tour of his exhibition pools.

Allan went in the water with me one last time. We pushed our board clear to the end of what seemed to be an enormous pool which ended up in some sort of floodgate. A siren sounded, and I heard grinding, then a cataract of water being let out into the lock. The artificial wave was several meters high; the trick was to surf its complete length, then dive off in time to avoid the crush of water against the cement wall which closed off the other end of the pool.

Allan called out the distances for me. I wasn't sure I could memorize them. Olaf came up with the idea of putting in a line of floating buzzers that would tell me where I should get off the board.

That same evening, after I had moved into Marineland, Allan took me to West Hollywood. It was night, I guess. There was no way to tell except that there was a whole lot going on, and when she was dropping us off the lady who picked us up told me to be careful, because it wasn't the kind of place for me. I would have really liked to know what part of L.A. *was* the kind of place for me. We sat down at the corner of Highland Avenue and Santa Monica Boulevard, in front of a service station that perfumed the intersection with the odor of diesel fuel. Zita climbed on top of the automatic newspaper vendor I was leaning up against. Allan left me, saying he'd meet me at a coffee shop called the French Market, a little further down, fifteen minutes' walk straight ahead on Santa Monica. I had never felt so alone. He was leaving the next day. I pulled Zita against me. She struggled, meowing. I couldn't understand why Allan insisted on making me wait at this streetcorner. I was in the middle of a desert, "in the middle of nowhere," and I was in the middle of one of the biggest metropolitan centers in the world. The passers-by were mostly men, from what I could judge by footsteps and rare outbursts of talk. Nothing amazing: there are seldom women out on foot late at night on any city street.

A few cars went by, slowing down in front of my newspaper vendor. Later on, I heard people describe West Hollywood as a "ghetto." The word didn't seem appropriate to me: that Angeleno district doesn't have a thing in common with the Mellah on Kerkenna.

I moved around a little. Right away a car made a U-turn in the intersection and pulled up beside me. The car window slid down: surely they couldn't have seen me before. Zita always did have a tendency to drag me into dimly lit corners. I learned to take my cues from reverberations, to put myself into the light. The girl at the wheel started up a conversation:

"Hello, I went by a little while ago. I didn't see you." The voice was young, and I could smell the odor of leather coming through the window.

Later on I would walk toward the purring motor, to place myself in front of their headlights.

A half-torn poster was flapping against a telephone pole. I didn't know what to say to her. She took my dead-set look for granted. She reached over to open the right door, and I got in, holding Zita on my knees. Only then did she realize that there was something funny. I wasn't merely a boy for sale.

"I'm blind." I wasn't about to go around carrying a sign. She remained silent for several moments, and I'm pretty sure she never did believe me. She was the first client I picked up on the streets.

I came back to this corner of Highland Avenue a lot afterward. A little further on, I relaxed in the Hollywood cemetery. A series of parking lots surrounded the tombs, and on an island with a little bridge was Rudolph Valentino's. It seems I looked like him, at least as he looked in *Son of the Sheik*. That's what an old actor, my second client, told me. When Allan left for Australia, I knew why he'd brought me to West Hollywood.

The morning Allan left, I continued training with Olaf, who provided room and board. If I wanted to eat at the park, I went to the cafeteria where the waiters read off a list of food for the day, throwing in uncomplimentary tidbits about the cook. My life was quite organized. Every day, about mid-afternoon I went up to West Hollywood, and sometimes didn't come back until early next morning. No matter when I got in, I had to dive into cold water and once more start that crazy race against the spray. Olaf wasn't giving me a penny as I hadn't become a profitable attraction yet. He was a shrewd businessman and he felt that if I claimed to be independent, it was up to me to make do.

I slept with secretaries and bartenders, engineers and old actresses, even a student at the University of California who wanted to take me to meetings of the gigolos' union. They expected more from a blind man than sexual services: piercing a taboo was a transcendental emotion commanding a high price.

A life of prostitution is dangerous. Without Zita, I could never have considered the street my territory. We formed an efficient couple. She often chose clients for me, became hostile as a prevention against others. Egyptian cats are not creatures of the drawing room; Zita could become a wild beast if another boy had designs on my intersection.

The long hours of waiting on the avenues of Los Angeles served as reciprocal training for Zita and me, schooling in street life. The sidewalks, the indentations of garage entries, all seemed to have been invented to foul up the blind. Zita has absolutely no memory. She's perfect for avoiding an obstacle, but completely incapable of going the same way twice.

I had to memorize a number of tricks to make it easier. If I was going to load myself down with memorizing street maps, I had to perfect the instinctive obedience training that Mrs. Hallowe'en had practiced with the cat: she came to obey several dozen different commands or questions. Oh! Never immediately or automatically, but in good faith, freely. "Car," with the "R" rolled out a long time, means I wanted to know if a car was in sight. "Stop," "Go," "Back," and a lot of other words meant something to her.

I don't know when Zita discovered I was blind. Late, I think, at the end of her apprenticeship, which lasted nearly a year the whole time I lived in Los Angeles. L.A. was the first city where I felt free to walk around. The first city where the falseness of the stereotypes that had alienated my freedom first appeared to me. I like L.A., the big squares of blocks of houses form an easy system of coordinates, and the automobile is queen. Later, discovering other cities in America and Europe, I didn't want to live anywhere but in cities. The idea that I formed out of simple sensations amid the drunkenness of my brand-new freedom of the interminable blocks of L.A. was later, such a complete contrast to the tight narrow streets of Europe echoing with sounds, which I had experienced for only two days.

I prefer cities and I prefer the night. The country is nothing but a desert for me where I cannot obtain a single clue. The city is alive with points of reference: rumbling motors, the sounds of cinema patrons, newspaper hawkers, clanking bottles and rustling paper; and odors too—so many odors Zita and I delightedly inhaled—of food, fruit, beer, medicines in front of drugstores, the perfume of flowers in the Hollywood cemetery, the odor of tar, of plaster and paint girding the walls of the film studios. It served me as a synthetic sight, joining together all the directional cues I already counted on. I counted the trees, or rather the reverberations that came from them as I walked. I memorized a construction site with an open ditch that smelled of acetylene, which Zita made me go around. I noted the slopes of all the avenues, and knew the general outlay of the map Allan had scratched onto the back of a postcard for me with his knife, pointing out the names of the bigger towns, Beverly Hills, Santa Monica, Venice, West Hollywood. Even in a car I wasn't lost anymore.

Since I usually went out at night, hitching there wasn't always easy. Coming up Santa Monica Boulevard, I kept thinking how big the city really was, a whole series of sidewalks as big as freeways and streets as big as runways. Wooden bungalows nestled in among tropical trees followed on the heels of drive-in stores, and all the noises and odors that no apartment buildings blocked arrived intact, unwavering. For hitching, all I had to do was make use of my handicap. I bought another pair of dark glasses. I stationed myself at the edge of the road, holding my arms out, with Zita perched on my shoulder. Cars stopped immediately. Seeing me put my glasses back into a pocket some drivers figured I was an imposter. So I'd have to explain that I didn't need dark glasses to cut down sun glare.

Zita and I became a single being with six paws. She sniffed the clients, the meals, the cars before she would let me get in. That cat—as she goes over her first exploits upon my shoulder—is a part of me today. I rigged up a little harness for her out of a light flexible nylon thread that left her practically free. She only had to guide me a few hours a day. When she'd learned enough, the harness became useless, so I gave it to Olaf, who used it to train baby seals. Her voice, the rubbing of her tail, signals upon or against my body were enough to tell me all I needed to know. I was pleased to be able to do without a canine guide. Zita is one animal never refused entry anywhere. She would go into all the bars, climbing around the glasses; she followed me into every bed. She must have been fairly pretty, or must have seemed expensive to be accepted where a cane or guide dog would have been a source of discomfort.

Anyway, Zita didn't need an excuse to be anywhere. Every place was home to her. She was adept enough to impose her presence without allowing that veil of pity to fall over me.

The people I slept with during those first weeks were stupefied when I asked for money. I always did it before I got in the car, so I wouldn't lose my corner. They didn't dare discuss my price. Some tried to gyp me, but it's easy to ask to change a bill at a restaurant or in a bar. Anyway my clients ran around with hundred dollar bills in their pockets like it was spare change.

The first week alone I put aside three hundred dollars, and it went up to nine hundred in following weeks: I'd never had so much money. Mrs. Hallowe'en gave me everything, but only a minimum of pocket money. Her friends' gifts—lighters and checks that she put in the bank for me—had made me a little nest egg. But with these Angelenos, dollars were found only in large wads, so large that I was able to slow down. I was only spending a part of it, stuffing the rest in a corner I reached by standing on my toes.

I didn't have the faintest idea what to do with my little treasure. I spent a lot of money on taxis, ordered the most expensive items in the best restaurants without even touching them. I was exhausted by late at night, and this money stashed away up over my head kept growing. I thought the money might come in handy one day, and I got an incredible thrill earning it so easily, after everything they had told us at the institute about how hard it was for an invalid to make a living.

All in all, I'd once more become the beggar that we have always been, we blind. Yet I didn't feel I was selling myself: I didn't have a well-defined sense of ownership of my body. I think you have to be sighted to believe in that, to be able to count your fingers, to look at a face that's yours in a mirror, a face that you can't see directly. To me a mirror is only something you use to fabricate a face, all the time repeating to yourself, "All that is me." You'd have to know the laws of perspective to really be an "I." I don't have a constant point of view about my body. Sometimes I even forget about parts, scattered as they are by localized sensations.

I asked myself what Mrs. Hallowe'en would have felt if she'd seen me transformed into one of those streetwalkers we had seen at the Villa Borghese. As for the clients, they weren't Laotian princes in exile or governor's wives, just everyday people. I began to take the initiative, to go up to them.

A sighted person lives in the crowd. A multitude of bodies and faces is there for him at every instant. In L.A., a deserted town, I knew the crowd. I can't identify a person without having touched him, embraced him entirely, and I was embracing two, three, ten a day.

I'm not saying I've only slept with people I liked. But by sleeping with many I've come to know the ways they were not pleasing to me, how ugly they were. The ugly interested me more than clients who obviously thought that they were good-looking, who told me straight out it was sad I couldn't see them.

Being available, and the ease with which I make love, are not crutches for my infirmity. Sex is a pathway through my alleged blackness. When I talk about ugliness, perhaps you think I mean it in the sense that sighted people use the word. I have an idea of what ugliness is, but it has nothing in common with the canons of painters, sculptors or photographers. It's arbitrary, invented from all those bodies. No law, no criteria can define in-visible beauty.

I learned about that fast world of the hunt and chase from other hitchhikers in shorts who hadn't made it on the silver screen, from tired old queens who always promised roles because they were in charge of film make-up, from high school kids with their school names embroidered in relief on their sweaters who hung out in front of the French Market until some car took them away for two hours and fifty dollars.

I never took anyone back to Marineland. I didn't want to

betray Olaf's trust. Coming back to the little savannah and the artificial bayou was a real relief. I never slept more than five or six hours between my training and my night ventures. The morning sun combined with alcohol and fatigue to form an exuberant mix when it came time for me to dive into the big saltwater pool.

I started to spread out away from the intersection in West L.A. A lot of clients lived in the area south of Santa Monica Boulevard. They would take me home by car, and I counted the number of turns and then went back on foot to the same intersection to pick up another client. The friendlier ones drove me back to my corner and they thought it was normal to be in this sort of relay race, where one hand took over from another, as they guided me into yet another car.

An automobile society is perfect for me. I really like gridwork cities with numbered streets, which most Europeans detest. Above all, I like best the pleasure spots, the nightlife areas in cities. I could never get lost in West Hollywood, no more than I could in the "Village" in New York, or Pigalle in Paris. You never get lost in a nightlife quarter. The night spots, where people hang around for pleasure or for money, are the ones where I'm most easily accepted, a blind paradox. The music from the bars and the bodies all form a network that's so easy to follow. Nobody thinks twice about one more extravagance as my blindness appeared to be. In the pleasure centers, my completely intuitive sense of geography works best. People out strolling are never in a hurry, are delighted to give you directions without thinking you're lost just because you're wandering around at three o'clock in the morning. Official pity stops at the doors of these ghettos. I can't really say I went completely unnoticed. In the space of one month, several hundred people had earned the right to say hello to me. At the very least, this popularity spared me the problem of going around telling everyone I was blind, or of having to wear dark glasses: rumor preceded me.

I knew dozens of people by their first names, their skins and their telephone numbers. And I lived alone; otherwise, after making love, I would never have been able to stand all those voices—men's and women's. Most of the American men dreamed of sucking off someone blind. They seemed to think that act daring, a sacrilege. The bars were allowing me in with Zita, where at the beginning they always objected, calling up their sacrosanct insurance as an excuse. But I'd become something of a local personality. Life was hurried, fast in L.A. To get away from it, I'd go to the movies. I didn't know anything more hypnotic than the sound of a film and people breathing in a large half-deserted room. One day I began to dance again.

All I knew about dancing was from the *zikr*, a circle of men pounding their hands and feet and repeating the name of Allah. Or the dance designed to chase away the "horsehoof genies," evil spirits.

Since Kerkenna, I certainly had occasions where I might have danced. The only thing standing between me and the dance floor was the reaction of people who could see: an imaginary obstacle, a phantom. Then a continuity formed between my morning exercise on the surfboard and the sound of the sea beyond the lock, and the roar of loudspeakers in the big discotheque where I began to go, Zita on my shoulder.

I slid out onto the dance floor. I sensed people making a circle around me, but I didn't stop. I suppose I was doing something completely different from the dancers around me. I imitated dancers from my childhood—blacks with billowing pants crouching on their heels dancing to the drum sound, with long tresses of black wool ending in big knots that swirled above their *chechias*. The disco rhythm was a little slower than what I had known on Kerkenna.

In a few minutes I forgot everything; where I was, what was around me, even Zita who moved away growling before this kind of possession. The moist air had become the clear skies of Tunisia. I took off my sneakers to once again feel the sensation of dust on the ground. Never mind that this dust was composed of cigarette ashes and broken glass: it was the dust of the dancing ground on Kerkenna, the dust from the desert swirling above the sea, swept into big clouds by the *sirocco* wind.

My body, my legs, my back all were finally disembodied. During the past four years I hadn't made a single gesture not calculated for the sighted world. At each refrain—marked by the old blacks on Kerkenna with an accelerating rhythm of their curved sticks on the drums to almost total anarchy—I would squat down, arms out before me, turning around in place, like I had seen them do.

The music changed, and the d.j. put on African percussion,

then sambas, no doubt for me. But I wasn't aware of anything: beaches of records melted into each other.

I tore myself away from the dance floor brutally, like coming up out of deep water. The square in Kerkenna had disappeared, I was drenched in sweat and it was night. Instead of hearing exhausted dancers huddled around a fire to warm their bur-nooses in the night's chill, I heard conversations coming from the bar.

A hand held out a mug of Coca-Cola to me, half of which I spilled. I gathered Zita onto my shoulder, scratching her head and whispering in her ear that we were leaving. She hopped back down and started to clear a path among the dancers, showing me the way out.

The guy who had given me the Coke followed us. I could hear him whistling behind me. From the reaction he was getting, he must have been fat and old; but he seemed to have made up his mind, and pushed aside the young men with clear skin and well-developed muscles on the dance floor, who were in his way.

He joined me outside, under the entrance marquee where I was calming down, listening to rhythm inundating the night. According to him, we had already seen each other somewhere. He shook my hand. We had not been formally introduced at that point.

He had a disagreeable voice, wheezy, plaintive, shrill.

He continuously made a little rustling noise, due to a mania for wiping his hands with his handkerchief, grumbling about excessive heat. He asked if I knew I'd been dancing in front of a mirror all night long. He knew I was blind.

Mirror, narcissism, the wheezing voice went on. Many of the people at those places I went to even needed a mirror to make love. At the mirror I had explored the icy surface with the palm of one hand, my reflected body the other, yet it remained a complete mystery to me.

He asked if he hadn't seen me several times at the corner of Highland Avenue, when he was filling up at the service station. I dryly told him it wasn't working hours for me and I was off-duty.

That didn't discourage him. He invited me to come have a bite with him at the big Mexican restaurant on Melrose. Couples from the discos devoured *tacos* in the midst of waitress' hollering, their rustling frilly costumes brushing by my face. I gave my *enchilada* to Zita, who finished it under the table: she liked spicy food.

Other boys came up to our table and I was reassured. I'd started to wonder if I hadn't run into some kind of crazy. They all talked business, and called him Fatsy informally, but with a hint of fear in their voices. One was a colleague of mine from the Boulevard. He started to negotiate something with Fatsy in a lowered voice. From time to time he'd let out "A hundred dollars? ... What a joke." They finally reached an agreement.

I asked Fatsy what line of work he was in. He told me he was a kind of lawyer. He was sad to see a gifted young fellow like me wasting myself like I was doing with the first man or woman to come along. Seemed like he knew all about my little sideline. I was unaware of my value, and was really making a mess out of things by climbing into just any old car. He suggested I go into business with him. All I'd have to do was wait around the telephone at the all-night bookstore on Santa Monica at the entrance to West Hollywood. The schedule would be the same as when I was usually at my streetcorner. The guy who ran the store was a friend of his, whom he had saved from prison several times after pornography convictions.

We made a deal: from then on, the cars came to get me at the bookstore, or sometimes a big black chauffeur-driven Cadillac that Fatsy rented for special occasions would take me to Beverly Hills, or into the residential suburbs of Orange County. The limousine won out in the afternoons, and a goodly number of little old lady bourbon alcoholics were among my new clients. The men were all young enough to make you think all the older guys had left Los Angeles; they paid better than the women. I had to turn half over to Fatsy. True, I wasn't paying for taxis anymore—a substantial savings in L.A.

I surfed on waves each morning, and upon bodies each night. Sliding from client to client, I mixed up their physiques, their voices. I might be talking to a day client and confuse him with a married woman from the previous evening who had inundated me with a list of her indiscretions.

People who choose to sleep with someone blind are afraid of being seen, or else regret having not been seen. I reassured the gentle ones, the shy ones. I was outside the hard world of physical images, which is the world of success. And Fatsy was right. All the narcissists found deep disappointment with me, less because I am blind than because I was not able to admire myself. They were the hardest to take as they wanted to see me seeing.

In my country a man has several women, naturally. The more girls he sleeps with—women, or even men—the more a boy is admired. And money in no way ruined that pleasure for me—a pleasure usually so quickly exhausted.

In spite of all those experiences, I will never really know how the sighted make love among themselves. To visually perceive a lover must lead to much more in performance. A sighted person could never have happen to him what has happened to me; I'd completely forget about that presence lying by my side, jump up in surprise hearing their voice near me again when he or she lighted the first cigarette after lovemaking. Once I tried to fix them in my memory by asking them to describe themselves. One woman responded, "Pink eyes, green hair." She was right: how could I check it out?

Listening to them talking during love, I learned the terrors lurking in the depths of sighted desire. I make love with clenched teeth, without a word or moan. They all orchestrated a cacophony of sighs, of supplications, or encouragement, ecstasies and wails, as if they wanted to compensate for the fact that I couldn't see them by redoubling their efforts to surround me with sound.

I would hear them closing the blinds, flipping off the light switch. I would feel their eyelids closed beneath my fingertips, as they were having their orgasms, or pretending to. They lived in fear of seeing or being seen. And I lived in innocence.

With me, they said, they weren't afraid anymore, weren't ashamed of anything, not even the ridiculous.

I quickly learned to keep away from masochists, hysterics and maniacs. Once I got mixed up with an exhibitionist. Later on, I found out she had thrown her French windows and doors wide open while we made love, so all her neighbors could take advantage of the show we put on.

There came a day, months later, when the fatigue built up from training and my work made me lose contact with these bodies, which had kept on multiplying.

Until then, in spite of some confusion, I would pick up an odor, a voice, a place. I made love several times with the same person without recognizing them, and I felt I was approaching the limit: the same limit the *peyote* made me feel: dissolution, bursting apart in others' hands.

In the intensity of sexual discharge, I now perceived strange misapprehensions. The color of the person's hair, the remark that my partner hadn't said aloud but had thought, appeared so clearly to me that I spoke them, astonishing my clients. Consequences of my fatigue? Fatsy didn't take that into account, and rubbing his hands with his handkerchief announced he had a long waiting list. He had brought me a magazine. I was turning it between my fingers, not quite knowing what to do, when he told me that my picture was on the front cover. I was on my surfboard, on the cover of a smart slick-papered magazine. Underneath the photo, which Fatsy had given them without asking me, was a story telling about my future show at Marineland. The magazine was calling me "The Blind Surfer," written as big as your hand all the way across the page.

I didn't know how they had found out about it. Olaf hadn't warned me. I was a really hot consumer item, a toy at the whim of people who were too big, too rich and too sure of themselves. They were using my blindness as one more advantage for selling their product.

The telephone calls and the limousine never let up for an instant. Everyone in Beverly Hills wanted to sleep with the young blind Arab whose picture they'd seen. I was invited to parties in pretty little bungalows full of green plants. I became public, "popular," as Fatsy said. Popular in the true sense of the term, since each one could claim to have access to my most intimate secret.

In the bars and restaurants, dozens of pairs of eyes followed us, Zita and I with whispering. It didn't mean anything to me to know I was being spied on, considered a curiosity, a sexual object, a boy for sale. First, I didn't see these looks. And there was a kind of magic in passing through so many hands, a magic which bordered on the narrow sex of their visual pornography. On Kerkenna, where there were a few prostitutes, the oldest, blackest ones celebrated at night the cult of Hawa—the one Europeans call Eve, Madame l'Amour—to keep from speaking her name and conjuring her up. She reigned in Los Angeles, too. She must have kidnapped me without my knowing it away from my little island, to deliver me up to this madness in a strange land.

My prices went up.

It was a very profitable form of popularity. Each look riveted onto me was another twenty dollars, sticking to my skin from the hand of an anonymous client. And look at me they did. Once they had bought me, they admired in me the reflection of their own wealth, which could pay for the most unusual jewel: me, coming for their pleasure from so far away, coming from beyond all things visible, to make love to them.

Fatsy himself introduced me to particularly important clients. I called him every day at five o'clock to get my schedule. One day he told me I wouldn't return to Marineland for two days, if that was all right with me. It was becoming more and more established in advance that it *was* perfectly all right with me. To earn a thousand dollars, all I took along with me was a toothbrush and a clean shirt.

Driving the limousine in person, Fatsy described a new client. I was going to the home of a bachelor scientist; he was from the Coast, more or less. For Fatsy, anyone who didn't live in the glorious state of California meant less. We went along the ocean for a long time, driving toward San Francisco. The sun was setting on my left. We went several hundred miles, and Fatsy veered right, toward the mountains. His conversation, a lot of muttering, betrayed his nervousness, he who came up with stars and politicians, and had even shaken the President's mother's hand at a gala for the Democratic Party in which he'd taken an active role. This scientist, Larry Home, had the stuff Nobel prizes are made of. Fatsy kept repeating this phrase with an air of satisfaction. He must have read it somewhere in a newspaper.

The stuff in question was certainly heavily guarded. About ten miles from the ocean was a big parking lot where drivers had to leave their cars. Little buses that probably ran on compressed air were the visitors' sole transportation, letting off a continuous whoosh. There were no roads inside the Valley, only dirt paths for pedestrians and these little air-cars skimming over the lawns and around lakes. We arrived at a guardhouse, which was the last thing I would have expected to find at the end of this dirt path we were following. The guards passed information back and forth on walkie-talkies, and after confirmation from our host, let us pass.

While the little bus was parking, Fatsy claimed to have been a student with Larry. He didn't want to remind him of it though, since it seemed Larry didn't remember. I expected to meet some old gentleman smelling like formaldehyde; what I found was a man who must have been about the same age as Fatsy.

The place where Larry Home lived seemed like a huge park, encircled by the echo of distant mountains in the evening air. It was already cold in the shadows of trees, and the air was much purer coming down from the foothills of the Rockies than in the L.A. basin. Fatsy hadn't given me any indication of its location. The place was called Neurone Valley and was a top-secret military post. Nothing but laboratories where people looked into the mysteries of the human brain. About a dozen of them—all with firm self-assured voices—were gathered in Larry's living room when we arrived.

No children troubled the calm in Neurone Valley. The couples living there went to the sauna, went swimming in the artificial lake, or in the sea at the end of the valley. They had their own disco, and most of them lived with women, whom they sometimes swapped. No one wanted kids: they would have just gotten in the way of the work. Except for the ones who were themselves scientists, the women stayed out all afternoon on their bungalow terraces getting tan and watching T.V. shows on the four special networks in the valley.

Larry and his friends never stopped working. They got up every morning at eight o'clock, loading up on amphetamines in a race against their thirtieth birthdays to find the secret that would let them live the rest of their lives on royalties. Larry had already discovered a lot of secrets. His voice was dry, rich, not disagreeable, terribly precise. He told me he had invented a new plastic material for use in brain surgery. Fatsy said that Larry was the victim of a serious illness, and I thought maybe he had cancer, or something like that. Larry didn't say anything about it and seemed to be in fine shape. He could have had blue skin for all I cared. He asked his guests to leave and Fatsy was next on the list. Larry didn't seem to recognize him. He gave him a check, which must have been enormous if you could judge by the way Fatsy folded it to put it in his wallet. Fatsy was clearly subservient, while Larry had an authoritarian voice, and was uneasy, maybe for my sake. He offered him a whiskey in such a tone that Fatsy immediately refused and slipped away, whispering that he'd call me just as soon as I got back.

Larry spoke in a rather abrupt manner, even when he was trying to be nice to me. He always seemed to be carrying on an internal conversation with himself, as though he had to make an effort to remember that he was the one who'd invited me, and not I who'd fallen out of a helicopter into his living room. He asked what I would like for dinner and started punching in the menu on a keyboard, a little like a typewriter, which he had me touch. It was a computer terminal. He tapped out a word, waited for an answer, tapped out something else. That went on for five minutes, during which time he asked me when I would like to get up, what temperature I wanted for my shower, and at what time, what kind of tea in the morning, how I wanted my meat—medium or rare— and lots of other things. He punched in all of my answers as I responded, and explained that he had just programmed the next twelve hours, from the aperitif—which appeared in a receptacle with a thunk—clear up to the door and telephone, which would give off a busy signal up until then. He had even come up with a program for music, and one for T.V., which he scarcely watched, and only with the sound turned off, to keep a constant eye on graphs in a little corner of the screen for some experiment going on all by itself in his lab at the other end of the valley. The way he talked, the valley floor was nothing but computer cables, as big and as numerous as gas and water pipes in a city.

We sat down to dinner on a big sofa filled with water. He took care of all conversation, asked all the questions, while the conveyor belt brought up our food. It seemed as though he finally remembered why he had had me brought there. He wanted to know everything: where did I come from; how had I become blind; what had given me the idea of turning my blindness to profit in prostitution. Before Larry, I had never accepted that word. He seemed to think Fatsy had put my eyes out on purpose, or that my mother had, like sometimes happens to children where I'm from, to make them into beggars who'll bring in an income.

He had me tell everything about the institute, and I could have sworn he knew as much about it as I. When I asked if he'd ever been there he evaded the question, saying that all institutes are alike.

The cat had settled on Larry's lap and let him pet her. She had never done that with anyone but me.

Larry got up and led me into the next room, and I realized then he was bald. It seemed as though he had been waiting for my little discovery, chuckling, leaning his bumpy polished skull toward me. He offered me another cocktail, which I refused, and two capsules of T.T.1, which he took himself. He was taking enormous amounts of drugs, and loads of vitamins to counteract the effects of the drugs. He claimed it was good for him, feeling those chemicals circulating around inside. He slept only four hours a day, consuming the massive quantities of drugs invented by his friends, which he was always the first one to try. And the minute I finished screwing him, he was fast asleep. The only other important detail is that several times he tried to gesture in front of my eyes without my knowledge; but I could always tell. My lashes feel the heat given off by a hand, even at a distance. I closed my eyes, which he didn't like, because he wanted to observe the phosphorescence deep down inside my stare.

Apparently, his pills had made him just a little bit off. But he was outstanding in his field, and he was rich. He woke up early the next morning and went out of the room without a word, leaving me alone. I could hear the sound of eggs being fried in a skillet. I got up, and went into the bathroom, tapping along the walls. They were made of a soft plastic like the floor which totally swallowed up sound. I was completely lost. I found the wash basin, and started brushing my teeth, thinking about how last night, too, he had left me alone to discover his house. My independence seemed to interest him.

The shower spray had been programmed the night before, alternately icy cold then scalding. I had left my clothes in the bedroom. I put on an old sweater and some jeans drying near the tub. When I came back out, after turning into the hallway and opening the door to what I thought was going to be the bedroom, I felt fresh air. I was outside, and I couldn't find the doorknob where I'd come out. So I walked all the way around the house and finally arrived back at the main door. Automatic sprinklers were already hard at work under the rising sun. I pushed the buzzer by the door under an awning, and heard Larry's voice answering on a tape, saying he wasn't home. I buzzed again, and again, until Larry came in flesh and blood to interrupt the Larry on tape who was repeating his message for at least the tenth time. He yanked open the door and screamed into my face, "Because I say I'm not here!" I was at a loss for words, and he could see it on my face. He was only a few feet away from me, and he didn't recognize me.

But surely he wasn't blind. I was perplexed. Usually I'm the one who forgets people as soon as we've made love. His voice became more gentle, and I could feel him moving his hands in front of my eyes again. I turned my head to one side, he laughed, and led me inside. Zita let out a ferocious meow, jumping up on my knees, and Larry apologized for his illness: he was prosopagnostic. I had him spell out the word, and then I recognized it. That was why he knew all about institutions. Prosopagnostics are a kind of amnesiac. I had heard some of my friends at the institute talking about them. A terrible illness: they can't recognize faces anymore. Larry couldn't recognize his own wife's face, and they had divorced for the excellent reason that he could never be sure it was the same woman. Tired of always having to wear the same color clothing—canary yellow—to keep him from making a mistake, she had left him. He only talked to his children on the phone. He recognized their voices perfectly, but on sight he always took one for the other. It was really disagreeable to him to find himself talking to complete strangers who sounded like his nearest kin. He had decided to cut off all relations with his family and to never have any regular intimate contacts with anyone. He would sleep with gigolos only once. He never looked at the people he worked with. They all wore the same canary yellow shirts with their names stitched on the front. His colleagues all took pains to have some particular, individual clothing distinction, so he could identify them.

When he was standing still, Larry had excellent sight, and proved it to me by describing my face in detail.

I was absorbed in thought. He was planning to send me back, after using me. I did the very same thing with my clients. I was shocked because now he was the one in the position of taking that initiative. My advantage was slipping away—the thing that made them sorry to see me go. He would forget me right away. For a minute I hated him: I felt we were in the same boat.

His illness was only a detail for him, one that rather simplified his life, reducing it to sex and work. He really took an interest in me. He had read the magazine article with my picture in it. He wanted to know where my sense of balance came from. And he asked me trick questions. I felt I had been playing cat and mouse with him ever since the previous evening, as though he too was convinced I was hiding something from him.

During the two days I spent at his place, he didn't lose a minute. As a present, he offered to make a complete optometric examination of me. He seemed so pleased when I said yes, that I began to suspect he had had me visit him more for my handicap than for sex.

When he met me, he was convinced both that I was a fake and that the article was one of Fatsy's rackets to up the price. He asked if I had kept my medical file, and I told him the truth: I'd never read it. He was meaningfully silent.

His early years as a visually handicapped child had made Larry become a student of neurophysiology. He was interested in anything that had to do with vision. By being skeptical of my blindness, he wasn't being insulting. He was having fun with it, like it was a good joke. He would admit that I had problems with my vision. But how could I demonstrate to him that I was blind? It was driving me crazy. He claimed to have watched me, and I didn't run into anything in his living room, where the walls were of brick and far from soundproof. He had me describe the big flower vase by the entryway, which I had never touched. I stood in front of it. I could tell it had a rounded shape, a little larger at the bottom, with a long neck. I could tell the general shape of an object from the sound that came back from it directly, or off the wall behind it. I sensed obstacles by premonition, somewhere inside my forehead, between my temples. I would have to turn toward an object to guess its shape. He listened to me eagerly and I realized I was cornering myself. It was so much simpler to suppose that I could see, if only a little.

By the evening of the first day, I had convinced him he wasn't dealing with an imposter. For the moment, I was all for the tests. He had changed his mind. I was blind from "hysteria," a term used not only for wildly screaming women, but for any act a person does without wanted to, yet wanting to.

He had calculated just the right time in his little deal with Fatsy to be able to bring to light the answer to the mystery of "the blind surfer." He took me in his jeep over to another house, on a farm. Chickens went scurrying as we pulled up and a man was feeding some ducks. Well, anyway, some living beings that were making noises like ducks, but might have had rabbits' bodies.

We went inside the house. The man feeding the animals was stuff Nobel prizes are made of, too. The room was filled with bric-a-brac that I was constantly running into: books, farm implements, television sets. He had me sit down in a dentists' chair straight out of the Old West. They set to work, moving around a helmet with a lot of electrodes sticking out of it, that they had me touch. To start off with, they looked at an X-ray of my skull. There were no visible lesions on my brain. I didn't know what an electroencephalogram was. I had never had one at the hospital. They gave me a little shot, and started arguing while I floated along in a pleasant half-slumber, congratulating myself for not having brought along Zita, who would have hated all those electrical discharges. The other man couldn't get the machine adjusted, swearing that it had been used just the week before. Finally, they must have found what they were looking for. They became quiet, watching a little screen. I couldn't guess what they were getting out of it all.

Eventually Larry stood up, and discreetly claimed victory. The other man was flipping the screen with his finger. He insisted there exist people who are actually blind, but who demonstrate normal rhythms. They consulted a thick book, some files, the computer. I was listening to birds flying around in the branches of the apple trees outside the house, on the other side of the wall. They had examined the inside of my eye with a laser, and I thought I could feel a little flame flitting over my retina. For a long time I had known that all the reflexes in my eyes were the same as with a sighted person: my pupils would react to light.

All the nerves in charge of eye *movement* can be intact, while the eye itself doesn't see. It's another nerve which renders it "sighted." Larry could hook up a projector right in front of my face if he wanted. The contractions of my eyes were coming only from heat and reflex. He had classed me in the category of "blindness by desire to not see," having me recall that at the institute I was quite familiar with blind people convinced they could see. The illness was symmetrical. My reply was that he couldn't believe I was blind, because he couldn't see it for himself.

He thought a little while, and recognized that I could never actually prove to him that I really was blind. The limits of seeing and not seeing were beyond—or outside—science. He had known of a case similar to mine, where some trauma had caused an abscess on the brain, which was later absorbed without a trace. The boy had been truly blind for two weeks, and had stayed that way by habit. In my case, perhaps prostitution was keeping me blind. I still thought I was blind, but maybe I really wasn't anymore.

Of course, I had suffered a blow. The scar was still there. It often happens that a wound causing a total blindness—briefly— becomes the cause of a total lack of vision by psychological habitude. He even knew of a case where a boy became blind during the first night of his honeymoon. According to Larry, I was blind to keep from seeing the people I was sleeping with. He understood it perfectly well, given the fact that the spectacle was surely not always entirely inviting.

How do you get an intelligent man to reason the other side? I knew I was sleeping with just anybody because I was blind, and not the reverse.

But my "alpha occipital rhythm" was normal, Larry said snapping his fingers, put off by my resistance. They started arguing again, while I drank some watered down coffee in a kind of graduated glass used for experiments.

I heard Larry's buddy whipping up something in the kitchen. He came back near me and I could smell the odor of manure and smoke from his clothing. I didn't know what in the world he was doing above my head, and I had to keep myself from sticking out my hand. There was a long silence, and Larry came to apologize to me. He had been wrong in not believing me. I was strictly blind. I wanted to know what the decisive experiment had been. They handed me a little kitchen knife, suspended from the end of a fine string. When you held it up, the point swung forward. They had swung it in front of my eyes. The thing was sufficiently small for me not to sense it, in which case I would have closed my eyes by reflex. I hadn't blinked. I didn't have the protective "blink reflex." This experiment was more conclusive than all the machines. They were so positive they would obtain the opposite result, they had tried this simple method only as a last resort.

Larry seemed a little disappointed. I was relieved. He had started to make me wonder myself.

He was disappointed, but definitely convinced. An object small enough and cold enough remains invisible to me. And you can't cheat with the blink reflex; a reflex of the cerebral cortex more ancient than the oldest mammals, according to Larry; an automatic reflex by which the eye preserves itself; a survival reflex no act of will can supercede.

Larry took me back to his place in the jeep. I confided to him how I thought that I could see one single time after the accident. I suppose that after the nerve was cut, the parts of the brain that create vision must have been intact, and could keep on working in some sort of closed circuit, especially when stimulated by a drug.

Basic translation: I was finally forming some idea of the brain. When I was a kid I thought the inside of your head was filled with white jelly, concentrated sperm, which flowed down through the spinal cord and into the genitals.

The explanations Larry gave were the first rebound my spirits had. No one had ever taken the trouble to help me form any idea of what had happened to me. Larry wasn't like other doctors. He could discuss it with me without yawning or patting me on the cheek. He didn't make himself intentionally incomprehensible. My studies hadn't been encouraged much but Larry thought that people become scholars when it's a question of their own lives, or of what colors their lives. Larry was the first person to ever praise my vocation of self-study, to unveil a bit of knowledge for me.

So, the prostitute from Santa Monica Boulevard discussed the brain with a famous scientist.

The brain: on Kerkenna, in Rome, the doctors had certainly talked to me about it enough, without ever realizing I had never even seen a model of it. At school on Kerkenna, the only teaching aid had been a map of the world donated by Tunis Air. Mrs. Hallowe'en was certainly not capable of giving me any scientific instruction, and her healers had remained wisely indecipherable. I knew I had suffered a blow to the back of my head, which in the most common terminology had "wrecked" my brain.

Later on, I had my files sent from the hospital in Rome to Santa Barbara, and the director had read some extracts aloud, stumbling over the words "cortical cecity." I didn't know anything about this barbaric term that sounded like it ought to have something to do with peeling fruit. I'd never had classes in Natural Science which went further than plants. Larry was the first person to allow me to get some idea of something so important to me. Like the kids at the institute, I thought that you see from in front. And the introduction of a little piece of metal in my neck hadn't at first been enough to give me any idea why I should be blind. Listening to Larry's minced-up definitions, I moved the center of vision to the back of my head. The zone where I had been affected was number seventeen, on both sides of a central line dividing the back of the brain. The neighboring portion, number eighteen, is known as Brodman's Area. Larry had been affected there when he was very young. He talked about it without emotion, unless it was to envy that certain Mister Brodman, maybe already dead, who'd had his name inscribed in Larry's own brain, like a street in the city you live in named after a general you would like to have been.

We went back to eat at Larry's house. Zita didn't want to leave the bedroom and she set up camp in the middle of the plastic waterbed which she threatened to flatten with her claws as she played with Larry. To avoid an inundation, he gave her a sleeping pill which she accepted without the least reluctance. Within two days, whatever came from Larry's hand had become familiar to her, she who had never accepted food from anyone but me. The pill wasn't simply a sedative: it acted upon a little bundle of nerves near the brain. When the cat started dreaming, instead of making symbolic gestures, she got up and started hunting exactly as if she were awake. She slipped away from me like she didn't know I was there. She didn't notice my hands, couldn't even hear me. She was chasing an imaginary mouse that existed only in her dream. Then, she started meowing in a raspy voice, calling another cat. I kicked at her a couple of times, but got no reaction.

All her impressions were coming from inside. I was afraid of a thing like that—a drug that made you act out such violent dreams. Larry assured me that the pill was harmless: the dreams wouldn't become any more violent. That tiny bundle of nerves usually serves to cut off commands the brain gives to muscles when you're asleep, in order to keep the body at rest. It couldn't do its job right in Zita because of the little pill.

When in a dream we're at the edge of a cliff, or a ferocious beast is jumping at our throats, we remain in bed. This little bunch of nerves drastically cuts the current going out to our limbs, but the brain goes on functioning all by itself, just as I had guessed: in a closed circuit.

Larry turned toward me with an engaging laugh, as if he were offering me a new cocktail. He had positively no sense of morality about drugs. Do I? Yes.

According to Larry, I now had available to me the only means to know if I was truly seeing when I dreamed. That way, we could have proved if my visual function was only disconnected, but still intact.

As much as the idea of being seen awake meant nothing to me, that's how repulsive the idea of being seen dreaming was to me. Why? I could only know by seeing myself dreaming. Like all his colleagues in the Valley, Larry had done it. He had filmed himself with an automatic camera. But with me, there would always have to be an intermediary, someone to see me, to describe me.

Under the effects of Larry's drug, dreamers didn't talk any more than in everyday life. Their movements had to be interpreted; their mimicry, the silent film of their adventures, their dream desires.

Larry swore he was just the person to do it: he was the ideal intermediary as he didn't know anything about me. At the end of the evening, I allowed myself to be tempted—I let him watch me dream that night. It was the only way to get to know about myself.

As I woke up, I anxiously began to question him.

Did I see? Did I act like a person who could see? How can you tell by looking at someone's face if he *is* seeing? During sleep, my eyes had started moving, not lazily, like when I was awake, following the sounds I heard by force of habit, or reflex. No. My wide open eyes were clearly seeing. Nothing of what was in front of me—which was Larry's face—but an interior landscape that my eyes were constantly sweeping.

I had made numerous gestures and Larry couldn't figure out what they meant. They evidently had something to do with my life with Mrs. Hallowe'en, about which I didn't feel the need to be explicit with him. I had also gotten up, squatting several times, then would kneel with my arms out on the floor. Larry didn't recognize the motions of Islamic prayer. I had done it several times, ten, twenty times, which meant my dream was made of days gone by on Kerkenna.

My prayer posture was intriguing to Larry. I gave him the key. During the experiment, while I was dreaming I had always turned in the same direction, making this prayer motion. He had tried to disorient me, turning me around, changing the position of the bed. No external signal could be reaching me to show where that one direction lay. I translated for him the first part of this verse from the second *sura* which I was made to recite as a child:

"We have seen you turning, unsure, your face to every side of the heavens; We wish for you to henceforth turn toward a region where you will be gratified ... No matter where you are, turn toward this shore."

Speaking of the shore, we went swimming at the end of the Valley at the big beach where the employees all went to unwind.

Stretched out in the sun eating hamburgers, we continued our discussion. I was fascinated by what Larry was telling me. I understood without having him draw me a picture. He came back to the prayer: he had checked with his compass, and claimed that I turned obstinately toward the Orient to pray—the true Orient of the rising sun—even while dreaming. It is true that on Kerkenna I also turned toward the Orient. In America, the direction of Mecca had not changed for me.

I hadn't prayed in years. No matter. I hadn't lost my intuition for the right direction. Larry didn't understand how the spirit could be gratified by one direction more than another. At the outside, he would have admitted a preference for place, but not for orientation. And how did this orientation manage to survive in dreams, cutting across the barrier of reality?

Already, a rift was forming between Larry and me. He saw the spirit as a perfect view of three hundred sixty degrees. He didn't understand how the spirit could turn toward something, without having a side to turn to. I was doing it every day, with sounds and odors.

I know a certain portion of the sky, the one you can feel, a home fire glowing in the hollow of your palm when you turn toward the rising sun with open hands; and it's as pleasing to my spirit as it is to my body. On a beach on Kerkenna, the attraction is all the more sensitive, as if the echo of the *muezzin* had drifted on the water from one sea to another over Africa. Here, the beaches face West.

Larry's spirit was instinctively turned toward the setting sun, because the dream adventure, the riches, are in the West for Americans as they are in the East for us, the people where I come from and Europeans.

His Orient was West. To follow me, he would have to fly over the Rockies, the plains of the Middle West, the smoke of New York, the Atlantic, Europe and Arabia. While by the Pacific...

Larry wanted to take me to Hawaii to start our experiments all over again, to find out what I'd do being closer to Mecca from the west than from the east. He poured sand from one hand to the other as he spoke.

In the brain, everything is arranged in a completely different order from the reality we perceive. In my head, the East was no closer to east on a compass than yellow was yellow. But I could swear I could actually feel the Orient point, the only, the true Orient. It was made of saffron and jasmine, heat and dust, and I squinted my eyes, involuntarily: the only remaining gesture, a souvenir of Kerkenna's blinding light.

What did I see in my dreams? I think Larry would have gladly cut two holes into my neck to take a peek if it could have been possible. I alone could perhaps have been able to interpret the movement on my face during my dreams; and I was the only one unable to do it. Larry was constructing a hypothesis aloud. You would have to have a flexible tape recorder—a supple mask to put over my face—which would be able to reproduce at will my recorded movements, for interpretation by touch. I found the idea excellent. I don't understand how you can be satisfied with a flat projection, when life is in relief, in depth.

The next day, when I was taken back to Marineland in an official car, Olaf was quite content for me to have spent two days off somewhere being tested. It hadn't cost him a cent.

Everyone knows that blind people spend a lot of time going off to have tests. Having decided to pick up just anyone, to forget about Larry, I went back to West Hollywood with Zita. He had too much of a hold over me: he had seen me dreaming: my independence had suffered.

I continued to meet Fatsy's clients. It was a useful habit. People drove me around, invited me places, and paid me. After I had drunk a little, I told some of them about my discovery of the brain. They were delighted to have come across such a cultivated young man. A man that raised turkeys gave me money so I could enroll in a university. I wouldn't have been alone. I knew at least two other guys who were paying their way through school by tricking on Santa Monica Boulevard.

Fatsy kept wanting me to call Larry. He didn't understand my reluctance. He had become an astrology convert, and wanted me to take part in séances. I refused, even though it would have paid well. I don't care for black masses. I take things more seriously than these Westerners. Fatsy did draw up my horoscope chart and discovered I would regain my vision thanks to a rich and powerful magician, who could only be Larry. I didn't try to see Larry again. He found me himself. My spirit-guide was remote controlled. To avoid him, and remembering his illness, I changed what I was wearing several times a day. The cat, anything by which he could recognize me, stayed at home.

The jeep pulled up in front of me one evening. I recognized it right away. Accepting Destiny, I climbed in without a word. Larry told me that he had been going through all the young guys with black curly hair he could find for two weeks listening to their voices and examining their eyes in the obscurity of his car. He found himself with dozens of Puerto Ricans, Mexicans, Filipinos, all with perfect sight. I would have been able to evade him a long time by "playing sighted," as we used to say at the institute.

He opened up a new vial of Angel Dust in my honor, which he snorted with a little spoon. We spent several weeks together, going out at night to a discothèque that Larry liked and sleeping in an apartment Fatsy loaned us in Malibu. Larry was very well known. In all the public places, even in nightclubs, people wanted to talk to him. I didn't really know very much about that kind of thing. I don't read the papers. I don't see the photos. I did notice that my prices were still going up. I was turning people down, starting with the younger ones who claimed to be beautiful or handsome. I was starting to get a feel for what it means to someone blind to live in the film capital of the world. How lucky I was to be able to keep a cool head in the midst of the greatest continuous show on Earth, in the heart of the richest image-making factory of our time!

Everyone I talked to in the bars worked in films. Looking me over as if they were taking measurements on a piece of land zoned for construction that they would just love to buy, they swore there was a fortune to be made from my face.

Larry tried to dance with me. He was very clumsy, at least to me. I dance only for myself: I'm the only one who can be my partner.

When we got tired, we'd sit down, and Larry would try to make conversation with me, screaming over people's conversations and the music, all of which came to me in fragments.

The public seemed to think Larry was stuck on himself: he didn't recognize a soul. They wouldn't have believed his illness even if they'd known what it was. They didn't believe that a face, their face, could be a mere construction in someone else's brain. They thought they *were* their faces: unique, material, their personal property, a variation of the face of God. I don't have a face anymore, and for me no one else does either.

A face is a landscape. A landscape doesn't exist away from the panorama from which you contemplate it. For me, a face is more like a hand, the shape of a body, of a knee. A simple comparison. I know perfectly well that a knee is not a face. The young people in L.A. were terrified at the idea of having to do without a face. They couldn't believe you can live without one.

Larry committed the worst offense against public figures and celebrities who were obliged to explain who they were, so he could identify them. Everybody was just a little bit afraid of him and they preferred to speak to me, while Larry turned his back to them and stroked Zita. I listen to everyone. All you need to answer is a smile.

Neither with Mrs. Hallowe'en nor at the institute had I ever run into such difficult relationships. The only things that counted were wealth, celebrity, or youth and beauty; rarely all of them together. And in this infernal dance all I had to exchange was a beauty useless to me.

The music and the movement in these places had an incredible presence. To avoid running into bar stools and customers I danced all the time. In dancing I'd found the best means to keep my equilibrium. Larry told me about a French philosopher who'd written that there is no perception without movement. By dancing, I was multiplying contacts without meaning to, exchanges of heat not to mention odors, which often left a lot to be desired. When I keep my index finger on Braille characters for too long I can't feel the points anymore. Perhaps a face is nothing more than that: the dream of a stock-still figure, like an I.D. photo, almost imperceptible.

I have always liked—been absolutely crazy about—movement. I had never been able to imagine Mrs. Hallowe'en at rest, and I wouldn't like to have seen her corpse. Larry felt suffocated if he didn't travel a couple of hundred miles in a day. I only perceive the movement of my body; I only feel my body when I'm moving. The old people at the institute sat rocking back and forth, softening the final blow, recalling a vaguely rhythmic existence as they dissolved in a fading world. This vice of "rocking" got us used to retirement as one of the maimed at a very early age. This swaying is only a compromise between our movement and the sighted's fear of others' stares. I discovered that in English the same word describes this slow motion of the blind and what used to pour out of the jukebox on Kerkenna. Our rocking was nothing more than a hobbled dance.

When I danced the universe seemed like a tactile ballet of motion to me, an army of insect wings, or those hummingbirds Mrs. Hallowe'en told me about which remain nearly still in mid-air, hovering on wildly flapping wings. A dance floor is not a world of stares, but of grazing touches, of lashes humming in vibration.

Sensations interlace. All the senses have their centers, Larry said, but each center is also a picture of what is happening in another center, whose echo reaches it more or less drowned out.

Larry had suggested that I compare sensation to the tone you hear on long distance calls. It gets weaker and changes rhythm as a function of the number of relays it passes. Odors reach us from an area nearby, right after the first tone, very close—a private line from our noses to our brains. For me, the French verb *sentir*, meaning to smell as well as to sense, to feel, always gives the strongest sense of presence.

I can resist music, but not odors. I haven't the least modesty about noises, but I'm almost afraid of odors, which are often the proof of impurity. I always use the word "sense" for "see," including meaning "to touch." In the beginning was the sense, Larry concluded, at the beginning of Evolution. What in the world was Evolution?

We spent another weekend at Neurone Valley. Larry had me touch real brains from calves, pigs, chimpanzees. The chimpanzee brain was still warm and very fragile. By pushing lightly with my thumb I could have taken off a chunk of this humid sponge stuck to my fingers. Within this quivering jelly, billions of little centers were devoted to interpreting the world.

Larry found my progress astounding. A sighted person cannot put together a representation of vision without including himself as spectator. I wasn't trying to find the "little man" sitting back behind the window of my eyes, or inside my head. My brain, a floating Medusa inside my skull, was only a relay, a tap, an element of the earth linked to the sensitive world by intricate multiple exchanges, a mosaic of highly refined tension that no single comprehensive center could reduce. But like a plant, the brain is capable of reassembling missing pieces to ensure the body's survival.

In the buried folds, the soggy milky cavities, signals were being exchanged, and after repetition upon repetition, a presence was formed which thought itself simple; a sensation, a vision, an odor, an ever modifying sum of infinitesmal chemical reactions, believed itself the center of the world.

Larry was quite pleased with how I was reconstructing sighted science without being familiar with it, as a finger can recognize a Braille character from two points when it can handle up to six points, or as the eye constructs a vision of the world which nevertheless has a hole at its center, according to Larry, from a "blind spot" that all the sighted people unconsciously carry around with them.

An abstraction which gives sighted students debilitating headaches is simple to me: thinking, without trying to see or form a spatial image, without reading or contemplating a map; feeling time, without picturing a flowing hourglass: I am unhindered by any symbol, by any comparison.

Larry told me that the best topologists—scientists who study physical space—were blind. My space is in relief, in depth, because it is comprised of the palpitation of surfaces, the very shapes of things.

California summer settled sleepily over the Valley. The center was deserted apart from a few guards who played cards and drank beer. That summer for want of being a seeing man, I became a reflective man. Idolatry is repulsive to me. At the institute, I'd touched sculptures made by Vidal, a blind artist from the last century: a bull, a horse in full stride. The animals were running in place, rearing up to capture a visual memory, to force it to reappear. This unfortunate man had spent his life carrying on in a language he could no longer understand.

During the time I lived with Larry, my conscious existence was being transformed. Studying my blindness in the abstract, I had the dizzying sensation of being on two sides of a sensation at the same time, of being the observer and the observed. As when I touch one of my hands with the other, both are at once the subject and the object of sensation.

At first I committed Larry's lessons to memory. I wasn't writing at the time. I had no perspective available to enable me to put together an idea of an ensemble, a whole. Larry agreed it was better that way. Because all paradoxes seemed so evident to me, my spirit wasn't tarnished by any visual comparisons.

But at the end of several weeks, my notions were getting all tangled. I was getting lost again; memory does have its limits.

Larry had a device built at great cost especially for me, one of only two in existence. He kept one and offered the other to me. I still use it today.

Scarcely larger than a cigarette package, it's a vivid bright red plastic, to keep it from getting lost, and is so solid even Zita's claws can't scratch it. On its longest side, six keys correspond to the six points of Braille, just like on a typewriter, to register each letter and I have to press down a certain number of keys at the same time.

A window where lines of Braille containing the text just struck appear one by one allows me to read it. I rarely use this. Above, another window gives a translation in visual characters. The text is stored line by line in a little memory bank contained on a super-microcassette spool, smaller than on any ordinary portable recorder. A hundred lines equals one second in time. One full cassette is worth dozens of volumes of Braille.

From the day I got it, I set out to learn how to write fluently in Braille. I never was able to read it very well. My old mental block still worked against all that laborious spelling, but in two weeks I was typing faster than the best stenos and without the slightest noise. Larry plugged the digicassette directly into a computer. That way it could avoid passing through human language; it also saved energy. He dictated series of numbers to me during the dead time of his experiments.

Concepts of relativity, of time and space, of the curvature of space, and how to program computers were easier for me to understand than forming any notions of perspective.

I understood the importance of delivering hundreds of messages per second—messages I didn't completely understand— which were gobbled up by the machine in the time it takes to sigh. It responded to my questions by means of its window, delivering a series of digits that I called out, whenever Larry's hands and eyes were otherwise occupied.

Larry was finishing a series of experiments on frogs. The heat annoyed the creatures. Flies were getting into the lab. Larry said I made a good assistant, devoid of squeamishness. Handling a blood-tinged eye had no more effect upon me than did messing around with a hunk of calves' liver.

After the experiments, I gave the frogs to Zita, who toyed with them awhile then ate them. You could hear her little jawbone crunching in a corner of the lab, and it was all over.

These batrachians are endowed with nerves that can re-generate, as they say lizards' tails do. Their optic nerves are easily cut with a little scalpel by delicately raising the eyeball. I could get a lot of practice hundreds of subjects lived in this basement, now transformed into a laboratory annex.

Larry would take out an eye and put it back into the cavity upside down, the bottom part on top, the top on bottom. I would bandage it. With other frogs, Larry exchanged the right eye with the left, sometimes even exchanged them *and* turned them upside down. Later, after I had taken off the bandages, Larry offered the frogs plastic flies hanging on a transparent thread in front of them. I could hear the frogs jump to catch them. All those we had operated on saw the world in reverse. Some tried to turn around to catch their prey in the air, behind themselves. Others looked for flies on the floor, which were really hanging up above them.

Every night, despite our shower programmed with vanilla scent, we smelled like fish.

Larry's point was made. Low, high, left, right—all are conventions of the sighted brain, not images of the world. There's nobody behind our nerves to correct the error. Because the eye is not a glass window, and our "high" is only the high part of the retina, we are only echoes, repetitions, mixed impressions, worldly matter, uncentered multiplicities, a cacaphony of electrical swarms, of miniscule chemical storms.

After the frogs, we worked a while on chimpanzees. We had to sacrifice three animals for the experiment to succeed. By injecting a colored dye into the chimpanzee's eye, then cutting fine slices out of its frozen brain, we obtained a plate that I then photosensitized and developed. Larry read the translation of the last big show the chimps ever saw: a neon bar, fixed on an axis which changed positions for each of them. According to whether it was horizontal or vertical, the brain mobilized different cells, forming an arbitrary design like the letter of an unknown alphabet, different each time.

Larry never kept me from going back to West Hollywood. My stops at the bookstore had been less frequent during the summer—which turned L.A. into a dustbowl of carbon monoxide. By autumn, I had dissected my fill of those creatures. Larry's obsession had arrived at an impasse. You couldn't dissect a living brain, still less a human brain. I stayed in L.A. oftener, and at Marineland where I'd only been able to practice at night during the whole tourist season, since they had invaded the entire zoological park.

Business picked up, and I settled into the apartment Fatsy had loaned me. Larry joined me when I didn't have other clients. One October morning, even before Larry's chronograph alarm had gone off, they broke down the door. There was Larry, in kimono and handcuffs. I understood by the sudden commotion that it was the cops. I raised my wrists ironically. They didn't dare put their iron bracelets on me. They threw my clothes at me and Zita. They had to open the cuffs so that Larry could get dressed while a cop read him his rights, racing down a paper saying he had broken the law on the protection of minors. I didn't understand. I wasn't a minor by age. In his office, the judge reminded me that his colleague in San Francsco had placed me under the care of an institution. I was a prolonged minor under the protection of the State of California, and in short, whomsoever touched me was tampering with state property. We had been followed by a detective hired by Larry's wife, which couldn't have been too hard to do: we went out a lot, and the magazine article had done the rest. The judge asked what my resources had been since I'd left the institute. I said that I worked at Marineland, and Olaf confirmed it. Fortunately, he made up pay vouchers, for amounts I really would love to have earned. Olaf needed me. The judge let me go. He had to wait for some documents from the other judge before he could hold his inquest, at which time he would decide whether or not to send me back to the institute. Olaf acted as my guarantor, swearing that he would have me take correspondence courses. And the judge's wife already had free tickets for October 17th, the opening night of my show. After leaving the police station, where I had slept a night, I barely had time to shave. That very same evening, in public, for the first time I had to do my number—I hadn't practiced in three days.

The floodgates opened up. I was carried off by the wave. Indian Summer nights in California are mild, and the water was almost warm from having been in the lock all day. My body sprang back automatically to the necessary torsion that would pull it out of the liquid tumult, and I dove at the last moment to avoid being smashed to bits on the retaining wall. Above me I heard the sloshing water hurled against the concrete, and the cheering of delighted spectators drawing back in a mass from the geyser of water that gushed toward them.

After that night Olaf added a spotlight to follow me; he would have installed fireworks on the surfboard if he could have. Followed by the projector over the phosphorescent water, I always went past the warning buzzers to create more suspense in the show. It cost ten dollars a head to get in.

Some nights I'd do ten, twenty waves, carried by the applause of the spray-swept crowd assembled in the dark. The show was such a huge success the outcome of my trial was virtually certain. I had become a permanent attraction of the park.

I questioned Fatsy as to what had become of Larry. He had no interest in the subject anymore: Larry wouldn't be a client for a certain length of time. After having confirmed the papers' announcement of the disappearance of Professor Home, Fatsy asked when I was coming back to work. As soon as he was released on bail, Larry had fled abroad before his verdict. They said it was something political. Senatorial elections were coming up, and Fatsy had become active in the management of a local Democratic club.

These political things are beyond me. I was really too tired for anything beside my act.

The blind surfer became an attraction listed in all the tourist brochures; the blind surfer and his dolphins. Olaf had noticed that visitors were deserting the other attractions which took place every hour here and there in the park, especially the dolphin tank. So he put them in my act. The poor things were so unhappy without spectators they were in danger of dying of sadness, pointing their noses for nothing at the edge of their abandoned pools. To communicate with them you had to use a whistle inaudible to the human ear, an ultrasonic whistle which I wore on a chain around my neck. Certain pitches they made signified impatience, others amusement, or announced they wanted to play. The language of dolphins doesn't express words, so much as desires.

The two dolphins became accustomed to my surfboard. They had been trained by a great old guy who taught me how to play with them. They had smooth expressive bodies, and would tap me on the nose with their heads whenever they wanted to play. They loved to playfully swat me with their tails as I swam toward my board. They would slowly slide between my legs; they liked a man's body, because they had always lived with men.

Then the shit hit the fan; again. Because it's unlawful to make animals work at night, the ASPCA lodged a protest and wanted the show stopped. While we were waiting for a second opinion, the show was moved to a sunset time. The worst rumors about me were flying around. Olaf asked if I would go on T.V. to show he wasn't holding me prisoner or mistreating me.

I didn't know very much about this television thing which I'd been hearing about non-stop since I'd first arrived in America. On Kerkenna, the first television had been turned on only a year before my accident. Even though the set held a place of honor in the café, there wasn't anything on it because there weren't any relays yet for Southern Tunisia. For me, television remained a loud radio that people turned toward to listen to.

The television announced that I would be on a show, "Good Morning, America," at nine o'clock in the morning. I wasn't even fully awake. I couldn't for the life of me figure out why I had to stay nailed down to that couch. I didn't know where they kept the camera. The microphones had barely started working when the other guests, across from me, started to rake me over the coals. I was a disgrace to the handicapped cause, I was the symbol of the commercial exploitation of the blind. One of them was paralyzed, and I could understand him being furious about my photos. The other represented some League for the Blind and kept knocking into the low table in front of him. I asked him why he felt dishonored by a show he couldn't see.

During the debate, I kept thinking about the viewers. Did the people who saw us believe we were in their homes? Weren't we just a moving picture, up over the oven in the kitchen? I couldn't talk to them, as the moderator insisted time and time again for me to do. Someone I can't hear doesn't exist for me.

At the end of Autumn, the League for the Blind put up a picket line outside the park entrance. To be on the safe side, and also because I was drained from the surfing, I completely stopped looking for evening clients in West Hollywood.

Now I never left my little bamboo pavilion on the edge of the miniature pond where pink flamingos posed. At the beginning of November, in the middle of the show, the two dolphins got particularly rough in their play with me. The old man thought they were carrying out courting rituals. They had no way of knowing if I was male or female he added, excusing himself. Ever since I had been playing with them, Zita had become extremely jealous. The next evening, when I jumped onto my board, she leapt from the edge of the pool, over the wave, and stationed her little snarling self on the edge of the board. It was too late to go back. I took the wave when I could. Instead of being petrified with fright, the cat just started walking between my legs, threatening the dolphins with furious meowing.

At the critical moment, I felt a whack from the tail of one of the dolphins, who had done it on purpose, instead of diving under the board and coming up on the other side like it was supposed to. I fell, in a moment that seeemed terribly long to me, rolled by the wave toward the concrete wall and the shouting of the spectators, who weren't pulling back quickly enough for me not to have the impression of falling smack dab in the middle of them. The rest was silence.

The Marineland clinic was like something out of a fairy tale. I wanted to talk to my neighbor. He answered in groans. The nurse brought him an entire platter of fish flailing about on a tray. My roommate was an old obese seal who wheezed all day long and suffered from rheumatism. He was just on the other side of a low divider. Across the room, an employee was moaning about his arm, broken by a shark. Zita got acquainted with a lynx who had the flu in the stall next door. My accident wasn't serious: I had cracked a rib and gashed a scar on my cheek. I took it all so lightly the nurse couldn't believe it. The clinic was comprised of ten little dwarf pavilions surrounded by reeds and plaster crocodiles. I slept away a long convalescence. They brought my meals on a cart.

Then someone knocked on the door and unceremoniously walked in. It was Fatsy's voice; he started right in telling me that he'd always known that show would never give me anything but trouble, and now, after it had happened, he was really glad to see me again. I noticed that his voice was already disagreeable to me, something I was trying to escape rather than listen to. He thought maybe I could start working West Hollywood again, because there wasn't a snowball's chance in Hell that the park would pick up the show again after my accident. He put a box of chocolates on my bed; even the outside wrappers were sticky after having spent hours in the sun in the back of his car.

I hesitated, then answered that it was out of the question. I didn't want to any more. I had a fever. I couldn't understand why he was still standing there, instead of leaving.

He scooted his chair back on the floor like you might clear your throat, and picked up the conversation in a different tone. I couldn't quite manage to grasp all of what he was saying, but he was wheezing his words now, like he was under the strain of some powerful emotion. He informed me that I owed everything to West Hollywood, and to him. Without him, I would've become a bum or been picked up by the police and dragged off to some asylum, which was where I belonged. He kept talking about snapshots. It seemed these snapshots existed, and if they were to be sent off to certain newspapers, it might be pretty fuckin' funny. He slammed the wooden door, yelling how he would leave me a couple of days to think it over. He was gone before I was fully conscious of the fact that he'd been threatening me.

That bastard had taken pictures, maybe with the help of certain clients. A scandal. Hah! A photo, for me, doesn't have the least value, even when it's of me. But then there was that judge, waiting to make a decision.

The whole bunch had conspired to send me back to the institute. I was in a panic. Fatsy had talked about my "image" in the public eye. Besides an absurdly organized world all around me that I had to reconstruct, right now I had a double on my hands who could get me recognized all up and down the coast.

I wanted to get up. I had to try several times. The floor swayed under me. Wanting something to eat, the seal next to me began to applaud. The old dolphin trainer came in, and I asked him to help me get my things together. He was nearly in tears to see me leave. I ended up leaving him the address of a hotel called the Chelsea in New York which I knew about from Mrs. Hallowe'en. She'd spoken about it only in a ready-made phrase: "If I were to be ruined to the point of landing in the Chelsea ..." So I figured the Chelsea was the cheapest place possible. I asked the old man to write a letter for me which I dictated to him; and I explained everything concerning Fatsy. I gave him both barrels. He deserved it. He had threatened me to force me to prostitute myself.

The nurse came in while I was packing. She started screaming in Swedish and left to find Olaf. Before they had a chance to get back I had climbed into one of the taxis always waiting in front of Marineland, and was driven to the air terminal. I had more than four thousand dollars on me: it was time to split from the West Coast. Sure, I'd found my liberty there, but I was also sure that if I stayed, they would end up getting the best of me, completely transforming me into a role in their dream, a dream where Larry's machines, sex for pay, and cold craziness were reducing me, even me, into an image.

During the entire flight, the stewardesses took turns trying to take Zita away, asking if anyone was waiting for me at the airport. I'd only been in New York once, at the Hotel Pierre, where Mrs. Hallowe'en took a suite which I practically never left. From the windows of the Pierre they said you could see the buttresses of the Chelsea, a little further down—as one can contemplate Purgatory from Paradise.

The taxi driver who picked me up at the airport whistled kindly when I told him I was blind, then asked how I managed to get around, to which Zita answered with a meow. The driver didn't know his way around town yet and finally admitted that he'd gotten there only a few planes before mine. He spoke French. He was Haitian, and it was nice to listen to him. I hadn't spoken my native tongue, French, since Mrs. Hallowe'en had died. He told me that taxi drivers here are always the most recent immigrants.

This Hotel Chelsea didn't have a revolving door. I've always dreaded revolving doors. When I was with Mrs. Hallowe'en, once I'd passed through, they locked me inside of the hotel better than the best iron bars.

It was raining outside and cold. I've never gotten used to the cold. Zita and I must both have looked like drowned cats in the lobby. I put my dark glasses back on, to warm up a bit. Over in one corner a drunk was humming. Behind the counter with its top up, a bunch of people were arguing in Spanish. A painter was trying to pay his bill with some frescoes he had done on the walls of his room. They started arguing again, about me, and they took me the cat and my bag into a big clanky whiny elevator up to the sixth floor. From there I took a right, and then another right, and the door at the end of the hall was mine; for twenty dollars a day.

I was living by myself for the first time in a hotel. I was as proud as a little kid wearing his first pair of long pants. The managers of the Chelsea—there were four of them—didn't ask me to sign a waiver of responsibility. In the course of my many wanderings, I usually found that doormen and hotel management always imagined me bringing on floods and fires, falling down stairwells...

Here, nobody gave a hoot if I were blind or not. The hotel is so far gone, insurance companies won't even cover it anymore.

I'd never had a chance to visit New York because I had only spent a couple of days there before with Mrs. Hallowe'en, in the Pierre, buried with my tape recorder and radio. While I was stubbing my fingers opening the window in my room, I recognized the smells coming in, thick and maritime, like a shellfish soup seasoned with diesel fuel.

I went back down to the street. On the curb I heard a lot of hooting. I had been noticed, barely missed being run down by an automobile. Little jets of hot steam rose from the basements like boilers on a ship. The mist disappeared in the Atlantic wind coming straight down Twenty-Third Street, the street where my hotel was.

New York is my first European city—Rome doesn't count: there, I was just an invalid in transit; nor did my lightning stopover in Paris count either—a European city to someone who had learned to get around in Los Angeles' desert of automobiles. Here, there were people on the streets, nonstop passers-by; a crowd of extras who might be turning the corner of the street only to resurface behind me moments later after a spin around the avenue.

For the first time—alone with Zita—I was getting around solely on foot. The whole city is meteorological. I can find my way by following the prevailing winds. Manhattan is an island, smaller than Kerkenna; or a boat, with the Hudson and East Rivers parading slowly by, reassuringly, to the right and left at the end of every street. Up in front, where the winds whip in from the open sea where I rode on a boat, clear to the statue slightly off to one side of the prow of this island/ocean liner. The aft, peopled with Blacks, is astern, beyond One Hundredth Street.

I have been going aft up north these last few days. Families were conversing outside, late at night. They were friendly to me, since I said I was Arab. They probably guessed, anyway.

Alone, for almost a whole year; alone as I've never been, even in L.A. It amazes me how I can manage to melt into this crowd so easily. More than anywhere else, I feel free, free to the point that I don't need to test my freedom by taking up where I left off in West Hollywood. Free, because here no one is preoccupied with my blindness. I could walk around naked covered with gold paint without a hitch. Who knows? Maybe there are people doing that all around me. At any rate, no stranger in the night is out to put me in an asylum.

Here recently, I have gotten to know a mixed family of Palestinians and Cubans who run a restaurant on Eighth Avenue, just to the right when I leave the hotel. I have couscous with crayfish there. There are a lot of Arabs in this city, more than anywhere else I've been. But they don't come from North Africa, and I realize they've already lived in big cities like Cairo or Beirut, which I can only imagine. The only Arab city I have seen is Tunis, when I was small.

This city is a boat, and the only people I frequent are the passengers from steerage. An entirely different world from the West Coast elite. I walk along the windy gangways, the avenues, that run parallel to the rivers. A group of Moroccan hippies has just moved in as squatters next door to the hotel. They play music all day long on the stoop of the building they're occupying. They had to take off the boards blocking the doorway to get inside. I have to speak French with them, since they can't understand my southern Tunisian: the French which was my basic language, which Mrs. Hallowe'en found to be the only correct one, which she imposed upon me from a tape recorder. I also speak Italian with the newspaper vendor, and Spanish at the hotel. I have the impression of being in a little Europe, a Europe someone has shaken in a blender.

I can feel the roll of the street that lets me know right away if I'm going toward the front, the rear, or across the boat. The back of the boat is called Uptown because you climb to get there, like to the bridgehouse on a ship. That's where you find the crew; mostly black, as I said.

I heard people say in L.A. that New York was gray. But it's full of the feel of the sea, the sun and spray. If I saw it as being one color, it would be light yellow, like the sun which seems alive in Central Park when the air is very cold. The sun tells me every second whether I'm going uptown or downtown, east or west.

On Manhattan, I don't need to carve out any map, the layout is so simple. The Portuguese guy at the desk downstairs in the daytime explained once how the number system works: the Avenues run north and south; the Streets east and west, and buildings go from zero to one hundred for the first block, and by hundreds more in the following blocks.

A city of mathematicians. I've always really liked figuring in my head. The Portuguese guy is so proud of the fact that only artists live in the hotel. There are thousands of artists here, like this woman living just below me who keeps busy typing between midnight and five o'clock in the morning on her electric typewriter, with occasional time-outs to pour a drink or to curse. Then there's the saxophonist above me, whose voice sounds like his instrument. Or the old hippie next door who doesn't even say hi, and doesn't make any noise at all except sometimes a faint clinking of a little spoon. Or the night visitors who come knocking and knocking on his door, too out of it or too stoned to give up. The employees in the office downstairs are all of different nationalities. They think I'm an artist. I talk about the show I did out on the Coast, without ever specifying what kind of show it was. Surfing already seems so far away, and I've developed a veritable allergy to beauty and wealth. In Los Angeles, I let myself be had by the appearance of the game. In New York, I almost feel at home, and I'm starting to get back into myself.

A self that the summer with Larry has profoundly changed, changed into an intellectual. The winos told me how to find the New York Public Library: the gathering place for all the used and abused people in the city. For the first few months, all I did was stay seated near subway entrances, or in late night coffee shops, listening to little bits of Europe that hardly understood one another. An old Polish baglady talking away with a Filipino vendor, for example, in snatches of English. Here, my freedom rests on what a blind man doesn't notice, or a foreigner either. With my accent and my mistakes in English, I'm as American as any of them, and they ask me for directions, thinking I'm an old-time New Yorker.

The library isn't very far from the hotel. Zita appreciates this little tangent because it takes us near the nice parts of Park Avenue, where cats like her are out cruising around. In the square in front of the library, she meets Persians, Angoras and Siamese. Since Spring she has been loading me up with little fuzzy bastards that I give to the cleaning ladies.

Inside the library, they wanted to kick Zita out. I ended up declaring that under the law of the State of New York, being blind, I was authorized to be accompanied by a guide animal. In all my meetings with judges I'd noticed they always started out with "Pursuant to the law of the State of . . . " The formula was the equivalent of their dignified black robes. I waited on the stairs while they went to consult their superiors. I could hear the voices of some young Blacks around me taking turns saying, "You want a joint, man? Five dollars for three, two bucks a joint. Wanna joint . . . "

The section for amblyopics has individual headphones that allow you to completely isolate yourself while you're listening to cassettes. This winter the only literature accessible to me is on tape. I had never listened to European literature: novels, philosophy: my culture was made up of encyclopedias at the institute and language manuals listened to in hotel rooms in the days of Mrs. Hallowe'en.

Up to then, I didn't have a good idea what a library was for. I'd never read much when I could see on Kerkenna, except my schoolbooks. I've always liked to be read *to*, even if the voice sounds stupid and stumbles through the text. When I eventually learned to decipher the Braille numbers with Larry, I could read aloud, my finger turning into a tonearm pick-up following the grooves of the record before me.

The library taught me silent reading. It's an enormous building in warm marble with resounding stairwells. You could stay for hours without people or librarians bothering you. In the index of the record-and-tape library, there obviously weren't any texts listed in Arabic, except for a selection of Middle Eastern newspapers. But there were two cassettes, one of which was the English translation of a work by the ancient Tunisian historian, Ibn Khaldoun, which I knew about from my childhood. I listened to the other cassette clear to the end because it was listed under "Arabia." *The Seven Pillars of Wisdom*, by Colonel Lawrence.

The section recorded in French was my favorite. The *Fondation La Fayette pour le bien des aveugles*. The texts were read by French actors, and *The Thousand and One Nights* by a woman who hammed up the text. The introduction claimed that the tales had been written by a Frenchman named Galland, when I know they've always been in Arabic.

My first trip through a library was really emotional. Around me, other blind people were rummaging around in the impressive silence. When I removed my headphones, the only thing I could hear was the gentle purring of other cassettes, and behind that, the grumbling of machines. I was encased inside the innards of the boat that is New York. Night must have fallen, and when they threw me out at closing time, I had listened to six cassettes in a row. It was cold, of course, colder than I had ever known; and Zita refused to get down on the ground. But the noises sounded different, stifled. I thought I'd gone deaf, all of a sudden, because of the cassettes, and I dropped Zita, even more terrified than she was. But the city reached through to me dimly, as though the air itself had thickened. I took a step, and felt the horror of a dusty plastic squashing under my foot, making a noise like tearing paper. I stooped down and picked up a little of it. The stuff was cold, like ice cubes in a whiskey, but airborne, light, melting, something like a frozen cotton candy padding. I could have sworn it was alive, moving in my hand as it melted: snow.

I had heard people talk about it, but I had never seen any, except in movies. The snow was burying the square in front of the library, and when I lifted my head I felt the cold brush of a few straggling flakes.

A catastrophe had swallowed up New York while I was reading. All that remained unburied in the entire city was this one library, protected by its mass, which smothered all the noises from the avenue.

The next day I discovered some snow still remained on the ground, and after it froze to ice the snow was transformed from a mysterious carpet into a wonderful way to break a leg. I fell twice, and even Zita scrabbled along the ground as she slid. In Central Park, the sun reflecting off the snow made an efficient mix of warm rays and icy air. The snow, the frozen air, was boiling, vaporizing in the sun without having time to melt. I took off my clothes and started rolling around in the billions of crystals that grazed my skin. A dog, two old ladies, some bicyclists and a lazy policeman made me get dressed again. As far as sighted people are concerned, you don't bathe in snow like you do in water.

I went back to the library every afternoon. I could converse with all the men and women who had written in every past, except mine: Arabic.

I complained to the head librarian about the lack of texts recorded in that language. He told me I was the first blind Arab to ever say anything of it. In general, the Arab immigrants here are not handicapped. He submitted my request to the administrative council, and authorized me to utilize a special service, for which they gave me a card, on which I didn't even know what they had written. It gave me the right to use a machine the library had just acquired. I sat down, and Zita's back went up as she dug her claws into my shoulder, contemplating the machine. I was in front of a big metal desk with a space to the left where I was supposed to place the opened book that I'd asked for. On the right there was a kind of window with a flat surface, like in my digicassette. I touched the screen, and some lines appeared in relief on the spot that before had been perfectly smooth. I explored a little more. Every tiny point that formed the screen was movable, and could go up or down to create depth. I tried to understand the marks, but I finally figured out I must have been between two lines, because there was a big empty zone in the middle.

All you had to do was move the camera on its sliding scale, up over the open book, so that the characters appeared, much enlarged, and in relief. That day I stayed there all afternoon. It was fantastic: now I could read *everything*, all the books, and even works of art; I could even learn about perspective. With a single knock, the doors of the entire cultural universe had opened for me.

From that moment on, I would spend my life in this office, in the welcome hollow core of the library in the midst of the city's murmuring. I rediscovered Arabic characters; I had lied to the head librarian when I told him I could read very well. Just touching them, bringing them out, recognizing them, with all the procession of feelings and images from the past parading by is— it's a joy. I skimmed over treatises on logic and some *falâsifa*, the mystical invocations of the Sufis, and especially poetry: real literature, works in calligraphy. These writers found its essential rareness and had distilled poetry down to the letter. Abou Nawas, Al Moutanabbi, and for me, the master of masters, Aboul Al' Al Maari the blind, the formidable, who wrote upon his own tomb of his birth: "Here lies the product of the blame laid on the shoulders of my father—a fault with which I never burdened anyone . . ."

If poets can stand the rhythm of slow deciphering, of detaching every individual letter, of scrutinizing it, I can scarcely do more than recall them from my old memories of the alphabet, where each letter has its own feel, a poetry which an Arab student would be ashamed of. I was absorbed body and soul in the miracle of this surface, where a trail was being blazed for me as sensitive as the one my feet left in the snow which turned the entire city into a museum of footprints. Only, reading letter by letter I wasn't able to absorb the enormous books written in tiny characters that were reserved for Arabic scholars. Anyway, the machine wasn't designed to accommodate Arab texts. It was made so that the book progresses slowly from left to right, not the other way around.

I've gone on like this for months, while the wad of bills stuffed between the bathroom cabinet and the wall in my room got dangerously smaller, to the point of falling on the floor, which happened yesterday. Every morning, while the snow was melting and Spring eased into Summer, I went to the library, which brought me back to French.

Today, I feel I have become a creature of books. You don't spend a whole year alone on the other side of a page. The Arab-Cubans on Eighth Avenue say I talk like a book. I think you call the result of solitary education an autodidact.

I am an open book. I've read everything in the library written by or about the blind. I am a uniquely open book, without a guide, who's reinventing culture.

In a room devoted to teaching methods, the librarian had me touch an enormous sphere made of bronze. It was a terrestrial globe, taller than I, which had been cast three centuries ago in Europe for the use of those infirm of sight. On its surface I could feel engraved points, which represented cities, and reliefs which were supposed to give the impression of mountains.

Fuzzy, too big, not even spherical to me—was that our globe—a world fabricated by the sighted for the blind people's use? A sphere that is too big to me is a flat surface.

Taking down my discoveries on my digicassette, I understood I had only seen parts of things at the intitute. All this civilization, kept at a distance from the blind.

Two centuries before the advent of the electric Optacon reader that I used, a Frenchman, Valentin Hauy, had the idea of using large characters in relief for the vision-impaired. That book, Hauy's books, had been for the blind, our refuge and consolation, our sole access to humanity. We took our first steps within the little crib of books accessible to us, all chosen by the sighted.

The books printed with the Hauy system disappointed me. The shapes of the characters weren't what I'm used to. Too old, I suppose. There was mainly this one enormous Bible in forty-five volumes, printed in Philadelphia in 1845, with characters in relief too small to be distinguished under the finger.

Summer came. It was cooler within the high walls of the library and along its marble corridors than it was outside. Skimming over characters eroded by time, I discovered a communication I had never experienced. Other blind hands had thousands upon thousands of times read this sign, arduously deciphered this phrase.

Since I began reading I have the impression of aging quickly, of joining an immense sunken continent of blind scholars before me. Since I live alone, communication which I'd possessed in the bodies that caressed me, was refined into caressing signs in relief. Books replaced sex.

A new model of the machine that converts the optical into the tactile arrived at the library. Moved by my devotion, the head librarian let me know I could use it. The principle wasn't any different than on the one I already used. But the stimulators weren't placed beneath one's fingers. I had to sit in a special chair, had to position under my shirt, right onto my skin, a harness armed with these stimulating stimulators. They translate the images and signs into pressure upon my back. The advantage over the earlier model lay in the size of the reading zone. With a fingertip, only a few points could be read simultaneously. I could recognize a design, read several large characters at once on my back. This meant I could become aware of several lines of a text at once, or the general composition of the markings of an engraving.

This exercise on the Optacon enabled me to acquire a sense of simultaneity. And I do mean exercise. I was continually tempted to turn around, to form the idea of the letter or the lines of a drawing behind me, on my back. Progressively, I stopped trying to localize them. Rapid brushing by a multitude of points ends up forming a near image.

Since the end of Spring, the unique exercise of "reading" with the skin of my back was draining me—and transforming me. I became so sensitive in that area that the least stare burned through me, the least contact made me shiver. As the nerves of my back became as sensitive as the bump in the middle of my fingertips, little by little, I had the increasingly absurd impression of being constantly watched. An impression that wasn't to let me go, sticking to me all the way to my hotel room, and which made me unsociable, suspicious.

Illustrations—at last! I pierced the mystery of what, for me, those flat pages without letters were. During the time I used the dorsal Optacon, I pored over a donated brochure that contained engravings with subtitles, telling the story of the benefactors of the blind. The Optacon permitted me to violate the secret of the sighted, to finally know how they were seeing me. This book, of course, was destined for little sighted kids. It was supposed to incite them to pity.

The series of etchings began with a group of blind musicians, at a festival called the Sainte-Ovide. It took me five hours with the help of the inscription to figure it out. It is still engraved in my mind. The musicians wear grotesque costumes too big for them, and big round solid spectacles with no glass in the middle. They're playing a tune they must know by heart, from music stands where the scores are upside down: lighted candles are beside them in full daylight.

In one corner, a gentleman in a buttoned suit and a hat is accosting a little character, a child dressed in rags. The kid is holding out his hand in the drawing, and the gentleman has just placed a round object in it. The orchestra is smaller than the two characters, the effect of what the sighted call perspective.

I had just witnessed the birth of European philanthropy for the blind. The gentleman was Valentin Hauy, who had given his name to that system of characters engraved in relief. The kid was a blind boy by the name of François Lesueur, whom Hauy adopted, and who—by recognizing a gold *écu* by touch—gave him the idea of relief characters.

The text seemed to insinuate that up until then no one had ever thought the blind could be gifted with intelligence. Other gravures showed the young Lesueur at Court with twenty other young blind children, reading from big books using Hauy's system. Still other illustrations showed a carnival float from the Festival of the Supreme Being, celebrated by a French religious sect during the Revolution. A group of blind people was singing a hymn written especially for them. Was the Supreme Being of the blind the same as for the sighted? Or was it the Great Blind One? This question never crossed the minds of the book's authors. As I followed the story of little Lesueur, the origin of philanthropy was revealed to me. It was born from the desire of those who could see to be rid of the sight of the blind. The grotesque orchestra was only there to represent the horror of the spectacle of the infirm, a dishonorable spectacle that had to be abolished. I had already heard this argument on T.V. in Los Angeles. This pervasive philanthropy hid their fears and indiscretions. It built institutions, encouraged the creation of a parallel universe, the universe of Braille, where it shuttered-in all the blind. It required humiliating signs, destined solely for the sighted: the cane, and especially the glasses, the better to hide those sterile eyes. It wished to prohibit them from being seen.

Another gravure showed young Louis Braille, at age fifteen, inventing his alphabet in front of an old soldier with a saber and moustache. The two figures are in front of a booth at an exposition of industrial inventions. The old officer, de la Serre, has invented an "*écriture obscure*," writing with eight points per character—a writing for spies, for use under cover of darkness. Thus, no candles would have to be lighted to give away their position. Louis Braille reduced the character to six points and had the Braille writing adopted by institutions. Those are the prisons I escaped. I can write Braille passably at the moment, although very slowly by hand, from right to left, like I used to write calligraphy at the Koranic school. You have to be able to write it very fast by hand, to be able to read it really well.

No doubt the points are easier to read with a finger than the dashes; but repellent things were also explained to me. If I had read only Braille, all I would have known of the world was what institutions wanted me to know about it. I prefer to spend hours decoding a secret of the sighted than learning a language created for the sole use of my counterparts.

I continued skimming over etchings, maps and photographs. The device with the harness, which gave a good impression of flowing script, transformed photos and paintings into a fog of impressions.

Fortunately, I was taken by another fever: communicating on my own. Since it's more difficult for me to read than to write— which accounts for no novel moving fast enough for me—I began to make intensive use of Larry's digicassette.

I began to write. The heat fermented what was in the garbage cans at the hotel. I don't know if I'm writing for myself or for anyone else. I'm writing with no hope of ever rereading it again, simply to calm my effervescence.

By the end of Spring—three months ago—I thought I was falling ill. I usually have very good health. Winter with no exercise and the New York air made it clear that I have to think about keeping up my strength. They'd be only too happy to get hold of me again, those doctors and judges who must still be on my trail. The symptoms began when I first started thinking I was being continuously observed. The institute's psychiatrist would have been delighted. For eight months now, I have been living on the East Coast, and I've forgotten L.A. But I was carrying within me some unknown weakness, a scar of the images Los Angeles had so fervently pumped into me. Other people's looks must carry an inaudible and unfelt venom which built up inside me. In the West, I lived every day of my life knowing I was being looked over, up and down, appreciated; I molded my posture to that without a thought. A subtle poison which, when it was withdrawn, perhaps made me ill.

I felt alone, yet I still kept trying to get away from imaginary stares, I closed the curtains in my room, made sure the light was turned out. My nervousness, when the nice weather arrived to stay, became an intolerable burning, in my back, in the very spot where I read with the Optacon, the spot where I also felt—even with the harness removed—a permanent stare reading me, without anyone else being with me.

I had to give up reading. My back was becoming covered with blisters. I was thirsty to meet another body. I had read too much, thought too much. I wanted to be like before: a spectacle, a show, unconscious of itself.

This impression of always being seen was ridiculous. I even felt it when I was in bed, where it had driven me to hide. Painfully, I put it up against the freedom that I had felt when thousands of spectators followed me with their eyes in the pool at Marineland. There are two kinds of stares. The intentional one is a single eye you can't put out.

Reading had created a third moral eye for me. I'm speaking of it in the past, because I've rounded the horn. The feeling of being watched never left me. I live with it, as you live with your infirmity. Up against the shyness and closed-in feeling that threaten me, I went once more to the only antidote I know: offering up the spectacle of my blind body. At the time, I thought my uneasiness might come from my being celibate. Since I had been in New York, I'd only had sex with my hand. I thought that might cause me to lose my strength. So, I slept with a girl I picked up in the hotel corridor, not exchanging a single word with her to break the spell. That too-hot night, I was taken to the police station by some subway employees: I'd forgotten to get dressed again before going out of the hotel. Now a Manhattan cop can tell about coming across a blind exhibitionist.

If I've reached a high speed for typing letters and words—the same speed I acquired with Larry for figures—my Braille reading hasn't gotten any better, and doubtless never will. Only Zita, perched upon my shoulder as I'm lining out the words, can see to decode the visual window which seems to be there only to taunt me. I leave it hooked up, and the text speaks line by line, coming out of me with no regrets, parading past, never to return again. Zita licks a paw every time the line jumps with a tiny click, which only she can observe.

If this text has a reader, you have just joined me. You are right here next to me.

Typing letters, I sometimes have the feeling of halfway poking my fingers into another universe, where they become the visible extremities of an entirely invisible body. Fingers striking keys without respite, composing a text that the liquid crystals in the window—otherwise useless—form and reform, form and reform. I write fast, very fast, hundreds of times faster than I will ever read.

Today, September 28th, it's still hot. I won't read any more, because I know our reading limitations now: we, the blind. At the institute, the more gifted ones, those who could read a line with their right index finger and follow another line with their left, never managed to dictate fast enough for the stenos who were also blind. We're condemned to stumble when we read, condemned to write as fast as we think. The library's immense collection of blind people's memoirs reassured me about that. A civilization of the blind would be a civilization of writings, but not of reading; a civilization where thousands of writers are consecrated to a void of thousands of texts without readers, mirrored, echoing cries thrown into a chasm.

I will not go to the library again.

I hardly have any money left. I'm going to start working in a show again, to heal myself. I met a troupe of dancers in the Arab-Cuban restaurant over on Eighth Avenue. Or rather, they met me. Just when I was hunting about feverishly for my fork, surrounded by punk music from the juke-box next to me, I heard a voice so sharp I thought it was a musical instrument asking to sit at my table. He was so tall his voice seemed to be coming from the ceiling. He talked about how tall he was to excuse himself. Being tall is an infirmity, especially in the theatre. They can't put you onstage with anyone else without creating a comic effect; which of course never makes me laugh. I'm rather small, compared to Americans. He knew I had already done some theatre work, because the doorman at the Chelsea and he were good friends, and they had talked about me.

We drank a few beers, and he took me to an ice-cold warehouse at the edge of the river all the way east, where they were rehearsing their show. I didn't understand anything about the staging, the movements, or how he could direct by screaming. It was supposed to be some sort of ballet; all I could do was mutter.

He had me come up to the stage and showed me a few simple dance movements. I began, and then stopped short, because I thought I'd had an accident. I felt heat rising to my face like my veins were about to burst, which made my head spin. They told me I had just blushed.

I blushed that day for the very first time. At Marineland, and in the worst possible sexual situations, I had never felt that way. I didn't find it disagreeable, the blood swelling my facial arteries, the heat radiating from my face. Solitude in the library had left its mark. I had no knowledge of what blushing is: a sign of self-consciousness among the sighted.

They were uneasy, coughing. During a break they told me about the show. They had taken me in and planned to build a show around me. I was a blind dancer, as in real life and behind me were other dancers, picking up my movements; you cannot know if they imitate me or if I imitate them.

During the last ten weeks, I've been practicing like mad. Under my influence, they've changed the music as we went along to more percussive rhythms. I think we're ready, even though I've never studied dance.

They're waiting for me at Phoebe's, a café on the corner of Second Avenue ten minutes from here. Even Zita knows the way. It's right near the theatre where we rehearse. At the other tables journalists and artists they all know call to them to stop over. They make a lively group, always getting up to say hello to a producer, or someone.

The main thing in their business is to talk about a show possibly more than to perform it. I don't listen. They bore me a little. They've guaranteed me fifty dollars per show.

While we wait for the opening, I don't have a cent. The director gives me enough to pay for my room and feeds me along with the others. I'll start earning money again in Europe: we're going on tour. I don't have an idea of what sense sighted people will make of the show. I'm curious about Europe. I've practically forgotten it. I only knew it in flashes, between Kerkenna, America and the institute. I'm going opposite the direction Christopher Columbus took. I've learned everything in America without ever having seen it.

Lamorne

Amar's picture on the cover of that American magazine stands watch above the little school desk where I'm finishing these notes. Down below as a new day dawns, that noise of broken dishes and drunken voices is from my wedding feast.

My marriage: it's already far away, as if someone else's wedding were taking place down there, someone else's empty dress lying outside Alix's office.

How could I have married a man who manipulated my life? I'm looking at this photo Alix hid from me, this magazine Antonio must have brought down from Paris; Antonio who's seeing Malika again. Amar's slightly flexed, tanned legs, his shoulders with muscles puffed out in front.

He's not only blind he's alone, because of me. I just found out that I yanked away the hand that had been guiding him. I'm searching for his troubles beneath the forced smile of his exertions, looking for traces of poor treatment those slavedrivers must have put him through once they had their hands on him, like some animal in a zoo. He's risking his life so he won't die of starvation. All he had was me, and I abandoned him; I've spent all these unconscious years at Lamorne, I who am entirely responsible for his defenseless isolation.

He had just lost his guardian. I was on that San Francisco bridge, he was surrounded by cops, he climbed into their car. The telescope closed off again with an angry clank. I had no more change. I ran, I followed the car which had already reached the toll booth. I ran frantically waving my arms clear to the shoreline, where the bridge access began.

I ran the whole way. I took off my coat because it was so hot. The sun was chasing off huge chunks of fog that hung on the hillsides, and I thought my chest would explode. I saw another police car. I tried to flag it down, but they went by laughing without stopping. I went back across the bridge again to the Presidio, a big park with turns and more turns and wooden houses where soldiers who lived on the base sat in shirtsleeves smoking. They didn't understand anything I said, and kept trying to hug me. It took hours to get back to the hotel. When I arrived, brought back by some officer from the Presidio, Philippe was meditating: He didn't want to budge. He claimed the homeopathic pellets had done me worlds of good, my color was really better: I was on the verge of a nervous collapse. I got into it with every telephone operator in the city trying to find the police station where they had taken Amar. I was just a witness, but at least I could have talked to him, seen him. Philippe had the hotel refuse to connect any more calls for me. Being upset like that was bad for me, nor did he want me calling Paris every ten minutes trying to reach Amar's sisters.

I wanted to go around to every police station and hospital, and—as usual—Philippe ended up giving me a sedative shot. I was burning with fever. I was on the point of getting hold of Amar and he was slipping through my hands. No one wanted to help me. I was in a sweat, biting my sheets.

None of the San Francisco police stations had ever heard of Amar. After three days, a lawyer from the Zen center thought to call the Marin County sheriff. He was the one who had arrested Amar because the northern half of the bridge was under his jurisdiction. Amar had gone off to some institute for the blind. His fate depended upon a judge, whom we telephoned. The judge was very cold. He asked if I was a relative, and like a fool I said no. He asked my name, saying he was going to write to Amar to let him know I wanted to see him. Amar didn't even know my last name. The judge seemed to think Amar should be protected from the people he'd been around the past few years. Only his family could get the institution's address. I gave up and decided to leave a message for him.

The only thing left was for me to go back to Paris, to see his sisters. Philippe wasn't any help at all: he was convinced you shouldn't help patients too much with their obsessions. He ended up buying the plane tickets only because my state of health had become disquieting. So disquieting, in fact, that on the plane they lifted the armrests on three seats to let me sleep.

A succession of lighthouse beacons: a black wall, a white wall. I spent days sleeping in a room at Sainte-Anne, next to Philippe's apartment.

Listening, I became aware of the gravity of my situation. It's true he didn't know I could hear everything. My ears became loudspeakers, painful with fever: I was in danger of dying.

The minute the fever was down, I went out trying to find Malika, but Malika was traveling and Amar's sisters refused to answer my calls and wouldn't open their door. I came back from these errands even more run down by fever. Philippe had me completely confined. I thought I was going to die when, as a last resort, he suggested I go with him to Lamorne for a few months.

It had been a custom for years between Philippe and I to say that I was "too nervous" or "tired." We avoided the word "ill." This time I was so sick, the name Lamorne gave me a little hope. Very carefully, by slipping into resignation, Philippe exhausted my resistance. The unfortunate coincidence of the accident on the bridge was a warning to me: I was putting a jinx on Amar. To find him again, I first had to find myself. I couldn't be the least use to him—lost in a hostile America—if I wasn't capable of governing myself. Pale and silent, nearly unconscious, I accepted the trip to Lamorne.

To those who frequented the psych wards of the early Seventies, Lamorne was the Ritz. I didn't know what the place looked like: I imagined a family of artists in front of a château surrounded by green lawns. Following all the events that had occurred, my transfer to Lamorne was inevitable. I'd become too unmanageable for Sainte-Anne. I was spying on the other patients and male nurses in the bathroom; making holes in the walls.

Philippe dragged me off in a taxi to fill out the papers necessary for my transfer and to buy me enough clothing to wear, since I'd left my bag in the San Francisco hotel. Everyone said Lamorne was very chic, very intellectual. Philippe wrapped me up in a blanket and put me on the train, first-class, to Orléans and I woke up with the conductor shaking me. In my dream, he had just replaced a cop in an American uniform like those who'd taken Amar away. To get to Orléans, I had to change trains in Les Aubrais. The conductor led me by the arm, like I wasn't even capable of walking, over to the "shuttle" as he called it. He had barely gone back to his train when I got off the connection thinking I was already at Lamorne. I walked into the countryside around the station—an industrial zone in the middle of some fields. It was muggy; a gray sun was somewhere under the clouds. To the right and left of the road, prefab buildings sent white light back at me. Workers were coming out of the buildings: their shift was over, they had lunchboxes in their hands.

Most were Arabs. I watched them go past, one by one, not listening to their smart remarks, staring at them, at their wrinkled, cracked faces. I started yelling back at them, asking what they were jabbering about, then everything began to spin, and the next thing I knew I was in a police car which was slowing down and all I could hear was the siren on the roof. Instead of the gray entrance to Sainte-Anne, a white château at the end of a long lawn rose in front of the headlights: Lamorne.

As soon as the cops helped me out of the car, I went straight for the steps of the château. I was weaving a bit and some young guy with long hair in a black polo shirt ran after me. He had just signed the cops' papers. He held me by the arm and pointed out a brick building under the trees. I told him I wasn't about to sleep in any stable. Then I felt weak. He carried me inside like a package and put me to bed.

Months passed in a delirium. Philippe appeared on the painted wallpaper of the room, deformed, monstrous. It was a mansard attic room with exposed beams, very pretty, very provincial. I was so exhausted I couldn't answer him. He stayed to hold my hand. The seasons passed. A long time afterward, I was looking at the window and the sunlit forest through half-closed eyes. I felt less out of sorts, so I got up. What I had taken to be a window was only a spot of sun upon the wallpaper. Coming through the real windows, from across the Spring landscape, were voices below me, and I saw a group which included Philippe, some women in tailored suits, some young girls who must have been nurses, the young guy who had changed out of his polo shirt, and some other blond guy with a moustache. They looked more like students than doctors. A white Mercedes screeched up and a thin young character with tortoise shell glasses and brushed back hair got out, like some devilish jack-in-the-box. He began to hug everybody, making quick gestures with his hands as he walked up toward the château: Alix.

Alix was head doctor at Lamorne. Philippe told me he had just returned from some congress in the Philippines: he would introduce me to Alix as soon as I could be up. The following week I was up. I began calling Paris again from the phone in the entrance to the building. I got hold of Malika, who acted very coldly to me. She hung up almost right away. As for Amar's sisters, it was impossible to talk with them: an Arab man's voice refused to call them to the phone. It was as though I had the plague, as though they'd found out about my role in his accident on Kerkenna.

I took one last plunge into despair and began crying at breakfast. It was the first time I was breakfasting in the dining room, at least in the front part of the dining room. A machine boiled water, and people made themselves toast and jam and went to sit anywhere, out on the lawn, out in the sun.

I was moving around; I was living, but my body felt bizarre. I wasn't unhappy, but completely flat, warming myself in the sun, not thinking about anything. I refused to talk, made as few waves as possible. It was painful. I would look at my hands, my feet, as if they were far away, hunks of rock stuck onto my body that I was forced to drag around. I didn't wash. I only dressed in a robe. The very sight of others was disagreeable to me. I wouldn't meet their looks; I didn't want anything to do with them. I could only look at faces on the sly, in secret. Seeing eyes was . . . I couldn't stand it! Deprived of my obsession, I began to doubt that Amar had ever existed, and I drowned myself in clouds as winter rain beat against the château: my second winter at Lamorne.

Spring came again. I would eat my little plate of food beneath the trees, in my own little corner as usual, a habit I thought would be eternal, until I didn't have any teeth, any hair, anything.

For the first time, someone tried to get into a conversation with me. Or at least I realized it for the first time. He had this one peculiar habit: he would talk to me and look somewhere else. He wanted to know if I felt less tired. And—miracle—I understood him, could talk to him. It brought tears to my eyes. He noted with a detached air that in his opinion the stew had certainly been well salted—just like that—and advised me to eat the meat and leave the vegetables. When I tasted it he smiled, and with a gesture that took in all the patients eating: "Meat for one and all, in the middle of the war ... it's marvelous, no?"

He was fat, well-dressed, with a rust colored suit and a red tie—all wrinkled. He told me his name was Monsieur Rodolphe and that I should come see him in his office. Sure enough, there was a plaque on a little office marked "M. Rodolphe, Assistant Medical Chief." The door didn't open. It was glued onto the wall: The Assistant Chief was set up in front of it, not inside. He brought me out of my slump. I didn't even know the layout of the grounds. I'd never been beyond the path between my room and the dining room. Strolling around the grounds with him meant perpetual amazement at every auto, at every bush and flower in the garden. When we walked even further, I was blown away by the most ordinary, dusty grocery and tobacco shop window displays, lost in the surrounding countryside. All this merchandise in the middle of a war, he commented. Monsieur Rodolphe's entire family had bought the farm the same day, killed by the last American bombardment at Boulogne-Billancourt.

It was Alix who told me Monsieur Rodolphe's story. I had finally gotten to know Alix. He had a real office—a big white room with couches of fake white leather filled with little plastic balls that crunched beneath me. The mantlepiece was white marble; the carpeting was white plush. If he could have, Alix would have had white wood burning in the fireplace.

Since I'd started talking again—since Monsieur Rodolphe had begun taking me on long walks around the country—Alix took an interest in me. The château was smack dab in the middle of crazy country. *Burdins*, the local people called them. I don't know why they were all concentrated there. Maybe there are a lot of drunks in that region. Other patients came from Paris, and had been put there because cow country is supposed to be good for them. There were two little towns, one to the north with a psychiatric hospital for men, another for women south of the château; all along the big road linking them, the *burdins* walked hand in hand, unpredictable. They all wore blue pilgrim's capes and smiled angelically at passing cars from toothless mouths, with little nods of their trembling chins. They weren't especially old, but they all seemed pretty vegged-out to me. They were public assistance patients, and the "residents" from Lamorne looked down on them because they weren't even schizophrenic ... just simple idiots and alcoholics. They were everywhere, even at night, in the most secluded hideaways, walking like spectres along the ditches, dark blue butterflies in the headlights' glare.

All these people walked, walked, all day long. I too started walking. Monsieur Rodolphe said we were on an inspection tour, and the *burdins* believed us, because they couldn't tell the difference between us and real doctors.

This region is in the center of France. Just think, all the crazies in the country are bunched up here to profit from the calm of the Loire. So Lamorne was surrounded by this crazy country, which knocked down property values and allowed them to put up patients in big buildings they bought for a song.

Every evening on the banks of the canals, you could hear music floating up from transistor radios, which the *burdins* all carried around. At twilight time, dozens of blue pilgrims' capes, their little box radios in their hands, came back to the farms where they lodged.

Certain ones would plaster themselves against the bars of the gates in front of the château each evening, drooling over the spectacle of our meal. Others would take their places along the road, transistors in hand—transistors the local shopkeepers sold at three times their price, because the *burdins* didn't have any idea of value. They carried on conversations with telephone wires, which they seemed able to overhear. They all became quiet, bowing low whenever I approached, then began talking again to themselves furiously, as if interrupted, as soon as I had passed.

While I was out walking, I noticed that the whole population lived off the crazy people—those in Lamorne as well as those on public assistance. Especially the farmers who, according to Alix, made fifty francs a day per *burdin* to lodge them in some pigsty which had been crudely repainted and barely furnished with a hanging, electric lightbulb. Unlike the inhabitants of Lamorne, the *burdins* were lodged by local residents, following an old custom of the area. From time to time they would commit a murder or rape. The inhabitants never got all worked up about it, because they all lived off the *burdins*, shopkeepers as well as the others.

To appease their uneasiness or to make the countryside move, be it ever so slowly, they spent their lives walking non-stop. To stay quiet, to be shut up inside four walls, would have been death. I felt myself becoming like them. The *burdins* were my border-line, a vision of what I might become. Thanks to Monsieur Rodolphe, who'd had the idea of showing them to me, I could remain on the other side of the château fence, among those with interesting conversational maladies. The *burdins* weren't all idiots, but I heard the shop ladies' laughter when in a funny trembling voice they would give the butcher orders for the peasants where they were living. And they would walk away with "two outta' five." Five steaks, two of them from scraps. Two "*burdin* specials."

The peasants' little girls would play with them, pinching them and giving them nicknames, since they often lived just on the other side of the walls of their bedrooms. They were hardly more than animals, but even so they were less unhappy than the old vegetables at Sainte-Anne. Hanging around Monsieur Rodolphe, I was reassured every day that I wasn't quite at that point yet. When Alix had started his clinic—buying the château with the inheritance from his father's chocolate factory just after the war—Monsieur Rodolphe had been his first patient. For twenty-five years he'd been a pillar of the household. He had known the hard times when Social Security didn't want to reimburse Lamorne because of Alix's nonconformist methods. When I asked Alix about the comedy of a fake office, he let me know that all the offices were fake, except his. In fact, nothing would have stopped Monsieur Rodolphe from really being the director if it weren't for the fact that the S.S. simply doesn't like changes of status. He would have made a really good manager. All he ever thought about was putting in supplies. He even attended the clinic staff meetings.

Monsieur Rodolphe had begun my cure. Alix wanted to finish it.

To Alix, Monsieur Rodolphe was nearly a guarantee. His presence was a permanent warning that sometimes doctors are crazy too. Near the end of this second year at Lamorne, Alix often spoke to me with an open heart. His plan was to have everyone participate in running the clinic. If he could have gotten away with it, all the patients would have been part of the administrative council. I pointed out that I didn't see why the S.S. would pay if there was no difference between crazy people and doctors. About then, Monsieur Rodolphe took me to visit a big rock with a hole in it, at an intersection about ten kilometers from the château. It was a "*déburdinoir*," very well-known in the area, a curiosity from the Middle Ages: a big millstone, with a hole as big as a head in the middle, you could see the sky through. In olden days, crazy people used to stick their heads inside—and were cured.

Without a moment's hesitation I stuck my neck into the opening. The rock was cold and humid, and it seemed as though I was in a guillotine. I didn't feel a thing, but I was cured. On the way back to the château, I decided to tell my life story to Alix, which didn't happen right away. Once I was face to face with him, I didn't know how to start, and he began to tell me his story again, because equality required that patients know as much about his life as he did about theirs.

Philippe was coming down every weekend from Sainte-Anne, and he was delighted to see that my speech had returned. When I compared him to Alix, I couldn't help but find Alix more amusing. Alix talked fast, answering the phone and wiping his glasses at the same time. He was more direct; Philippe would get all mixed up and chew on his moustache. Alix dressed in a deerskin jacket and Italian moccasins, while Philippe always showed up wearing his dead-leaf threadbare suits from *Samaritaine*. Alix's hands always gestured, while Philippe's were clammy and still. With his black hair brushed back and his Fifties style, Alix looked a little like Arthur Miller. Philippe, pardon my saying so, looked like a wet cocker spaniel.

Alix finished telling me the story of the clinic and Monsieur Rodolphe. Without alluding to the fact that I had stayed so many months without speaking a word, he asked me incidentally, as if he'd just noticed my presence, why I was there. By habit, I turned toward Philippe. In front of Alix, he was like a bird facing a snake, silent, completely fascinated. All of a sudden, like a sink that's just become unstopped, I began to talk, telling him about my past, all of it jumbled out of order. Alix coughed and suggested I start over again—from the beginning.

Whenever I was speaking with Philippe, I've always had the

impression of talking us into a swamp, where he and I were constantly losing our footing. Alix didn't seem like a doctor, at least not like a psychiatrist. He was open-minded.

I stretched out on the sofa and felt more relaxed. Alix had Philippe leave on the pretext of welcoming a new patient. He walked around his office and sat near me. I could smell mint aftershave lotion. I realized Philippe had already told Alix about my past. He already knew me pretty well—my family, my life in Paris—and I said to myself that I was a part of Lamorne's society now, and that he was getting ready for me to stay a long time—a real long time.

At Lamorne, there weren't patients; there were only "residents," Alix said. Just like at the *Comédie Française*.

Later, when I was explaining that I had no intention of spending my entire life in insane asylums, Alix described Lamorne as a little society which wanted nothing more than better exchanges, on both sides of the bourgeois barrier between patients and doctors. His hands were cold, then nervous, as he tried to prove his point on the abolition of barriers to me.

We had two or three discussion-sessions per week, sometimes with Philippe joining us. Alix suggested that I might easily become a monitor at Lamorne, that I had a warm secure future awaiting me. No one had ever offered me work in a psychiatric hospital before, and I thought it was rather nice. As a reward, when he started to unbutton his fly while he petted my little pussy I let him get away with it. Then I gave him a tap on the noggin and left.

I discovered all the activities that made up Lamorne—a real Club Med, outstanding in its field: horse riding in the park, a minibus service to go to town, an open air theatre where monitors organized shows.

The monitors were young longhairs who did the typing and filing in another building and kept to themselves all day, except when it came time for their shift. It seems they were afraid of the patients.

No one had real names at Lamorne. People knew each other only by first names like Alix, or last names like Monsieur Rodolphe. No one knew Alix's last name. As for me, who had always refused to answer to my official first name, I found this

way of doing things rather to my liking. They had accepted
Andréa without running off to find my identity card.

I described to Alix my meeting with Amar, the accident, how
his family now refused to help me get back in touch with him. As I
unfurled my tale, I realized how absurd it was of me to have kept
Amar's sisters from knowing that I knew their brother. I had
hidden it simply because I considered myself guilty; but by hiding
that, I revealed it too. While I was talking to Alix and Philippe
was taking notes, I understood how I had put myself into such an
impasse, acting as though I were guilty, yet without admitting
anything. The first time I saw Amar again I should have gone and
spoken to him as if nothing was wrong. Maybe he'd even
forgotten me, or forgiven me, if he ever even knew my part in it
all.

I pondered for a long time and told them they had no right to
analyze me together. It was against all the rules. Alix wasn't
bothered. Unlike my analysis with Philippe, where I'd spend an
hour being silent, here I was having solid discussions, yelling to
interrupt them. It was a council of war held on the subject of the
inside of my head.

They wanted to know everything about my parents, my
brothers and sisters, the dirty things I did when I was a little girl.
They had blood samples taken where they found a natural L.S.D.
Alix asked me to talk about all my lovers—that really seemed to
turn him on.

Alix had caught on that I was fascinated by Arabs, he decided
I was persecuted by them. I protested. I've never slept with a
single Arab.

I caught on really quickly to the fact that Alix never
pronounced Amar's name, as though he had put it in parentheses.
In the Spring, when I got to the part about the bridge in San
Francisco which I didn't recall precisely, they decided to try
hypnosis on me. Alix held a silver ball on a thread. When I came
to, my arms were still stretched out in front of me, like in a dream,
pushing something out of my way. I didn't know what I'd
admitted under hypnosis. Alix and Philippe were holding a secret
meeting from which I was excluded.

They gave me formal notice that I must give up my "myths."
That's what they called Amar. They had decided not to believe in
his existence. As far as my meeting and running after him went,

forget it, all "myths."

Deeply troubled by Alix's apparent good faith, I wavered. I hadn't invented Amar, but neither of them had ever seen him. He was only a symbol in my battle with myself, in my determination to make myself unhappy, to be at fault. I would become Alix's wife.

From the very beginning of my analysis, I'd become a personality at Lamorne. Alix parceled out his other patients to his assistants to personally treat me. After a while, the visitors—intellectuals from Paris in duffle-coats and deerskin jackets, movie people, other doctors—who came to spend a weekend with the crazies, really took me for a member of the staff. Alix had me undergo a strictly controlled medication cure, which made my past and my passion for Amar somewhat unreal to me. One day I met Antonio who'd come with a group of anarchist visitors to store bombs in the clinic basement. I didn't have anything to say to him. Alix locked him up to question him about me. I didn't attach the slightest importance to it. I wanted to reorganize my life, to erase once and for all this stupid drama I had myself made. I taught Rock steps to all the monitors who went dancing in the Paris clubs on Friday evenings. I had been made a weekend monitor.

Some time after my hypnosis, Alix showed me an article he'd done for a psychiatric review which was all about me: he had this Dada idea that war syndromes went on and on. I was supposed to be a belated victim of the Algerian war, along with some Japanese lost on island in the Pacific who think they're still at war with the Americans and, of course, Monsieur Rodolphe.

The article ended with "To be continued." To cut the ground out from under Alix's feet, I decided to prepare the continuation with my own little story myself, which I'm writing this very minute, the first part of which I'd written right after the San Francisco episode. I didn't start to work on it right away. I wanted to go over my recollections first. I had a hunch that in Alix's explanations, some camouflaging was going on. Today, I know exactly where; so I'm writing to balance out his lies.

Alix was becoming more and more forward, caressing my breasts and bottom while we talked. At the same time he was making little signals to Philippe, who thought I was going to break my vow to never sleep with my psychiatrist. Like all intellectuals, Alix was degenerate enough that it would have been fine with him if all three of us slept together.

I began to talk about leaving. I'd had enough of this farce. I didn't want to be sick anymore. Alix and Philippe were alarmed. They were in the middle of a big book based on my case, and at all costs needed me there to finish. They'd charted out an evolutionary curve over the years. My decision to leave was a catastrophe they wouldn't underwrite.

That's when Alix proposed to me. As he said, it was the most practical thing to do. I was surprised and flattered, but I hesitated. It was the first time anyone had proposed marriage to me. I was afraid I'd regret it if I said no, so I said yes.

I went to phone the news to my mother, who never thought I would marry a real gentleman. All the residents and monitors offered me a bouquet. Alix's former wives—some were those doctors in tailored suits I had seen—came by to congratulate me. They mentioned in passing how much alimony Alix was sending them, and told me to be sure to go over the marriage contract with a fine-toothed comb.

Alix would just as soon have married me in secret, stopping off at the town hall one day when we were shopping in Orléans; dressed in civilian clothes, in a civil ceremony. I had always told my family I'd be married in white, and I demanded a wedding all in white even though I wouldn't invite my brothers, just to piss them off. Alix's Italian parents were delighted, and they came over from Padua. I ordered a bridal gown from Orléans, and the patients decorated the château with white ribbons and bouquets of plastic orange blossoms.

When we got back from the town hall, Alix lit up a little cigar and said quite satisfied, that henceforth we would always stay together, all three of us, right Philippe?

Philippe said yes, sounding very touched. He had just asked to be transferred to Lamorne. He seemed to think that he'd married me by proxy.

It all came to a head that afternoon when Alix fucked me. Philippe didn't want to leave the room. We had to throw him out; he was furious and disappeared somewhere to go sulk.

At the château, everyone assembled on the lawn. Monsieur Rodolphe gave the welcoming speech in the name of the residents, wishing us long years of happiness without food rationing. The monitors gave Alix a special copy of his *Review*, with the articles by him on me. Half the residents' band was playing the trumpets fanfare from Aïda, the other half "Happy Birthday to You," and one resident wearing a red sweater and excited by the festive atmosphere was singing The Internationale. The monitors had made a while bathtub full of punch that they surrounded with gold paper. They set it on fire and passed out paper cups to everybody, despite Alix's objections. Don't think the residents didn't rush right over.

We dined at a huge table in the courtyard under the trees, and even though Alix had forbidden serving wine because of the residents, the longer the meal went on, the more exicted they became. By dessert, several patients had begun, each in his own way, to refute Alix's theories by smearing their faces with whipped cream or soaking their pricks in condiments. Not counting some who were bleating over the leg of lamb bone saying "baa, baa," others were hiding under the table because the fruit salad refused to speak to them.

Everyone had dressed in white, just as I'd asked. The only white clothes at Lamorne were medical smocks, which no one ever used, kept in a closet in case of an inspection. All the guests looked like nurses or doctors unless they were simply going Roman, wrapped up in sheets.

I turned to my husband. He wouldn't stop humming Philippe's name. See, Alix was acting really strange himself. He kept trying to eat his fork and knife, using the chicken wing and drumstick as utensils. And he had started on this discourse that no one was listening to, proposing that henceforth, the doctors would be elected by the patients. I started feeling faint myself around sunset. I heard the voice of one monitor—the one with a big black beard. He was laughing so hard, he was holding his sides, telling Alix that the entire pharmacy had been ripped off, and poured into the punch by Monsieur Rodolphe. Alix scrambled to his feet screaming and shot away from the table holding his hand in front of his mouth to find the john. I shook my maids of honor, but one—a Japanese monitor—was trying to eat the cake with bread sticks, and the other, a Ph.D. who'd married Alix once upon a time, could only yell out the amount of her alimony as the rest of the table fell apart.

I got up to join Alix and grabbed hold of the tablecloth.

Someone had my sleeve. I turned, furious. Philippe: he'd reappeared, pale, his moustache standing on end. He was the only one who hadn't drunk the spiked punch. I had forgotten about him since the scene that afternoon. He'd boycotted the party out in the barn, covering his ears. Straw was sticking out of his suitcoat pocket. He was trembling and there was a tear in his eye: he was jealous.

He wasn't jealous of Alix—he was jealous of me. He interrogated me in a strange, strained voice. How was Alix? Was he big? Was I satisfied? I had really played my cards just right, hadn't I?

He'd thought we were going to play *ménage-à-trois* even in bed. His limp body jumped in spasms of sorrow. He was the turkey in the farce. No one wanted to sleep with him. Despite the drugs, I was very cold. The fasting shrink was stepping out of his role, crumbling to pieces right in front of my eyes. I was more lucid than he. I pushed him away, a bit too brutally. He stuck to me; his tears were glue and his sadness, putty.

As the blood rose in his face he became aggressive, with a spitefulness long-hidden under his easygoing manner, the spitefulness of a raging queen. I looked at him, agape. A metamorphosis: the good little poodle was now a rabid greyhound bitch.

I made him repeat his insinuation: I didn't understand. He said through his teeth that a murderess had better think of the police first before deciding to chase off someone who'd served her ten years and had his friend stolen away. I thought he was talking about Kerkenna. I wasn't even convinced anymore that I was responsible, not for the time being, at least. And anyway, I hadn't killed Amar. He dotted my "i's" for me. Under hypnosis I'd admitted to murder. You couldn't lie under hypnosis. Was I really so stupid that I'd never felt the incredible nature of a coincidence like that on the bridge? Had I come onto that scene just at the right moment strictly by chance?

The whole scene came back to me in a flash, like before my big fever: a whirlpool of space between the truck and trailer, the thin old fragile shoulder bones cracking almost under my hands, the whooshing of this unbelievably light thing in the wind smashing off the bumper of the truck, a bouncing ball of reddish rags flying across the railing. I held my head in my hands, as that horrible half-plucked giant chicken held a drumstick in its hand, giving me the eye from the back door of the truck.

Philippe always said he had never believed in Amar; Alix had nearly convinced me that I was a victim of autointoxication. Pushed to the limit, Philippe was giving me the final word in their conspiracy. There had been a crime, and the only witness was blind. They'd decided to bury the whole business in the secrecy of their office, for me and for them: Alix to make me his wife, and Philippe out of friendship for us both.

Philippe collapsed sobbing into the dessert, begging me to forgive him for the harm he'd just done me, bellowing that he'd betrayed the Hippocratic oath. He was calling Alix with a voice so heartrending that he came out of the toilet, wiping his mouth, still weaving on his feet.

I went into the château, struggling and yelling at all those birds around me whose piercing cries were really getting to me. I wanted them to shut up! I passed in front of Alix's office, and went in to rest a minute. On the desk I saw a magazine, half-hidden under the leather pad. On the cover was that photo across from me now, the photo of Amar in red swimming trunks, on a surfboard, an enormous greenish wave reaching up behind him, captioned "THE BLIND SURFER." I tried to read the article, but my eyes wouldn't focus. I didn't understand where the picture had been taken, I didn't understand the text. One piece of evidence was slapping me across the face: in his pique of jealousy, Philippe hadn't made up anything. Alix was keeping from me that he knew Amar existed, that he'd picked up his trail. I was his protector's murderess: I had pushed the old lady under the truck. He didn't want me to find out. For more than two years, Amar had been without protection and it was all my fault.

Down below, in a moment of lucidity Alix locked the big gate and threw the key over the wall. Finally, he'd shut off the electricity by taking out all the fuses. I found Philippe with him in his room, their lips locked together, spit running down Philippe's moustache and Alix's glasses. Alix got up and tragically declared that he loved Philippe.

That scene took place two hours ago, in the early morning. I asked for five thousand francs a month alimony, plus ten thousand in advance. I decided to get a divorce. He was so afraid I'd go spreading around that he's homosexual, that he accepted right away. I was sorry I didn't ask for more. I asked what was going to become of their book, but they'd decided to change the subject to "Love Relationships Between Analysts."

I'll be catching the train for Paris in a little while. I just phoned the place where Amar was working in Los Angeles, from the phone number in that magazine. It's daylight over there now. The clinic will pay for the call. The operator at the place switched me over to the dolphin section where I got hold of an old man who speaks Spanish, and he told me Amar wasn't working there anymore. Since I had learned a little Spanish with Carmen, I asked where Amar had gone to. He didn't want to say and the clicks of the telephone meter were counting off silence. I had the bright idea to tell him I was Amar's sister, so then he talked a little more. Amar was in New York, in a hotel called the Chelsea. I'd always thought Chelsea was in London.

What a mistake to think he was an invalid!

I'm ending my thirteenth week in New York, picking up these notes where I left off at Lamorne. I've just reread them. I came here thinking I would be indispensable to Amar, that I was responsible for whatever happened to him. I saw myself as Antigone, guiding him my whole life.

Amar doesn't need anyone. I'm not here for him, but for myself. He doesn't even know I exist. I live with him without him knowing it. The first few days, I would hold out my arm to help him every time I'd pass him in the hotel. I stopped my gestures in time, before he could catch on. I need him. It's better if he never remembers my existence; he has so much to forgive me for.

I came back to America myself, no medicine, and no one here to suspect that I was just getting out of the twilight zone. Ever since I've slept with Amar my attacks have stopped. I speak very little, I dress in jeans and a black pullover sweater and I've cut my hair, which makes me look a little older. After all, I'm a divorced, respectable, woman.

It's so cold even my periods are late. I'm in New York, in a landscape of flat tarred roofs and water tanks that you can see from Sabine's window, with the Empire State Building lit with colored lights.

Sabine is my French friend, the only one I run around with here. I live three floors above Amar. I speak only French and haven't learned a word of English. Alix has started paying alimony by wire to my mother, who forwards it here with little comments written on the stubs. She can't deal with my broken marriage. I don't want to give my address to Philippe and Alix, because it would be just like them to come and get me. They agreed they would do everything for the divorce by mail.

I arrived at Kennedy airport at the end of Spring with only a canvas bag so the immigration officers kept me a long time. When I came outside, it was already late at night. I didn't understand a thing about the taxi system. One took me by force. The driver was Polish and spoke Italian and wanted me to be Swedish because of my hair—I, who detest Nordics. I said "Chelsea," to him. I thought it was really well-known. We got to an intersection of big avenues with towers at the end, and he showed me a street and asked, "*Quello?*" I didn't know what to say. He took me in front of a big building, I paid and went into this enormous marble entry hall. The man at the desk was dead drunk and asked for my card. I didn't understand which card he meant, but he didn't insist and gave me a key for the eighth floor.

In the room, I figured out that I wasn't in a hotel—not even an American one—but in some kind of gigantic youth hostel. On the roof was a pool and a bar; the tennis courts were on the ground floor. Thousands of young *nanas* like me from every country in Europe were holed up in that hostel.

Across from my bed, on the other side of the street, was a building like a fortified castle, or at least a brick apartment building made to look like a castle with red paint slapped onto its facade. I could see a sign from my window and leaned out to read it. I saw the famous metal stairways along the front that are a specialty here. The sign said "Chelsea Hotel."

I almost went back downstairs to have them cancel my room, but they'd made me pay twelve dollars in advance, and I didn't want to lose it. I looked up at the facade. Only a few windows were lit up, which isn't surprising, since it was four o'clock in the morning. I had never looked at windows so much, lit up at night like that.

One window was his.

I didn't think about it right away. I heard a cat meowing and climbing, running along the horizontal lines the folded-up fire-escapes make on the building. She went past, up above the hotel sign almost level with me, looking for a male, and I recognized her: the feline beast that accompanied Amar in Paris.

She went in one of those guillotine windows that was slightly open. I went onto the fire escape on the side of my building and walked straight ahead so that I could be across from and a little above his window. And I saw him stretched out in bed.

He was sleeping with his eyes open and the light was turned on. He was paler, thinner than in the magazine photo and shadows gave him an enormous mouth which opened and closed a little as he breathed. Since the street was so wide, I couldn't see all the details of his face, but there was no doubt: it was him all right. I was interrupted in my contemplation by a voice behind me—the guy whose window I was standing in front of. He opened it, and I went in. He was a student from Holland. He laughed and agreed to swap rooms with me, even though this part was reserved for guys. He had a master key for the door that connected the two sections on each floor. From that day on I have never stopped observing Amar: his face, his hands, especially his eyes.

They are sand and lichen in the morning when the sun climbs above the big bridge leading to Brooklyn, and the moist street odors rise. They're the color of the North Sea when it rains on the tar-covered terraces and blue canvas awnings. Come sunset on the big west river, and they're dark green, flecked with gold. But at night, they become a phosphorescent milky blue, almost like the eyes of his cat.

I've gone over them a hundred times with binoculars. I'm certain. In the dark, above the wrought iron stairs on the red brick building lit up by a hotel sign, his eyes send out a faint glow of light. Most people, I suppose, take it for reflections. But I know it's luminescence, coming from inside.

From the "Y" I had a perfect view. He never closed his curtains. Daylight doesn't keep him from sleeping. Even when he is sleeping, he often keeps his eyes open, humid and luminous in the tranquil room.

His eyes don't speak to me, but they send me emotions. Not ideas, or things that you see—only colors—colors he does not know. Colors and feelings.

He lives alone fortunately. From the window of the "Y," thanks to the binoculars, I tried to imagine I was shortening the distance; that I was in the room beside him. Another person living in his room would have noticed me.

So I slept with him after all these years, almost by accident. The act didn't have the importance I'd thought it would. I saw the beginnings of his moustache, and a little tattoo I hadn't known about in the hollow of his chest. The color of his skin had changed too. It was deep brown in the photo, like on Kerkenna. Here, getting paler, it became a drab olive with hints of green. His curly hair, his lashes, his long brows became even blacker, and two creases are forming at the corners of his mouth which he almost always keeps closed, except when he's asleep.

He hardly ever makes love. I've seen him come back with girls who live in the hotel, like that horrible nag with a pony-tail who's always typing on her machine, sitting in a lotus position on the carpet of her room just below his. He doesn't do anything with them. Wrapped up behind the curtain, I wait for them to leave. I'm the only one who's slept with him.

Sabine pushed me into his arms. I knew her from Paris but I never would have recognized her. I'd met her ten years ago. One morning shortly after I'd arrived, I went up to the pool at the "Y." I'd just gotten up. I didn't go in swimming. Just seeing the rain outside on the terrace sent shivers up and down my back. Someone was swimming early, making a lot of noise, smacking hands and feet against the water. She dove in one more time with a big splat and finally dried off, exercising as she moved away.

I was the only other living soul there. She came beside me and spoke English. I answered in French and we realized we even knew each other. We'd met at a party at Marie-Flor's, years before May '68. Sabine lives at the Chelsea almost all the time. She goes out every day to roller skate with some Blacks who carry big transistors on their shoulders, far away on the other side of the bridges. She's tall and dark, has saggy breasts and wrinkles at the corners of her eyes, and a red nose due to cocaine. She gets her tan from a lamp and lots of sports. She doesn't drink, and she's very well-preserved. I went with her, in her bathrobe across the street in the rain. We went up to her place on the top floor of the hotel, so I could give her news about the women in Paris: she meant the feminists I hardly knew.

So I went to her place for a drink and when I left, three hours later, it was to go get my bag at the "Y" and take it to her apartment at the Chelsea.

It's all white and there are three phones in the kitchen alone. She spends all her time on the phone, either answering that someone is on the other line, or else saying that she isn't there. I stay next door in the living room because she has a huge, very private apartment atop the hotel. In the big room: seven movie projectors, three placed next to each other on the sofa. All over the walls little pieces of film are hung up everywhere on nails as well as yellow and red film leader.

She pays her hotel bill by making a current-events film every month called "The Chelsea News," made up of interviews of personalities who live at the hotel—Brazilian punk singers, or homosexual poets. She gives news from each floor, the construction work, any attack or rape in the hallways. She shows the film in the bar downstairs. From time to time she throws in some porno, at an extra charge. She can't stand the French in New York, who always think they're on top of everything. I don't give a hoot what goes on in New York.

Sabine claims I'm starting to look like Amar, that I've taken to walking like him and, ever since the day he had a fever, I have chills and nausea. She comes back to the apartment with Puerto Rican guys who wear body-molded sparkly tee shirts, and bitches about my lack of imagination, my getting stuck on a Tunisian in New York. Since I slept with him, everything sexual leaves me completely indifferent. Apparently it doesn't do anything for him either. I try to be as far away as he is from my own image, to not feel any emotion if someone talks about my body. Sabine sometimes sighs looking at him, and says we'd make a lovely couple.

The first day I was at her place, she said why didn't I come to snort a little coke in a quiet room on the ground floor with her and the hotel bookkeepers. Coming back in the elevator we found ourselves with Amar.

My head was spinning. Sabine started pushing me on him. I could tell through his jeans that he had a hard-on, even though he seemed to be absolutely as usual, caressing that cat who'd already tried to put me in front of a firing squad. When the elevator opened at his floor Sabine shoved me out. I was turned on because he was standing so calmly with that bulge, not batting an eyelash. When he took me by the hand and led me to his room, I followed. We made love without saying a word and I made my escape into the hallway, crying, pursued by the cat.

I thought about sleeping with him so many times, I think I became frigid. Since I gave it up, everything's peaceful.

Since I started to watch him live, I knew I wouldn't try to "see" him anymore as Sabine says, to meet him again, to be in his presence. My presence with his? His alone was enough for me. At first, I was watching to keep an eye on him. I couldn't believe he could be so independent. Even today, if he were in danger . . . By staying at a distance I equalize myself with him. Since he can't "see" me, I prefer he doesn't know I watch him. I'm not watching for me, but for him. I make him see himself: I'm the shadow—of someone who can't see himself.

I've gotten into the habit of following him at a distance. He goes to the public library; it's as big as the *Panthéon*, and is about ten streets from here. Sometimes I've gone in. I caught his profile looking straight ahead while his hands explored a book in front of him. I didn't know blind people read with their fingers.

I don't like to be too close to him. I'm afraid. I could go up to him on the street, make like I was his wife, or a person accompanying him. Maybe he wouldn't figure it out and no one else would notice.

I don't try to get close to him. The cat walks around him, guarding him like a dragon. She recognizes me and she spits and raises her back whenever I pass.

In three years, he's changed less than I have. When I was little, there was only one boy in my class, because he was the son of the *concierge* at the girls' school. I really would have liked to be the only girl in a class of boys. Not so they'd all be after my ass, but because I wouldn't have had a way to compare, to know I was a girl.

When I look at him, I'm physically moved. Like the little boy in my class, he's one of a kind in a herd of people that see. He can't compare. He doesn't seem any taller to me now than six years ago on Kerkenna. He isn't a man yet, more an adolescent. Being blind must keep you younger. His body is strong, although he doesn't have hair on his chest and just a little fuzzy wool around his sex. But he's barely a man because he doesn't have a piercing stare: he's a man without defense, without attack.

When I slept with him, I didn't try to get him to recognize me. I thought that was exactly what I needed; but when I want to speak I had a lump in my throat and I got dressed without a word. I left the room while he was still washing up.

I can't live with him, face to face, like an ordinary man. I'm never face to face with him since he doesn't see me. He's not face to face with me, either, because I don't see his look. I'm closed up in him, an extension of him.

When I hooked up with him, he didn't suspect a parasite, an outer shell. Now I don't want him to know I exist. I'm not looking for a return engagement. I don't need him to see me. It's enough that I see him.

I've changed a lot, gotten thinner. Since I can't stand the food here, Sabine makes me canned sauerkraut and pasteurized camembert that an airline attendant friend of hers rips off Air France. I don't go out of the hotel except to follow Amar, so I hardly know anything about this city. So what? The hotel is a city in itself. Hundreds of people live here.

Sabine is always saying that she lives here because nobody cares what you're doing or what you're wearing. And the city is just a collection of maniacs living side by side. None of the people I've met ever gave me a problem; they weren't surprised about anything. I can follow Amar in a crowd and they don't turn around and look at him, despite the funny way he walks; a little stiff, legs spread apart, with his strange eyes that move without focusing on anything, and with that cat beside him. Neither the guy I borrowed the room from at first in the youth hostel nor Sabine were surprised to meet a voyeur. They admitted that I was possessed by my *idée fixe*, which is to know every minute where Amar is and what he's doing.

Sabine says: "To each his own." She also says that reciprocal love, European style, isn't in vogue here anymore.

Entering his life, all I've done is cause catastrophe. I'd be a jinx on him. I've become so superstitious I don't sit where he has sat, don't touch an object he's touched, without first wiping it off.

Sabine decided to help me. Below her window on the street side there's only a big ventilator cupboard that separates us from him. One night going out the window we lowered an enormous bathroom mirror and fastened it onto the fire escape, the mirror turned toward the hotel. After we'd nearly let the whole thing fall onto some passers-by, we finally got it into place with rope. The next day, the cleaning lady had an absolute shit fit. To shut her up, Sabine promised to do a story on her in the Chelsea News. From the street, the mirror is just a brown spot, barely visible through the ladder railing.

By taking out three rotten plates of the fire escape platform, we were just above Amar's window. It opened and he leaned toward our noise. We held our breath: I could have run my fingers through his reflected hair.

Sitting in the living room, where I glue together film clips for Sabine, I can see him perfectly, especially at night with the light on in his room. From him to me across the windows and the floors, there is no more distance than from one end to the other of a big apartment. When he's standing, he's as big as my hand. Picking up the binoculars, I can verify if he's closely shaved. The binoculars are only an accessory now. Long periods in front of their eyepiece is tiring.

Now, I do sort of fear physical contact with him but I can't get enough of his image. After a while keeping an eye on him has become second nature. It has happened that I would caress myself with his image, especially when he undresses to get into bed and he thinks he's alone in his room. But since I went to bed with him, I swear there is nothing else sexual between us since there isn't anything between us: there's only him and me. I forget myself a little looking at him. Sometimes I'm afraid he's going to burn himself on the kettle when he's making tea, or that he'll fall down the elevator shaft—or into all the other traps that he so skillfully avoids.

I made myself his shadow: a guardian angel who never has to intervene.

How can you tell he's blind? Only by his expressionless gaze. His hands, his mouth, his legs speak: his eyes, never. I sometimes manage to find something when he's leaning out the window. With the binoculars, I see a little vein beating just under the eyelids; I can see the pupils follow a police car siren without seeing it or when he looks up toward the sky because it's raining. Yet, his eyes don't express anything like what I find in Sabine's if she's looking at the same spectacle. You can't see what he sees there, or what he thinks about whatever he's seeing: they only express the interior of his feelings, undistracted by anything outside himself.

They're mysterious wells that no reflection overshadows.

I sleep during the day a lot while he's at the library, after I've done some tidying up and watched him out of the corner of my eye as he cleans up to go out. To keep him in sight, I open all the doors in the apartment, even the bathroom door. I'm as well as married to him, long-distance. I often watch him while he's sleeping thanks to the light kept on all night in his room. I don't know if he started suspecting something, because for several weeks he began to systematically turn out the lights as he went to bed. Sabine has a remedy for everything: she turned the light switch around in his room, opening his door with a master key. When he thinks he's checking to see if the switch is turned off, he turns it on.

He fools around with some tiny instrument day and night and is never without it. You'd think it was a harmonica with keys on the side. I thought it was a musical instrument, but I can't hear any sound. According to Sabine it's probably a little calculator. Yeah. He must be counting in his head. I can see the creases over his eyes. Accounts to infinity, lost in there, which he never rereads.

I watch him making coffee, open the window, and stay in bed wearing headphones, reading with his ears ... who knows what; all kinds of stuff! He has a whole slew of cassettes. I put on records while I watch him moving, breathing, scratching himself, and especially tapping away on his little gizmo.

Sabine is starting to feel like I have lived in her place just about long enough. Amar had visitors the other night. It seems he's become an actor and they're going on a European tour. The receptionist said in a few days. I'm going to leave with him. Someone has to look out for him.

By the way ... I have the results from my tests. I'm three months pregnant.

Such A Clearsighted Liberty

Ladies and Gentlemen of the Jury:

I am imprisoned, and I am more free than you...a society of the blind would no doubt be more free than yours could ever be. No one there would think of posting watch over another. Constrained to speak to you from the exterior of the reality to which you belong, I am utilizing terms which I know you will accept to make myself understood...like "blind" and "look." I use them only for convenience to get a message across. What sense this message makes to the sighted, I do not myself know.

I feel free, in prison, compared to my penitentiary companions, who never stop crying for the vision of freedom, of Nature, of cities they have lost.

I'm not crying for a lost vision of freedom. At least since I have been in a cell I no longer feel observed by the sighted world. The penitentiary walls prevent the outside from seeing me more than they keep me from being footloose and fancy free.

They say a prison is a place of isolation. On the contrary the only problem here for me is a sort of promiscuity. My fellow prisoners are terribly noisy, as is the whole system: meal carts, slamming iron doors, the jangling of loud keys: incessant racket.

You have condemned me to a maximum term. I must pay with a lifetime of prison for the fact that your habits and your moral rules are as arbitrary to me as your perceptual world: I who come not only from Arabia, but from a continent that is invisible.

Like all sighted people, you do not understand that we do not speak of the same world even when we use the same words. We are in two parallel universes that sometimes coincide, to my shame under the odious form of pity. Still, they remain distinct.

Your power over me is truly blind since it is a dictatorship over a dimension which you affirm that I lack. In the name of what morals have you condemned me? Do you know the morals of the blind? By reducing me to be measured by your sighted prejudice you imposed moral torture upon me during my trial. I did not dare protest—and suffer the fate of a martyr. My attorney attempted to demonstrate that I was of lesser responsibility because blind, and the prosecution that I was that much more culpable because I had exploited that respect due the infirm.

During the preliminary hearings, your experts got it into their heads to demonstrate that I was sighted, to add lying to my guilt. The absence of the "blink reflex"—once they knew I was familiar with the principle of the experiment—seemed to them the sign of a hardened criminal, capable of having his eyes put out before he would admit to being sighted.

Finally, in the absence of my innocence, the court admitted my blindness. They must have been waiting a long time in the labs for a young blind man condemned to a long term—someone they could force to make up his mind, one way or another. The insistence of their examinations became clear.

And so I do not excuse myself for what I have committed through being blind. I knew perfectly well that transporting fourteen kilos of pure heroin was illegal. I could easily have claimed ignorance of this substance. I did not try. My attorney reproached me often enough for that.

How comical it was, the exasperation in your questions to yourselves, ladies and gentlemen of the jury. I had committed an affront to your good conscience: I'd swindled your charity.

I had the misfortune to be picked up on territory under American jurisdiction. To get picked up: slang was never more appropriate for me with my horror of stumbling. I did not feel a thing, not the least warning.

There are only "lifers" in this lost Nevada penitentiary. I have been stagnating here six months, if you can stagnate in the sun. They let me keep my guide-cat, Zita. She is getting uneasy from a dearth of mice and birds and small living beings to chase in prison.

My companions and I are in the section for swindlers and delinquent intellectuals: counterfeiters with whom I compete to recognize banknotes by touch; other drug smugglers; embezzlers, computer thieves; white-collar criminals. Life is less different for me here than for my counterparts. I was already cloistered in New York, and in Europe I was working hard. They let me keep my digicassette, so I can continue to write.

Everyone respects me on the exercise ground. Even those from the murderers' blocks, where there is no discipline other than that they provide themselves and where the guards do not even enter. The guards are a little bit afraid of me too. Not afraid of being slashed with a knife, but of the hex that I might put on them.

They know that I'm just passing through. The old prisoners say that's how it is: when a young one in good health gets pinched, they send him up for the maximum, and then offer to reduce the sentence for "voluntary participation" in medical experiments. The penitentiary is a warehouse for medical testing, even for the Army. I am waiting for this experiment they want to impose on me. I do not know what they want to do with me. They say I will not suffer ... on the contrary.

Above the walls separating me from the assassins' block, I can hear a cloud of backfires amid dust. They are going 'round and 'round in circles on the motorcycles the administration authorized them to bring in piece by piece and to reconstruct. They go around in black leather, circling under the burning sun, giving themselves the illusion they are on the outside.

I am in the murderers' good graces. They think I'm a new kind of hardened criminal. Unlike the judge, they think a handicapped outlaw is even more courageous.

I started out being a smuggler a long time back with Mrs. Hallowe'en's friends. Until now, I did not feel the need to relate the whys and wherefores of my incessant travels: I acted as a courier. I was building myself quite a little nest egg, as she put it.

I could never stand the white cane, the symbol of infirmity. "Being blind," I had to carry it anyway, to catch planes, to pass customs. It was her idea to use it for numerous items in which she trafficked: diamonds, jewels, currency, gold. She always loved contraband, even though it wasn't necessary for her. Naturally when I began to travel in Europe again with the dance troupe and they proposed that I resume my "transports," I accepted. I never take drugs myself; it disturbs my sense of equilibrium. But they offered me more for four or five shipments than all the money I'd earned 'til then.

I've always needed a lot of money. It's the price of my independence—taxis, restaurants expensive enough to not deny me. I am always obliged to spend more than others to be free. Only deluxe establishments accept the blind.

The idea of a blind person needing money seemed to really shock. As did the police reports confirming that I'd prostituted myself in Los Angeles. You were ready to pardon me much, but not for destroying the image of blind purity you had fashioned for me.

I tore up the suit of pity that you'd woven and through the intermediary of the institute imposed upon me. That's what condemned me most in your eyes.

I arrived in Europe via Barcelona: my first European city— apart from that brief passage through Rome to consult Italian doctors just after my accident seven years ago, and a twenty-four hour visit to Paris just before the accident in San Francisco.

For a while in Europe I began wearing dark glasses again. The tight crowds everywhere, the narrow streets, the sounds bouncing off high buildings—worse than inside a train station—were disorienting at first. The dark glasses protected me from the sighted. At least, that way the closed-in mob wouldn't bump into me.

There is no outdoors in European cities. You are always inside, even when out in a square.

I always go out late at night, I prefer it to daytime. One evening, I was drinking an orange juice at a bar in the Calle San José, at that time of night filled with people. Next to me someone was wearing fur despite the heat ... someone so heavy the stool creaked. It was a man dressed like a woman. A bunch of sailors came in drunk and got it into their heads that they were going to marry us, or at least to pay me a trick using the transvestite. I don't know who ever gave them the idea a blind person can be so easily fooled and would have ever taken him for a woman; I would never make a mistake like that, unless I could see.

This kind of nonsense should be familiar to you.

People believe that the blind are sexless, virginal, indefinitely preserved in the formaldehyde of goodwill. In two centuries you have sewn us a robe of charity which forms a chasm all around us more surely than the rattles of lepers, turning us into fleshless beings, ridiculous eunuchs.

In Europe, I visited the blind quarters of your large cities; blind schools, blind museums, blind workshops line the streets, emblazoned with the names of your philanthropists.

Like us Arabs, you have had your blind soothsayers, your blind knights and kings, your blind Crusaders—like the three hundred followers of Saint Louis the King of France, whose eyes my ancestors are accused of having put out. I have touched wooden letters in Rome created five hundred years ago.

Once upon a time two centuries ago, you invented philanthropy, discussing whether or not the blind were gifted with feelings. No one had figured that out before. Philanthropy has done much more than care for the blind: now you can hide them. You convicted me without pity because I betrayed my role—to be the living emblem of your philanthropy.

You've decided the blind too have souls: they no longer needed bodies. You've created a new immaterial witness, a purely intelligent being without sex or bodily needs, a philanthropic blind which your "dignity" can then smother.

The Prosecutor dwelt upon the period I'd spent in an institution as proof I'd been given every opportunity.

Every opportunity of being an eternal eunuch. Because you are all philanthropists, *I* must be virtuous, *I* must be immobile, *I* must be shut away for my own good. Because of philanthropy, *I* should not walk alone, nor wander at night, nor dance, nor make love.

Philanthropy begins when you forcibly take my arm and make me cross a street I don't want to cross. It continues when you wish to prohibit the handicapped from being seen. You suppose that I am fragile as glass. For my well being you protect me, a ward in isolation. You suppose I'm transparent, without secrets, without intimacy. And your philanthropy is most complete when you can be scandalized by a crime committed by someone blind.

I am endowed with feelings, but denuded of morals—your glaring, short-sighted morals.

The least I could do was to use your own blindness toward me—your blindness—for my action.

I turned weakness into strength.

When I arrived in Europe, show business was my work. A trade I'd learned here in America. Because I am an American Arab more than a European Arab.

When I tell other prisoners I was a dancer, they're shocked. They seem to feel there is something degrading for an "invalid" to parade around in a show. They prefer me as a gigolo, or a drug-runner.

I don't know why so many people are so afraid of exhibitions of the blind. Is it for our sakes? Or for theirs? A blind person is not someone who doesn't see—you can only do that from the inside—but he is someone whose sight can upset children; someone you have to wall off, keep invisible from the world's eyes.

Through dancing, I escaped my handicapped condition, escaped being a prisoner of sight. A stage is a material quality of air and floorboards: a mixture of dust and electricity, and stifled coughs and the breath of the audience. They never had to tell me when the spots were lit: I could hear them. Darkness talks too: scraping seats, sneezes, whispers, scanning glances. The spotlight silences all that.

In that moment, all movement takes on a marvelous importance. Your arms sweep through thousands of spiderwebs caressing your face, the close-knit aerial fabric of their riveted attention. I love to be looked at, and the most idiotic sighted people are those who think they're being discreet by turning away for my sake.

Maybe I've always preferred to put myself on display. Spectators' looks are an unconscious burning, which the heat of the dance brings alive and makes almost unbearable; and which gives me the feeling of existing more fully.

I never stopped feelng I was being watched in Europe all those months that I was dancing; it reached the point that I would turn around in the most deserted street feeling looks on me.

I had learned by heart movement after movement, sequences I executed under the director's hand as he guided my legs, turned my shoulders. On stage, the relationship was reversed and for the audience the other dancers seemed to be imitating a choreography I supposedly was inventing.

I have always loved music and dance above everything else, even when little. I spent my childhood waiting for the return of *Achoura*, the carnival of the eighteenth day of the year. Its marking off Winter from Spring provided me with the rhythm I grew up with, while my adolescent days flowed by. I wore a green caftan, a silk turban the same color, and a little sabre like a real sheik. At thirteen I sometimes dressed up, contemptuously, in the variegated *derbela* of the blind beggar and went tapping my way around. Dancing was at the dawn of my life. Much later, traveling, I learned of the existence of another form of movement different from those I knew. It was a clever way of moving only inside yourself, which you call thinking.

I did not know how to read quietly or how to feel any emotion without movement. At the school on Kerkenna, the sheik who had us recite the *qasîda*—fables in verse with a single rhyme, monotonous as the desert dunes—taught us a gesture to mark out the rhythm. I am incapable of saying a poem without making that gesture. I could not talk about music; I could only sing it, dance it. Now I know how to talk about everything without moving anything but my fingers or my lips.

The same sheik on Kerkenna told me how poetry had been invented with the birth of the Prophet, by a Master who was walking in the Street of the Blacksmiths in the old town; the *medina*.

I hardly ever went in the Street of the Blacksmiths in our *medina* when I was little on Kerkenna: I was afraid to. Since the town was really small, the two streets—the street of the dyers and the street of the blacksmiths—were only one with sulphurous fires and stagnant ditchwater that looked like blood or bile which came up to your heels, and the constant hammering of punches shaping teapots and trays.

When I became blind I understood what the sheik had meant. The hammers improvised rhythms which answered one another as they worked, overlapping, filling the perfumed air that enveloped me like a net. I would stay there for hours, and my mother had to take me back to our house by force . . . the house where I vegetated in silence, repeating a jumble of endless litanies.

The inventor of rhythm must have been a blind blacksmith. Inventing rhythm, he found music and poetry . . . or he must have at least closed his eyes to find it. All musicians do that I'm sure if they want to concentrate on a melody. Music and poetry were first of all arts of the blind that the sighted have clumsily annexed. Dance, as well, which is nothing more than blind rhythm in motion.

The sighted often think that music "represents," because the musicians and blind poets who had worked for them finally made them believe they were describing the same things the sighted could see. The musician and the poet felt nothing less than— liberation from the image.

In the show business world, I was not seeking images. The feeling of the hall, the sensation of the spotlights whose burning I confused with people looking upon my skin: these are not images.

It was makeup which made me like the theatre most. Not for the pleasure of appearances, but for making my skin feel like a screen sensitive to lights: an animated painting. Even with a thousand stares fixed on me, my skin is not outside. The surface of the world turns toward me.

Under the repeated tweaks of the makeup girl's pinches, my face became a hollow fingerprint, a mask I could feel at every point from my chin to the roots of my hair. I do not believe a bare face is more real than a painted one. On the contrary, I felt it more present when made up than not. But on the other hand, it is nothing but a nuisance for me to wear clothing, because I have no impressions but those coming from inside me, and my movements are hampered by these floating obstacles invented by your modesty.

If there were an art of blind painting, it would be an art of skin painting, and each work would be a unique tattoo, living and present for a single spectator; he who would wear it inside himself until it was so well incorporated would lose any sensation of it.

I was lucky to begin my blind life in America. I became free through sex and theatre. If I had not had those means of mixing into the crowd of my contemporaries, I would have only been a creature of an institution released from captivity back into the wild, unable to take a single step without assistance. Mrs. Hallowe'en fortunately was not a philanthropist and anyway she always preferred animals to me. The only people with whom I feel equal are those who want my body ... not my welfare.

Skins are images. My memory is an immense warehouse

where hundreds of skins are drying side by side, men's and women's, each with a unique and different grain.

When I left Tunisia for America, I had to make myself over, rebuild myself differently from what I'd been. I never would have been able to be free had I stayed my mother's helpless invalid, if I stayed a blind young Arab lost in some rockpile. It took a shock, as the experts say, the shock a fifteen-year-old boy could feel being transported here six months after the accident that blinded him.

Lost in the midst of a foreign crowd, deprived of any point of reference, I had to invent my own morals. I am a moral America. My rules of life are a discovery I had to make myself. I could not imitate your behavior ... I could not see it.

I must discover alone—beginning with my self—the civilization of tact, of touch, that you have kept from being born. You understand my morals are not the same as yours: I do not know the spectacle of pain, the show of misery, the family circus, the beauty pageant. I do not know what draws tears from you, or makes you smile. I have not cried much in my lifetime. That emotion is reserved for the sighted. Smiling—that idiotic muscular response in some collusion which escapes me—is only a mechanical action for me now.

At the police inquest you recounted how I was a former "prostitute" and had "homosexual tendencies." I do not attach the same importance to sex that you do. For me, making love is a simple prolonged handshake: the shortest path to being able to know another human being. Here, in prison, I continue to accept propositions from the penitentiary bosses. There is a racket for anything in prison: cassettes, records, food. But nobody considers me a faggot. These hardcore men who bashfully caress me, have put me outside the norm. It is I who am the man.

The only women's bodies I ever saw as a child were at the *hamman*, what you would call a Turkish bath, when I went to find my mother; and they were hidden in steam. Sometimes, at the *wadi*, I would catch a glimpse of little brown bodies speckled by the sun through the fig-tree leaves. I have also seen women in films, but I was already blind when I first made love with a woman.

A man's body is more familiar to me. Before, I saw myself in the mirror a lot. I have contemplated my own image surrounded by jasmine. And I played sex games with boys my age on the island.

I have no sexual tastes, in your sense of the word. The imaginary is reserved for the sighted. Thus, I am not homosexual. Only the distance, which I cease to be able to touch, marks the end of my possibility of compassion. A person in his death agony, if he is silent, is already gone for me, and a body kept away out of reach of my arms does not yet exist.

So numerous are these bodies that have made me into something else, washed me of all regret. And I have never known if they were beautiful. For you, beauty builds up the difference between the two sexes, yet it is only of a visible order. So, after having mixed up so many bodies, having felt them all different and so difficult to recreate, how can I not mix up the sexes?

The poets call the beloved being Al Habib. He is all sexes.

There: that's what I would have told you at the trial if stupor, rage and my lawyer's advice to be prudent hadn't held me back. I will not send this letter. It will remain, in French and in Braille, on my digicassette. I have sold my body one more time, accepting participation in this series of experiments. I have withdrawn my right to protest. From his very first visit, my lawyer knew precisely what was going on: an exorbitant sentence followed by reduced time, due to my cooperation. They hiked up the sentence in proportion to my experimental value. Other than blindness, I am fully intact. Since I'm warned about what's behind their game, induced to accept it, I regret nothing. It is much harder to wait for the moment when they'll transport me to the Army hospital, especially the way my fellow inmates congratulate me on maybe being "cured," "being able to see again." They wouldn't talk that way had I been blind from birth. They cannot imagine the blind could have any desire more powerful than wanting to see. There exist fish, even mammals, that are blind. People admire the bat's radar, but the idea of blind humanity makes them vomit in terror.

I am not a militant for blind rights and I don't wish to demonstrate how oppressed we are. Being blind is mere accident, insignificant: a purely individual quirk.

But this quirk is radical. All I have to do is to make the world visible, and I know that your civilization of vision is but one absurdity among others, coldly, nearly unanimously upheld.

I know since those tests at Neurone Valley that no one in the world can "cure" me. I am so far from that desire, the new experiments scare me. I have to swear a vow of secrecy, never to reveal anything about the techniques to be used upon me or anything else about our deal, either.

They will be transferring me to the hospital soon, I suppose for several weeks. Afterwards, I will be outside again, under judicial surveillance. I don't miss freedom—the sighted freedom symbolized by the space between two steel bars. I miss the wind. I want to rediscover the winds of, the breath of, cities I don't yet know. The wind is my element, my sensual distraction, my countryside. I used to bathe in it hours at a time, a weathervane subject to an endless tumult of sensations. When I was a kid, we celebrated the change of wind on the island. One morning, the wind from the sea would replace the wind from the desert, announcing rain. Then we would organize the Festival of the Wind, reciting in chorus the appropriate *sourate* to attract divine benedictions the wind carried. My mother boiled colored eggs and my sisters made up little paper squares where they wrote down the bad words, the words the wind was supposed to take away, and then the good words, which were to be dissolved in a glass of tea and swallowed.

The wind brings health and sickness, swells the chest and looses the flocks. The wind is the communal respiration which links peole to the world and which makes me a part of Reality.

The cities where I went were primarily territories of the wind. Geographic maps for the blind should be made of breezes, of air in motion, instead of those ridiculous models that I found.

I want to go back to the cities of the wind, which guides me and supports me. The heavy wind of coal smoke and cannery row, the rumble on a balcony—Barcelona *ramblas* reaching through wrought iron to me from faîence tile; the deep and powerful breaths harbored in New York Harbor; the stifled fog of loden cloth and fur outside the *gallerias* in Milan. I do not know the winds of Asia; but I miss the Pacific. I have so many winds to discover yet.

You do not see the wind. You are part of it. The wind is in me, around me, upon me, everywhere and yet so near. It returns to me my elementary existence, it wipes away the precautions of visible distance. It is my freedom made flesh. Zita is climbing up on me, holding her too-warm nose up to the fan. In vain. The walls of this prison have arrested the wind.

Vincennes

Andréa ... I have kept my old first name, which only Léopold, if he still exists, knows replaced the one I was baptised with; knows because he's the one who invented it.

I started to make a name for myself when I arrived in Paris. I mean, several names, in the bars on the "Champs ..." and the drugstores of Saint-Germain. I changed my name like my shoes, depending on the style of the guy I was picking up. There are people who look like they go out with Isabelles, others that sleep with Jackies.

At the horsepistol they kept trying to get me to sign the register. I'd always scribble down an illegible first name. Philippe would come to my rescue. At Lamorne, I became Madame Alix before I had time to become Andréa again.

I always thought that keeping the same first name for two or more lovers carried a curse. A first name, like a handkerchief, should only be used for a single person. Afterwards, you must throw it away. When you don't have lovers anymore, you don't have any first name either. That's what happened to me. Sleeping with Antonio, I became Andréa again because that was the name I was using when we first became lovers and he thought it original. It made me feel like I was slipping back into my old clothes from the Fourteenth Arrondissement.

I followed Amar through airports all across Europe. I even had to ask for an advance on my alimony from Alix so I could continue. I saw the show Amar danced in thirty-seven times, with ear plugs toward the end, so I could just look at him.

Since he's in prison, I miss that life of guardian angel. which wasn't always easy. I had the feeling that his daughter in my belly was benefitting from his radiance, that she was nearer to him if I stayed within sight of him. I would take a table alone in restaurants, despite waiters' smiles, a table not too far away from where he dined alone too. He never spills anything. He listens for dishes to be set on the tablecloth and feeds his cat under the table. Other patrons would watch him out of the corners of their eyes. He had the waiters read his bill to him, then he would add it up on his little red calculator.

The restaurant was near the theatre. The waiter told me that Amar was the blind dancer. They didn't dare ask for autographs: they thought a blind man wouldn't know how to write. During those first months in Europe he was a celebrity everywhere he went. I'm not sure he ever really realized it, so he certainly couldn't realize when it was all over.

I was a part of the troupe without being in it. Since I was there every night, the stage managers and stagehands knew me. As did the *concierges* of the hotels where they stayed and the theatre ushers. I was often there from four o'clock in the afternoon. They just figured I was part of the staff, or thought I was the "little friend" of someone in the troupe.

I followed everything: afternoon rehearsals—barely awake— reheated dinners in local *brasseries* for fifteen or twenty people after the show, the freezing cold theatre wings that smelled like feet. From the cracked-open door to his dressing room I could see his bare chest in the mirror, an old lady patting powder and make-up on him. I didn't speak to him. I never touched him. I was around.

His skin kept on getting paler, because of the makeup. The tattoo, a serpent coiled around fire, had become a blackish blue.

He had visitors in his dressing room and at the hotel. People who weren't theatre people. From then on, I became afraid for him.

In each hotel I left suitcases full of clothes bought in Spanish *supermercados*, a local Uniprix, the Italian *La Standa*, a boutique in Berlin. I stockpiled clothes from all the crowds where I followed him to throw off his barely vigilant attention.

He loved wandering around in crowds. He needed this anonymous throng, those thousands of people out on the go who always pulled aside as he approached. In Europe, he'd started using his white cane again—a collapsible one, made of aluminum—and his dark glasses, which he wore upon his forehead, when he sat alone on a bench.

I would watch him in the crowd, warn him of false steps. I would hold open subway doors and he would thank me, never surprised the crowd always had the same face. The crowd had bled into me, made me indistinguishable, lost among shapeless forms. The other actors in the troupe, even the cat, no longer noticed me.

I lost my voice, or almost did, during that time, because I never used it. I figured if he had any memory of me from Kerkenna it would be of my voice. It had become very husky, bizarre to hear when I was talking to myself. To get closer to him, I became multifaceted. I got rid of colors that were too bright, not from fear of attracting his attention, but of attracting others. Fortunately he is solitary by nature. He takes walks with his cat every morning. I changed perfumes, changed the way I walk, my heels, my jewelry, anything that made noise. My coats too, because he might have recognized me by the sound of fabric brushing against me.

I had never learned to dress by sound and odor before rather than by appearance—to blot myself out, instead of underlining my presence. It's harder than finding something sexy to wear to a party. The unrecognizable demands infinitely more work than any other style.

I would often get up and offer him my seat; I would find him a chair on a promenade. I could go up to him, sometimes, catch him by chance in the crush of a bus. But he never paid any attention to me.

Sometimes I would follow him in the silent crowd. I had never so much felt how silent a crowd can be. All you hear is thousands of footsteps, a continual hopeless shuffling in grayness. The passersby walking, not speaking, in underground halls along sidewalks where he'd hesitate, tapping his new collapsible cane. Someone was always there to send him in the right direction... someone nameless who was half the crowd—I never dressed up as a man.

Nothing of what he did escaped me. You can't hide from your shadow. I felt the catastrophe coming without being able to warn him.

*

My disguises weren't protecting me from Amar so much as from others—a change of perfume would have been enough to throw him off ... the smugglers were more difficult to observe.

I didn't know what their game was but they carried gold cigarette lighters, wore three-piece suits and crocodile shoes and carried attaché cases.

The first time I saw them was in Barcelona. I wasn't the only one to notice them. All three, Amar and the two others, were there, too well-dressed at the café across from the Opera. From my table, I could only see the end of their table. Some fat guy alone at a table sitting with his back to me blocked my view. When they left, he folded his newspaper and got up too. I was to see the fat guy again several months later at the end of the year.

The dance troupe was playing for three days in a renovated train station in Berlin. I was staying in the same hotel as the dancers, on a big modern avenue called Tustermann Way, or something like that. I don't speak German. I was at the window, looking at the long flat modern buildings with a church in ruins in the middle, when I saw this same fat guy get out of a taxi.

He was so fat he had to make three tries to get out of the car. Once out on the sidewalk, he lit up a cigarillo, looking up at the hotel sign. He went inside. I called the desk and asked for train schedules to Istanbul. While the person at the desk was trying to find his way through the timetables, I heard the fat guy ask if Amar was staying at the hotel. He even knew him by his last name. He left right away before the receptionist had time to ring up Amar's room. In the next few days, other men came to see Amar. I wasn't able to hear because they were running the vacuum cleaner in the hallway. They do that a lot in Berlin. The visitors were the same: two young well-dressed hoods with the same attaché cases as in Barcelona.

I didn't think anything of it. We were leaving the next day for Paris. I almost didn't get a seat because the plane was sold out. And because the airport is round, made of a hundred corridors, all glass and all exactly alike, I lost a lot of time looking for the check-in counter. I asked for priority seating, since I was pregnant. Right then I saw the fat pig spying on Amar walk up to the counter, out of breath and sweating. He asked for a seat for Paris too, but I had taken the last one. He started yelling in

American. When he saw Amar come in, he shut up. He started chuckling, not noticing me, and took off toward the American police. This part of the airport was in the American sector. A policeman was sleeping behind a glass partition a little further down, under that flag with all the stars and a plastic gold eagle.

Some of the stagehands said hi to me because I had ended up getting to know them. Amar was carrying his cat in a basket. As was my custom I had attached myself to a different group than his.

Amar had his cane in his hand, but he never used it to guide himself—only to clear away passersby.

The hostess picked up her telephone and her voice came out of the speakers above our heads with the first boarding call. She had the priorities go into the waiting room—just Amar and I. I stayed seated, silent, at the other end of the bench. I thought about his daughter sleeping inside me, just a few yards away, without him even knowing it.

The hostess started to examine the others' tickets, to let the rest of the passengers enter.

Then I saw the fat guy coming back with two cops swinging their clubs. They came directly into the waiting room through a glass door they had a key to. Amar was absentmindedly playing with his cat, teasing it with his cane. They walked straight toward him.

I wanted to scream. Nothing came out. From always having kept still in his presence, my voice wouldn't obey me anymore. The cops put their hands on his shoulders and the fat guy slipped off to the restroom while the older cop took the cane, turning it in his hands. He undid it and took out a long string with little plastic bags full of white powder hanging from it, just like a magician's wand. The other people from the troupe watched the scene through the glass. They started hollering to get in. After he had thrown me out, the other cop closed the door, and they went off to get some plainclothes cops. They took Amar away, shoving past the troupe director who wanted to know what the hell was going on. The last one to leave was the old cop, carrying the cat basket, swinging at the end of a string. I saw the fat guy come from the other direction with a greasy smile, returning to the departure counter. Now there was a seat available for Paris.

*

The hostess repeated the boarding call, and I was biting my glove, not knowing what to do. The people from the troupe were hesitating, too, but the hostess pushed them toward the gate, and I followed the wave of movement while the director—absolutely at his wit's end—was looking for a telephone to call the lawyers and at the same time asking everybody who could play Amar's part. The fat guy was still smiling and making like he was reading the *International Herald Tribune.* Since the troupe was bunched toward the front of the plane, I was forced to sit just behind him. I looked at his neck the whole trip, refused all the bonbons from the stewardess and imagined I was a very well-honed hatchet. I couldn't save the father of my child, but I could save his honor—with a vengeance.

I hadn't been back to Paris in nearly a year, and I arrived like a foreigner, completely blown away that the customs agents spoke French. I stayed right behind the fat guy. He picked up a suitcase on the ground level while I pretended to look for mine. He took a taxi to the Rue des Pyramides, and I followed in another cab. I was quite used to tailing people, because of Amar. But in this case, I couldn't be seen. I took down the address of the hotel, then telephoned Philippe, who wasn't at Sainte-Anne. I took out the old notebook I wasn't using anymore and tried all the numbers until I finally got Marie-Flor, who was just leaving for Japan where she was in charge of a design collection. She left the keys to her apartment near the Bastille with the concierge, who wasn't Spanish anymore.

Marie-Flor had made sure to tell me to take it easy on the phone. She might just as well have told a nicotine fiend not to smoke. I called Sabine in New York, remembering she had a lawyer lover. It took me two days to figure out how to turn on the heat so I slept with my sweater on, even under the covers. Sabine called me back and told me that Amar had been transferred to a penitentiary in America, because according to the cops, the drugs he was trasnporting were supposed to end up in the United States. She also said he would go on trial in the United States since he'd been arrested in the American sector of the airport. She was off to the Bahamas with her lover and they didn't have time to get mixed up in all that.

I called Malika. I was ready to try anything, even humiliating myself in front of his sisters and family to save him. Antonio answered. I was so nervous I told him to meet me at the Tambour, a café at the Bastille open late at night. He came and started to flirt with me—if you can call it flirting when someone pinches you under the table and crunches your feet—without even considering what a state I was in.

I missed Amar; I still miss him every day because I got into the habit of centering my life upon him. Antonio thought I was at Lamorne all that time. He came back to the apartment at the Bastille with me, and fucked his brains out. I asked if he still had that 38 revolver, and smoking a cigarette and looking at the ceiling, he said yes.

I picked up the fat American's trail without any trouble just by hanging around in front of his hotel in the Rue des Pyramides. I slid along after him several weeks. He only went out to eat hamburgers at the Wimpy's on the Champs Elysées, or in the evenings to have a drink at Harry's Bar near the Opéra. Antonio came from time to time to screw.

Antonio admitted—seeming somewhat troubled—that Malika told him that Djamillah and Alissa never wanted to see me again. Someone had told them I'd been on Kerkenna. Each time I saw Antonio I asked him for his 38, so he finally agreed to take care of the matter himself ... no questions asked. I knew that if Antonio found out the fat guy was an informer he'd love to shoot him. I told him just enough, without mentioning Amar's name, to make him think the fat guy had ratted on me. I must have been convincing. Antonio said he didn't want to give me his gun because he claimed it had such a strong kick it would bowl me over. I showed him the guy from the sidewalk at the corner of the Rue Sainte-Anne. The fat guy was just coming out of Harry's Bar and he raised his arm like he was going to hail a taxi, but there wasn't any taxi. There was just a big fat bullet to pop open his head, the insides of which ran down the street. Antonio had spread his legs apart holding the pistol with both hands in the middle of the street, and the fat guy had crumbled, lowering a bloody hand from his forehead.

I felt the little girl in me jump for joy. Her father was avenged. The curtain in the bar slit open and jazz music and screaming spilled into the street. Antonio calmly set off for the Avenue de l'Opéra, pulling me by the hand. I got loose and went back to the fat nobody. The people who had come to the threshold of the bar pulled back quickly and lowered the shade with a metallic clink.

I knelt down. The fat guy had a convulsed violet face, as though he'd had an attack the moment the bullet was expanding his mind. His coat was turned open and I rummaged through the pockets. I wanted to know why he had turned in Amar. I grabbed a big wallet, and I could hear footsteps behind me and a hand grabbed me by the shoulder. Fortunately, it was Antonio. He dragged me away, clear over to the Pyramides subway while the cop's flashing lights passed by.

We went back to the Bastille by subway. I lit a fire in the little marble fireplace no one ever uses, using as fuel those wooden marionettes Marie-Flor collects. I spread out all the contents of the wallet on the fur in front of the fireplace while Antonio took a bath, pouring in all the bath salts in the cabinet: currency, papers, a little green notebook, an envelope.

I put aside a wad of dollars which I didn't count, but which Antonio flipped through when he got out of his bath. I asked him to translate a clipping with the fat guy's photo from an American newspaper, already old and yellowed. The article said he had been on trial and convicted after being denounced because he'd been a "pimp," three years before. Antonio didn't know what a "pimp" was. That had happened in Los Angeles.

In one of the billfold's pockets was a photo of Amar, hidden in an envelope. He was inside an apartment—nude. The photo had been taken through a window whose corner you could see, but it was fuzzy. He was standing and had a hard-on.

The photo went back two or three years. He had an almost adolescent body, with long thighs and little fuzzy hairs around his sex. The notebook was filled with hundreds of names in alphabetical order ... columns of numbers, payments. I continued for the next several days to fuck with Antonio, exciting myself mentally with the photo. As he coldly told me, the bastard was turned on because he was getting it on with a pregnant woman.

I didn't tell him anything about Amar. I didn't show him the photo. I asked him not to tell anyone—not even Malika—that I was in Paris. I was thinking about going back to New York right away and waiting for Amar to get out of prison. But when I phoned her for whole evenings at a time in the Bahamas, Sabine explained to me that, normally, he should be out after about two or three more incarnations. That meant a really long time.

I was so brought down I dropped the receiver.

There was every chance in the world he would never even know his little girl. He would have to be proven innocent to be retried. And Antonio had knocked off the only person who knew who had put that white powder into his cane.

I still had several weeks left before I was supposed to go into delivery, and I wanted to do it in Paris so the child would be born French. After that I'd go to America. I would get the judges together and tell them: *voilà*—his daughter. I would ask for permission to visit and tell him everything—the bald tire, the murder, the long shadow, the fat guy's death in Paris.

They'd lock me up with him. We would have a little cell that I could decorate like a French flat. The baby could play on the upper bunk as I read to Amar.

I was forming these plans as I watched the comings and goings of the nurse Philippe and Alix had given me for the last weeks of my pregnancy—which were really painful. The delivery was painful too, because of my old screwed up abortion. Finally, a boy came out of me instead of the girl I always thought I was carrying.

I was so afraid the baby was going to be born blind that the first days I didn't even look at it. Philippe and Alix took care of everything while I went back to the Bastille to finish up my convalescence. Every day they brought me the baby, who had a brown tint and cried loudly, and wanted to suck my breasts with all his might till I had to peck on him to make him let go. I never had a drop of milk and I didn't want him to deform my breasts. When I was finally sure he really could see normally, I made a place for him in the apartment, in an old cardboard box stuffed with cushions. The nurse continued to feed him. I was really too tired to get up every two hours. Some days later, they came to bring me pills. Alix was playing with his glasses and seemed really bothered about something. He said he would like me to leave the child with him. Philippe and he had always dreamed of having a child. He was ready to recognize it. After all, he *was* the father, no?

I was stupefied. Alix insisted that the air at Lamorne was much better for a child and he finally laid down his glasses and asked me in a heartrending voice if I didn't want to come back down there too, with our son.

I wiped his glasses and gave a handkerchief to Philippe, who was crying too, repeating over and over: "Come back with us, come back with us." Then I took the baby in my arms. I looked at its brown, itsy-bitsy wrinkled face, puckering to cry again; and I wondered how Alix could possibly believe he was the father of this little son of a sheik. He blew his nose and just at that instant said in a tearful voice how wild it was how much the baby looked like his Italian grandmother.

Just like that, the baby found a father and a home, which is more of an asylum. I didn't try to explain anything about Amar to them. Both were so emotional about the idea of becoming a couple with a kid that I was sure the little tyke would have a good family atmosphere. They started begging me to come with them. I said I'd come along a little later on, acting really tired so they'd leave ... which they did, delighted, cradling the baby between them.

I stayed in bed several days more until I started squabbling with the nurse and threw her out. I didn't want to eat, I didn't want to drink, I didn't want any medicine. Alix and Philippe sent a bouquet every day to say it with flowers. All I was thinking about was the child's father and his three life terms in prison. I didn't know they could send you up for longer than life.

I took out the pictures of him—the only things I kept from my past: the magazine cover where he's surfing and the photo I found in the fat guy's wallet, which was a little fuzzy in daylight. I liked the fuzzy one best.

While I was examining the negative the envelope fell. An address was written on it in the same handwriting as the figures in the notebook ... an address in Europe written over another in the United States, which had been scratched out: Prof. Larry Home, Department of Neurology, University of Vincennes.

I had already seen that name somewhere. I opened the notebook to H, and there it was: Larry Home ... with an impressive list of payments in dollars—more from him than from any other name in the book. In old French francs it came to milions.

This Larry Home had paid a king's ransom to that fat hog for Amar. Without untangling everything linking these three together, it was clear that the organizer had been this professor, and he was now living in Paris, or rather in Vincennes.

I called Antonio at his paper and asked him to go there with me.

The name on the envelope was marked on notices for students with his class hours under this heading: U.E.R. *de neurologie* . . . Unit for Educational Research, or something like that.

The department in question was in a long prefab buiding set in the mud at the edge of a trash field. Antonio and I were starting across the mud puddles when some guy on a scooter went by splattering me and stopped in front of the building. When he took off his helmet I could see he wasn't a student as I'd thought, but at least forty or more, completely bald, with round metal glasses. He started to untie a basket attached to the luggage rack.

I leaned on Antonio—a dizzy spell. He had taken a cat from the basket . . . the same cat I'd left in Berlin. It was her all right— the same white patch on her forehead, the same bobbed tail. She turned toward me. She recognized me and walked toward me, spitting. The guy called her, like you would whistle for a dog, and she obeyed. He walked away, mumbling to excuse himself in English. Amar couldn't be far away. How had he gotten here from an American prison?

Larry Home was definitely American, the admissions secretary confirmed. I used to know her from the Rosebud on Montparnasse. She had been placed in the university by her old man. I didn't know it was that easy to become a student. I filled out all the papers, while she filled me in on how this Amerlock had left his country to escape some sordid morals scandal. Then she asked me to be on the anti-vivisection committee she was forming with some other secretaries in the department.

Alix and Philippe were really happy to see me signing up. That way, I also got Social Security for the kid, who could sure use it. In fact, I was looking for some way to get closer to the laboratories. I was convinced that Amar must be hiding there with the help of that crazy cue-ball brain and his assistants.

Antonio and I continued together in the dirty sheets of the Bastille flat. He was fucking me but I was a dead woman, my hands behind my neck watching his thin back moving up and around while I thought about the obstacles I would have to force: the armored door to the labs. The bald queen never went in or out without meal trays. Surely for Amar; since he'd already eaten at the cafeteria.

Antonio talked to me sometimes about Amar's sisters, who now hated me, and about one of their pals named Hassan. I remembered the guy in the postman's uniform who was with them the night I saw Amar in Paris. They didn't know anything more about him than I did ... probably less. They thought their brother was in an American penitentiary, and they were sending him gazelle horns and green tea. I was convinced he was here in Paris, not far away from his cat.

The bald queen (everybody knew he was a fag) was also a famous scientist. A cortège of students surrounded him whenever he crossed the lawn, along with the cat who raised her paws in scorn as she sidestepped all the old wet hand-outs stuck together on the ground.

I enrolled in his course to keep better tabs on him. He let absolutely no one go into the lab where Amar must be eating and sleeping after his escape from prison. The plastic shutters by the parking lot were hermetically sealed. The only time he cracked them open one instant I saw a seated silhouette from the back, head hanging down, sadly rocking back and forth. My heart skipped a beat. I wanted to get closer. When he caught sight of me, he closed the curtain.

The bald queen spoke seated at his desk while the cat ran back and forth between the rows of seats. I was with the feminists, who all sat in a group up high and on the left. They wouldn't allow any men in that corner. They would interrupt and ask why the brain of a man was considered superior to a woman's. It was all over my head. The class was half in English with a Canadian student doing the translating. In the front row, a group of Blacks sold wooden statues they carved during class. And nobody listened. You could barely hear because of the disco which had been put in for the employees next door, which opened at nine o'clock in the morning.

I found out that most of the profs, as well as the students were foreigners. The students were Arabs or Blacks; the profs English or American or Australian. Nobody understood anybody, which didn't prevent them from talking or interrupting the teachers. They give a degree to all the Arabs who've slept with them and who write about it in magic marker in those john stalls without doors. In all this disorder, the finagling of Professor Home in his lab went entirely unnoticed.

The secretary from the department of neurology was a good friend of the secretary in the admissions office, and secretly working to provide the anti-vivisection committee with information.

The bald queen might have already had the Nobel Prize to hear her talk ... if it weren't for his morals, she added. She thought that one day or another they would give him amnesty and he'd go back to the U.S.A. He had already made the trip once some weeks before, for the first time since he had been at Vincennes. They said he had pulled off some tremendous experiment.

They didn't have the least little key to the neurology labs. Everything in there was top secret. The professor kept it with him. He managed everything with the help of an American student entirely devoted to him. She had gone through their lab coats for me—in vain.

And the trash cans that came out of that lab! ... clotted blood, animal limbs that were still moving mixed in with thrown-away coffee filters. The professor drank it by the gallon.

I soon became president of the anti-vivisection committee, which counted the majority of departmental secretaries among its members; and we set up a table in the hall between other groups—one against rape, another for the independence of the Canaries—Islands. We had our own banner too and our own megaphone, which made quite a concert with the others.

The bald queen went by without ever seeing us; he never smiled. He shut himself up in his office as soon as class was over, and spoke with a calm, dry little voice. He was ugly, full of tics, and his eyes were so hard they shone like cut gems. The rare times I saw him laugh I heard a wicked crackling, like a stove full of dry firewood.

He never said hello to anyone. He was so absentminded that one day when he caught me going through his papers, I explained that I was the new replacement secretary and he didn't bat an eye. Our anti-vivisection slogans in the hall got no reaction. You could have sworn he saw us every morning for the first time.

Finally I discovered an airline ticket in his box. He had already booked his return flight on Pan Am to Los Angeles for the end of the next month. I had to hurry. I couldn't guess what he had up his sleeve for Amar. I was afraid of Home. I felt he was powerful and evil. The very idea that he touched Amar gave me goosebumps, as if he had placed those hands of his in rubber gloves upon my own skin. But despite all the chances I'd taken, my continual presence around his lab didn't seem to have alerted him.

How to break into that lab without a scandal—because a run-in with the police wouldn't do Amar any good. I circulated around looking for a way, without even noticing the posters going up all over for the strike.

At the next meeting of the anti-vivisection committee, I started to get the group fired up by denouncing the assassins of frogs and rats who hid in the Science building labs. Around the rooms we met in, filled with cigarette smoke, students milled in and out carrying posters, buckets of glue, leaflets calling for a strike and occupation of the building for the next day.

The next day—yesterday—I arrived by bus. Big gray buses were parked in rows all along the alleys in the woods. Helmets shone in the leaves and big shoes crushed the grass. When I entered the hall I was caught up in the cyclone, and all of a sudden there were three hundred of us in the office of some bearded guy wearing a charcoal gray sweater—the university president. He was stuttering promises that the cops would not enter.

I could hear Antonio's voice among a bunch of black leather jackets calling for a mass meeting. I elbowed a path through and he gave me a big hug. He was hyper and overexcited. His group, a bunch of real nice young hoods, was taking tables apart and making clubs of metal legs. They wanted to get ahead more than other students. I chose to go with them. Antonio was giving orders to an Arab acting as his second—that ugly Arab named Hassan.

Antonio had just gotten out of the clink at the time Amar was passing through Paris. He didn't know him, and he wasn't interested in him. I would rather he never knew. He loved fucking me so much it would have hurt him to know I was hunting someone else and that he was just a tool. I had already liquidated two of Amar's enemies—the old lady on the bridge in San Francisco and the fat American in front of Harry's Bar. All this uproar would give me a chance to get into the bald queen's lab.

At the rally everyone decided to take part in the defense of the building and started erecting barricades. I spoke for the anti-vivisection committee and suggested occupying the Science building and the labs to liberate the animal prisoners. The room broke out in applause. Outside, the science students and profs passed through two lines of cops to get to work like nothing was going on. I saw the bald queen go by, the cat sticking her head out of her basket, coldly regarding all the tumult. I went back in the rally to hear Antonio denounce the laboratories that worked for American imperialism—even for the American Army.

At that very moment a girl came in with her hair disheveled and her skirt torn, saying the cops had just busted the entire committee for the independence of the Canary Islands, whom they'd caught ripping off faculty letterhead paper. Antonio yelled that we had to take the Americans hostage and exchange them for the committee prisoners.

The whole assembly left in a thunder to occupy the Science building. It was on the other side of the sports grounds and we went past demonstrating. The cops loaded their guns with grenades which they passed out of buses on the other side of the fence. The president climbed on a car in front of the prefab building and began a discourse on how there were outside agitators involved in the whole thing. I went to find a wastebasket in one office and climbed up on the car hood and crowned him with the wastebasket full of cigarette butts. The students applauded and entered the building, scattering into offices to find rats with wires sticking out of them imprisoned under glass globes, or frogs with five feet, raised in mineral water. They let them all go, and they started running and jumping everywhere. Antonio got a commando team together to search the building. A series of dull explosions vibrated outside and I saw Amar's cat jump through a ventilator shaft, chasing frogs to gobble them up in the middle of the fracas.

I wasn't the only one to see her. Hassan, Antonio's ugly buddy looked at her as if he'd seen the devil. To get through all the offices, Antonio had started taking apart the hinges to the lab door which was already cracked ajar. Who should appear but the bald queen shaking like a leaf. He started talking in English. None of the dozen or so Portuguese or Arabs there, nor Antonio could understand English. Outside, the cops had started lobbing teargas grenades onto the sports grounds to break up the biggest part of the demonstration.

All of a sudden, the bald queen stuck his hand in a coat pocket to take out his passport and show he was American. I yelled "Careful! He's going to shoot!" and I saw a little round hole just above him in the wall. I was deafened several minutes by the detonation.

The American dived back, crossing the bay window in the sound of smashing glass. Outside, a squad of cops had slid along the wall, and a guy in street clothes carefully sighted Antonio through the window and fired. I turned around. Antonio was slowly swaying, his legs still apart holding his 38. with both hands. He fell in a heap amid the smoke climbing the linoleum tiles and vining up from the window. A red spot was growing on the back of his shirt. The students scattered all over the building, constructing barricades out of televisions and computer terminals.

I leaned out the window. The cops had drawn back and taken shelter behind their shields to avoid the ricochets off the fire-resistant glass the students were holding. A sort of gigantic turtle of cops slowly waddled toward the building, their long clubs dragging on the ground, their shields side by side above their heads.

In the background a little bald silhouette was running toward the parking lot. I let out a scream of rage. My deafness from the gunfire was gone. The yelling, the noise of clubs and whistles from officers in gold helmets directing the maneuvers safe behind the buses all went through my head.

There was also a moaning interspersed with gargling coming from down on the floor. I bent down. Antonio wasn't quite dead and he was trying to talk in spite of the blood dripping between his lips. *Pompino! Pompino!* was all he said, so I undid his fly to suck him off and he came in a few seconds—just as he went.

The students began to loot. They were taking furniture and typewriters out of the offices. No one was paying any attention to me. I could finally get into the lab. When he took off, the bald queen had left the door open.

The lab interior was silent and black. The blinds and double windows were closed and the soundproof ceiling stopped all the outside ruckus. I looked for a light switch calling out for Amar.

My hand found so many switches I was afraid I'd be electrocuted. All I could hear in response was a groan. I found the switch, flipped, heard a roar and was pushed up against the wall by Antonio's pal Hassan who'd followed me into the dark.

A creature the size of a child wearing a raincoat burst between us, running on its long, hairy arms and legs at the same time. Wires dragged onto the ground from its head. Two white plastic electrical plugs had been planted in the middle of a shaved pink area on its skull.

I opened the blinds. The ape—it was an ape, sure enough—was running across the sports grounds getting tangled up in its wires, and then was hanging over the goal. Over behind the buses and plainclothes cop had pulled out his revolver quick as Bernard Blier and was calmly taking aim.

I turned around. Hassan had disappeared. The office was empty. In the corner was a chair with broken bracelets where the ape must have sat. I overturned the cartons, the furniture, shelves, microscopes. In the bottom of a drawer was something red, no bigger than a harmonica, with keys on its side. I could see Amar's hand playing this very instrument. He'd used it every day. I picked up the device and slid it into my bag . . . thinking he must be dead.

I left with a group of hoods, taking shelter behind some broken-up tables. They made me keep my head down. I walked in a daze seeing nothing.

We went back across the sports field, just as a grenade landed inside the goal line. In the big hall, ten megaphones were yelling contradicting orders all at once. I crossed the hall to reach the parking lot where I stuck out my thumb to hitch—in tears.

I saw Hassan beside a yellow postal scooter, putting the cat into a mailing carton he'd made some holes in with a knife. I recognized him when he stood up after putting the package on the back. Hocine was his name, not Hassan—Hocine, Amar's childhood friend, who'd wanted to work for the post office, a real ugly one. He was the only one who'd followed Amar from start to finish like me. The only one who knew Amar was blind because of me: the only one who could tell Amar's sisters.

Scarves of teargas wrapped around the trees in the evening light. Hocine stopped in front of me. He held out his hand and I climbed into the basket. I'm holding the little machine tight against me—the little machine that never left him, where he could read the time, and which he'd counted on. Hocine is crying too, because of the gas, the cat is clawing frantically at the box. She . . . she won't forgive me.

The Hidden Writing

I want so much to *not* see anymore—if only for an instant!

I keep on desperately closing my eyes trying to find myself again. All I do is make the image sharper, more pitiless.

My fingers run over the digicassette keys in the obscurity of the night. Writing, I forget the crackling, the buzzing like a dying bee inside my skull. I write in darkness to hide myself from what I cannot stop seeing. Even now, I see blackness. The machine never stops, and black night is sometimes streaked with a brief runaway electron.

I've cried, I've pleaded. They shrugged their shoulders, sighed that I would get used to it, gave me tranquilizers.

They left the machine running, and the machine does not have eyelids in front of the lens of its tireless camera.

It is night time, and they've put out the indirect lighting that bathes my room. The machine does not sleep, or sleeps with its eyes open.

The blackness—which I did not know—reassures me a little. I had to see it again to rediscover the dark: on Kerkenna it was always peopled with stars; at the cinema the entrance lights always made it somewhat imperfect.

I see black, a black that's a little bit phosphorescent, a television with nothing to show but night. Not like my nights before, my blind nights which were really my days, but the desolate night of this little cell upon an ice floe.

On my head I feel the cold helmet grip my temples. I am exhausted, broken but I cannot sleep, so I am mechanically typing out this text, thinking that at night they do not watch.

They have annexed me to a cathode-ray tube. My prosthesis at least lets me know when they watch me. They never thought I'd write in the dark. They did not pay attention to the digicassette because I didn't show them that it has memory. They think it only serves to calculate and to tell time.

I can write without seeing. I can even write *only* without seeing. My moving hand is more myself than the absurd vision this machine has glued onto my internal window. I know I could direct the camera toward my own hand, and could reread myself at last "in black." When I was at the institute, we used to say that sighted newspapers were printed "in black," that is, not in Braille. Black is a sighted idea.

I continue to write "us" for the blind. It is one way to resist the electronic machine.

When I was in Europe an old blind man told me how Braille had been used as a code for resistance fighters in the last war. I remembered my reading in New York. The old officer who'd invented Braille had called it *écriture obscure*, "hidden writing," to throw off spies. I am derailing sighted espionage by writing at night instead of sleeping.

I think no one in the world thinks about me or worries about my fate. Not even those half sisters whom I saw only one day and who are all that remain of my family. My father has never recognized me.

The cassette is half full now. I have no replacement. What will happen when it is full? I marked down the address my sisters left me in Paris in black stick figures. I remembered it as it contained the word *Plaisance*. And I traced a magic sign to punish any violators of my secret.

By turning the pulley near my head I can sweep the room clear to that ray of light which must be filtering under the door from in the hallway. Or I can turn my gaze to the window—a vast pane of glass, hermetically sealed at night with automatic metal shutters, behind which is only the sad light of the Pole. Four thousand receptors nestle in the shadow of my skull full of energy, ready to once again sweep with their electronic wash. A dull stare, which for an instant is only the vague crackling of phosphors lost in space.

I never use the camera on myself. This stare, which is inside me, is actually situated outside me. It passes behind me, making me be here upon my bed and there above the bed at the same time, taking in the entire room. My eye hangs from the ceiling, my body is stretched out on the floor.

Since the operation, I have not stopped asking them to unhook the machine. They don't understand. They expect an explosion of gratitude. I have cried without my vision fogging. I have gone on strike and not responded during training sessions. They spoke to me as to a stubborn child.

They bound my hands, they placed the camera out of my reach, which only redoubled my pleas. They excused themselves, repeating that I would soon be grateful to them. For months now, all I've wanted is to be blind again.

I calmed down so I might cunningly resist, fuzzing my mind against the constant buzzing. They undid me. They put the camera into my hand and I screamed with horror. It was as though my hand had become my arm's eye. I tried to smash it. They insisted that the sweeping is so rapid I couldn't possible feel it. They're mistaken. When the light is turned on for one horrible instant, in a second a luminous point fills my visual space, from upper left to lower right, in streaks that form an image. Then the screen fills up, the immense limitless screen that can turn in on itself; the terrifying screen they placed inside me, which hides the world from me. Since I see, I no longer hear, I no longer sense.

Food has no more flavor when I see the aluminum trays the nurse brings in. I can contemplate them by moving around the zoom, 'til I'm nauseous.

My first memory after the operation, my first visual memory: a row of masks, the whole lower portion of each face lost in a blazing whiteness that extended to their chests, their arms. I could hear a voice among the others, a voice speaking American which I recognized. One face had a skull shiny with sweat moving its lips at the same time that I heard its words.

Another doctor put a finger to his lips, holding another finger out toward me. The voice was silent: Larry's voice.

He disappeared from my field of vision. The image was so ugly I retched to think I'd slept with him. He came back with a four-pawed monster with a flat head sitting on his shoulder. She meowed, and I knew then it was Zita and I wanted to reach out my arm to her.

Then, with Larry gone, they began to talk about a helmet.

This weight, this swarming in my skull ... but the words were very close and the faces quite far away, lost in a crowd of doctors. They came back toward me as if they had walked down from the ceiling, across the air, falling on me. I felt sure I was lying down, yet my point of view was that of someone standing.

The internal screen had no limits, but it stopped progressively someplace behind my head on the edges of where I could not see. And the sound seemed to come from somewhere different than the image, though exactly synchronized. I closed my eyes and I made the horrible discovery that the image still remained, unmodified.

They had given me not the possibility, but the obligation of seeing. They had butchered my brain to introduce me to the sighted world.

I was too weak to talk. I felt a hand placed on my shoulder and a voice was softly speaking. The mouth saying these words was in front of me, but the sound came from behind. It was not the sound that threw me off—it was the image.

I started to struggle. Right away I felt a sting in my arm. Before I sank, the image started slowly moving, turning around the blazing white room. I saw a cot with a sheet covering a shape, a body, a somber head upon a pillow, covered with a huge helmet. At the same time I felt a hand beside me turn a knob next to my arm. The vision of the head was getting larger and larger in my own head. I opened my mouth to scream and the head did the same. The black hole of my mouth filled up the screen, and I fell into myself.

I woke up and I was anesthetized with no other sensation than a line of fire crossing my head. I looked for the cat, called to her, but nothing came.

At this latitude there is no true night, no true day. My artificial light smothered the gray outside of the ice. In a few "nights" I learned a lot. Science was being poured into me during my sleep ... a tape recorder beneath the pillow which shuts itself off the moment I wake up. They think I will accept the machine much better once I understand how it functions.

By turning the camera knob I can see a shiny surface which goes right to that line between the paleness of the sky and the whiteness of the ice; a line which must be the horizon.

To keep me from wanting to escape, Nootka—which is what they call my nurse—has told me we are in Alaska and that it's minus twenty degrees outside. When the transport came to get me at the penitentiary visiting room, the director made me put on warm clothing. The other prisoners were at the windows and I could sense their envious breathing all around me. They thought they were seeing me off to a liberty which in their eyes I could enjoy.

The military plane with a drafty cabin and hard seats landed somewhere in the extreme North. They transported me in some big vehicle which made a lot of noise throwing ice off to the sides as it shook in its tracks.

I said I wanted Zita and they told me she had gotten loose during the trip. They were lying since I saw her when I first woke up. They simply wanted to separate me from my blind habits, to keep me from continuing to be guided by her, to force me to collaborate with their seeing machine.

The scar on my neck grew up to the top of the skull. Between the skin and cranial bone, they had slipped in a second skin, made of some metallic plastic which contains their four thousand miniscule radio receptors. All these wires are bunched together to cross the cranial bone just at the spot where my wound had left a hole.

On the surface of my brain, they placed a rubber plate with four thousand electrodes the size of the head of a pin which discharge electricity at the receptors' command. They are very proud of this system. Otherwise they would have been obliged to leave an open wound to bring a cable out of my body. The helmet containing the emittors is linked to a television camera up above my bed. Each luminous point corresponds to a radio receptor, and each receptor is tuned to a slightly different frequency. Everything is built to last. The brain perceives vibrations made of multiple tiny excitations more easily than a single huge discharge, Larry told me.

A guinea pig for how long? Ten years? Twenty? They showed me a gym room and a cinema for the base personnel. I am going to live here in "re-education." They say I have a brilliant future—an expression I now understand. In a few years, they'll replace the machine—which is heavy and difficult to transport—with a synthetic eye which they showed me some designs for. An eye made by competing labs—all in the Air Force, because it uses transistor crystals like those in a satellite's eye—crystals which transform light directly into electricity.

They are re-educating me to see, as you might have to be re-educated to walk, except that it all adds up to paralyzing me . . . keeping me from feeling, by forcing me to look.

Supreme torture: the image gets better every day. That luminous gross approximation has become a painting in relief, with objects near and far, but all of it inside my head. That takes away all desire for grasping, for eating or caressing.

Each imprint in a man's brain is unique in the world, like a fingerprint upon the deep recesses of the eye. Larry must have given them mine. They sure didn't waste any time. And as I learned to see again, I've also corrected the machine.

To be really sure of the results, they had to have a talking subject. I've spent hours indicating the exact position of each phosphor, taken separately such as I saw it in black space. They corrected the position of each point on the emittor helmet.

I remembered the world in color from Kerkenna. They offered to artificially tint my vision with a little computer linked to my digicassette. Now I mix in reds, flames. I am like a sick person in a computer bath. They show me geometric figures, people's portraits, maps. I must describe what I see, the most painstaking thing I know of. When I refuse to work, I have meetings with the psychoanalyst who goes on forever.

From time to time, they bring in a video tape machine and movie cassettes. They hook it up in place of the camera cable, and I have a two-hour private screening. Even the least violent action in the film leaves me dangerously exhausted, as if I had lived it. But really, all they ever put on are musical comedies, treacly sap that invades me, drowns me, asphyxiates me.

I asked for my digicassette so I'd be able to tell time. I have trouble reading the clock dials for the sighted, used as I am to brushing the time it gives in Braille. When they figured out they could hook it into the computer by punching instructions in Braille, they ended up letting me have the digicassette. But I've never managed to find the set of commands that says "unit Off."

So I can contrast the image, make it lighter or darker, distort it, superimpose it, double it. They thought all these games would give me a taste for the machine but I get intense headaches from it, especially when color is added. I have seen the snow blue, then red, moving like the sea. I saw the covers of my bed turn into volcanic eruptions when I moved my knee; I've seen the nurse's head in negative, solarized, in the blotched colors of some mad painter.

The black surgeon suggested I use the digicassette to create landscapes and people. He showed me how to do it, breaking the image down into program elements. I drew the basic shape of a house and a tree as I knew them. The house I entered was always too big or too little. I got lost inside or stuck in these visions of voluntary dreams. I stopped, but I kept the digicassette—to be able to write in the dark.

No calendar. Maybe I've slept for a thousand years. The supplies come in only to the camp entrance by "Caterpillars" they shake the ice from far away. They never bring letters or newspapers. The snow puts time to sleep.

Now that I see I don't have sex anymore. I don't even want to bring myself off anymore. I am now two, permanently. Not two skins, not two bodies, but two spirits—each watching the other. At first I thought this missing excitation came from the injections and from my weakness when they had to force feed me because I went on strike to make them pull the plug.

Dozens of people were taking care of me. Masseurs made my muscles function despite myself. They broke my strike—which had consisted of doing the least possible. They made me exist against my will with that love all mechanics have for their machines.

I asked for exercise. Since I started seeing, I was immobilized in a bed. Since I could not go to the exercise room with the helmet and camera, they had to take it off an hour a day. Moving, for me, finally means not seeing.

They were so afraid I would interrupt my apprenticeship, they went to a lot of trouble to grant me this hour.

As soon as I took off my helmet I regained my world of sound. My body was in good shape. They'd taken good care of it. After all, I was walking around with ten million dollars' worth of electronics in my head—as the psychologists never stop congratulating me.

I see Nootka the nurse as really small, maybe because of the slanted angle of my vision. She has prominent cheekbones, and her eyes are rather tight. She was born in one of the Eskimo villages razed by the ice-dozers when they constructed the base. She speaks a funny Kalmuk-English. She is the first person I can look at without feeling disgust. She's sort of fun, really—a shapeless *djinni* from my childhood: an ice fairy. She sympathizes whenever I complain.

I tried to ask her for information about the base. She went on the defensive right away. She became quiet, and her face became somber and I thought she was blushing as she nervously arranged my pillows.

Every time she touches me she jumps, like I'm some kind of electric battery. I think she secretly admires me. She almost envies all the electronic paraphernalia that surrounds me; it impresses her. She always asks what I see, as if she were a spectator with a bad seat at the movies.

I have a pain in my head, rheumatism, as soon as I try to read with the camera. The letters all bump into one another, the drawings blink. Only my left hemisphere is fixed: the most important one; the one which directs the right leg and hand. The right hemisphere is still blind. In fact, all that I have are my left visual fields. When I draw a line, looking at it through the camera, I find it curves left. If I could walk wearing this prosthesis, I would always tend toward the right.

My seeing brain is a pilot desperately trying to counter an endless skid, a boat tiring against a dominant wind carrying it off course.

Yesterday, the black surgeon suggested I visit my own brain. He wasn't kidding. They used a sort of laser device that X-rays in depth and in relief. They can plug it into my own interior screen. I crossed the skeleton of my face under my own skin. Beyond, blue masses were palpitating gently under my forehead.

The radiography dropped down a little to the level of my eyes. They movements were slow, almost acceptable, a slow motion ballet within the soft mass of my hemispheres. The computer was sculpting details into lines and colored masses; the convolutions, the jumble of my brain lobes. Behind my eyes, I now climbed along two red cables to an intersection just behind my nose. By rolling a little on my back and sliding down a bit more, I could get the camera to offer a vision from down under. The two big cables were each divided in half, and half of each cable crossed the other in a living knot of tangled nerves, shaken by electrical spasms.

Under, above ... I was floating under the crown of my own head, skimming over two whitish continents—my hemispheres lined with valleys—that I sometimes dove down into. Long luminous filaments ran across this gelatin. They existed only on the left hemisphere—the only one to "see," to see itself. I turned over on my side and rubbed my temple—an ivory white partition high as a wall. Then I arrived at the back. I was situated behind my brain inside my skull. I slid toward a big dark spot spilling over the back left half—a black spot in relief like ebonite, which penetrated deeply, invading the delicate translucent substance as my vision plunged me into myself, even deeper, into the valley between the two hemispheres, deeper than a ravine, never ending ... the ravine where imagination hides: the calcarine fissure—the location of my operation.

At the bottom of the ravine in the milky half-light surrounded by the muted beating of my own blood, I wrapped myself in myself, bathed in the lymph of my chasms in a desperate search for that moment when I might finally contemplate me seeing myself.

The doctors are delighted to see me keeping busy with the machine. As a reward for this wisdom, today I was led by two M.P.'s wearing boots and helmets who walked like robots all the way to see an official who considers himself responsible for my detention. They had always refused interviews before. Clearing his throat, he read me a long paper with stapled pages—some of which he skipped over entirely. His breath stank of catsup. He put the papers down ... It was an agreement between me and the U.S. government which stated that I made a gift of my body to science. I pointed out that it was a little early for my autopsy.

He changed his tone of voice to say that what was coming next was off the record: I was a living scientific wonder. I should think of all the other blind people and all the discoveries my operation would allow. They absolutely needed my cooperation ... and were determined to get it. I reminded him that in prison they'd promised me a speedy release following the experiment.

They would free me, when my psychological state permitted, and nothing would be a better index to that than my adaptation to the machine. That was to be my pass to the sighted world. It would take as long as it had to. In twenty years, I could have a villa with a heated pool on an iceberg, like the base officers. Be released? The question was obscene.

I'm having a lot of trouble falling asleep. There's a lot of noise in the room, a tiny mouse gnawing under the floor. Under the floor? No mouse could ever tunnel through that much ice. Or behind the wall? You would think it was a signal, another prisoner tapping on the wall. I'm not allowed to get up more than three times a night, which I carefully ration. Whenever I get out of the helmet a light comes on, and they allow me only to relieve myself—not to dream.

I walked all the way to the wall. As soon as I left the bed, the noise stopped, as if someone heard me coming. Another sensation stopped at the moment I lifted off the helmet . . . a sensation that I only found again by putting the helmet back on: the phosphors, which I don't see any more, I've become so used to them . . . phosphors dancing a saraband, writing a luminous telegram.

The noise was from the phosphors—it corresponded to their rhythm. My mind refused to believe it: I not only had luminous parasites, but now they had become audible too.

The noise and the succession of flashes became so strong during the night that I told the nurse about it. The doctor came and took the helmet off, talking about parasites, static. This isn't static. The sound and images follow some order . . . dashes, dots . . . Since a short while ago, I'm huddled up in my sheets, because it seems as though I can still hear the noise of this irregular cavalcade—still see the luminous spots.

I hear it again . . . The phosphors, too. I yelled, I beat my head . . . But, I'm not wearing the helmet . . . The nurse came and told me I was having a nightmare . . . No—I see them—I hear them . . . They're not in the helmet . . . They're in my head . . .

The black doctor came. I was trembling like a child. The Morse code continued. To distract me from my terror, he wanted me to take down the dots and dashes. I took a piece of paper and for half an hour marked down shorts and longs—dots and dashes . . . The noise and light got weaker; it disappeared by morning, leaving me exhausted. The black surgeon thinks they may be currents produced in some internal circuit of my brain: another self talking to me in Morse code inside my head.

I slept all day and just woke up in a sweat. The noise and the phosphors have stopped. I'm all fuzzy, as if they'd given me a drug for sleep. I got up and staggered. No noise, with or without the helmet. No light. I've gone deaf!

No, not deaf. I hit the wall and it made a sound. Not the same sound as before ... a stifled, flat sound. The room was soundproofed while I slept. The walls are covered with metal plates—a soft metal I can scratch with my fingernail. They've buried me alive in a lead tomb!

I wonder if I'm not in a nightmare the machine makes for me. Yesterday I was in such a state of exasperation I hit the lead paneling of my room until the frantic nurse went to find the doctor. He came in wearing a bathrobe. I turned the lights out and slipped off the bed. I'd arranged pillows under the helmet. He came in and while he was talking to the camera that was supposed to be me I jumped him.

The on-call night doctor was a wimpy little student. I could feel his bones ready to crack when I pulled his arm behind his back. He yelled but I put my hand around his throat and threatened to strangle him if he didn't tell me the truth. I listened for anyone else coming. The insulation worked both ways. I twisted his arm again.

He moaned that everything was going to be all right. I could feel him lying. I turned a little harder until his arm was ready to break. He fell on his knees and, terrorized, came up with an explanation. Receptors out of sync because of acids created by the prosthesis' electrical activity, oscillators sliding into other frequencies, frequencies, frequencies...

I'd become a living radio receptor. It wasn't my brain sending me these codes but some ham operator maybe a thousand miles away.

The waves got through to me better during certain hours. He rubbed his arm, continuing to talk without me having to push him. The accompaniment of light with the noise came from the transformation of a brain center called the angular gyrus. Normally, it coordinates sound and image in the brain. I asked what would happen if a lot of other receptors came untuned. He'd never thought electronics was the only possible case since they'd begun observing me (without my knowledge) because of these new phenomena. He wouldn't be surprised if an autopsy proved that my brain had adapted itself to a situation never before encountered—a functional adaptation, trying to integrate the implanted radio receptors into a new me ... a deeper me, which was practicing, perfecting itself, upping its powers as a practiced ear can pick up an infinitesimal sound out of general background noise and by amplifying it bring it to conscious perception. He left; I didn't try to detain him. I collapsed on the edge of the bed and the door latch thudded heavily like the closing of a tomb.

They came to get me this morning. As soon as I was out of the room, the phosphors came back weakly. In the corridors I ran into the black surgeon, he was furious with the other doctor. I told him I would like to know why.

Perhaps a dozen people were sitting around in a big room where they took me: old people, with big shoes that creaked, the odor of leather, brief words. Once again silence and transparence in my head. This staff room must have been bombproof. I thought I had been brought before some sort of tribunal for having strong-armed the little night doctor; but no, they wanted to know if I still heard the signals—and how long they lasted.

They spoke about me in completely objective terms while I stood in front of them, between two soldiers, as if I were an electrical phenomenon. I interrupted to say that I was a Tunisian citizen and I wanted to see my ambassador. One military man coldly told me that spies didn't have ambassadors.

Spies? I started yelling and kicking the guards. One landed a punch that knocked me senseless. When I came to, I was in the same place, sitting, and one old man was clearing his throat while the black surgeon handed me a glass of water and a tablet, and mumbled a protest.

This old man—the oldest military man, one who all the others moved aside for in a clinking of medals—softly tapped a stick against his leather boots. He came up to me and put his hand on my head and started talking like a grandfather calling me "son," combing his hand through my hair.

I wanted them to operate on me immediately to take out the prosthesis. He told me to be strong; it was impossible, right doctor? The other answered yes, not very convincingly. The old man's voice brightened. It certainly wasn't my fault—at least I was not voluntarily guilty ... but the facts were there. What I'd written on that paper—those optical and aural signals in Morse code—were nothing less than the secret code for firing the American defense network's H-bomb missiles.

His voice swelled. Surely I understood that I was living an exceptional adventure. He gave me his handkerchief, smelling of lavender, to wipe my forehead. The country needed me. He'd spoken to me harshly only in view of the importance of the secrets I'd stumbled upon. The country ... What country? He waved a paper in front of me and announced that it was a certificate of American citizenship which would be delivered to me if I cooperated.

We went into another room—the base listening post. The signals came back—very strongly in my head—really easy to read: a strong white light and a supersharp whistle. I was very close to the transmitter. They wondered how my brain could extract the information out of the general fog of radio waves, reconstitute it and the code, you might say, intuitively. A hybrid being, an electromagnetic being, was being born in me.

Back in my room, I put the helmet on again and engraved in my memory the high frequency ranges the technicians had given me in the form of a big plastic rule. I'd already moved from ten million impulses per second to thirty million.

A frequency, a rhythm, a pulse, a beat ... The rhythm of a wave, or of a living being. Some electronic alchemy was being produced in me that associated my living rhythms with the babbling of those waves. Like a listener turning the knob on his radio, my brain enlarges its reception band, multiplying the possibilities available to the circuits in my prosthesis as it searches for better reception, beating to the varied rhythms of the higher frequencies.

The hammers in the Street of the Blacksmiths could not strike millions of times a second, but these impulses infinitely exceed anything else the rest of me can conceive—the rest of me, huddling, threatened with extermination.

Faster, faster, faster my independent brain becomes giddy with acceleration, elaborating bit by bit, a half-alive listening post: a center in my brain, just as there is a center for visual attention, and a center for auditory attention.

Higher, even higher in frequency, the wavelengths become

shorter and shorter.

This run of frequencies is my last visual memory. I will never put the helmet on again. They don't need me as a sighted subject anymore.

Yesterday evening, the little Kalmuk nurse turned out the lights very early. She took away all my things and put them into a metal case. This morning, when she brought my coffee, I sensed that something was happening on the base.

The trip began ... a trip to I don't know where, I don't know how, but which I greeted with relief, because it rid me of my sight and the helmet.

That helmet: my old friends at the Institute would give ten years of their lives to wear it—if only for a minute.

The nurse took a long time buttoning me up, letting her hands wander. We walked surrounded by a pack of guards along the cement corridors, onto planks put down over ice, onto a metal catwalk that vibrated and hummed as the icy wind blew so strong it froze my ears. I almost couldn't hear the phosphors which had reappeared the minute I'd left the insulated room.

Some hands took hold of me around the waist, as though they were going to throw me in the air. I was afraid and screamed. I heard laughter and felt myself being passed like a package along a metal ladder down deep, really deep. Had they cut a hole in the ice? The air down below does not smell stuffy. It's slightly invigorating. It comes out through an opening above the wall. By climbing onto the upper berth, I can breath in deeply. I feel a lot better. The noises in my head have disappeared as well as the phosphors. There's no helmet in this iron cell which I have completely explored. All I hear is purring, a reassuring hum, reassuring because it's outside: the hum of ordinary machines, with pistons and motors. No more signals, no more hallucinations, no more helmet. Are they taking me back to the penitentiary?

The days pass. The military men make me go each morning into a slightly larger cell across a narrow corridor where you have to step up over the threshold. They want to know if I've heard or seen anything, and I answer no ... I was answering no until yesterday. Then the tapping started again—at first in the middle of the night and finally in the middle of my rest period. It disappeared. They asked me to note whenever I heard it. The next day it returned even stronger. They seemed to have predicted its return. They're recording everything—the exact times the signals are strongest, the sequences I call out—flashes and entire half-seconds of overwhelming reeling accompanied by crackling sounds. They're making some kind of game out of this information. I don't know how they're making their emissions stronger. No doubt as a function of my responses. Tonight, the emission was so clear I was unable to sleep.

Nootka just came in, very upset. She gave me a glass and four tablets and was so nervous she spilled half the liquid, then had me go to bed, even though I've only just now finished lunch. After spitting the pills back out, I started typing on the digicassette. I hear muffled noises against the walls of my cell from the corridors—long narrow corridors they've never let me explore. A drumming now—and a shock—such a shock I nearly fell out of my bunk. My cell had been picked up by a giant who threw it back to Earth. A bell started chiming next to my door but no one came to stop it. New shocks kept on convulsing my cell. I must be on a boat and not on the base.

The door clicked and Nootka came running in. She flung the door shut; a wave of icy water smelling of rotten fish was trying to get in at the same time. I jumped off the bunk and helped her turn the handle. We were in water to our ankles. She hid her head on my shoulder, clutching at me, which let me understand that with the last detonation the lights had suddenly gone out—that always drives the sighted crazy.

I put the nurse into the bunk bed. She didn't want to let me go and howled that we were all going to die. I told her they were coming to help us. Surely there must be lifeboats on the ship.

She was seized by a nervous, crazy laugh. Then she began to sob again, asking how a lifeboat would help us beneath miles of ice sheets.

If I'd never seen a submarine on Kerkenna, at least I'd heard of them. We're stranded at the bottom of a washed-out sea under tons of icebergs, under roaming polar bears, and around us silent schools slide by—the blind fish of the deep.

I stretched out beside her on the cot. As she was shivering I took her in my arms and awaiting death we made love.

She is sleeping at my side now, and the air is thickening

around us. Nothing more is coming through the grille. She is on my left arm, making it go to sleep. I don't want to awaken her. She moans in her sleep—words in a language I don't know. And, all of a sudden, some words from the *sourate Ya Sin* came to my lips:

Thinking I was going to die I began to scream.

She woke up and I thought the emissions were beginning again. Fortunately she heard the noise too—outside. We pounded on the door with our fists. A metal scraping is coming toward us.

We opened the door and I fell into the moist and icy cold arms of a diver wearing a rubber wetsuit. In the corridor the water was climbing to our knees—water so cold it seemed like liquid ice. The diver had a round object in his hand: a flashlight. I went back into the cabin and grabbed the digicassette. Why wasn't Nootka following our rescuers? She had stayed in the cabin, frozen where she was. The sight of the diver terrified her. He spoke to her using a language I recognized. Mrs. Hallowe'en had spoken a few words of it: Russian.

He slid me into a watertight trunk which other divers hauled up to the surface: a floating box with room for only one person. I don't know what became of Nootka.

On the frozen dock I asked about her this morning, but no one spoke English. The Russian police who've just interrogated me said she'd died attempting to escape. I cannot know if that's true of if they're only trying to make some impression on me.

They consider me a spy. The more I protest that I'm Tunisian, that I know nothing of what the Americans were trying to make me do, the louder they yell at me and shake me. They think the truth will fall out of me like a ripe fruit.

The Russian Army sank the whole American crew of the spy submarine on which I'd found myself. All witnesses to my innocence are thousands of miles below. On the other hand the Russians had me listen to my voice reading aloud the signals I received. They'd recovered the tape and all the officers' notes from the American sub.

The strength of the emission didn't vary ... only my position—the position of the sub, changing over the days, cruising around following my indications: looking for the best place to eavesdrop, the best place to listen in on codes for Russian missiles ... until they'd penetrated U.S.S.R. territorial waters.

My presence on the submarine, it's route, the text of the signals I transmitted: nothing more was needed to put me before a firing squad, as the interpreter never ceased reminding me. Since those hours of waiting at the bottom of the sea, I've become used to the idea of death.

The Russian military men are just like the American military men except they have only one voice—that of the interpreter. They immediately asked me to collaborate, filling me in on the pillage of the third world by the imperialists. I told them the story of my operation. They're convinced that I'm lying, to cover up my exact role. They're desperately trying to figure out what a blind man could possibly be doing on a spy submarine. My story of the radio receiver in my head was judged ridiculous, impossible, even metaphysical, by their specialists. They think I'm simply an excellent technician playing dumb: a radio technician.

I asked for an X-ray. They took one. All they saw was a vague black spot, a consequence of the accident that had left me blind— a scar. Their equipment is old and not too precise.

I wanted to give them a demonstration, but since I've left the submarine, all emissions have ceased: no phosphors, no noise. I can't ask them to open my skull again. Maybe my brain digested the prosthesis? As much as the cards seem stacked against me, hope has returned.

They were immersed in admiration of the digicassette. The base commander wanted me to give it to him. I had to remind him that not knowing Braille, it would be of no use to him. I'd had the foresight to close off the visual window where you can read the text "in black." I gave them a demonstration. The machine could tell the time and make all calculations in Braille. They didn't even think of its memory bank. I'm keeping it for myself, for a night when no moon shines in the barracks where they've locked me up.

I hear wolves or dogs howling in the distance. The guards snore; they sleep without getting undressed. Fortunately, they've given me an insulated leather jumpsuit lined with lambswool, which is so hot I can sleep nude inside it.

I spent the day with the base political commissar and with a member of the U.S.S.R. Academy of Science. They're even more stupid than I thought. The Academy is convinced that I'm a medium—that I practice thought transmission and read the secret codes in the minds of Russian officers. The professor—an old man with a goatee named Vassiliev—made me go through the most ridiculous experiments I've ever participated in, and now I seem to be embarking on a serious career as a guinea pig.

Professor Vassiliev speaks a little English. He's been experimenting with thought transmission for thirty years, as did his father before him, at court under the Czars. He lives in the Kremlin. The bigwigs there don't do a thing without asking his opinion. He is the president of the parapsychology section of the Academy of Science. He strokes his goatee, he is polite and delighted to have found a new medium. He tells me his memories of Rasputin, carefully noting my reactions.

He has a colleague, seated on a goatskin, somewhere on the coast of Kamchatka, who's supposed to be sending me mental messages. I'm seated on a chair, isolated by sheets of glass, and I say "white" or "black" every two seconds, following what I feel, without thinking—especially without thinking: in short, by chance.

I asked Vassiliev how the Communists could believe in children's stories, in magic even my mother would not take seriously. He was puzzled. They undertake their experiments in all possible seriousness. My "correspondent" has before him a machine which draws white or black cards at random, and they compare the series that this guy has seen to my answers. They moved the correspondent and due to fatigue I really started to see whites and blacks.

Vassiliev returned triumphant. I had gotten two per cent correct—beyond the limit of chance. How can my voluntary chance be compared to a machine's?

I've just calculated that at the rate Vassiliev is going, he'd got thirty years before he'll reconstitute the first phrase of a code.

In the evening we play checkers in the barracks. He introduced me to his successor—his grandson—already Secretary of the Academy of Science. They see me in their lab for life ... a family medium of sorts.

I'm entirely of their opinions. I stroke these two naîve ninnies; lead them by the hair of their chins. I've had time to think about a way of getting out of here. Vassiliev is too scatterbrained to notice that I have no more reservations about going for the weekly visit to the medical lab tomorrow. Vassiliev has an ingrate guinea pig on his hands who wants out of his lab.

*

Above me a blizzard blows and the ground is carpeted with ice when I touch it with my left hand—the one I'm using up against me to push the digicassette keys. My right hand no longer feels a thing. I have a hard time even moving it. The girls think it's a little frozen, but I feel it may be more serious than that.

The emissions started in again with renewed power. My head is crossed by geometric figures that light up like neon signs and the right part of my body is numb from top to bottom. I can only write with my left hand, using my thumb for two keys. It's only a little slower that way.

My body is half numb from being tinkered with by doctors. Poor body: passed through all those hands by God's will. The more the mysterious malady gnaws at my brain, the further away my body seems—used up by the stares it has brushed against, insensitive, distracted from my attention, slipping little by little into non-being.

I'm very careful to not let anything about the gravity of my state show to the girls. They would panic and probably turn me over to doctors in Anchorage. I don't ever want to see another doctor again. I haven't any more time to lose. I have a task to accomplish in California . . . to find the man who turned me into a living semiconductor.

The girls are huddled all around me in mountain sleeping bags, down caps and mittens. They put the entire sail over my chest. I'm not cold—at least I don't feel the cold inside my thermal jumpsuit. I'm listening to the noise in my head. It started up again and changed. The moment I wasn't hearing anything was ony a respite—a crossing of a vast empty space along a graduated scale of radio waves, between the military and the commercial stations. Radio waves reach me now full of undefinable music, knotted around the Pole—intermingled ribbons—snatches of the whole world's conversation. As we move away from the Pole, day approaches. Reception isn't as good now. A while ago, following the colored puzzles that took shape inside me, I could hear hoarse words, quiet moans. Three notes of music as suddenly clear—as if they were played next to me. I'm half-dreaming or else one of the girls is crying out, disturbed in her sleep.

The nylon bubble we're sheltered in is held in place by stakes driven into the ice at the halfway point between Alaskan and Russian waters: just over the border, if their instruments are correct.

While the wind toys with the inflatable tent—a polar wind so much like the wind of the desert—the half day sends voices from the high frequencies off to siesta. I got away like a breeze. They didn't know how slick a blind man could be. When they took me to the medical check-up, like every time before, a guard held my arm. I slipped the digicassette into my boot while I was getting undressed and wedged a little piece of wood torn off of my bunk under the door of the doctor's office.

They had me stretch out nude on the cot and then began to take my blood pressure. I complained of cold. The doctor moved an object next to me that he put upon a chair. I touched it, and yow!—it was a little round incandescent radiator that he usually kept in his office. Each person added his own heating because the base's central heating was insufficient.

He turned to write down my blood pressure. The guard was whistling softly behind me. I took a deep breath and gave a healthy kick to the middle of the radiator using my right foot. I hardly felt a thing. There was the noise of electrical burn-out. A motor fouled up somewhere on base and the guard was swearing, bumping around, trying to find my cot. He caught my arm just as I was opening the door I had stuck ajar, but he let me loose to strike a match and I slid past, letting the door slam closed on his nose—a door which opens in one direction.

I slipped into my jumpsuit and ran out without zipping up into the corridor, boots in hand. They must have all been in the dark, judging from the number of people that I bumped into. Guards were hitting one another, knocking over furniture.

I followed the cement corridors as far as I could hear them. I passed intersections where my footsteps echoed endlessly and arrived at an abandoned area of the base that smelled like piss and mold. I touched a wall in front of me. I was in a cul-de-sac—a concrete circle whose only opening was the corridor from where I'd just come.

I could hear barking. I recalled the ferocious dogs guarding the camp. I was so afraid I started feeling the walls again. Then, standing on my toes with my arms way up, I could sense something over my head—an iron bar, suspended in nothingness—a ladder that called with icy air that it would suck me up into it. I jumped and grabbed hold of the bar, got my bearings and began to climb. I climbed an hour, maybe two. Once, barking came from far below. I remained motionless, stuck in my concrete tube, convinced the men below would see me when they looked up. If this endless chimney I was clambering up ended in daylight ... The dogs turned back, following my trail in the wrong direction. Some voices spoke down below, their eyes riveted on the chimney raised toward me. They followed the dogs. Maybe it was dark outside, or maybe the chimney simply led to another concrete cul-de-sac. I was so tired. I didn't know if I was climbing up or down—only that the air was getting fresher, numbing my hands through the jumpsuit fabric. My right hand and leg responded poorly.

Despite the cold, I was sweating—sweat that froze on the ladder bars. The emissions of phosphors and the crackling were picking up the closer I got to the surface. I was hearing verses of songs, snatches of orchestral music—as if the entire world had been poured over me through that little round hole in the sky—in a cascade of waves. The receptors had reached what's called frequency modulation: F.M.

I came out into icy air, lifted off a poorly welded grill and had to take shelter behind the chimney I'd been climbing, because the wind was so violent. I was on an ice covered surface which had melted around the concrete shaft I'd just left.

I walked straight ahead, my arms outstretched, and found an iron railing. I leaned over. The wind whistled below. I was on a platform which might be a thousand feet high where the conduit I'd climbed reached its apex.

I touched the beginning of another ladder that took off from the platform, which I immediately climbed down. It stopped after a few steps—into a void. I hung from the last bar. My feet encountered nothing—so I said a little prayer and let go.

I was spread-eagled on ice, several feet below the platform. Ice. I'd never touched it in such huge quantities. It was slick like glass and salty to taste. I started walking, my back to the wind, following only one rule: to put the maximum space between myself and the point AB.

The cold burned my face, even my feet through the fur-lined boots. I started to run to get warm and my tears froze in the corners of my eyes.

Even though the ice was so smooth that I fell with every step around the platform, as soon as I moved away it took on curious and discouraging forms. I was running a frozen obstacle course—hard, cutting obstacles. The ice rose in slopes, gentle at first then more and more angled—a smooth slope with no hand bars. I had one sole means: shoot off on the flat part and grab at the summit—a crest of smashed cutting ice behind which was another crevice, the start of another slope...

This ice was the sea—the frozen sea.

I walked several hours, eating a bar of disgusting grainy Russian chocolate that I found in my pocket. The wind carried away bursts of voices, drum rolls, comets streaking through my head. I fell frequently, but the jumpsuit softened the blows and I wanted to hold out as long as I could. I knew the Polar night was just beginning and would last several months, and that the obscure half-night light reached out all around me.

Then I fell, convinced that nothing more could happen to me, and I lay in my furry upholstery listening to radio waves babble.

Kaleidoscopic shapes appeared in the center—just in front of me—infinite helices spinning in the void, turning into flowers, fireworks, then reversing and curving out again from center toward periphery.

The frequency modulations went over me relentlessly, like the hands of a pianist over a keyboard made of nerve endings. That night, lost in the hollow of an ice wave, enchanted, I witnessed the birth of music in my head. The chance sputtering changed into hints of voices—entire sentences reached me—reconstructed by my new brain from billions of stimulations running through it—translated into abstract colored images. Commercial jingles, concert applause, station identifications reached me intact, on the heels of visual sensations. All the voices of all the hosts in the world were concentrated in me in a mad hysterical communication, to the rhythm of fleeting words, songs, screams, laughter. And still I nodded off.

The grating of steel scraping ice awakened me. I stood up to escape. Someone jumped me and got me in a hold.

They loaded me into their vehicle, talking among themselves in Swedish, and rubbed my face with alcohol. They are so tall and strong that at first I thought they were men. They began to disinfect my scrapes under the jumpsuit, laughing hard because I was naked underneath.

We got going, and I heard the wind whistle around us. When I lowered my arm to touch the ice, they held me back. I was on a sled which wasn't being pulled by anything, yet which seemed to fly over ice waves.

One of them—the oldest—speaks a little English. Their sled has a sail, and we avoid the ice waves by continuously sliding in the hollow of one frozen wave which makes an enormous arc from Siberia to Alaska. They are three sisters—world champion sail-sledders—and they have permits to cross the Bering Straits. They couldn't figure out where I came from. They weren't at east until we'd crossed the American border.

I asked how they'd found me, and she put her finger on my jumpsuit and burst out laughing: "Red!" I laughed too. I'm not especially wild about them knowing I'm blind. My Russian jumpsuit is bright red. Tomorrow, I'll leave before they meet their reception committee ... They advised me to see the immigration officer right away, just before Anchorage, near a private little airport mostly used for business. They're happy to get rid of me. They've lost fifty-three minutes from their scheduled time because of the extra weight I added.

The three big fingers, then the index finger by itself, then the little finger.

The three big fingers, then the index finger by itself .... On the Braille keyboard you can make the word *je* with only one hand. *Je*; I. My left hand is writing *je* right now—this left hand continuing to work all by itself, taking itself for a speaking subject—this subject of a body lying stretched out in the back of a rusty car without wheels, upon a stack of old tires—in the middle of a field of broken abandoned automobiles ending at a beach. Across the fence you can hear the sea.

Some sheet metal is flapping in the early morning breeze. It wasn't hard to get in—just jump over the fence in front of the gas pumps. The garage man only comes in the Summer and Spring has just begun.

The cab driver was really surprised that anyone would go swimming at night in red coveralls in this kind of weather. On the beach, a couple was embracing inside a hollow like a big shell they'd dug in the sand ... a couple of nightowl nudists no doubt, who took off when they heard the sand crunch under my feet.

Wind sweeps the terraces, whistling through piles of chairs and folded umbrellas, meandering around little booths with boarded-over windows where hot dogs are sold. The "resort area" of this suburb south of San Francisco only comes alive during the season ... The region is inhabited only by technicians who work in local laboratories. Not a cry disturbs the gulls as they peacefully devour the last sandwich remains.

"Hello—this if Fresno, broadcasting on a frequency of 98 megahertz. Here is our musical program for the morning..." The voice was so clear that another groggily answered, croaking hello in response. That night, fighting against the hertzian tidal waves, I doubted myself—this me that was sleeping less than ten miles from Neurone Valley—who was familiar with the beach at the edge of the astronomical observatory where Larry often went.

Yesterday morning—a hundred years ago—the Swedish sisters stuffed the pockets of my jumpsuit with cereal, with smoked herring soaking in condensed milk, and with two fifty dollar bills. I jumped off the moving sled while they all braked together with their feet in a shower of shaved ice, so they wouldn't have to strike the sail and lose any more time. I walked straight in the direction they indicated and a quarter of an hour later my nearly paralyzed right leg set foot on American soil—which is to say another sort of dirty ice. The emissions became less sharp. The ground reflects radio waves less than ice. Opposite the sea, a road runs along the coast sprinkled with the ends of driveways leading to houses that gave out breakfast smells. A tractor noise throbbed: a snowmobile. The driver was going to the airport. I went into the main lounge and straight to the tobacco counter, where I bought a pair of dark glasses. I had myself led to the first-class waiting room and gave some money to an employee who recognized me as blind. There were no customs controls. The only passengers were businessmen who had come with their own planes to hunt in the Great North.

I began a conversation with the first arrival who told me all about his life in the smoked salmon business. He was already half-crocked. What was left of me answered in short phrases: Yes, student ... hitching ... proving the blind also knew how to make do. He slapped me on the back and took me to the runway. My broken body was chocked into his tiny jet between folded rifles and elks' heads. He went on drinking Canadian whiskey straight from the bottle, talking during the entire trip, turning his head toward me to keep me from falling asleep.

Once in the air, the radio emissions calmed down. Frequency modulation must remain close to the ground. He stopped in San Francisco to refuel at another little business airport where there weren't customs controls either—at least not for planes coming in from Alaska. After that a taxi driver got my last fifty dollars.

It drove away slowly, as if the driver was expecting me to call him back. His radio was turned on. Leaning against the gas pumps, I had to wait for the noise to die down. The motor dwindled away but the radio stayed inside me, accompanied by visions of whirling smoke that went from blue to shining black.

This place smells like cold motors and rancid oil. To the left is a tow truck with a hook and chain. To the right, hanging tools—a little screwdriver that slid into the jumpsuit pocket—rows of loose parts on metal shelves, one of which was a real heavy pipe. It fits nicely in my left hand, and is about half as long as my forearm.

At the junkyard entrance, a big limousine was lifted up on beams and didn't have doors: a place to crash. My left hand found the knobs: a radio on the dashboard that worked.

Three fingers, two fingers. I ... am I still able to write *je* this morning? Three fingers ... My left hand felt around on the radio pushbuttons, looking for the FM band. In the middle of the spectrum the same stations were playing in my head the same grand organ light-show that vibrated out of the dashboard speakers. The same? Not quite. Two different versions on a theme, executed by two different orchestras. A Spanish voice was crooning, a ballroom orchestra's sugary violins were playing—pink, white, blue ... a fireside guitar, in the far background; the stamping of an insurrection of percussion, exploding like muffled rockets. As the day wore on, voices came back stronger—housewives' voices in praise of detergents, shopkeepers telling about their wonderful wares—big sale, don't wait, buy now; vamps so pleased they didn't smell anymore; sleepy-voiced announcers, covering a tidal wave of secrets, news, marking America's awakening.

Music conjured up by a flood of lights, unfurling colors being born on the fringes of still other tones in a sieve of syrupy melodies—bursting slow-motion disco explosions. This music wasn't real music that an ear can hear. It made up the aural translation of a luminous translation. A tangle of corpuscles in search of each other behind my neck were even obeying my hand—the hand turning the knob which picks the stations, climbing from frequency to frequency, to the rhythm of what was going on up under the skull, to the far end of the radio's frequencies, the end of the race, stuck between two intermingled stations.

The audible kaleidoscope was brutally interrupted and the sun popped out on my arm through the glassless widows. My reheated blood was flowing better.

Fortunately, no one found it bizarre for some character to listen to a radio full-blast all night long in an auto graveyard. No one. There isn't anyone around this morning: not a single car in the parking lot. I walked its length from front to back, one side to the other, to warm myself in the early sun. I'm dragging my right leg, and my right arm is still numb, but the emissions have stopped again. I wanted to say the word *je* out loud, but I'm having trouble pronouncing words. Speech is starting to not be there, as in aphasia . . . but *JE*, I still have language and I can still type in Braille. I must have had a minor stroke last night, after getting over the fence.

I am reincorporated. I hear perfectly well the sound of the ocean to my right. On my left, I feel the wind come down the valley where the road which will lead me to Larry goes. Left; Right. How can I have retained those notions when the left half of my brain doesn't even function anymore, except probably to transform radio waves into light and noise, robbing me of even articulate speech? I will go left on the road; the sun on my forehead will provoke electrical storms in my head on the left side at the back of my neck. Paralysis is winning out, like cold in a tired swimmer's body—my back and ribs on the right.

At the intersection of the beach and the road to Neurone Valley is a telephone booth. I picked up the receiver dialed zero and asked the operator for Professor Larry Home's number, in Neurone Valley.

I had to speak three times. My mouth refused to separate the words. She had to look it up. "Home, office, or mobile?" She had to go through recent listings.

The operator's voice repeated her questions dryly. Larry now had three numbers; only one was listed in Neurone Valley. I took down the number for his car phone on my digicassette. She could connect me with the Neurone Valley switchboard if I put in twenty-five cents. I didn't have twenty-five cents. I stammered out one question: since when had Larry come back to the center? She didn't answer, furious at having been taken in by some clown who didn't even have a quarter.

I asked what day it was. I didn't know. She told me, then hung up. I stood in front of the silent receiver. Larry must have come back just after my operation: amnesty for services rendered, doubtless.

I hung up then picked up the receiver again and dialed Larry's car. I had to start again at zero, and the numbers were escaping me. I let it ring and ring and let the receiver hang on the end of the cord.

Two trucks gave me a lift to the base entrance. The first was driven by Mexicans and I sat in the middle of a load of vegetables. The second driver was a technician from the center, who never stopped looking me over. He couldn't decide if I was really blind or just some joker who'd found this dark glasses gimmick to snag rides.

As a last resort, I know how to play blind—tapping, my arms out in front, in the middle of the highway until someone stops.

The technician from the center was becoming definitely suspicious. I had him let me off below the ramp leading to the valley entrance where there's a little Mexican village with a refreshment stand. He calmed down: I must be a Chicano.

I waited for him to leave. The sun was already hot and I was only sweating on my left side. I was still cold on the right, even in the jumpsuit.

The technician's pickup stopped on the ramp. Was he looking in my direction? I heard the guard's voice at the entrance. Apparently, the technician was leaving his truck there and taking a shuttle inside the valley.

I went up the length of the slope, through dried out shrubs planted on each bank. The parking lot went clear to the edge of the valley. On all fours I slipped between cars. In the first row were three or four jeeps. I couldn't pick up any telephone noise.

I'd have to put my ear against the glass.

After about ten minutes, I heard a muffled buzz, straight in front of me. I went to the second row and found it. I whacked the pipe against the taillight, covering it first with my sleeve so it wouldn't make noise. I undid it with a screwdriver. Just in the nick of time. The guard's voice approached. He asked what in the world I thought I was doing there. I answered without turning around, just turning a little to one side, that Mr. Home had asked me to replace his broken taillight. I imitated a Chicano accent. He asked where the tow truck was, and I motioned with the screwdriver that it was down below. He planted himself behind me and I felt him looking at the weird red overalls I was wearing, under which I was half-sweating to beat the band. Before he had time to go to the railing to look for the tow truck, someone was honking at the gate. Inside the car, the phone was still buzzing away.

He went back to the guardhouse. The traffic never stopped: the afternoon exodus. I put my screwdriver away and went down the road, surrounded by the motorbikes of base employees going out for a swim between noon and two o'clock. The sun was blazing. I crawled back to the car, and after having forced open the little window with the screwdriver, I stretched out on the floor under a blanket, between the front and back seats. I cradled the receiver and all was quiet. A suffocating long time went by. Then I heard his voice, swearing when he saw the smashed-in taillight. He opened the door I'd relocked, sat down with a groan—never glancing behind—and took off down the ramp full speed. I heard him open the glovebox, then I quietly sat up. Against the floorboard my left side had really begun to ache and I couldn't lean on my right arm anymore. He pushed the cigarette lighter in, and saw me in his rearview mirror as he straightened up, just as I nudged the end of my pipe in his back.

He couldn't see my hand and let out a little cry, like an animal caught in a trap. After several miles he found his tongue again and said there were a few hundred dollars in his wallet. If I wanted the car right now I could have it. He swore he wouldn't press charges. He was talking in a choked, hurried voice. It was hysterical that he didn't recognize me. I didn't know what to do with him, now that I had him. In a little boy's voice he asked where we were going. I felt in very good humor. I simply groaned

"Right" at the intersection, and while he was slowly taking the turn I could feel his mind vaguely searching for that familiar voice.

I had him stop at the edge of an open field covered with tamarisk which surrounded the observatory where he sometimes used to take me for walks. When I pushed him a little with the end of the pipe to make him get out of the car, Larry's back jumped. I opened the door myself and lost contact with his back the instant it took him to get out of the driver's seat. I could hear him hopping onto the gravel and take off running. My left hand touched an icy forehead. A new rush of radio waves stronger than ever burst inside me. The noise of a terrifying war, sown with bombardments, machine gun fire and screams, left me dazed for several seconds ... time enough for Larry to escape. A wave of commercials followed—so strongly that I stumbled. I recognized the sound of a television—a deformed sound, simplified: made of western-six shooters, interruptive gongs of "words from our sponsors," honey-sweet voices, trumpet fanfares. And against this background, Larry's silhouette stood out, clear as a bell: I mean against the background images formed by these sounds— the crazy interplay of injected shapes and colors that accompanied the soundtrack.

Larry was running straight at an enormous obstacle which rapidly grew bigger as I ran too—some immaterial obstacle. An obstacle sending waves directly at me ... a wall of images and sounds. It rose and grew hollow above us like a gigantic dome the closer I got. Then Larry leaned against the base of this dome standing upon its side, turned toward me and reached down for a rock. I said, "Larry," in a weak voice and threw the pipe straight at the kneeling silhouette. There was an insignificant moist heavy thud and the silhouette fell forward at the foot of the radio-telescope antenna.

I went closer. A sticky warm soup was pouring out of his forehead. I tasted it—slightly salty. I recognized the taste of a poorly cooked steak. There was no more breathing. Larry was dead.

Another stroke in my brain. The next to the last, perhaps. The hand taps all by itself—a hand with the index finger now completely numb. The images appeared in the hottest sunlight—

just after Larry's death. Pictures that haven't stopped blending all afternoon—gushing out of the sun's furnace above this head.

Polarized faces moving orange lips with green shadows to announce unheard of misfortune, women smiling songs in violet, the sputtered yellow and blue hissing of synthetic music. And most of all, explosions—explosions by the hundreds—daughters of a great solar explosion that would ravage the nerves of the earth's population—explosions at the ends of gangster's revolvers, from cannons, tanks, boats; explosions are the only times image and sound ever perfectly coincide.

The television images producing their own sound, as though sound was producing its own images: higher in frequency to billions of pulses a second, and more. The funnel swallowed itself, reabsorbed itself; and the head has become lucid again, but it is now separated by an uncrossable void from the hand that writes. The hand is left, the head right. Left of the head is an enormous ear, but in reality it is behind the skull—an ear that now only hears a confusion of noise accompanied by dying lights: the noise of the radio waves returning. The left hand can touch, can pinch the body, which is now leaning against some cold mass: the concrete base that supports the giant antenna; and the hand tirelessly continues to push the little warm keys, forming words that it can no longer speak.

The body must seem as if it's standing—standing against the antenna strut which is turning, following the sun with a rustle of wind in its metallic lace.

The sun is setting, striking only the back of the neck of this body which turns its back to it, while the eyes remain in shadow, The dark glasses have slipped to the ground.

Tens of billions of vibrations per second ... beyond radar, at the very extremes of the wave spectrum—where the atmosphere lets nothing pass but light, and nameless rays zoom in from the cosmos.

Footsteps make the steel and latticework antenna resonate ... And the sun has appeared at the lowest infrareds—a turning ball hestiant to leave the nothingness. The sun that heats the back of the neck but which appears in front, striking the prosthesis with its accurate whip, pulling nearer the center as the colors become clearer in a sinuous curve that no earthly sun has ever traced.

The sun in the back, but the sun in front too—a sun that is not

centered, but on the extreme edge of the visual field—and which
is moving, crawling toward the middle ... a sun of synthesis,
manufactured by millions of emittors reached all at the same time
by millions of billions of beats per second—the frequencies of
visible light finally attained. That astral body climbed to yellow,
exploded in green, melted in blue and was gently absorbed in
violet in a tinted earthquake. All around, timid people, isolated
but still forming a crowd, gathered, speaking of the clouds
darkening the west that night over the sea. The sun existed only
for me—invisible to others—lost beyond the ultraviolet. The
body started to disperse again, while hands began to palpate it
determinedly. Night must have fallen. Matches crackled; steps
stumbling upon the metal.

Billions upon billions: the zeros jump right off a meter gone
berserk. Billions upon billions of microwaves accelerating without end, each shorter and faster than the one before.

X-rays coming from the universe, cutting out silhouettes—
skeletal lovers entwined, caked together against pillars of steel.
Cosmic rays—distant signals from the far reaches of the galaxies
... messages so rapid they flee to transit light years after having
for an instant pierced the skull, crossed the inner ear. Supersharp
whistles and long icy moans from constellations; sidereal rattles;
striped disks of suns turning in the void; gongs rolling secretly in
space ... the whispers of immense voices next to the ear—
electronic trumpets forever announcing a final burst that doesn't
come.

Was this really the music of the spheres?—or the soundtrack
of some space opera film from a T.V. station on the coast? The
cassette slips more and more to the ground; the fingers become
numb. The head fell backward without being able to completely
fall, the group is so compact now. The veil was torn, and the sky
appeared. Sky formed in the head—a planetarium sky—a great
black dome sewn with radio-sources of silver and gold. The eyes
are closed to see better. Faster, higher—the waves push a sidereal
surfer into the void: the entire sky without a horizon, without
limit—the sky where the ghosts of astral bodies emitted beyond
light superimpose, the splendor of dead galaxies still sending their
now cold rays.

On Kerkenna to evince God, the *hadjis* who've been to Mecca
imperceptibly move a finger in a gesture almost loving—a rosary

reduced to the essential. Almost in the same manner, the fingers pressing the keys are barely moving. The world is rolling onto itself like a sheet of paper—dividing into four parallel images, then into a hundred, then into a thousand bursts—each an entire scene carved like the facets of a diamond ... dances of the *Achoura* in the dust, black marble lobbies of a funerary and deserted hotel with echoes of a hobbling cane where a rubbing feline shadow slides. The quaking of ultra frequencies have reached the whole body—a quaking so rapid it seems to shake the spider's metallic web; the wires of the netting clink together: the earth itself, the concrete base where the antenna is anchored trembles too. The group broke with piercing screams—the body slid to the ground—a ground made of jolts and hiccoughs—a drunken ground. On Kerkenna the same women's shrill screams announced the volcano's awakening when the ground shook under the feet of a furious giant onthe move, with his head below, under the rock crust.

In the race to escape the sheets and girders of metal falling from the sky, someone crushed the little red device that his left hand had just let go. There was a crack of plastic, the snap of a released spring and a little white rectangle flew off into the night, rolling down the rocky slope.

At the base of the antenna the car manuevered, the motor revving, between the road and the giant domed antenna, turned now toward the moon which had just emerged from behind clouds. Shivers still convulsed the huge black arms and the wire network pulling away from the white concave disk.

The car headlights continued to turn, the wheels to spin grabbing at the gravel.

What a stupid idea to go there for a breath of air after the baths! We'd pulled up in front of the radiotelescope. It was pretty in the moonlight. As we stopped the car, we wondered if it was a military zone. Reassuringly, other cars were parked in the field. We recognized some. The little van belonging to the owner of that porno moviehouse on Highland Avenue, the Chevy convertible and Mustang of that doctor and lawyer who always cruise together, and a lot of others. There were even some French people. One fellow wore a red leather jumpsuit. He was really handsome, leaning against the strut of the huge antenna. You can find that kind of clothing in the Castro Street boutiques. We didn't go up to him. A guy that good-looking, all by himself—it's kind of fishy. He looked Mexican or Arab; drugged; swaying back and forth, keeping one hand in his pocket. Maybe he had a knife.

When the quake came, we left. It was the third that day. We didn't want to hang around under that enormous metal maze during a tremor. When we were turning around, the headlights swept across the antenna base. That's when we noticed it—right in front of the wheels. We'd nearly run over it, so we opened the door and picked it up.

It was a cassette—an audio cassette—smaller than a commercial model, with an Arabic name written on each side, and an address in Paris in Roman script.

Winding the u-turn, our headlights returned to the radio-telescope. The handsome guy had climbed up onto the antenna, and was crawling over its surface—a little red spider. His clothing got snagged on some wire, and he slipped right out of the jumpsuit. There was another tremor, and he fell, naked, into the ocean.

How can one believe it? Yet this cassette certainly exists, here in the little glass case across from my office at Lamorne, between a Japanese idol incense-burner and a music box from Freud's time.

But who still dares to speak in the silence now restored on these cosmic ruins? Who deciphered this text and ultimately joined to it the tale of those parties who desire to remain anonymous and who were present on that beach that night?

It is time, reader, to lift the mask. My name is Philippe Marcoeur. I am a physician. I am a psychiatrist in this tale, wherein, I must say, my patient often passed the bounds of reality: in particular when she endowed me with delirious relations with a man whom I respect, whom I admire, who is my master, and still today, her husband.

My patient has never been divorced except in her imagination. Her husband and myself allowed ourselves this innocent ruse for this very sick woman whose case I have followed for fifteen years, and whose adventures I am publishing today.

"*A cura di ...*" say the Italians speaking of the editor of a specific text: "In the care of". Never was an expression more just.

Fifteen years, since my internship in Lausanne: fifteen years during which she never ceased to deliver herself entirely to me.

Bursting of the ocular globe by deep, infected lesions lacerating the cornea and zonula of Zinn. To the right, in the pulp of clawed flesh of the ocular muscles, a hemmorhage of the interior chamber, with shredding of the iris; and this trembling upon movement of the globe, which indicates passage of the vitreous into the anterior of the lens; persistent hypertension—diagnosed in the following days—which led to a secondary glaucoma, depriving my patient of her remaining eye, by good fortune, perhaps—before she was able to contemplate her appearance in a mirror. When they brought her in to me, the blood had dried in large blotches upon her face, and one could see the very white cheekbone, between the large brown lips of the wound. The vitreous was slowly running, coagulating on her cheek.

These panther's wounds came from a cat ... a little cat with a bobbed tail, restrained now in a cage by an officer of the law, tranquilly seated, licking its claws ... bloodstained claws.

Such was the final price paid by my patient for a long,

perverse, amorous illusion.

I found this cassette in the pocket of her coat. Grabbing for it, she provoked this reaction from the little wild feline. Its' finders, respecting the inscription on the case, sent it along with a letter to the address indicated.

It was necessary to find a responsible party to settle an astronomical hospital bill. The young Arab ladies who live in the apartment the cassette had been forwarded to declare the animal lived with their half-brother. On its collar, the cat wore a number under which it was listed with an International Pedigree of Felines. I thus discovered the cat belonged to an elderly lady of the demimonde, who had bequeathed to it a considerable fortune at her death in San Francisco.

Fortunately for my patient, the aggressor was amply situated financially to repair the damage it caused. A Swiss bank, administering the account on behalf of this cat—identified by her number and pawprint as Zita—verified that she is the wealthiest animal in the world. Today, from a villa on the edge of Lake Léman where she is aging comfortably in a gilded cage, she pays my patient's upkeep.

And Amar? According to the American police whom I consulted he was unquestionably a dangerous heroin smuggler, trafficking on a large scale, who for a time had been detained in a Nevada penitentiary, before he escaped. He's never been the object of any experimentation whatsoever—it's forbidden by the Constitution of the United States. Even his blindness was contested by the police. It seems we are witnessing the birth of a new form of criminality, absolutely without scruples, which no longer hesitates to assume the most pity-evoking appearance. This autodidactic mythomaniac is a true assassin. The body of an American professor was discovered on the beach. The murderer had formerly known the victim in a lengthy career as a Los Angeles prostitute. Was it vengeance for some unknown denunciation?

The delirious nature of the last portion of the cassette deciphered by me—thanks to a device miraculously fallen into my patient's hands—must remain inconclusive.

There remain those crimes which my client has been accused of. The first, in San Francisco, was—from all evidence—the work of the young male prostitute who at that time believed he figured in the elderly woman's will. My client was "covering for him," as the police say. A second crime, at Harry's Bar, was on the other hand, well established, although in that instance she was little more than an accomplice. After consultations with some magistrate friends and thanks to the understanding of the district attorney, an acquittal was rendered without the patient having to appear, since the events had occurred during a time in which she was in a state of mental incapacity.

I've read this text to my patient, who believes it—if I may dare say—blindly.

Before me lies the peaceful tableau of Lamorne Clinic: on its grassy lawn, seated in a chaise longue, is a young woman whose scarred face is difficult to distinguish in twilight.

Next to her is a visitor of Mahgreb origin, an employee of the Postal and Telegraphs Dept. whom she'd known on Kerkenna. He is holding little Abd el-Kader on his knees, and they are speaking of the past. In the grass, at his feet, is one of those transistor radios with which unscrupulous merchants inundate our ill, babbling out election results. The Left won. Alix is practically a minister of state.

In a while when the sun has set, she will accompany her guest to the gates, wandering, tapping across the lawn, and then she will return to her seat with the child in her arms. She might let him fall but I keep a constant eye on her from here. I will hear the sputter of the yellow scooter taking off, and she will turn on the little radio again. I will have to go take Kader from her, because she will stay in the evening damp a long time turning knobs, listening to the background noise—that crackling coming from elsewhere—which to her is a voice.

Docteur Philippe Marcoeur
Lamorne, May 1981